"I need to kno…
Tell me…you rei…

The Cajun's dark eyes w…
his face contorted in misery. She hated seeing him suffer.

"Nicole," he repeated, and held a hand out, summoning her to come closer.

At that moment, the morning sun broke over the tops of the trees and shone through the open side door of the helicopter, casting his rugged face in sharp relief. For the first time, she could truly see the man who'd risked his life for her. Her heart clenched, and the prickle of déjà vu returned. He seemed so familiar…

"I…need—" He stopped, clenching his teeth and growling in torment. "Please…I need to know… you remember."

"I remember," she lied, leaning closer to be sure he heard her.

"Then say my name, Nicole."

And in a heartbeat, an echo from her past yanked her back five years to a hotel room in New Orleans. Her heart wrenched, and tears spilled from her eyes.

"Oh, my God!" She curled her fingers into the hair at his nape and buried her face in his neck. "Daniel…"

Dear Reader,

As I was writing *Soldier's Pregnancy Protocol*, I found myself more and more fascinated by Alec's missing partner, Daniel LeCroix. What had happened to him? I asked myself. Just who was this mysterious Cajun? Even though he was not "on screen" most of the book, I felt his presence throughout writing the book. Secondary characters sometimes take over, demanding their own story be told. By the time I finished Alec's book, Daniel's history with Senator White's daughter was already playing out in my head.

I was thrilled to have the chance to write Daniel and Nicole's story…so much so that the opening chapters of *The Reunion Mission* almost wrote themselves. This is a true story of my heart, even though I shook my head at times wondering what I'd done to myself by having characters who needed to speak not just Spanish, but Colombian Spanish, and not just French, but Cajun French. (Yes, there is a big difference!) I hope you enjoy Daniel and Nicole's story as much as I enjoyed telling it…

Oh, and keep an eye out for book three in the BLACK OPS RESCUES series. I hope to have Jake's story ready soon! As always, more information about all my books is available on my website, www.bethcornelison. com.

Happy reading,

Beth Cornelison

THE REUNION MISSION

BY
BETH CORNELISON

Printed and bound in Spain

First published in Great Britain 2012
by Mills & Boon, an imprint of Harlequin (UK) Limited,
Eton House, 18-24 Paradise Road, Richmond, Surrey TW9 1SR

© Beth Cornelison 2012

ISBN: 978 0 263 89574 2
ebook ISBN: 978 1 408 97256 4

46-1112

Harlequin (UK) policy is to use papers that are natural, renewable and recyclable products and made from wood grown in sustainable forests. The logging and manufacturing processes conform to the legal environmental re...

Pı...
by...

Beth Cornelison started writing stories as a child when she penned a tale about the adventures of her cat, Ajax. A Georgia native, she received her bachelor's degree in public relations from the University of Georgia. After working in public relations for a little more than a year, she moved with her husband to Louisiana, where she decided to pursue her love of writing fiction.

Since that first time, Beth has written many more stories of adventure and romantic suspense and has won numerous honors for her work, including a coveted Golden Heart Award in romantic suspense from Romance Writers of America. She is active on the board of directors for the North Louisiana Storytellers and Authors of Romance (NOLA STARS) and loves reading, traveling, *Peanuts'* Snoopy and spending downtime with her family.

She writes from her home in Louisiana, where she lives with her husband, one son and two cats who think they are people. Beth loves to hear from her readers. You can write to her at PO Box 5418, Bossier City, LA 71171, USA or visit her website, www.bethcornelison.com.

To Keyren Gerlach Burgess, who believed in me and helped bring Alec, Daniel and Jake to life.

Thank you to fellow Mills & Boon® Intrigue author Gail Barrett and her friend, Margarita Unger, for their help with Colombian Spanish translations.

Thank you also to Jennifer Malone and her father, Monte Bonin, for their help with Cajun French, as well as answering questions about Cajun culture.

Thank you to Sara Beth Salyer for sharing her name (as the winning bidder in the Brenda Novak Diabetes Auction for a Cure) and allowing me the honor of paying homage to her beloved kitty, Oreo, as characters in *The Reunion Mission*.

Chapter 1

"Left perimeter clear." Shifting his night vision goggles, Daniel LeCroix peered through the inky blankness of the Colombian jungle, his body humming and ready for action. He focused on the large tent at the far end of the rebel encampment. No sign of soldiers who slept in the canvas shelter. Lowering the night vision goggles, he cast a glance to his partner, who monitored the camp through an infrared imaging camera. "What do you have?"

Months of preparation had led to this moment. With their objective moments from fruition, he'd be damned if he'd let anything screw up their mission now.

"No movement," Alec Kincaid confirmed. "Looks like the guards watching the ammo are the only ones awake." Alec stowed the infrared imager in his pack and slid his NVGs into place. "Ready to move?"

Adrenaline spiked in Daniel's blood, readying him for battle. "Hell, yeah. Let's go."

Silently, he and Alec dropped from the tree where they'd been perched for hours, watching the faction of rebel soldiers who held several captives in the remote camp. Only one of the prisoners interested Daniel.

Nicole White. A U.S. senator's daughter kidnapped from the medical mission where she was working and held as a political pawn.

Freeing her and returning her safely to the United States was their sole objective tonight.

Leading with his sidearm, Daniel crept down the steep, vegetation-dense hillside to the clearing in the narrow Colombian valley where Nicole had been held for close to thirteen months.

Would she recognize him, remember him?

Daniel shoved down the jangle of anticipation that skittered through him when he thought of seeing Nicole again. Touching her. He had to stay focused on his job if they were to get out of that jungle alive.

When they reached the crude wire fence at the edge of the camp, Alec pulled a pair of wire cutters from his pack and quickly created a hole large enough for them to crawl through on their bellies. Daniel wiggled through first, then Alec. Using hand signals, Daniel directed Alec to the right. Daniel walked backward, following Alec and guarding their six. Keeping to the shadows, they made their way toward the back of the camp where Nicole was being held.

As they rounded the tent where they'd determined supplies were kept, Alec stopped abruptly. He pointed to the guard stationed at the entrance of the supply tent.

I've got this one, Alec signaled, then soundlessly dispatched the man before the guard even knew he had company.

Behind them, a squeak drew Daniel's attention. The door to the ramshackle latrine by the perimeter fence opened, and a soldier stepped out, shining a flashlight toward the camp.

When the beam passed over Alec, Daniel tensed. Just as the man swung the light back and opened his mouth to shout a warning to the camp, Daniel fired a single head shot, and the soldier crumpled. Despite the silencer muffling the gun's noise, Daniel knew someone could have heard the telltale pop. They had to hurry.

By unspoken agreement, Alec set a faster pace toward the fenced area where Nicole was being held. Farther down, they encountered two more guards, playing a game with dice as they monitored the cache of arms stacked in crates under a tarp. Skulking through the night like panthers, Alec and Daniel snuck up on the duo and took them out, as well.

All clear.

With Alec keeping watch, Daniel hurried to the fenced area where the rebels held their captives. The cages holding the prisoners were little more than dog pens, and two teepeed sheets of rotting plywood provided Nicole's only protection from the elements. Rage flashed through Daniel seeing the squalid conditions in which Nicole had been forced to live. Gritting his teeth, he funneled his fury into cutting through the fencing of her cage, then crawled to the tented plywood where she slept.

She wasn't alone. Daniel frowned but dismissed the small form huddled beside her. His mandate was clear. Nicole was his only objective.

Shifting his attention, Daniel held his breath as he caught his first up-close glimpse of Nicole in five years. Her long slender legs and feet were bare. Dirty cargo shorts and a sleeveless T-shirt hugged her womanly curves, and the fetal position in which she slept heightened his sense of her vulnerability. Her arms pillowed her head, and her tangled blond hair spilled over her cheek. Even disheveled and grimy, she was still every bit as beautiful as he remembered.

Daniel's heart performed a tuck and roll, and he allowed

himself the briefest moment just to look at her and thank God she appeared unharmed. But even a few seconds of delay were an indulgence, and he steeled himself for the task ahead. It was go time.

Five years earlier

Daniel stood at attention, watching the parade of national and state dignitaries dressed in their best black-tie finery make their way into the governor's Mardi Gras ball. His buddies at the New Orleans Naval Air Station thought he was crazy for volunteering to work security for the ball. But when he'd heard that Louisiana Senator Alan White would be attending, he'd known he couldn't be anywhere else that night.

Daniel had prepped his Navy dress whites for the event, counting on the other rumor he'd heard to be true—since his wife's death last year, Senator White had brought his daughter, Nicole, as his companion to public events such as this.

Even as he conjured a memory of the last time he'd seen Nicole, a limo flying American flags from the antennae pulled up to the front drive of the antebellum mansion where the ball was underway. Daniel held his breath as Senator White emerged from the backseat, then turned to offer his hand to someone inside the limo. A chill filled the air that February evening, but the weather had nothing to do with the tremor that rolled through Daniel as a graceful young blonde woman stepped out onto the driveway. An ice-blue chiffon gown hugged her curves, and she molded her mouth into a stiff smile as she started toward the stairs on the senator's arm. Jeweled combs winked in the porch lights and held her long hair swept up in a twist, exposing the slim column of her neck.

Daniel tracked her progress with his gaze as she approached, his mouth dry and his gut in knots. With her hand tucked in the crook of her father's arm, Nicole cast a surveying glance to the other partygoers, issuing perfunctory greetings. The politician's daughter, groomed in social graces and good public relations. American nobility, so far out of his league Daniel had to squelch the urge to laugh in bitter irony at the lengths he'd gone to tonight just for a chance to see her again. His studious gaze caught her attention, and Daniel flashed her a lopsided grin. "Hello, Nicole."

Her steps faltered, and a look of confusion dented her brow. "Do I—?"

Daniel blew out a deep breath. He'd been crazy to think she'd remember him after so many years.

But then her face brightened, and she pulled her arm free of her father's to step closer to Daniel. "Boudreaux!"

His heart kicked up a zydeco beat as she seized his hand and squeezed his fingers. "Boudreaux? Is that you?"

He grimaced mentally. As much as he'd wanted her to remember him, her use of the derogatory nickname her friends had given him didn't bode well for *what* she remembered about him. He tugged his mouth into an awkward smile. "Yeah, it's me."

Delight lit her eyes and brightened her grin, and hope stirred in his chest.

"Oh, my God! Look at you!" She canted forward, circling his shoulders with her arms and pressing a social kiss to his cheek.

Stunned by her hug, he was a beat too slow returning the embrace, and his brain snagged when the sweet floral scent of her hair hit him. His body's reaction to her touch, her scent was immediate and carnal.

Still holding the sleeves of his dress whites jacket, she levered back and let her gaze take in the length of him. "I almost didn't recognize you in this impressive attire." She flashed a flirtatious grin and tugged at the breast of his jacket.

"Good Lord, everything they say about a man in uniform is true!"

Daniel rallied his senses, determined not to come off as a flustered sap and to preserve the dignity his uniform required. "You look beautiful, too."

Understatement. She was breathtaking. He'd thought so five years ago on her prom night, when he'd been his cousin's date and met Nicole for the first time.

"Nicole!" Senator White had backtracked to fetch his wayward daughter, not quite managing to hide his irritation. "What's going on?"

Had she been hugging the son of one of his golf buddies rather than a security guard, the senator wouldn't have been nearly so piqued, Daniel wagered.

Nicole extended a hand to her father, waving him closer. "Daddy, I want you to meet someone. This is—" She hesitated, cutting an embarrassed look to Daniel.

"Daniel LeCroix," he finished, offering his hand to the senator before she defaulted to the nickname that mocked his bayou roots.

She twitched her lips in an apologetic grin. "Daniel. Of course! Forgive me. I'm just awful with names!"

Her father arched an eyebrow and heaved a sigh. "To my chagrin. She once called the chairman of armed services by his predecessor's name."

Folding Daniel's free hand between her hands, she faced her father again. "Daniel is the boy who brought me home from prom my junior year." When her father's expression remained blank, she added pointedly, "He's the one who rescued Boudreaux from the storm drain for me!"

Adrenaline kicked Daniel's pulse, and he jerked a startled glance toward her. *Boudreaux?* She'd named the kitten—?

Nicole met his questioning look with a secret smile. "What else would I name him?"

"Ah, yes. Your cat. I remember now. Well, it's nice to meet you, Daniel." The senator offered Nicole his arm, and his raised eyebrows, warning her it was time to go inside. "Nicole, this young man has a job to do, and our hosts are waiting."

Facing Daniel, she squeezed his hand and gave him a lopsided smile of regret. "It was wonderful seeing you again, Daniel."

He returned a polite smile. *Don't leave.* "You, too, Nicole." Then to the senator, "Sir."

The senator met his gaze with a hard look that darted to Daniel's rank insignia on his uniform. "Lieutenant."

The senator's tone carried a warning, a reminder of Daniel's place and the social gap between a boy from the bayou and the senator's well-bred daughter. As if Daniel needed reminding. Though he was proud of his Cajun roots, he was always striving to be better than the next guy—at basic training, in the classroom, in operations—trying to prove his detractors wrong, silencing those who singled him out or who bought into erroneous stereotypes regarding his heritage.

Nicole squeezed his hand before she released it and flashed a rueful smile as her father grasped her elbow and led her inside.

With a cleansing breath, he resumed his watch, shoulders back and hands clasped behind him. Though he stood at rigid attention, his mind writhed with a tangle of emotions.

He'd accomplished what he'd set out to do tonight. He'd seen Nicole again. But, in light of the tumult inside him, coming tonight might have been a mistake.

Nicole needed air. Shoving her way through the crowded dance floor, she hurried to the front porch and gripped the railing as another shudder of disgust rippled through her. All evening she'd put up with the leering glances her father seemed not to notice, but when the president of the Chamber of Commerce squeezed her bottom on the dance floor, she'd had enough. She'd bet her father's fortune that his "friends" never treated her mother with such disrespect.

Thoughts of her mother, stolen from her by cancer just four months ago, brought moisture to Nicole's eyes. She cast a longing gaze toward the parked cars, wishing she didn't have to endure the party any longer, and she spotted the white dress uniform and broad shoulders that had sent her pulse racing earlier that evening.

A smile ghosted across her lips. Daniel LeCroix. She wasn't surprised he'd joined the armed forces. Even in her brief association with him on prom night five years ago, she'd seen his valor, his kindness, his integrity. When her date hadn't deigned to get his hands dirty to retrieve the stranded kitten, when her friends had all abandoned her for "wasting time" on the rescue, only Daniel had stayed behind to help her instead of going to the dance. Daniel had ruined his rented tux moving the sewer grate and climbing into the drainage pipes, then had walked her and her new pet home. And left an indelible mark on her heart.

Nicole couldn't help but wonder how different *tonight* would have been if he'd been her escort instead of her father.

The night's not over. Her breath stilled. Ditching her father in favor of Daniel would be waving a red flag in her father's face. He'd never forgive her for the snub and the damage to his well-crafted public image.

But had her father respected her feelings when she'd complained about his friends' untoward advances? A flash of anger spiraled through her. How long was she supposed to put her life on hold to be her father's PR darling? She was already a year behind her class in nursing school because of his last election campaign and months of filling her mother's shoes as his companion at high-profile events and parties. As much as she loved her father, she just didn't want the high-society lifestyle he thrived on.

Inside, the orchestra began playing the ballad from a popular Andrew Lloyd Webber musical, and Nicole sighed. Fixing her gaze on Daniel, she crossed the porch and approached him. "Dance with me?"

He cut a startled glance her direction. "Nicole." His gaze shifted behind her, obviously noting that she was alone. "Why aren't you inside?"

"I needed a breather. Too much hot air in there." She twitched a grin and hitched her head toward the party. Stepping closer to him, she held out her hand. "So will you dance with me? This is one of my favorite songs."

His gaze locked on hers, his regret obvious. "I can't. I'm on duty."

She moved close enough to slide her hand along the polished buttons of his dress whites. She could feel the strong, steady beat of his heart beneath her fingers, and the life-affirming cadence struck her as powerfully virile and maddeningly sexy. "Just one dance. No one will know or care if you just danced this one song with me." She slid her arms around his neck and twined her fingers in the close-cropped hair at his nape. "Please."

His mental battle played across his face, the tug-of-war between duty and desire. "Nicole…" Closing his eyes, he settled a hand at her waist and halfheartedly tried to push her away.

Suddenly the idea of losing this opportunity to dance with Daniel, because of the rules of his job, or her father's code of conduct, or any other stuffy social convention or arbitrary legal dictate, made her want to scream. She fisted her hand in the back of his dress coat and refused to be budged. Tears of frustration and rebellion puddled in her eyes, and she raised her chin to meet his gaze.

"Screw the rules, Daniel. I want to dance with you."

His dark eyes narrowed on her, and hands that had pushed her away now touched the bare skin exposed by the low cut in the back of her dress. The warmth of his fingers against her night-chilled skin spun a delicious tingle from her head to her toes. A groan rumbled in his throat as he flattened his palm at the small of her back and drew her close.

A tremor of anticipation spun through her when she aligned her body with his. The stiff creases of his uniform and the sensual play of his muscles tantalized her through her sheer dress. Resting her cheek on his shoulder, she melted in his arms, moving with him when he swayed and shifted his feet in a slow dance. The tension that had pounded at her temples slipped away as he held her, and Nicole could almost pretend they were alone, the only two people in this corner of the world.

Daniel skimmed a hand up her spine, sending sparks of shimmery heat through her blood. When he reached her nape, his thumb caressed her sensitized skin with lazy, hypnotic strokes.

"You know," he murmured, his deep voice a low, sexy rumble, "I always kind of regretted that we didn't make it to prom that night. I'd been hoping I'd have the chance to dance with you."

She smiled and curled her fingers in the fabric of his dress coat. "Then this dance was long overdue."

He drew a slow deep breath, then let it out on a hum of pleasure. "And worth the wait."

"Agreed." She snuggled closer, inhaling the crisp scent of soap that clung to him. She closed her eyes and savored the moment. But all too soon the ballad ended and a faster song began. Daniel stopped dancing, but he didn't step back right away. He didn't have to tell her he was thinking about his guard duty, the rules he'd already broken for her.

Nicole mentally scrambled for a way to extend the precious minutes she'd had in his arms. She wasn't ready to say good-night to the thoughtful Daniel she'd gotten to know on her prom night, the honorable soldier concerned tonight for his duty, the sexy man whose touch made her feel thoroughly feminine and on fire.

"I should—"

"Be my date tonight," she interrupted. Lifting her head, she met his dark gaze and gripped his arms to keep him from moving away. Hoping she sounded enticing and impulsive rather than desperate, she flashed a grin. "Come inside with me, and we can spend the rest of the night dancing."

His expression dimmed. "I can't leave my post. Not until my replacement arrives at midnight."

Hope swelled in her chest. "What if someone else covered your post until then? Robert, our chauffeur, is trained in security and often works protection detail for my father." She reached in his front coat pocket, pulled out the cell phone she'd felt there while they danced and dialed.

Daniel opened his mouth to argue, but she turned a shoulder as Robert came on the line. Within minutes, a scowling and skeptical Robert was in place at the front steps, and Daniel had no more excuses not to join her inside.

A giddy sense of victory swirled through her when Daniel finally relented and followed her up the porch stairs. Her triumph was all the sweeter when she thought of the buffer Daniel would provide between her and her father's tedious friends.

Daniel offered her his arm as they crossed the porch. "Is this going to cause a problem with your father?"

Nicole hiked up her chin, remembering the blind eye her father turned to his business associates' behavior toward her. "Maybe. But I don't care. It will teach him a lesson."

Daniel frowned as they stepped into the foyer. "I don't want to get in the middle of some family thing...."

"Don't worry." She tugged his arm, pulling him into the-ballroom, where the volume of music and voices made conversation difficult. "I've got this."

Daniel could feel Senator White's dark glare following him as Nicole led him out onto the dance floor. When she'd explained why Daniel was at her side, the senator had clearly been unhappy with her stunt, and something in Nicole's manner had rankled Daniel, as well. But once he had Nicole in his arms again, the senator faded from his thoughts. With Nicole pressed against his body, his hands on the silky skin of her back, the delicate scent of her surrounding him, he forgot anything beyond that moment, this woman. And the fire that consumed him.

When she threaded her fingers through his short cropped hair or angled her head to flash him a smile with equal parts of sweetness and seduction, his blood ran hot, and his need wound tighter. Months of anticipation and longing coiled inside him.

He'd spent the past five years thinking about Nicole and regretting the chance he'd let slip through his fingers the night he'd walked her home with her new kitten. His sense of honor and propriety, along with a belief that she was out of his reach, had lulled him into inaction when she was sixteen. Since that night, he'd sworn never to miss another opportunity, in any form, when it knocked. For a kid from the bayou, life didn't offer many lucky breaks or second chances.

As they moved together, she chatted amiably, filling him in on her years in nursing school, her mother's illness and recent death, her dream of working overseas in one of the many poor communities where health care was so desperately needed. She quizzed him on his career plans with the Navy, his last tour in the Persian Gulf, his specialty in weapons and explosives.

"Why weapons?" she asked with a frown.

He shrugged. "Because…I'm a guy, and guys like guns and things that go boom."

Her frown turned to a scowling pout, and he was slammed with the urge to kiss her plump raspberry lips. He swallowed hard and determinedly refocused his thoughts. "Because…" he said, schooling his face. "It was where I was needed. It's what I'm good at."

Her smile warmed. "I bet you're good at a lot of things."

He grunted in acknowledgment and brushed his thumb over her bottom lip. "Better at some things than others."

Her pale blue gaze heated, and she canted closer, tracing his ear with her finger. "Do tell."

Lust sent a scalding jolt through him, and as his desire-crazed brain scrambled, weighing discretion against temptation, a firm hand clapped him on the shoulder.

"I'm cutting in," her father said, effectively dousing the flames licking Daniel's veins.

Nicole stiffened. "Actually, I'd rather not." She pulled away from her father's grip and gave Daniel a confident smile. "Daniel was just about to take me home. These shoes are killing me, and my headache from earlier is back."

"Nonsense." The senator took her elbow and guided his daughter off the dance floor. "If you're ready to go home, I can leave now, or have Robert drive you back to the hotel."

"No, Dad, I—" Nicole turned, met Daniel's gaze with a silent plea in her eyes.

Firming his jaw, Daniel wedged through the crowd and cut the senator off at the edge of the dance floor. "The hotel is on my way, sir. It would be my pleasure to take Nicole home."

Nicole beamed, freeing her arm from her father's grasp. "I'll be fine. Good night, Dad."

Daniel seized the chance to pull Nicole toward the front door. He could feel her father's glare burning holes in his back as he escorted Nicole outside and toward the parked cars.

She looped her arm in his and leaned into him as they crossed the grassy lawn. "Thank you. If I'd had to dance with my left-footed father or one of his ass-grabbing friends again tonight, I think I'd—"

Daniel stopped short. "Ass-grabbing?"

She snorted derisively. "Oh, yeah. Right before I came out and found you, the sleazeball from the Chamber of Commerce copped himself a feel."

He tensed and fisted his hands, feeling the thrum of anger pounding at his temples. Performing a stiff about-face, he stalked back toward the mansion. "Show him to me."

Nicole slipped off her high heels and jogged to catch up to him. "Why? So you can defend my honor by punching him in the dentures?" She blocked his path, and when she met his gaze, her eyes sparkled with mirth. "I'm flattered by your chivalry, but save your energy."

He sucked in a deep breath, struggling to calm his raging pulse. "It's just…when I think of some creep with his hands on your—"

She laughed and ran her fingers up the front of his jacket. "You wish you'd thought of it?"

He scoffed and caught her hands in his, tugging her closer. "Believe me, *cher*. I thought about it plenty."

She laced her fingers with his, her expression coy. "Then why didn't you?" She tugged his hands behind her and planted them at the small of her back. "I think I'd like having your hands on me."

The coil of lust inside him yanked tighter. With a groan, he slid his hands down the silky fabric of her dress to palm her bottom. He curled his fingers, testing the supple flesh beneath her dress and tugging her closer.

She sighed her pleasure, and when she tipped her head up, her eyes zeroing in on his mouth, he captured her lips with his. Moving one hand to cradle the base of her head, he held her in place while he explored the taste and texture of her kiss. She clutched at his back, returning his passion and meeting the thrust and parry of his tongue. A sound somewhere between a whimper and a purr rumbled in her throat, and the seductive mewl threw kindling on the fire already blazing in his blood. He wanted her so much he hurt.

"Nicole," he rasped, barely recognizing his own voice, "let me take you home."

"Only if you promise not to leave me at the door." She nibbled her way down his jaw to his ear. "Last time, in high school, you left me…aching for you." Nicole looped her arms around his neck, pressing her breasts against his chest. "I'm still aching for you."

He half moaned, half sighed. "The feeling is mutual."

When he slipped his hands under her dress and filled his hands with her bare bottom, she gasped. "Daniel…"

He shifted his hand, delving a finger into the moist heat between her legs, before the slam of a car door reminded him they were in public. If not for her reputation, he'd take her there in the grassy lawn of the antebellum mansion. But he wouldn't subject her to any scandal or scorn from her social set. Grasping her arms, he kissed her forehead and levered back. "Not here. Which hotel are you staying at?"

She gave him the name of a posh hotel on Canal Street, and as he led her to his truck, he stooped to pick up the shoes she'd kicked off earlier. They seemed ridiculously small to him—size 6—with dangerously spiked heels. "How do you walk in these?"

She grinned. "Very carefully."

He smacked another kiss on her lips before closing her door and circling to the driver's side. The thirty-minute drive to her hotel was torture. He fought the urge to pull to the side of the road and toss her in the backseat, or stop at one of the many lower-rent motels they passed. But Nicole White was not the kind of woman he could take to a second-rate motor inn. He would wait another half hour until they reached her hotel room. Even if his body was strung tighter than a guy wire.

If it killed him, he would wait. For Nicole.

Chapter 2

Present day—Colombia

Nicole woke with a start when a large hand clamped over her mouth and a low male voice growled in her ear, "Don't make any noise."

He gaze flew to the dark figure hovering over her, and panic flooded her brain. In the night shadows, she could tell little about her attacker, except that he was large, and strong, and dark featured. When she squirmed, trying to find Tia, terrified this man could have harmed the little girl, the man's hold on her tightened.

"It's all right, Nicole. I won't hurt you," he whispered, his mouth so close to her that his lips brushed the shell of her ear and his warm breath fanned her neck. In the fog of her fear, it took her a moment to realize he'd used her name. And that he spoke English.

She snapped a startled gaze to his, straining to make out

his face while her heart drummed an anxious beat against her ribs. No use. In the blackness of the jungle night, she couldn't see anything distinguishing about his face.

"I'm an American operative. I'm here to take you home. Do you understand?"

Home. The word held such sweet promise, she couldn't help the whimper of relief that squeaked from her throat.

Her attacker—no, her *rescuer*—loosened his grip on her mouth. "Promise to be quiet?"

She nodded, and tears of joy puddled in her eyes. She was going home. *Finally.* And Tia could get the medical attention she needed. Nicole's heart soared, even though the prospect of escaping the camp filled her with a chilling fear.

As he removed his hand from her mouth, the man dragged his fingers along her chin, brushing her hair back from her face and wiping a tear from her cheek with his thumb. The intimate gesture startled her, and the first uneasy whispers that something was off tickled her nape. He hovered, scant inches above her, and she searched his face, wishing desperately she could see him better in the darkness. Then, with a troubled-sounding sigh, he dipped his head.

And kissed her.

Nicole's breath caught, and her pulse scampered on a fresh wave of panic. Had he lied about his intentions? When her initial, paralyzing shock passed, she gained the frame of mind to resist. But hesitated.

His lips were gentle. The tender caress of his mouth surprised her, intrigued her. Filled her with a sweet warmth. Her body responded to his kiss as if she'd known him her whole life…and yet the edgy prickle at her neck bit harder.

A groan rumbled from his chest, and he broke the kiss to sit back on his heels, muttering a curse under his breath. "Sorry. I shouldn't have done that."

"Damn right, you shouldn't have! Who are you?" she whispered fiercely.

He tensed and angled a hooded glance toward her. "Your ticket outta here. Get up." His tone was gruff now, in contradiction to his soft kiss, and she shivered, despite the clammy heat of the jungle. "I brought shoes and socks for you. Size 6, right?"

"I—yes. How did you know?"

"It's my job to know." He slid a pack off his back and pulled out a pair of boots. "Can you walk? We have a difficult hike ahead of us."

"I can, but Tia's weak." She glanced to the sleeping girl, whose age she estimated at eight years and who'd shared her cage for the past several months. She'd come to love Tia like a daughter, bonding with the terrified child as she protected her from the cruelty of their guards. "She's had a fever and hasn't eaten in days."

Her rescuer followed her glance to Tia and shook his head. "Forget it. She's not coming with us." He shoved the boots at her. "Put these on. Hurry."

Nicole's chest tightened. "What? She has to come. She'll die here if I leave her!" She shifted her gaze down the row of night-darkened cages. "And what about the others? There are twelve of us being held here!"

He clamped a hand over her mouth and growled in her ear. "Keep your voice down." He grabbed the socks up and shoved one onto her foot. "Our objective is to get *you* out. Only you. We can't take anyone else."

She snatched her foot away. "Why? Because they're not American?" Disdain filled her voice, but she didn't care. "Their lives still matter. We can't leave—"

"No. Only you. We only have provisions for you." His tone brooked no resistance, and he tossed a boot into her lap. "Hurry up."

"Then…take Tia instead of me. Please. She's just a child. This is no place for an eight-year-old girl."

He glanced at Tia again and jammed fingers through his short black hair. Hope fluttered in Nicole's chest. Clearly the idea of leaving a little girl behind bothered him.

He released a ragged sigh and cupped a hand at the nape of Nicole's neck. "Don't do this. I have been planning this rescue for months. I'm here to take *you* home. You, Nicole." He kept his voice low, but his tone vibrated with fury and frustration.

An odd sense of familiarity sketched down her spine. Something about his voice…

"I will not do anything that could jeopardize my objective. Got it?"

Nicole's temper spiked. "Did I ask you to save me?"

She felt him tense, his fingers digging into her scalp. "Get your ass moving, or I'll carry you out of here."

A frisson of fear slithered through her. Indecision. Anguish. "I won't leave her. If you don't take her, I'm not going, either." To prove her point, Nicole shoved the boot into his chest and let it drop.

Even with the night shadows, she couldn't miss the lethal scowl he narrowed on her.

"Lafitte!" another male voice whispered just outside her plywood shelter. "What the hell's the hold up? Haul ass!"

Her rescuer bit out another curse, in French this time, and pivoted to where Tia slept. Bending over her, he scooped the girl into his arms.

Relief and gratitude swept through Nicole and left her trembling.

When Tia woke and whimpered in fright, the man clapped a hand over her mouth…which only frightened Tia more.

Quickly Nicole scrambled over and stroked Tia's arm, squeezed her hand. "It's okay, *mija. Es un amigo.*" She tugged the man's hand away from Tia's mouth, then tapped her own finger to Tia's lips. "Shh."

Nicole didn't miss the irony of hushing a girl who hadn't spoken a word since arriving at the camp, traumatized and alone. Tia raised wide brown eyes so full of blind trust that Nicole's heart twisted. She prayed trusting these men, attempting an escape with them, didn't prove a deadly mistake.

When Tia quieted, Nicole jammed the boots on her feet and crawled out of her plywood lean-to in time to see her rescuer pass Tia off to the second man.

"What the hell?" the second man whispered harshly.

"Change of plans," he grumbled under his breath, then stalked back to Nicole. "Ready?" He offered her a hand up, which she took. When he'd pulled her to her feet, he drew her close, and she grabbed one of his muscular arms while she found her balance. "We have to move fast. If you can't run, I'll carry you."

Judging by the size of the arm she held and the width of his chest, she had no doubt he could carry her for miles. The notion started an odd tremble low in her belly. She shook her head. "No. I can run."

"Good. Keep your head down, and do exactly as I say, *when* I say. Got it?" His tone and face were hard and unyielding.

She bristled a bit at his high-handedness but swallowed the sharp retort that came to mind. Under the circumstances, she'd forgive his bossiness. "Got it."

He seized her hand and hauled her with him as he moved to the hole cut in the cage that had imprisoned her. The second man had already carried Tia out and was headed toward the perimeter fence. She scurried through the gap and glanced warily around the dark camp, her heart thundering.

Two shadowy dark figures lay unmoving in the dirt by the weapons cache, and a sick understanding crawled through her.

Her rescuers had killed those men and who knew how many others in order to reach her. Bile rose in her throat, and she fought the urge to vomit.

As he rose to his feet, her rescuer shoved a cumbersome-looking pair of goggles on his head, then pulled a large hand-gun from the waist of his fatigues, reinforcing her recognition of his deadly skill. Her breath hung in her lungs. Apprehension shuddered through her.

Before she could reconcile this lethal soldier with the man who'd kissed her so sweetly and dried her tear moments ear-lier, he grabbed her arm and ran. She stumbled, trying to keep up with the pace he set, and gritting her teeth, she forced her exercise-deprived legs to move faster. She refused to slow him down, be a hindrance to their escape.

When they reached the hole cut in the perimeter fence, she had precious seconds to rest while the first man shimmied through the hole on his belly. As they coaxed Tia through the gap, Nicole gasped for breath, already winded. The pitch blackness of the jungle loomed beyond the fence that served not only to keep prisoners in, but also to keep wild animals out. Their escape route lay through that dense, wild terrain.

"Nicole." Her rescuer waved her toward the hole in the fence. "Come on, *cher.*"

The endearment reverberated in her head as she dropped to her knees in preparation to crawl through the hole. She recognized the colloquial Cajun French term, pronounced *sha,* which she heard often in her home state. "You're from Louisiana."

He stilled for an instant, and she felt more than saw his gaze boring into hers. "Yes." Before she could respond, he put a hand on her head and shoved her down. "Go!"

She did, with Cajun Man at her heels. Already the second man had disappeared into the thick foliage with Tia. Once through the fence, her rescuer dug in his pack and gave her a pair of goggles like the ones he and his partner wore. "Put these on."

She obeyed, then marveled at the green images that leaped out of the blackness of the night. Night vision goggles. Of course. She studied him with her newly enhanced vision, but he, too, wore a pair of goggles that obscured her view of his face. The goggles only confirmed for her that he was dark-haired and broad-shouldered and had a heavy layer of stubble covering his cheeks and chin. She'd had little chance to familiarize herself with the goggles before he grabbed her hand and pulled her into the jungle.

Behind them, a voice shouted in the camp. A warning. An alert. Someone had discovered the dead guards or her empty cage.

Cajun Man's hand tightened around hers. "Damn! Go, go, go!"

Through the overgrown jungle, she heard the rebel encampment waking, engines starting, angry shouts. He tugged her arm, urging her to go faster, and adrenaline fueled her feet.

Their escape path led them up the steep side of a mountain, and soon her muscles trembled from exertion. Nicole used her free hand to grab limbs and roots, anything she could use to help pull herself up the incline as he hauled her forward by the hand. She couldn't quit, had to find the strength to press on. Letting the rebel soldiers catch her now would mean certain death.

Wide-leafed branches slapped at her legs, her face. Around her, the eyes of nocturnal animals glowed in her goggles, and she fought the fear that threatened to suffocate her. She had to keep moving, keep running. Keep putting one foot in front of the other.

Finally, they reached the top of the incline, and the terrain leveled out. Cajun Man never slowed their pace. The foliage thinned out in places making their progress easier. Many minutes later, when Nicole thought she might drop from exhaustion, he slowed at last and led her behind a wide tree trunk where his partner had stopped with Tia.

She gulped oxygen and collapsed on the ground beside the little girl. Tia crawled close and buried her head in Nicole's chest.

"Where are we?" Cajun Man asked his friend, who'd pulled out a small gadget she couldn't identify in the dark, even with her night vision goggles.

"Chopper's still a couple miles north," his partner answered.

Her heart beat so hard she could barely hear their discussion over the pounding pulse in her ears.

Turning, Cajun Man crouched in front of her and squeezed her shoulder. "How are you holding up?"

She nodded, unable to find the breath to speak.

"And the kid?" He jerked his head toward Tia.

"Scared," Nicole panted. "But…all right."

The night vision goggles helped her make out general forms in an unnatural green glow, but the details of Cajun's and his partner's appearances were still a mystery. She shoved aside her frustration with not knowing what her rescuers looked like. What did it matter as long as they got her and Tia out of that jungle alive? It didn't. Yet she couldn't quash the eerie prickle of familiarity his voice evoked.

He handed her a flask from his pack. "Drink."

She waved his offering away. "I'm okay."

"Drink," he repeated more forcefully, shoving the canteen into her hand. "I can't have you passing out on me later when I need you to run."

Capitulating, she uncapped the flask and tipped it up to her lips. She almost groaned in pleasure as a sweet fruity drink bathed her tongue. An energy drink. How long had it been since she'd had anything but foul water to drink?

Brushing Tia's hair back from her eyes, Nicole gave the canteen to the girl and helped her take a sip. When the little girl tasted the sweet drink, she clutched the canteen tighter and tipped it higher for a bigger gulp.

"Hey!" Cajun snatched the container back. "That's gotta last until we're outta here. Those of us who are hoofing it get priority."

Tia shrank away from him, huddling closer to Nicole with a whimper.

Nicole bit back a retort. She had to remember that this man had risked his life to save her and had brought Tia along against his better judgment and despite the limited provisions he'd made. She raised her chin and worked at keeping her voice nonconfrontational. "Could you please try not to scare her? She's just a kid, and she's already been through a nightmare."

He paused in the act of stashing the canteen in his pack, cast a side-glance to Nicole and heaved an impatient sigh as he shoved to his feet. "Enough rest. Let's move." He faced his partner and gave a nod. "Alec?"

His partner stowed his own canteen and stepped forward to help Nicole to her feet. Cajun Man lifted Tia into his arms and led the way with Nicole following and his partner—Alec, he'd called him—bringing up the rear. Though they were no longer running, they moved at a fast clip, and Nicole had trouble keeping up. The distance between the Cajun and Nicole widened by the minute, until, maybe an hour later, Alec finally cupped his hands around his mouth and made a shrill noise, something between a bird call and monkey. Cajun Man stopped, setting Tia on the ground, and Alec grabbed Nicole's arm to hustle her forward.

"This is taking too long," Cajun Man said as they approached, clearly agitated. "You go on," he said to Alec. "Take the girl and tell Jake to get the chopper ready. I'll stay with her, and we'll be there...whenever." His tone was full of frustration.

"Roger that." Without further discussion, Alec lifted Tia into his arms and disappeared into the jungle foliage. A ripple of apprehension shimmied through Nicole. Not that she didn't trust the Cajun, but having her rescue team halved felt like a dangerous move.

"Are you sure that's a good idea?" She pressed a hand to the stitch in her side.

"Normally, no." He paused, the silence taut with recriminations. "But under the circumstances—"

She grunted defensively. "I'm sorry I'm slowing you down. But all those months in a cage without exercise have left me out of shape."

He faced her and cocked his head as he studied her. The jungle shadows and his night vision goggles made him look like a strange insect from a sci-fi flick. "I know that."

His tone was softer now, almost apologetic, and she slumped at the base of a tree. Yanking off the cumbersome goggles, she rubbed her aching temples with the heels of her hands. His mercurial moods baffled her, set her on edge. "Look, I appreciate the risks you've taken to get me out of that stink hole. I'm doing everything I can to cooperate. But sometimes it seems like you're..." She waved a hand, searching for the right word, then dropped it limply to her lap again. "I don't know...mad at me or something. Have I done something to tick you off?"

Cajun Man was silent, and without her goggles, he was nothing but a looming figure in the blackness. For a moment, she thought he wouldn't answer, but finally he murmured, "Not you. Your father."

Her pulse kicked, and she sat taller. "What does any of this have to do with my father?"

"Everything," he growled, then sighed heavily. "And nothing."

She huffed her annoyance with his cryptic responses. "Which is it?"

"Let's just say it's bitterly ironic that I'm the one who'll be bringing you home to your father."

She blinked, befuddled by his word choice. "Ironic? Why?"

She sensed his hard gaze as a tingle skittered down her spine.

"Because your father tried to kill me."

When here?"

Chapter 3

A laugh of disbelief erupted from Nicole. "No way! My father is not a murderer." She scoffed and shook her head, amazed she was even debating such an absurd topic. "I may have had my differences with him in the past, but he's an upstanding citizen and an honorable man. He's a United States Senator, for heaven's sake."

The Cajun dropped quickly to a crouch in front of her, and she felt the stir of his breath when he jammed his face inches from hers to growl, "Not anymore. He was censured and later resigned."

Nicole's chest tightened. "Why?"

"Because he's a traitor to the United States."

She huffed indignantly. "That's a lie! He'd never—"

"He did," Cajun snarled. "I can *prove* that he negotiated with a terrorist and gave up classified information vital to national security, trying to get you released." He paused, breathing hard. "And while I respect his goal—clearly I've risked my own life to get you out of this hellhole—I would *never* have betrayed my country to do it."

Nausea swamped her gut, and she shook her head, trying to clear the confusing jumble of information that buzzed through her brain. "I—I don't believe you."

He grunted his disgust and impatience. "You don't have to believe me. I know what I know."

Nicole worked to form enough spit in her dry mouth to swallow. She fumbled to put her night vision goggles back on, to try again to identify her father's accuser. "Who are you, and what is it you think he did? I'm sure there's a logical explanation."

Cajun Man shoved to his feet again and angrily slapped a low-hanging branch out of his way. "A few months ago, he betrayed two American operatives working a top secret mission in enemy territory. He was trying to win your release, but…clearly, it didn't work."

Nicole's stomach swirled, acid biting hard. "Wh-what happened to the operatives?"

He didn't answer for several seconds, and dread screwed tighter in her chest.

"They took it upon themselves to rescue you, despite what your father almost cost them."

Nicole drew a silent gasp as the earth beneath her pitched. "Y-you…?"

Rather than answer her, he flicked his hand, motioning for her to stand up. "Come on. Time to go."

She gaped at him, too numb to move. "So…what? I'm some kind of pawn in your vendetta with my father?"

"Sounds about right. And it evens the score between you and me, too. Don't you think?"

She shook her head, stunned and confused. "Am I supposed to know you?"

He snorted derisively. "Says a lot that you don't."

"Look, stop talking in riddles and tell me what's going on! Who are you?" As hard as she was trying to keep her voice low, frustration and anger sharpened her tone.

"Get—" A loud pop cut the Cajun off and echoed through the dark jungle. Then a series of nerve-rattling cracks. Cajun Man barked a curse and yanked her to her feet. "Snipers! Run!"

Staggering, Nicole ran, fueled by fear. Cajun Man led the way, returning fire with his handgun. Around her bits of bark and dirt flew. The snipers' bullets zinged past her. She charged forward, blindly following the Cajun.

Suddenly, with an agonized scream, he fell.

Nicole skidded to a stop and dropped behind the modest protection of a fallen tree. The Cajun dragged himself forward, clutching his left leg, and an icy chill raced through her. She scrambled to his side. "You're hit?"

He pushed her away. "Forget me and go!" he rasped. "Straight ahead. Alec has the chopper—"

"I can't leave you here!" She moved closer and, with the help of her night vision goggles, she saw the bloody mess that was his knee. "Oh, my God!"

Despite her medical training, her gut pitched. He had to be in excruciating pain. Staying low to avoid the continuing rain of sniper fire, she whipped her shirt over her head. Unmindful of her dishabille, she tore the shirt at the side seam.

"No time!" He batted her away when she tried to staunch his bleeding. "Go!"

Tears filled her eyes. "And leave you here to die? How heartless do you think I am?"

He rolled his head back, teeth gritted and his thick neck arched as he growled in pain. "Nicole!"

Desperation and adrenaline spurred her to action. Wrapping her shirt around his knee, she tied the fabric off, then grabbed the front of his shirt in a fist. "Get up, soldier!" He wasn't the only one who could bark orders. "You *will* go with me. Now!"

She shoved her shoulder under his left armpit and struggled to get him upright and still stay behind the protection of the large tree.

Indecision bit Nicole. The Cajun was twice her size, and they were surrounded by snipers. How was she supposed to get them both to the helicopter safely?

The Cajun clearly read her dilemma, and with his superior strength, pried himself out of her grip. "Leave me, damn it! Run!"

Emotion clogged Nicole's throat, but she choked out, "Promise you'll follow." He jerked a nod that didn't quite convince her, but the hail of bullets seemed to be closing in. She stuck her face in the Cajun's and shouted, "I'll bring Alec back for you."

"No!" he yelled as she turned to run.

Moisture not only blurred her vision, but in the hot jungle, her night vision goggles steamed up. Giving up on the goggles, she yanked them off and tossed them behind her as she plowed forward. The first thin rays of morning sun filtered through the jungle canopy, and with the watery light as a guide, she rushed toward what appeared to be a clearing ahead. The whir of a motor reached her over the pounding of her pulse and the pop of gunfire.

Please God, let that engine be Alec with the helicopter.

"Alec!" Screaming for his help took almost more breath than she had left. Surely he'd heard the gunfire. Where was—?

A hand grabbed her arm and swung her into the thick vegetation. She swallowed her gasp, recognizing the tall, dark-haired man still wearing his night vision goggles. "Alec!"

He shoved her behind him. "Keep your head down!" Leaning against a tree branch with an automatic weapon propped on his shoulder, Alec fired into the trees. "Jake's got the chopper ready. That way!" He freed a hand long enough to push her toward the clearing.

She jerked away. "Where's Tia?"

"On the chopper with Jake."

She nodded in relief, then gasped, "Your partner was shot. We have to go back for him!" She started back the way she'd come, trusting Alec would follow.

"Nicole, wait!" He grabbed at her retreating back, but because she'd shed her shirt, he came up empty-handed. "Nicole!"

"Hurry!" She didn't wait. Desperate to reach the Cajun, she pumped her legs, knocking palm fronds out of her way with her arm, retracing her steps, using tree trunks for cover and the thick foliage to camouflage her progress. The sun was slightly higher now. Shadowy forms separated from the thin gray light that seeped through the jungle ceiling. Terror coiled around her like a python, squeezing her chest, but she forcefully battled the fear down. She had to keep it together. Not just for her own sake, but for Tia. For Alec and for the Cajun who, even though he hated her for some unknown offense, had risked his life, taken a bullet in his leg, saving her.

Alec, moving so silently she didn't hear him until he was upon her, pressed close behind Nicole, his automatic weapon at the ready.

The snipers' fire had slacked off, although she still saw an occasional muzzle flash in the upper branches followed by the chilling thud of a bullet hitting the ground.

"Go back to the chopper. I'll find him," Alec growled.

They'd only gotten half of the way back to where she'd left the Cajun, and something deep inside her wouldn't let her leave the jungle without him. She'd opened her mouth to argue, when one of the dark shadows moved with a lurch and a groan.

Nicole's heart stutter-stepped in admiration and compassion. Despite the obvious pain he was in, the Cajun was struggling toward their extraction point. As he neared, she made out the branch he used as a crutch while he dragged his bloodied leg behind him. He'd taken off his goggles as she had, and no longer had his backpack. Everything in his body language, from his rigidly set jaw, taut mouth, fisted hands and forward canting body as he staggered through the jungle exuded a sheer grit and steely determination. This man was a warrior. A fighter. A survivor.

Your father tried to kill me.

Nicole shook her head to clear the baffling accusation from her thoughts. She'd have time to work through the Cajun's assertions later. Right now, they had to get back to the helicopter.

She hurried toward him with Alec on her heels. Hearing them, Cajun jerked his head up, along with his gun.

She inhaled sharply. "Don't shoot. It's us."

He blew out a harsh breath. "Damn it, Nicole! I told you not to—"

"I know what you said," she countered, as Alec wedged himself under his partner's left arm, and Nicole moved to his right side. "I chose to ignore your orders. I knew and accepted the risk of helping you." She tensed her legs as he shifted some of his weight onto her and limped forward a couple steps. She angled a quick glance at his grimacing face and couldn't resist adding, "I figure it evens the score between you and me."

He stiffened. Whipped a startled look toward her. The thin dappled light still cast his face in shadow, but she felt the intensity of his glare. Without commenting, he hobbled forward. "Faster. I can take it."

"But you're—" The rat-a-tat of an automatic weapon echoed through the jungle behind them, getting closer.

"Don't baby me," he snarled. "Let's move!"

Holding tightly to his arm, his waist, Nicole half jogged, half staggered as she and Alec all but dragged the Cajun. He screamed in pain but demanded they keep up their pace. By the time they reached the clearing where the chopper waited, her legs were jelly, and her arm muscles quivered. As they left the line of trees, Alec shoved his weapon at her and hoisted his partner over his shoulder in a fireman's carry. "Cover us!"

Nicole gaped at the automatic weapon in her hands and shuddered. She'd only seen guns like this one fired. Had never held, much less fired, one.

But a new hail of bullets peppered the clearing as Alec ran for the chopper door with the Cajun across his back. Nicole swung the big gun up and fired toward the muzzle flashes in the jungle. Spinning on her heel, she darted across the open field, praying that everything she'd heard about moving targets was true. She kept her eyes fixed on the open door of the helicopter. Inside, she could see Tia in her pink shorts, huddled with her hands over her ears.

Alec dumped his partner unceremoniously on the floor of the chopper, then ran to the copilot's seat, yelling to the pilot, "Take off, cowboy!"

Panting for breath, Nicole dove into the open side of the chopper. The instant she was aboard, the helicopter lurched off the ground. Her stomach pitched as they ascended and swooped over the treetops. Dropping the weapon in her hands as if it were a rattlesnake, Nicole gasped for air and took a mental survey. She was in one piece, even though nicks and cuts on her arms and legs trickled blood.

And Tia was safe—even if the gunfire and tumult had clearly revived whatever nightmare she'd survived earlier. Nicole scuttled awkwardly across the rocking helicopter floor until she reached the frightened child.

With a whimper, Tia wrapped her arms around Nicole and

buried her face on her shoulder. Tia's warm tears dripped onto Nicole's skin, reminding her that she'd sacrificed her shirt to the Cajun's knee, so she wore only a bra. She closed her eyes and sighed, unable to find the energy to care. Modesty seemed a ludicrous indulgence in light of the situation.

"Nicole…" The strangled-sounding voice was almost lost in the roar of the helicopter turbines.

She raised her head to meet the Cajun's gaze. His dark eyes were wild with agony, and his face contorted in misery when the chopper hit an air pocket, jostling him. She hated seeing him suffer, no matter what vile allegations he'd leveled against her father. Whatever his reasons, his agenda, he *had* saved her—and Tia—from that cesspool prison camp.

"Ni-cole," he repeated and held a hand out, summoning her to come closer.

Giving Tia a reassuring smile, she untangled herself from the child's grip and moved to his side.

Nicole grasped his hand with one of hers and stroked his stubble-covered face with her other hand, wishing she could do something, anything to ease his pain. At that moment, the morning sun broke over the tops of the trees and shone through the open side door of the helicopter, casting his rugged face in sharp relief. For the first time, she could truly see the man who'd risked his life for her. Even with heavy black stubble covering his jaw, mud smudged on his cheeks and his features drawn in a grimace of pain, her Cajun rescuer was a devastatingly handsome man. Her heart clenched, and the prickle of déjà vu returned. He seemed so familiar.…

"I…need—" He stopped, clenching his teeth and growling in torment. "Please…I need—"

Tears puddled in her eyes. "What do you need? Tell me."

She had no idea what medical supplies, painkillers or other provisions the helicopter had, but she'd move heaven and earth to get him the best care when they were back in the States.

He drew a couple shallow breaths, his jaw tightening again. "I need to know…you remember." He swallowed hard, his eyes drilling into hers. "Tell me…you remember."

His request, and the obvious emotional distress behind it, rattled her. Witnessing his physical pain was hard enough. She opened her mouth to ask what he meant, but the tortured plea in his eyes stole her breath and her resolve.

"I remember," she lied, leaning closer to be sure he heard her.

He held her gaze for a moment, sweat beading on his forehead and expectant hope lighting his gaze. Then he scowled darkly and jerked his gaze away. He ground his back teeth together and scrunched his face in agony.

With lightning speed, he seized the back of her head and wound his fingers in her hair so tightly her scalp prickled. She gasped, as he pulled her down so that her face hovered right above his. "Then say my name!"

She stared at him, stunned by his vehemence and trying to reconcile the nagging intuition she'd had since he'd kissed her at the camp that something didn't add up. The niggling familiarity of his voice. Her body's response to his touch.

"Say my name, Nicole," he repeated, raggedly this time. "I want to hear you say it."

And in a heartbeat, an echo from her past yanked her back five years to a hotel room in New Orleans. Her heart wrenched, and tears spilled from her eyes.

"Oh, my God!" She curled her fingers into the hair at his nape and buried her face in his neck. "Daniel…"

Five years earlier

"What do you think?" Nicole asked as she struck a pose wearing Daniel's uniform hat. Only his uniform hat. "Could I be in the Navy?"

From the hotel bed, Daniel stacked his hands behind his

head, a move that emphasized the broad cut of his bare shoulders and the muscle definition in his arms. He sent her a seductive grin. "What I think is that I'll never wear my dress whites again without thinking how much better they look on you."

Nicole dropped her pose and crawled across the bed to him, letting her fingers walk up his chest. "Personally, as hot as you look in your dress whites, I have to say I like you out of them even more."

She flashed him a wicked grin, earning a playful pat on her fanny before he captured her head with his hand and dragged her close for a hot kiss. Despite having made love to him four times already in the past few hours, the heat of his mouth on hers, the stroke of his fingers along her thigh sent a thrill through her blood and made her body quiver in anticipation of another mind-blowing climax. She'd never, in her limited experience, known a man who could so thoroughly and continually elicit such a powerful and carnal response from her. He'd explored every inch of her body and unerringly found and finessed erogenous zones she'd never known she had.

Breathless, she plucked a condom from the bedside stand and ripped it open. "What do you say, Boudreaux? Are you ready for me?"

Holding her gaze, he took the prophylactic from her and covered himself. "Now I am."

In a deft move, he kicked the sheet off his feet and flipped her to her back. She gasped, then laughed as he straddled her, pinning her arms over her head with one hand and running one finger along the side of her midriff. She squirmed, trying to get away from the teasing touch. "Stop," she said, giggling, "I told you I'm ticklish."

He arched a sexy black eyebrow, and his dark brown gaze burrowed into her. "And I told you what would happen if you called me Boudreaux again."

She squealed in mirth as he lightly trailed his fingers over her most sensitive spots. "Stop!"

He traced the curve of her hip and down her leg. "What's my name?"

"Boudreaux!"

He shook his head and tickled his way past her naval, then circled her nipples with one finger. "Say my name. My real name."

She chuckled, flashed a saucy grin. "Afraid I've forgotten it?"

His head cocked to one side. "Have you?"

"No."

"Prove it." He tweaked the tip of her breast and shifted his weight so that his erection nudged between her legs.

Just the promise of what was to come coiled desire in her womb and chased the teasing grin from her lips. The fiery sensations crackling through her were no laughing matter. She wanted him inside her with an urgency that was primal and overwhelming. She angled her hips, straining toward him. "Please…"

Even when she wrapped her legs around him and arched her back, he waited.

"Say my name." His tone held no humor, and his eyes shone with a hunger and passion that stirred a tremor deep in her core. He brushed a kiss across her lips and nuzzled her cheek. "I want to hear my name on your lips when I'm inside you."

The sensual rasp of his voice stroked her, wound her anticipation tighter, while the poignant intimacy of his request seized her heart. She threaded her fingers through his hair and raised her lips to his ear. "Daniel. Daniel LeCroix…"

Nicole whispered his name, rolling the *R* in a sensual purr that vibrated through him and stoked the need that pounded through his veins. His body thrumming, he drew a ragged breath and buried himself inside her. "Ah, Nicole...*cher*..."

A sexy gasp caught in her throat, and she moaned as he filled her. Her body gripped his, and a protectiveness, an overwhelming need to possess her, drove him to hold her closer, thrust deeper, take her higher. When they'd made love the first time, he'd thought he could get his fill of her and satisfy the fascination with her that had begun on her prom night years ago. Instead he found the more they made love, the more he wanted her and the more he lost his heart to her.

With a mewling cry, Nicole bowed her back and shuddered as she peaked. "Daniel!"

The first pulse of her body milking him shattered his restraint, and primal noises rumbled from his throat as he followed her into a mind-numbing climax.

When the maelstrom passed and the sensual haze began to lift, he knew he was in trouble. His caring this much about her gave Nicole power over him. Rather than getting her out of his head, she'd found a way past his defenses and into his heart.

He tried to move away from her, needing distance to clear his head, but she wrapped her arms around his neck and tucked her body against his. "Hold me, Daniel. Please, hold me."

And he did. Until they fell asleep, wrapped in each other's arms. Until the first light of morning peeked through the gap in the curtains and prodded him awake.

Until her cell phone chimed on the dresser, and she rolled out of bed to answer it.

He flopped onto his back and watched her through his eyelashes as she, in all her naked glory, stumbled groggily across the room. The sight of her smooth skin and sultry curves sent a fresh rush of desire thundering through him.

Nicole plucked her cell phone from the dresser and checked

the screen. Her shoulders sagged, and she groaned before she thumbed the answer button. "Hi, Dad."

Daniel tensed.

"Yes, I was still asleep. Why?" She gasped, and her back stiffened. "Oh, no. I completely forgot. I'm so sorry." She sent a quick glance to their bed and winced. "Yeah, I know how important it is to you."

He propped on one elbow, watching her, and she mouthed, *Sorry.* Then turning, she headed into the bathroom. "I'm getting in the shower now. I'll meet you there."

Disappointment plucked at him. He'd hoped they could at least share breakfast before they parted ways.

He heard her turn on the shower and flopped back against the pillow with a sigh. Tossing back the covers, he climbed out of bed and strolled to the door of the bathroom to ask her if she wanted him to order room service. But the door was locked.

Frowning, he raised his hand to knock.

"Yes, I did spend the night with that guy from the bayou," she said, her voice haughty, her tone dripping disdain. "In fact, I had sex with him. Many times."

The taunting tone of her voice sent a chill through him. He lowered his hand and listened with his heart in his throat.

"I'm perfectly clear on your feelings about him," she scoffed, and he heard a thump. "Maybe that's the point."

A sinking sensation knotted in his chest as he saw last night through a new lens. The smug grin she'd given her father when she'd introduced him as her date for the rest of the night. Her repeated use of the Boudreaux moniker. The dark suspicious looks her father had given him.

His sense of being caught in the middle of a family feud had been more on target than he'd realized.

"Because I could, Dad. I can sleep with a Cajun or a frat

boy or the whole naval fleet if I feel like it. I'm not a little girl anymore. You can't dictate my life."

Daniel staggered back a step from the door as if pushed, as if kicked in the gut. Blindsided. Sucker punched. Deceived.

Had last night been nothing but a rebellion against her father? A walk on the wrong side of the tracks so she could flout her father's ideals?

"Who says there'll be a next time?" she said. "Maybe I'm ready to go back to Houston and finish my nursing degree! It's exactly what Mom would have wanted!"

As her argument with her father grew more heated, Daniel raked a hand through his hair and battled down the bitter hurt and anger that roiled inside him.

She'd used him. She'd seen an opportunity to hook a man her father saw as unworthy and dangle her tryst in the senator's face. A sharp ache of betrayal raked through his chest, and he snatched his pants and dress jacket from the closet.

Nicole's voice became a muted drone as he dressed and put on his shoes. By the time he gathered his hat and cell phone from the nightstand, a sour disgust, with himself and with Nicole's betrayal, had risen like bile in his throat.

The shower was the only sound from the bathroom when he gave the room one last glance for anything he'd missed. The rumpled bed served a vivid reminder of what had transpired the night before. He might have been making love to Nicole, but he'd gotten screwed.

Nicole sat on the floor of the shower, silent tears tracking down her cheeks. She had to pull herself together, couldn't let Daniel see how deeply her father's attitude hurt her. Somewhere during the night, making love to Daniel, she'd realized the only way to get her life back under control was to make a clean break from her father. She couldn't be the daughter he wanted her to be, and trying was suffocating her.

Losing her father, so soon after losing her mom, made it all the harder to break free. But if she needed any reminder how differently they viewed the world, it had been obvious when her father had referred to Daniel in such derogatory terms. She'd thrown the words back in his face, hoping her father would hear how elitist he sounded, but Alan White couldn't see what she saw him becoming. And it broke her heart.

Shutting of the water, Nicole dragged herself from the shower and dried off, deciding how much to tell Daniel about the argument he had to have overheard. The truth, of course, but how much of the truth? She was still grappling with the truth herself.

Finally, pulling on the plush robe the hotel provided, she headed back out to the room to face her future. And found no one there.

Chapter 4

Present day—New Orleans

Daniel woke slowly, keeping still, using all of his senses to test his surroundings for possible threats before opening his eyes. He'd been trained to assess every new situation carefully, especially if he was at a strategic disadvantage. Which he was, based on the throbbing ache in his knee and no memory past struggling to the chopper amid gunfire.

The beep of electronics and the murmur of distant voices, too muted for him to distinguish what language they were speaking, met his ears. He lay flat on a soft surface and had covers over him. A bed. His knee hurt like the devil, and he had tubes and needles poking him. His head felt a little muzzy, likely from some kind of painkiller, but he began to build a picture. He could smell antiseptic and...roasted chicken? His stomach growled.

So he was in a hospital room. But where?

And someone held his hand. That fact made his pulse trip. Who—?

He cracked his eyes open, peeking out through his eyelashes, careful not to alert his company to his waking…just in case.

Nicole sat in a wheelchair beside his bed, her head lolling to the side, her eyes closed, her lips slightly parted. Asleep. She wore a blue hospital gown and an IV bag, hanging from a pole attached to her wheelchair, was hooked up to her right hand. As when he'd found her asleep at the prison camp, he was struck by how beautiful she looked, despite the circumstances. And how vulnerable.

On the heels of that thought, he flashed to the jungle. To Nicole pushing herself to keep up despite her obvious exhaustion. To her feisty determination not to leave him behind when he was shot. To her stubborn protectiveness over the little girl.

No. Nicole White might look vulnerable, but a tenacious streak ran through her.

He angled his gaze to their joined hands, determined not to read anything into her presence in his room. Hands he remembered as delicately feminine and soft were now chapped and showed the wear of harsh living conditions. Her once well-manicured fingernails were short and ragged, her skin marred by cuts and bruises. The physical reminders of her ordeal caused a twisting sensation deep in his chest.

Oh, my God! Daniel… He'd blacked out shortly after her eyes had widened in recognition. Finally.

Disappointment pinched him.

But…the jungle had been dark, their situation had been perilous, and their last meeting had been over five years ago. His appearance had changed some over the years.

Still…it stung that she'd not known him immediately. Especially after the intimacies they'd shared their one night together. Daniel sighed. One night five years ago and one night ten years ago. Maybe he was asking too much to think she'd remember him. And even if she did recall everything that had happened that night in New Orleans, where did that leave them?

He had to remember who her father was, the *reason* they'd only had the one night, the way she'd used him....

A spike of bitter resentment seeped through the golden memories and gnawed in his gut. Nothing was settled between them. Clenching his back teeth, Daniel eased his hand out from under hers, careful not to wake her, then shifted in the bed to give her his back.

He sank into his pillow, prepared to nurse his black mood when a soft knock sounded at his door. A sweet and familiar face peeked around the corner.

"Daniel, you awake? Can we come in?" His spirits lifted as his partner's very pregnant wife waddled into the room, Alec behind her, and gave him a bright smile.

Daniel nodded, then hitched his head toward Nicole and signaled for his visitors to be quiet. As Erin Kincaid bent to hug him, he whispered, "Hey, gorgeous. Thanks for loaning me Alec. I brought him back in one piece, like I promised."

She squeezed him and gave his injured leg a side glance. "You promised you'd *all* come back unharmed."

He grunted. "Oops."

She sent him a withering frown and stepped away to allow her husband to greet him. Alec and Daniel clasped hands briefly, tightly. Words weren't needed. Alec was like a brother to Daniel. A brother who'd been through hell and back with him on many occasions. A brother with whom he'd trust his life.

"How's the knee?" Alec asked in a low voice.

"You tell me. I'm a little foggy on what happened after we got airborne. Sit-rep?"

"Pretty simple. We got the hell out of the jungle. Oh, and the snipers? Not from the camp. They were kids."

Daniel frowned. "What?"

Alec nodded. "No lie. Kids, about ten to twelve years old, posted in the trees to guard someone's cash crop. I saw the coca plants once we were in the air."

"Kids. Jeez." Daniel shook his head. "Okay, go on."

"Then we swapped the chopper for the Cessna you'd arranged in Bogotá and flew straight back to the States." Alec, who'd clearly had time to shower, shave and change into street clothes, moved a chair near the bed for his wife. "We were wheels down in New Orleans by early afternoon, some ten hours after extracting the target. Objective complete. Mission accomplished."

His partner crossed his arms over his chest and sent Daniel a satisfied grin.

Erin tipped her head to give her husband a worried frown. "Your last mission. You promised."

He sat on the arm of the chair and kissed Erin's hair. "Yes. I promise."

Daniel watched his partner and his wife with regret. As much as he liked Erin, as happy as he was for Alec, he couldn't help wondering about the future. He'd been Alec's partner on the top secret black ops team most of his career. What was he going to do now that Alec was retiring from active duty?

Daniel touched his thigh, just above his throbbing knee. Would he have a black ops job to go back to, or would his injury sideline him, too?

"I was looking for something more specific. I assume you've talked to the doctors here." He gave Nicole a meaningful glance. "Is she okay? What happened with the kid? Did Nicole tell you anything about her captivity on the flight home?"

Alec arched a dark eyebrow, and the glint in his blue eyes told Daniel he hadn't missed the question Daniel left out. "Nicole's fine. A few dings and some dehydration, but nothing a night in the hospital won't remedy." He folded his arms over his chest before he continued. "Tia is in a room on the pediatric floor getting IV fluids and a psych evaluation. At the moment, the hospital staff and government authorities here believe she is your daughter."

Daniel snapped his gaze up to Alec's. "*My* daughter? Wh—"

"Think about it, Lafitte. Nicole is blond and blue eyed, well-known in the States. No one would believe the girl was hers. And with your tan complexion and dark hair and eyes, you look more Hispanic than Jake or I do."

Daniel dragged a hand over his mouth. "What am I supposed to do with her?"

Alec held up his hands. "Easy. Nicole is working on cutting through the red tape involved in having Tia here without a visa, without knowledge of who her parents are, without consent of the Colombian government...."

Daniel shut his eyes and blew out a frustrated sigh. "I couldn't leave her. Nicole refused to go without the girl, and we didn't have time to argue."

"And when she looked at you with those big sad eyes, your heart melted. Right?" Alec smirked.

Daniel scowled. "Well, yeah. I'd have to be made of stone not to be sympathetic to a scared little girl. Especially in that hellhole. It was no place to leave a kid."

Alec's grin spread. "I was talking about Nicole's sad eyes, but it's good to know you have a soft spot for children, too."

Daniel cut a quick glace at Nicole, who was still asleep, then glowered at Alec. "Wiseass."

Erin and Alec exchanged a knowing grin, then fell silent. Daniel lowered his gaze to the lumpy silhouette of his injured leg under the thin blanket. Questions he hated to ask, dreading the answers, hung with a palpable tension in the quiet room.

"They operated on your knee, patched it up as best they could. You have several pins and screws holding you together at the moment." Alec's voice held a note of apology, commiseration. "The bullet went all the way through, which is good. If it had bounced around in your leg, it could have torn up more arteries, and you'd have bled out. Nicole, being a nurse, got busy once we were out of the jungle and stabilized your leg. She stopped the bleeding, kept tabs on your vitals and found stuff in the trauma kit to keep you knocked out for the ride home."

His gaze drifted to Nicole, almost of its own volition, and his chest tightened when he pictured her laboring over him to save his life. He swallowed hard, despite the cottony feeling in his mouth, and shifted his gaze to Alec. "But…"

To his credit, Alec didn't pretend not to know what Daniel was asking. His partner's brow furrowed in sympathy. "But the surgical repairs aren't a permanent fix. You'll be able to walk with a cane and some therapy, but you're gonna hurt like hell for a while. They recommend a joint replacement in the near future." He hesitated and pinned Daniel with a penetrating gaze. "Your days in the field are over. I'm sorry."

Daniel's gut wrenched, and he battled down the swell of panic with stubborn denial. "Maybe not. Maybe with physical therapy—"

"The team's already issued your deactivation order. I talked to the chief earlier, tried to get him to hold off until after your surgery, but…he was adamant. He can't take a chance in the field with an agent who's suffered a knee injury like yours."

Daniel gritted his teeth, and his hands fisted in the blanket. "He can't take me off the team without even talking to me! How—"

Nicole inhaled a sharp breath and jerked awake, a wild gaze darting nervously around her surroundings. Daniel kicked himself mentally, knowing his angry volume had woken her.

After a few shallow, panted breaths, she seemed to realize she was safe and melted wearily back into the wheelchair. Then noticing the attention she'd drawn, she scooted upright from her slumped position and, rubbing her neck with her hand, sent Daniel, then Alec, curious looks. "I fell asleep."

"Apparently." Daniel gave her a measured scrutiny. He was all too familiar with the time it took to decompress after a trauma, after being held captive and fearing daily for your life. Nicole had a tough road ahead.

Erin introduced herself, and the women exchanged polite greetings before Nicole's eyes locked on Daniel's, all traces of her earlier distress and confusion gone. "How do you feel?"

"Well, let's see…I've got a blown-out knee, a screaming headache and I just learned my injured leg means I no longer have a job." He gave her a churlish smile. "I'm peachy."

Nicole sat back, her expression wounded.

"Daniel…" Erin scolded quietly.

Guilt kicked him, and he tore his gaze from hers to glare at his feet.

"Come on, Lafitte," Alec said. "I know you're ticked about being taken off the team, but don't take it out on her."

"What, are you my mother now?" he growled.

Alec scoffed. "Fine. Clearly you need time alone to process all this." He stood and held his hand out to help Erin to her feet. "When you're ready to talk, you know how to reach me."

Daniel angled a look to his partner and Erin, his guilt and despondency grinding harder into his conscience. "Sorry," he mumbled.

"She's the one you owe an apology to." Alec aimed a thumb toward Nicole, then headed out the door with Erin. "We're heading back to Colorado tomorrow, but we'll stop in and say goodbye in the morning before we head out. Oh, yeah, Jake said to tell you he'd stop by later."

Daniel nodded an acknowledgment to Alec, then shifted a contrite glance to Nicole.

She grabbed the wheels of her chair and turned toward the door. "I should go, too. I didn't mean to be gone so long, and I don't want Tia to wake up alone."

Nicole rolled the wheelchair around the end of his bed, and Daniel saw his opportunity to set the record straight with her slipping away. "Nicole, wait."

She stopped but didn't look at him.

He clenched his teeth, mad at himself for taking out his frustrations on her and uncertain where to begin the conversation they needed to have. "I shouldn't have snapped at you. This—" he waved a hand at his knee "—isn't your fault."

When she raised her gaze, her eyes were bright with tears. The pain in her expression sucker punched his gut.

"I came down here," she started slowly, softly, "to thank you. For rescuing me. For bringing Tia with us." She shook her head and swiped moisture from her cheek. "I don't think I said it before, but I can never thank you enough for—"

"Forget it." He shrugged. "I just did my job."

"No. What you did went above and beyond—"

"Have you seen your father?" he interrupted, uncomfortable with her gratitude.

Her mouth tightened, and a chill filled her eyes. "Not yet. He was in Washington when I called him. He's on his way here now."

"What will you tell him?"

She drew her eyebrows together. "The truth. I have nothing to hide from him." She cocked her head, her expression steely. "Do you?"

He jerked another negligent shrug. "I'd be more worried about what he might hide from you. You deserve honesty."

"Oh? Have you been honest with me?"

"Always."

"Then answer this—why did you leave?"

He frowned and squeezed the sheets in his fist. "What?"

She rolled the wheelchair closer, her eyes shining with blue fire. "Don't pretend you don't know what I mean. On the helicopter, you were eager for me to remember that night. And, yes, I remember it. Vividly. And the morning after."

His gut pitched. What had he said while delirious with pain?

He clenched his teeth. "Then you shouldn't have to ask why I left."

Nicole's eyebrows lifted in surprise. "Excuse me? We barely said good morning. I went to take a shower, and by the time I got out of the bathroom, you'd run away like a roach when the lights turned on!"

Daniel scoffed. "A roach? Really?"

"Sure. It fits. I came out of the bathroom to find nothing but our condom wrappers scattered everywhere like trash after a Mardi Gras parade." She jabbed a finger toward him, and color rose in her cheeks. "You got your wham-bam and left without even a 'thank you, ma'am.' At least hookers get paid!"

Acid roiled in his gut. "Is that what you told your father? 'Cause that would explain a lot."

She blinked and sat back in the wheelchair, clearly startled. "My *father?* What does he have to do—?" She cut herself off abruptly and held up a hand. She inhaled a deep breath and shook her head. "Forget it. This is neither the time nor the place for this conversation."

Daniel shook his head. "Why rehash it at all? It's ancient history."

She shot him a skeptical frown. "You don't believe that, or you wouldn't have needed me to remember you."

Daniel scowled and shifted his gaze from her, hoping she couldn't tell how close to the truth she'd come.

"That's what you said, you know. 'I need to know you remember.' You were agonizing over it."

He shook his head, avoiding her eyes. "I had a shattered knee. It was the pain talking."

She sighed, a resigned, heartbreaking sound in the dim hospital room. "It might have been pain talking, but not pain from your knee."

He jerked his gaze to her, ready with denials, but she turned and wheeled her chair toward the door. "I have to go. Tia needs me."

The door swished closed behind her, leaving Daniel in the dark and silent room alone. He closed his eyes and let the raw ache of memories and regrets roll over him.

When she reached Tia's room on the pediatric floor, Nicole was still shaking all the way to her marrow. She paused outside Tia's door to gather her composure, not wanting any of her own upheaval to upset the girl. When she'd woken from her inadvertent nap in Daniel's room, she'd experienced a few terrifying moments of disorientation. Even now she felt as if a delicate thread wound through her, pulled so taut it cut into her soul. A thread that vibrated like a plucked wire, humming with images, sensations and sounds from her months in captivity. Even though she'd showered three times in the hospital, the rank smell of the prison camp lingered in her nose, and for an instant upon wakening, she'd thought she was back in Colombia.

Nicole drew a deep ragged breath and plowed shaky fingers through her hair, fighting for control, fighting to dampen the humming wire of tension that coiled inside her. It felt like that thread could snap at any moment, and everything she knew and relied on would unravel.

As if mentally breaking free of the Colombian prison weren't enough to contend with, the devastatingly handsome man in the hospital bed downstairs took her life in a freakishly surreal direction.

Daniel was back. She'd thought she'd moved past the hurt and longing associated with that torrid night years ago, moved beyond the handsome and heartbreaking enigma that was Daniel LeCroix. Yet here she was, trembling and fighting back tears, her emotions in turmoil again. Over Daniel.

Who'd braved the Colombian jungle and stormed the enemy camp to free her from her hellish captivity. Who'd accused her father of unspeakable crimes. Who, based on the ache sitting in her chest, still owned more of her heart than she'd realized.

A whimper in Tia's room yanked Nicole from her reflection, and she pushed through the door, quickly rolling her wheelchair to the side of the girl's bed. Nicole shoved all the tangled feelings for Daniel and lingering trauma over her imprisonment down, determined to hold herself together for Tia's sake. She couldn't afford to suffer a breakdown when this precious girl depended on her.

A nurse in pink scrubs was at Tia's side, cooing reassurances and trying to get a temperature reading with a thermometer that fit in the ear. But the frightened child would have none of it.

"Hi." The nurse smiled a greeting to Nicole. "I'm Sophie, and I'll be Tia's nurse tonight."

Nicole forced a friendly smile. "Hi, Sophie. I'm Nicole." She turned to Tia and leaned closed. "*Mija,* it's okay. She won't hurt you."

Tia's dark gaze latched onto Nicole's, and the girl lurched toward her, mewling in fright.

"I tried to explain that it wouldn't hurt," Sophie said.

Nicole nodded. "She doesn't speak any English. At least, not that I can tell. In fact, she hasn't spoken at all since—" Nicole hesitated. *Since she was dumped in a dog pen with me in a rebel army camp in Colombia.* Somehow she wasn't sure sharing the gritty reality of their situation was wise. She didn't need a media circus or the gossip mill interfering with her efforts to locate Tia's real parents through the proper channels. "Since she's been in my care."

"Has she been scheduled for a psych evaluation?" Sophie asked, finding Tia's chart at the foot of her bed and flipping it open to read.

Nicole nodded. "I was told they plan to have her meet with a trauma expert soon."

"What happened to her?" the nurse asked, giving Tia a sympathetic look.

Climbing out of the wheelchair to lie on the bed with Tia, Nicole sighed and smoothed the girl's hair. "I don't know. She was already in shock when I…took over her care."

Sophie glanced at Nicole's IV line and tipped her head to a curious angle. "I heard you all were camping somewhere and got stranded. The guys who brought you in said they found you two and the girl's father last night while they were hunting."

Nicole blinked, needing a moment to catch up, reconciling the cover story in her mind. When they arrived at the hospital, Alex and the pilot, Jake, had claimed Tia was Daniel's daughter. Now, she nodded, and tried to skirt around the lies intended to protect Tia and avoid trouble from outside influences. "I think she's calmer now, if you want to try again to get her temperature. Maybe you could show her how it works on me first?"

Sophie moved close again to take Nicole's temperature. "See? Doesn't hurt," she said and smiled at Tia.

Nicole hugged the little girl and rubbed her arm while the nurse checked Tia's temperature. "It's okay, *mija*. It's okay."

"Ninety-nine point two," Sophie read off the thermometer, then stashed it in her pocket. "Her fever's way down now thanks to the antibiotic and acetaminophen."

Nicole said a silent prayer of thanks that Tia's illness had apparently been nothing more than an ear infection. She'd feared something far worse, such as malaria or dengue fever from a mosquito bite.

Sophie headed for the door. "Well, I'll be on duty all night. Call if you need anything."

Nicole smiled her thanks, and as the door swung closed, she snuggled down on the bed with Tia curled against her in the night-darkened room. They'd spent innumerable hours in just such a position in the rebel camp. Nicole had done all she could to protect and shelter the traumatized child and had grown to love her as if she were her own daughter.

But she's not yours, her conscience prodded. Nicole closed her eyes, resigned to the task that lay ahead—locating Tia's real family and returning the girl to them.

The scuff of feet and crack of light from the hall woke Nicole about an hour later. She squinted groggily at the tall man silhouetted at the door.

"Nicole? Is that you?" The familiar voice broke with emotion.

"Daddy!" She untangled herself from Tia quickly and clambered from the bed.

Her father met her, pulling her into a tight embrace, before she'd made it more than a couple steps. "Nicole, darling... oh, thank God!"

They held each other and cried for several minutes, both too emotional to speak. Finally her father pulled a handkerchief from his pocket and wiped his face while Nicole swiped her cheeks with her fingers.

Her father cleared his throat. "I've been so worried about you, darling. Having you back is the answer to so many prayers." He tucked the handkerchief back in his pocket and cast a searching gaze over her. "You've lost weight, but otherwise you look healthy. Did they hurt you, darling? Are you really okay?"

An image of her captors flashed in her mind's eye, and the thread of panic inside her tugged tighter, a garrote threatening to choke her. Gritting her teeth, she swallowed the sour taste of bile, then inhaled deeply, slowly through her nose. *Hold it together. You can't fall apart.* "It was no picnic, but physically, I'm fine."

Her father narrowed a hard look on her that demanded her honesty. "And mentally?"

Her heartbeat stumbled. What could he see in her eyes? She shoved the tremor of doubt down deeper and refused to shy away from her father's scrutiny.

"Let's just say…some of my memories will take some time to get over. But I'm a White, and we're fighters. Right?" She forced a smile to reassure him.

His graying eyebrows knitted in a frown, and he drew her back into his arms. "Oh, Nicole, I tried everything I knew to get you released."

She squeezed her eyes shut, hearing Daniel's dark accusations in her head. *He betrayed two American operatives….*

"But even with all my connections, I couldn't—" He stiffened and levered back to meet her gaze again. "So what happened? How did you get away?"

Nicole's mouth dried. She'd only just gotten her father back. She wasn't ready to light the powder keg that topic would ignite. "I…was rescued." She turned and motioned to the bed where Tia slept. "*We* were rescued."

Her father leaned to peer around her at the bed, and a frown pocked his brow. "Who is that?"

"I don't know her real name. I call her Tia. She was kidnapped by the men who were holding me and put in my pen a few months ago."

His face darkened, and he stepped closer to the bed for a better look. "She's just a child!"

Her father's volume woke Tia, who sat up on the bed and whimpered in fear before she spotted Nicole and reached for her.

Nicole's heart twisted in pain for Tia's suffering, and she sat on the edge of the bed to stroke the girl's back. "I'm guessing she's about eight, but I haven't been able to get much information from her. She's been so traumatized that she hasn't spoken at all since her kidnapping."

"Not at all?"

Nicole shook her head.

Studying Tia with concern darkening his expression, her father dragged a hand along his jaw and sighed. "Am I right in assuming she's in this country without the proper paperwork?"

Nicole winced. "Well…yeah."

His shoulders slumped. "Nicole, I know you want to help her, but it's not as if she's one of the kittens you like to rescue. You can't bring her home with you like a pet and—"

"Shh!" She held up a hand to quiet him when he raised his voice and Tia cowered closer to her. "I know that."

"There are laws," her father argued in a quieter tone, "both American and international that supercede—"

"I *know!* But I couldn't leave her alone in the jungle with those thugs that kidnapped her!"

Her father scrubbed both hands over his face and jerked a nod of acquiescence. "Do you have any clue *whose* she is?"

Again Nicole frowned and shook her head. She met the

little girl's wide brown eyes and felt a tug at her heart. "My guess would be she's the daughter of someone important or powerful—a chief of police, a drug lord, a military leader or government official, maybe?" She paused and glanced to her father. "I was hoping you would use some of your connections to help me cut through red tape and find out where her family is."

He grunted and lowered himself in a chair at the side of the bed. "I don't know if my connections are worth much anymore. I, um…" He ducked his head and glared at the floor. "I resigned from office a couple months ago."

Nicole's chest tightened. Did she confront her father now or pretend not to have heard Daniel's side of recent events and wait for her father's explanation? Five years ago, she would have played along with whatever charade her father presented. But she'd grown up in Colombia. She'd endured too much and come too far to let herself fall back into her old role as the pliant and obedient daughter. She swallowed hard, forcing down the seesawing nausea that gripped her. "I heard you were forced out of office. That you were censured."

Her father's head snapped up, his expression startled. "Who told you that?"

For a moment, she clung to the belief that his surprise meant she had the story wrong, that he was poised to deny all of the horrid charges against him. She pulled in a cleansing breath and squared her shoulders. "The man who risked his life to save me—Daniel LeCroix."

But her father's face paled, and that hope drained from her, leaving her cold and shaking. Her father's bleak and stunned expression told her every ugly accusation Daniel had made in the jungle had been true.

Chapter 5

"What did LeCroix tell you?" her father asked darkly, his eyebrows dipping low over his eyes.

"Just the highlights. Running through a jungle while under fire was hardly the best time for an in-depth conversation."

Her father blanched even whiter. "Under fire?"

"I did say he risked his life to get me out. They all did—Daniel, Alec and Jake." She paused, her chest squeezing when she thought of the devastating injury to Daniel's knee. "Daniel was shot in the knee. His career is over."

Because he'd rescued her.

Her father stared at her, his shock still evident. "Why... wasn't I informed about this rescue mission before now?"

Nicole laughed without humor. "You're hardly on speaking terms with them. I don't think they rescued me as a favor to you as much as an in-your-face thing." She sobered. "Daniel said you betrayed him. You betrayed the United States by trading top secret national security intel for information about where I was being held."

Her father's back stiffened, and his face grew stony and defiant. "I did what I thought I had to in order to get you back."

"By giving up a team of undercover operatives to the enemy? They could have been killed! And what about the work they were doing? The breach to our operations down there to stop the flow of drugs and root out terrorist cells and—"

"You're my daughter!" her father shouted. "I couldn't leave you down there to die!"

His raised voice frightened Tia, who snuggled closer with a whimper and buried her face in Nicole's chest. Nicole stroked Tia's black hair and crooned soothing words, even though her father's admission churned inside her.

She hated to think she'd been the reason for her father's vile act, his fall from grace. More than that, she hated the idea that Daniel and Alec could have died because of what her father had done. For her.

And then Daniel had turned around and planned a high-risk mission to rescue her.

Nicole sighed and rubbed her temple. Daniel's actions were illogical, confusing…and humbling. She could *almost* believe he'd saved her life because he still cared about her. Except his snarling, icy attitude toward her would indicate otherwise.

So what about his kiss at the prison camp? He'd been tender and sweet. Like the lover he'd been five years ago….

Nicole shook her head to clear it. Deciphering Daniel's confounding behavior was not her priority at the moment.

"So what have your lawyers said? What have you been charged with?"

"Nothing related to…my deal with Ramirez. At this point, I don't think either LeCroix or Kincaid has reported what I did."

Nicole gaped. "Excuse me?"

"Don't ask me why." He sighed heavily. "There was a nasty mess one night this past January that I was involved in. And while General Ramirez, a known rebel leader and drug smuggler, was apprehended, my lawyers are working on a defense as to why I was there. I don't know what LeCroix and Kincaid told the authorities about that night but—"

"Daniel and Alec were there?"

Her father frowned. "He didn't tell you?"

Nicole rolled her gaze to the ceiling. "Apparently there's a *lot* I haven't been told."

She heard her father shift in the chair and exhale heavily. "I'll make a few calls and see what I can find out about the little girl. Are you sure she's Colombian? Not from Ecuador or Peru—"

Nicole lowered her gaze to meet her father's and shook her head. "Daddy, I'm not sure of anything anymore."

His expression softened, and he leaned toward the bed. "I love you, Nicole. You can be sure of that."

Tears prickled in her eyes, and she blinked them away. "I would appreciate any help you can offer. I know the authorities will try to take custody of Tia from me, and I can't let that happen. She's alone and scared, and she needs me. Until we find her family, I have to protect her."

The next morning, Daniel sat on the side of his hospital bed and rubbed his injured leg. Even with major painkillers in his system, he hurt like hell. He'd snatched only erratic moments of sleep last night while his conversation with Nicole replayed in his head.

It might have been pain talking, but not pain from your knee.

Maybe so, but the physical pain had lowered his guard, allowed emotions he'd kept securely locked away for years

to resurface. In light of the current throbbing in his knee
and the promise of continued pain for several weeks as he
healed, he'd better find a way to jam all those dangerous
feelings for Nicole somewhere safe and out of reach. Better yet, he should avoid any further contact with Nicole. His
mission was complete. He'd saved her from the Colombian
prison camp. The end.

"Whenever you're ready," said the nurse who stood beside his bed, waiting. She handed him a pair of crutches, then
reached for his arm to help him to his feet.

His doctor had left orders that Daniel put some weight on
the bad knee and practice walking on the injured leg so that
the joint didn't get stiff and inflexible. Daniel clenched his
back teeth and hoisted himself from the bed onto his good
leg. The nurse moved in close to steady him, and he waved
her away. "I can do it."

"Now put some weight on the other leg, and use the
crutches to take a step."

Daniel did as directed and bit back a scorching curse word
when a nearly blinding pain shot from his knee up his leg.
His bad leg buckled, and he wobbled on the crutches. *Fils
de putain!* His leg hadn't hurt this much when he'd been
dragging it behind him in the jungle. Of course, he'd had an
ample supply of adrenaline coursing through him, blocking
his pain at the time.

He squeezed the hand grips on the crutches harder and
sent his nurse a warning scowl when she tried again to steady
him. A cold sweat popped out on his brow and upper lip, but
he took a cleansing breath and planted the crutches another
foot in front of him. Braced. Shifted his weight.

He let another string of Cajun French curses fly, but he
didn't sway this time. While his nurse gave him trite words of
encouragement, he took a couple more steps. A bead of moisture rolled down his temple despite the chill air-conditioning,

and he clenched his teeth until his jaw ached. But he was walking.

Big ef-ing deal. He used to run a five-minute mile with a forty-pound pack on his back. Now he had a nurse praising him for each step as if he were a baby learning to walk. He glared his discontent and frustration at the woman. "Look, when I run a marathon again, compliment me all you want. For now, I could do without the false cheer."

The woman's face reflected a moment of hurt and surprise, and regret for his curtness kicked him in the gut. Before he could apologize, a voice from the door stopped him.

"Still in a grumpy mood, I see."

Daniel mustered all his strength not to falter as he jerked his gaze toward Nicole. Thirstily, he drank in the sight of her, taking note of her street clothes and the return of color to her cheeks. She looked damn good, in fact, if still a bit thin. "Been discharged, I take it?"

"Yeah. Something like that."

He pivoted on his good leg and hobbled back to his bed.

Nicole hesitated a few seconds, as if uncertain she should enter the lion's den, then she moved closer. The nurse propped his crutches near the head of his bed and stepped out of the room, giving them privacy to talk.

He scrubbed a hand over his face, hoping she didn't see him surreptitiously wipe the sweat from his brow. "And the girl?"

Her cheek twitched in a grin as if his simple inquiry about the child was gratifying to her. "Tia is supposed to be released later this afternoon, so I have to work fast to get approved as her guardian while the embassies search for her family." She fidgeted with her purse strap and took another step toward his bed. "My father is pulling some strings with a judge or two he knows to make the arrangements."

Daniel grunted and swallowed the snide retort that would

only alienate himself further from her. If this was goodbye, he didn't want her last memory to be him acting like a surly ass. He inhaled deeply, rubbed his aching knee and blew out a cleansing breath. "Well, good luck. I hope things work out for you."

Another awkward smile twitched at the corner of her mouth. "Thanks. When you see Alec and Jake again—"

"Alec and Erin went back to Colorado." As happy as he was for Alec, starting a new life with the woman of his dreams, Daniel couldn't help the kick of envy in his gut. "Her doctor didn't want her so far from home this close to her due date."

"Oh." She shifted her weight, clearly disappointed. "I'm sorry I missed them. I wanted to tell Alec thank you again." Nicole locked an earnest gaze on his. "When you talk to him—and Jake—please tell them how grateful I am for their part in our rescue."

Daniel jerked a nod. "Sure."

She tore her gaze away from his and stared at the floor while she chewed her lip, toyed with her earring. Even without his body language training, he'd have known she wanted to raise a difficult topic, probably delve into their history again. The last place he wanted to go.

She lifted troubled eyes to his and opened her mouth.

"Do you have a cell phone?" he asked before she could speak.

"Uh, yeah." She blinked, clearly caught off guard by his question. "My dad got a new one for me this morning."

Daniel held out his hand. "Let me see it."

Furrowing her brow, Nicole eyed him suspiciously before she dug in her purse and gave him the phone.

He tapped the on-screen menu to open her address book, entered his cell phone number and passed the device back to her. "Your father's not the only one with valuable contacts. If you have trouble with ICE or Homeland Security because of Tia, I'll do my best to help cut through red tape." He nodded to the phone, which she studied with a spark of intrigue lighting her eyes. "That number is the best way to reach me."

She tapped her screen a couple times, and on the tray table beside his bed, Daniel's cell phone buzzed. He arched one eyebrow, and she flashed a nervous grin. "Just checking."

"Thought I'd given you a fake number?"

She straightened. "No, I—" A blush rose in her cheeks as she fumbled. "I was making sure *my* phone worked." She ducked her head and made a production of stashing her phone.

A chuckle rumbled from his chest. "Right. And now I have your number, too."

Her chin shot up, and wide blue eyes latched onto his. "Oh. Yeah." She wet her lips. "Will you use it?"

He tensed, but his gaze never wavered. "I'm not sure that'd be a good idea. Things didn't work out so well for us last time."

She folded her arms over her chest and frowned at him. "And whose fault is that?"

"There's plenty of blame to go around."

Her shoulders slumped. "You're probably right." Heaving a sigh, she slid her purse strap in place on her shoulder. "Pity, too. Before that morning, I thought we had something pretty good between us."

So did I. Daniel bit back the reply. No point dwelling on could-have-beens. "Takes more than hot sex to make a relationship work."

Nicole scowled. "I know that."

She continued to glare at him, but he saw the heat that flared in her eyes. Heat that said she was remembering the sultry tangling of limbs and slap of flesh as their bodies writhed together. Daniel's body hummed as his brain easily conjured an erotic image from that night.

She cocked her head at a haughty angle. "Relationships take time…to learn each other's interests and tastes—"

"They take trust. Respect. Honesty," he snarled. He growled his frustration and waved her off. "Forget it. Like I said, it's history. Leave it alone."

"What makes you think we didn't have trust or…respect or…?"

"Leave. It. Alone," he repeated, his gaze drilling into her.

She threw up her hands and shook her head. "Whatever." Spinning on her heel, she stalked to the door and yanked it open.

Daniel's pulse stumbled, and acid gnawed his stomach. He was about to blow it again. He'd spent his final minutes with Nicole fighting about the past rather than repairing the tensions between them. But if he saw no future between them, why did he care so much where their relationship stood?

He squeezed the bedsheet in his fist. "Damn it, Nicole. Stop."

She waited for him to speak but didn't turn.

His heart thundered as he searched for something to tell her. *You complete me. You make me want to be a better man. We'll always have Paris.* He pinched the bridge of his nose as a parade of clichéd movie lines filled his head. Finally, he sighed and muttered, "It was a good night. But…we were too different to make it work."

She sent him a sad look over her shoulder. "It was a *great* night. But you didn't give us a chance to work."

Nicole disappeared into the hall, her hurt and disappointment still hovering in the air, reverberating around him. Daniel sank back in his pillows as a shard of hope lodged inside him like a splinter. Was it possible he'd read the situation wrong that morning years ago? Had he missed the most important opportunity of his life—the chance to be with Nicole?

He closed his eyes and swore under his breath. Hope was

a painful, double-edged sword. Just when he thought he'd finally cut Nicole out of his life, she cast a new light on his dark memories from their past.

Despite assurances that Tia could be released from the hospital that afternoon, legal red tape and delays kept Tia in the hospital another 24 hours. But Nicole made the most of the extra time, pushing the Department of Children and Family Services to complete an emergency home inspection and interview that allowed her to be appointed Tia's temporary legal guardian. Nicole took Tia to her father's New Orleans garden home, making a mental note to add apartment hunting to her to-do list once matters with Tia were settled.

"Hello?" she called as she and Tia entered the kitchen through the back door. "Anyone home?"

"Miss Nicole!" A thin, prematurely gray-haired woman bustled in from the laundry room and rushed to hug Nicole. "You're home! And safe, praise the Lord!"

Nicole beamed and embraced the woman who'd been her father's housekeeper for as long as she could remember. "Sarah Beth, how good to see you!"

Nicole introduced Tia to Sarah Beth Salyer, who traveled with her father to his many homes depending on where he was in residence at the moment—Washington, D.C., New Orleans, Baton Rouge or his ski cabin in Breckenridge. The two women caught each other up briefly on their respective status quos, then shared another tearful hug.

"I've taken good care of your Boudreaux and Oreo. They're around here somewhere." Sarah Beth searched the floor for Nicole's cats. "Probably on the sun porch."

Nicole's heart swelled. "Then the sun porch is my next stop. I've missed my babies. Want to meet my kitties?" Nicole asked Tia in Spanish.

The girl's face brightened, and Nicole had her answer.

Sarah Beth led them through the house to the sun porch, and Nicole spied Boudreaux on a chaise longue chair, basking in the sun.

"Hey, old man," she cooed, crouching next to the chair and waving Tia over.

"I'll start lunch for you, all right?" Sarah Beth headed back toward the kitchen.

"Thanks, Sarah Beth," Nicole called and scratched Boudreaux behind the ear. The kitten Daniel had rescued for her ten years earlier stretched and purred when she ruffled his fur. He was thinner than she remembered, but his yellow coat still looked glossy and sleek. Tears pricked her eyes when she thought of that prom night years ago when she'd first met Daniel. She'd lost a piece of her heart to him that night, and Boudreaux had been an ever-present reminder of Daniel's kindness and gallantry.

Leave. It. Alone. Why was Daniel so reluctant to discuss their past? Unless she meant less to him than she'd believed. He'd never professed any undying affection or loyalty, so maybe the tender emotions had all been one-sided. But if that was true, why had he risked his life to get her out of Colombia?

Tia's giggle pulled her out of her reverie. Oreo, the black-and-white tomcat she'd found as a kitten, had strolled over to greet them. She'd rescued Oreo at a work site while on a church mission trip to rebuild storm-damaged houses. The tomcat rubbed against Tia and butted her hand with his head. In return, Tia patted Oreo and laughed each time he bumped her hand asking for more attention. Nicole silently blessed Oreo for helping bring Tia out of her shell.

When her cell rang, Nicole dug her phone out of her pocket and checked the caller ID, foolishly wishing the caller was Daniel saying he'd changed his mind about having that long overdue talk about why he'd abandoned her. Instead, the call was from Washington, D.C., and she answered with her heart in her throat, praying for good news about Tia.

Leaving Tia to play with the cats, Nicole stepped into the next room to take the call.

"Miss White, this is Ramon Diaz. I am an attaché with the Colombian embassy. I believe we have a lead on the identity of the girl in your custody."

Relief washed through Nicole so hard and fast, her knees buckled, and she dropped onto the nearest chair. "That's wonderful! What did you find out?"

"She fits the description of Pilar Castillo, the daughter of Mario Castillo, a prominent judge in Bogotá whose family was attacked on the way to mass several months ago. Castillo's wife and other daughter were murdered, and Pilar was taken hostage. The BACRIM— that is, the *bandas criminales* or band of criminals—" Nicole kept silent, not bothering to tell him she was well familiar with the term for the many criminal gangs and rebel groups terrorizing Colombia "—claiming responsibility has used Pilar as leverage in blackmailing Judge Castillo regarding several critical cases he has presided over this year."

Nicole's stomach roiled, imagining the terror Tia—or Pilar—had witnessed, seeing her mother and sibling slaughtered. No wonder the poor child was traumatized. "Are you sure Tia is Pilar? Do you have a picture you can fax to me?"

"I do, and I have a picture of the judge you can show the girl. I'd ask that you send me a picture of the girl for cross confirmation from the father."

A picture of Tia? Nicole thought a moment. "I can take her picture with my phone and text it to you. Will that work?"

"*Sí,* that works," Diaz replied.

Nicole jotted down the cell phone number to text to and headed out to the sunroom again. Nicole had her own test in mind. Tia was still playing with Oreo, dangling a string for the cat to bap and giggling at the cat's antics, and Nicole watched for a moment, savoring the sweet sound of her laughter. Finally, she said calmly, "Pilar?"

The child froze, then jerked a wide-eyed glance up to her.

Nicole's pulse drummed as she stepped closer and squatted next to the girl. "Is that your name? *Es ese tu nombre?*" she asked. "Are you Pilar Castillo?"

Fat tears puddled in the girl's eyes, and she nodded.

Nicole pulled her into an embrace and rubbed the girl's back. "Oh, *mija*. We found your father. You'll be going home soon."

Nicole pulled the page from the fax machine in her father's home office as it fed from the printer. The image of a swarthy middle-aged man in a black robe stared back at her. Pilar's father, Mario Castillo.

"Chicken salad?" Sarah Beth asked from the office door, a plate in hand.

"Sounds heavenly. I'm starved." Nicole's stomach rumbled, and she thought of the many days in the prison camp when she'd eaten foul canned meats and stale crackers, dreaming of Sarah Beth's cooking. "Is Tia still on the sun porch?"

No, not Tia. Pilar. That would take a little getting used to.

"I think so. I set a place for her in the kitchen. Should I get her?" Sarah Beth asked.

"No, I'll get her. Thanks." Nicole folded the picture of Judge Castillo, jammed it in her pocket and headed toward the sun porch. Not wanting to upset the little girl and spoil her appetite, she decided to show Pilar the picture after lunch.

She'd just reached the French doors leading to the sunroom when she saw a hulking shadow cross the far wall.

Pulse jumping, Nicole swung through the door and took in the scene in a glance. Intruders had broken in.

She watched in horror as a dark-skinned stranger descended on Pilar.

Chapter 6

Pilar saw the man and screamed.

Boudreaux and Oreo spooked and scampered away. The man tripped over the bolting cats, landing on one knee. Pilar stumbled out of the man's reach, only to back into the grasp of a second man who appeared from the shadows.

"Pilar!" Acting purely on instinct, Nicole burst through the door, grabbing a decorative statuette from an end table. As she darted toward the first man, she hefted the figurine and smashed it on his head as he fumbled back to his feet. He toppled with a groan, clutching his head.

The second man had reeled Pilar in and held her against his chest, her legs dangling, as he fought to subdue her flailing arms.

"No! Let her go!" Nicole rushed forward with no thought for her own safety. Everything inside her had focused on freeing Pilar from the man's grip. She reached for the little girl, battling the man's arm when he tried to push Nicole away.

An all-out fight for Pilar ensued. He pulled Nicole's hair. Wrenched her wrists. Bit her arm.

In return, Nicole gouged at the man's eyes. Clawed his face. Scratched his arm. She realized they were in a tug of war with Pilar as the rope. The poor girl was being pulled like a Thanksgiving wishbone. To spare hurting Pilar, she needed to let go, but—

"Augh!" the man cried out and crumpled, grabbing his crotch.

Nicole hauled Pilar into her arms and spun away. On some level, she knew Pilar's flailing feet must have kicked the man in his family jewels, but she funneled her energy on one thing. Running. As she dodged a chaise chair, heading inside with Pilar clinging to her, the first man rolled on his back, snarling. He raised something small and black. A flash. A loud crack. *Gunfire!*

Nicole kept moving. Adrenaline fueled her legs. Panic buzzed in her ears.

"Nicole!" Sarah Beth stood by the door of her father's office, waving her in. "Hurry!"

Behind her, Nicole heard a shout. Another crack of gunfire. A crash and pounding footsteps.

A third gun-wielding man materialized from the kitchen. Aimed. Something hot stung her neck, but she ignored it as she charged across the living room and into her father's office. Nicole headed to the protection of her father's oversize desk and set Pilar on the carpet beneath it. Sarah Beth slammed the massive mahogany door closed and threw a bolt lock.

Loud thumps reverberated through the room as bullets pocked the office door.

"Get away from the door!" Nicole shouted to Sarah Beth.

"The second door—" the housekeeper said, pulling a thick metal door from a side pocket in the wall.

And Nicole remembered the construction project her father

had ordered in the months after Katrina. The central room of the house, his office, had been reinforced for hurricanes with iron beams, metal sheeting and a heavy secondary steel door. A safe room.

She ran to help Sarah Beth roll the heavy door over and lock it in place.

"We need to c-call 911," the housekeeper said, her voice shaking.

Nicole nodded and, with trembling hands, she reached in her pocket for her phone. The first tears of fear prickled her eyes, blurring her vision as she tried to steady her hands enough to hit the right spots on her touch screen. Meanwhile, Sarah Beth snatched up the desk phone and dialed.

Nicole stumbled behind the desk and slumped on the floor. Pilar huddled close, hands over her ears as she whimpered.

Her own panic, vivid with images from her imprisonment, crowded her brain, drawing the thread of tension inside her tighter. It would be so easy to give in to that pull toward chaos, but Nicole battled it away, one breath at a time. *Keep it together. For Pilar.*

Struggling to clear her mind, she thought of the Kevlar vest her mother had bought her father years ago after he'd sponsored his first controversial bill and received a series of death threats. The bulletproof vest was upstairs in her father's closet. No help.

Blinking away the moisture in her eyes, Nicole stared at her cell phone screen. Right now, she only wanted one man.

Daniel. Who'd saved her in Colombia. Who'd taken out her captors. Who'd made her feel safe.

The shouts and deafening thumps on the office door told her their assailants hadn't given up. And they were chipping slowly through the first barrier.

Nicole swallowed the bitter taste of fear that rose in her throat and struggled to steady her hands. Her thumb skipped to the button to bring up her contacts. With a stroke of the screen, she scrolled to the number Daniel had programmed in her phone just yesterday. And hit *Call*.

"Going home soon?" Jake asked as he strolled into Daniel's hospital room, wearing his trademark cowboy hat, and took stock of Daniel's latest attempt to put weight on his injured leg.

"Not soon enough. I feel useless sitting around here all day." His leg hurt less today and could bear more of his weight, but Daniel didn't harbor any illusions of a miraculous healing. His immediate future included walking with a cane at best and knee-replacement surgery as soon as it could be scheduled, followed by weeks of physical therapy.

His black op teammate—correction, *former* teammate, since Daniel had been canned—helped himself to the only chair in the room and stacked his hands behind his head. Jake narrowed his navy blue eyes on Daniel. "Looks like you're making progress. Your doctor give you an idea when you might bust this joint?"

Daniel shrugged off the question. He had nothing waiting for him when he left the hospital, so he hadn't given his release much thought.

Setting his well-worn cowboy hat on the table beside him, Jake rubbed a hand over his short-cropped sandy-brown hair and hedged. "Have you…talked to the chief about a job at headquarters?"

Daniel's cell phone chirped, and he hobbled toward the tray table where he'd left it. "I don't want any damn, soul-sucking desk job."

Jake turned up a hand. "You have one of the best minds in the business. You could coordinate missions, develop strategies—"

"Screw that." Holding Jake's gaze, he snatched up the

phone and dropped heavily on the side of the bed. "I'd rather leave the agency than push paper the rest of my life." He jabbed the answer button and barked, "What?"

"Daniel!" He knew the voice instantly, recognized the tremble of fear, heard the steady crashing in the background.

He jerked to attention, stiffening his back and squeezing the phone tighter. "Nicole, what's wrong?"

Jake sat forward, meeting Daniel's gaze.

"Men broke in…at my father's. They…tried to grab Pilar." Her voice was breathless and full of tears.

Daniel signaled Jake with his free hand. *Shoes. Pants. We're moving.*

"Are you hurt?" His own fear for Nicole sharpened his tone.

"We're in the safe room, b-but…they're shooting at the door, at the locks."

Jake whipped out a large pocketknife and sliced off the left leg of Daniel's jeans above the knee. With one hand, Daniel worked the jeans over the brace around his injured knee, while Jake shoved Daniel's shoes in front of him, ready to step into.

"Daniel, I…I need you," Nicole said, her voice breaking.

A fist closed around his heart, and a shudder rolled through him. *I'm coming, cher.*

Jamming the foot of his good leg in a shoe, Daniel lifted his arm for Jake to pull out his IV line. "Call 911," he grated, his own voice made rough with emotion. He thumbed disconnect and slid the phone in his jeans pocket.

Jake tossed him a shirt, and Daniel jerked it over his head and grabbed his crutches. "Let's roll."

"Daniel?" Nicole shouted, numb with disbelief. "Daniel!"

No answer. *Call 911,* he'd growled. And hung up on her. *Hung. Freaking. Up.*

Fury, hurt and disappointment coalesced inside her, a bitter brew. Her life was in peril, and he'd fobbed her off to 911. Never mind that the cops were in a better position than a hospitalized and injured Daniel to come to her rescue. Common sense did little to dull the sting of his rejection. His curt refusal to get involved.

She swiped at a tickle on her neck, and her fingers came away bloody. The sting she'd felt on her neck. Had a bullet grazed her? The bright red on her hand made the vibrating tension wire inside her tug tighter. She swallowed hard and sucked in a calming breath.

Don't lose it. Keep it together.

Sarah Beth was still on the line with the emergency operator, giving them the address, detailing their unfolding horror. From the sound of it, the men at the office door were making progress getting through the first door and could blast the lock on the inner steel door any time.

Nicole crawled under the desk with Pilar and wrapped her arms around the whimpering child. The men would have to come through Nicole to get to Pilar, and with her own fear jammed deep down inside her, Nicole was ready to put up a fight.

"I have a 9 mm in the glove box," Jake said as they roared down the highway in his pickup truck toward the address displayed on his GPS. "Take it."

Daniel opened the compartment in front of him and took out the weapon. After checking the chamber to make sure it was loaded, he shoved the gun in the waistband of his jeans. The GPS showed them nearing the address a Google search listed for Alan White's residence. Daniel checked his watch. Nicole had called eight minutes ago.

From under the brim of his cowboy hat, Jake shot him a dark glance, but Daniel saw the keen look of preparation in his eyes. "All right, man, this is your show. What's the plan?"

"Park one street over. We'll approach from behind. Obviously, you're more mobile than I am, so you take lead. I'll cover you. Nicole said they were in a safe room, which means center of the house, no windows. If our targets are still there, they'll be working on getting inside that room." Daniel didn't bother elaborating on what it meant if the gunmen weren't still at the senator's house. He shoved down the frisson of panic that swirled in his gut at the notion of anything happening to Nicole. He had to stay in battle mode. Had to focus.

Tossing his cowboy hat on the back seat, Jake pulled to a fast stop on a residential street lined with multilevel garden homes. Shouldering open the truck door, Daniel grabbed his crutches, cursing his limited mobility when he needed speed and agility more than ever.

"Go." He waved Jake away, and they started across the neighbor's lawn. By keeping his weight off his bad leg, Daniel could plant the crutches and swing his good leg forward in a large hop that moved him at a decent clip. As he approached the senator's house, he scanned the scene, picking out spots he could dive for cover if a gun battle erupted, choosing the best point of entry, searching for the best vantage point to survey the scene. As they neared the back garden gate, a steady thumping reached his ears. He hobbled up beside Jake, who'd pressed himself against the back garden wall to peer through a crack in the gate.

"What d'ya got, cowboy?" Daniel asked, finding the padlock that secured the gate had already been cut off.

"Garden's clear. Back door's ajar." Jake moved to get a different angle view. "Brick grill pit twenty paces to the left. No window to the right of the open door."

Daniel jerked a nod confirming their destinations. A sheen of sweat beaded on his brow as he pushed open the gate. Senses alert to his surroundings, heart pumping, Daniel hurried to the protection of the grill pit. Then while he covered

Jake, his teammate skulked to his position by the door. Flattened to the wall of the house, Jake reconnoitered the situation inside. Using hand signals, Jake waved Daniel closer. In four silent hops, Daniel took his position next to Jake. Propping his crutches beside him, he pulled out his gun. Balancing on his good leg, he leaned against the house for support.

More hand signals…. *Three tangos. All armed. Two by safe room door, third watching front yard by window.*

Daniel nodded and craned his neck for a look. The men at the door of the safe room were chopping their way through the wood frame around a steel barricade with an ax.

The goal of any operation was minimal casualties. Dead men couldn't give up valuable intel, lead them to those higher up the food chain.

The contingency plan, if they met resistance, was simple. Lethal force.

I'll go high. You take a knee, Daniel signaled. *Take the lookout. Head shot.* Which left the men by the safe room for Daniel.

Jake jerked a nod, sank to his knee and raised his sniper rifle.

In the distance, Daniel heard the wail of approaching sirens. Inside he heard a woman's scream as the men with the ax broke through the door frame. No time to wait.

Adrenaline charged through Daniel's blood. He funneled the surge of energy into focus, concentration, training.

"Freeze!" he shouted. "Drop your weapons and lie on the floor! Now!"

The three men turned. Both the lookout and Daniel's target raised their guns.

In a heartbeat, Daniel and Jake reacted.

The concussion of twin gun blasts pounded his chest. The man by the front window dropped. One down. Jake shifted his rifle and re-aimed.

Daniel's target staggered back a step, then clutched his neck. The third man dropped the ax and scrambled for his weapon.

Daniel re-sighted and squeezed the trigger again. Plaster splintered from the wall behind the ax man. A miss. *"Merde!"*

The man Daniel had shot in the throat slid down the wall but raised a handgun. Daniel finished the wounded man with a second shot that hit its mark.

Ax Man jumped behind a massive entertainment center and returned fire. As Ax Man shot at Daniel, Jake darted inside, running in a crouch until he reached the sofa.

"Drop your gun and get on the floor!" Daniel repeated.

Axe Man fired again, keeping Jake pinned behind the couch. Daniel needed a better position, preferably inside the house if he was going to help Jake. Gritting his teeth, he did a quick mental inventory of his surroundings, strategizing. Keeping his injured leg straight in front of him, Daniel slid to the ground, then crawled on his belly and elbows into the house. When Axe Man spotted him and opened fire, Daniel log-rolled until he was behind the couch with Jake.

Staying on his stomach, Daniel peered around the couch and zinged a few bullets near Ax Man's head. While Daniel distracted the gunman, Jake snuck from the other end of the couch to the opposite end of the entertainment center. He gave Daniel a hand signal, and Daniel took his cue, firing at a vase near the front window. The gunman jerked his attention across the room where the vase shattered. And Jake pounced. Before Ax Man could react, Jake took him down and held him pinned to the floor with a knee between the gunman's shoulders.

With adrenaline numbing his pain and his crutches still outside, Daniel hobbled over on his injured leg and disarmed Ax Man. He gave Jake a nod of thanks. "Get whatever information you can from him before the cops arrive."

"Roger that."

A whimper filtered out from the safe room, and Daniel's chest constricted. "Nicole!" He pounded a fist on the steel door. "Are you all right? Open the door. It's Daniel." He paused, listening, but blood whooshed in his ears, drowning out all but his own thundering pulse. "Nicole!"

Chapter 7

Nicole snapped her head up. In the silence following the barrage of gunfire, a familiar voice called to her from outside her father's office. "Daniel?"

Heart in her throat, Nicole eased Pilar into Sarah Beth's lap, then scurried to the battered reinforcement door. She threw the massive bolt that locked the steel door in place and struggled to push the door back in the wall pocket. Once the barricade had slid a couple inches, a large male hand grabbed the edge and shoved it aside in one powerful thrust.

Nicole's breath caught seeing Daniel's brawn filling the portal, a gun in his hand and a concerned scowl furrowing his chiseled face. *Daniel.* Fierce, handsome and…*here.* A familiar thrill tripped down her back and settled low in her belly.

"You came," she rasped in disbelief and joy.

His frown deepened. "Of course I did. You were under assault. You said you needed me."

"I know, but…you were in the hospital."

He lifted one eyebrow. "I checked myself out."

Nicole blinked, her ears still ringing from the gunfire and her post-adrenaline crash muddying her brain. "But you… hung up on me."

Daniel jerked a shrug. "I mobilize faster if I'm not on the phone."

"Your knee—"

"I'm getting the impression you're not glad to see me." He narrowed a dark penetrating stare on her and stepped closer. "Did you really think I'd ignore your call for help?" The intimate whisper and deep pitch of his voice sent a ripple of pleasure to her marrow.

"No." Maybe that's why her first instinct had been to call Daniel instead of the police.

He reached for her chin and swiped his thumb across her damp cheek. "Who are they? What did they want?"

Nicole took a few seconds to answer, needing time, unlike Daniel, to mentally shift from the deeply personal moment they'd been sharing back to the frightening business at hand. "I don't know who they are. I've never seen them before in my life. They were trying to take Pilar."

His eyebrows drew together. "Pilar?"

She nodded. "That's Tia's real name—Pilar Castillo. Her father is a prominent judge in Bogotá. I was in the process of confirming her identity through the Colombian embassy when the men attacked us."

A muscle in his jaw twitched, the only outward sign of what was going on behind those dark eyes. "You're bleeding." He touched the stinging spot on her neck.

"It's just a nick. Slap a Band-Aid on it, and I'm fine." She forced a smile, hoping he couldn't tell how shaken she was knowing that a bullet had only missed her carotid artery by a few inches. *Keep it together.*

He scowled his discontent. "You can't stay here," he said

at last. "You're not safe until we figure out how Pilar's location got leaked."

A chill shimmied through Nicole. Not safe in her own home? Two days ago, when she'd walked on U.S. soil again for the first time in months, she'd believed the nightmare was behind her. She'd been wrong.

Nicole glanced at the dead man lying in the hall behind Daniel, and her stomach roiled. "So what do I do? Go to a hotel?"

The front doorbell rang, interrupting any reply from Daniel. "This is the police. Open the door. We have reports of shots fired."

"I need to deal with the cops now." He gave her shoulder a squeeze. "But I'll be moving you and the girl to a safe house as soon as possible. Be ready."

A safe house? She opened her mouth to ask for elaboration, but Daniel spun away and limped on his bad leg toward the front door where the police knocked loudly. Nicole turned and staggered back into her father's office where Sarah Beth and Pilar still huddled together behind the large desk.

"Is it over? Is it safe to come out?" Sarah Beth asked, her face still pale with fright.

Nicole held her arms out to Pilar, who tumbled into her embrace, and nodded stiffly to Sarah Beth. "The police are here, and Daniel…"

She shuddered and tried to erase the image of the blank stare of the dead man in the hall. Daniel and his teammate had arrived just in time. She didn't want to think about the lethal means they'd employed to save her, Pilar and Sarah Beth.

Over the next couple hours, the police interviewed everyone at the scene, including the surviving man from the trio that had attacked the women. Nicole's father arrived minutes after the police and surveyed the ransacked house in horror. Nicole rushed to her father and hugged him tightly, reassuring him over and over that she was unharmed, only shaken by the attack.

Jake and Daniel showed the police their military credentials, and the preliminary ballistics assessment supported their claims of self-defense in the deaths of the two intruders. Pending an investigation, no charges were filed against them, but everyone, including Pilar, was required to accompany the cops to the police station so their hands and clothes could be tested for gunshot residue, along with other evidence collection.

The first long shadows of evening stretched across the parking lot of the New Orleans P.D. by the time Nicole and Pilar were released to go home. Jake and Daniel, leaning on his crutches, met them on the sidewalk as they exited the police headquarters. Nicole assessed Daniel's clenched teeth, the lines of pain and fatigue around his mouth and eyes, and concern burrowed past her own weariness. "You should go back to the hospital. You need rest and painkillers, and—"

"No." He shook his head, his eyes grim, uncompromising.

"Daniel…"

"No. We're going back to your father's place, but only long enough for you to pack a few necessities. Jake's agreed to drive us to the safe house I mentioned." He hitched his head toward the street. "His truck's down here. Let's go."

"Daniel, wait. Don't I get a say in this?" Nicole squeezed Pilar's hand and squared her shoulders.

Daniel's stern expression hardened further. "There's nothing to discuss. These men— whoever they are, whoever sent them—aren't going to give up just because this attempt to take Pilar failed. This is bigger than just an attempted kidnapping, and you're in their way. They won't hesitate to kill you to get the girl."

Nicole released a shaky breath, nodding. "I get that. But my father can hire men to—"

Daniel's chin jerked up when she mentioned her father, and Nicole hesitated. "Hold on. You can't think my father had anything to do with this!"

Pilar inched closer, casting Nicole a wary look when she raised her voice.

Daniel arched one eyebrow. "I can't?"

"Damn it, Daniel! Do *not* try to pin this on my father!"

Raising a hand to quell her argument, he leaned toward her, pitching his voice lower. "He may not be behind the attack, but we can't rule him out as the source of the leak. You told him about Pilar, didn't you?"

"I—" Nicole snapped her mouth shut. She had. Her father had promised to make phone calls to locate Pilar's parents and smooth over any red tape regarding her presence in the U.S.

Daniel clearly took her lack of response as capitulation. "Until we know where this threat against you and the girl is coming from, I'm not going to trust your safety to anyone else." Pivoting with his crutches, Daniel moved aside to let her precede him to Jake's truck. Sighing her resignation, Nicole led Pilar to the street and climbed inside Jake's dual-cab Ford F-150.

When they reached her father's house, Jake ran interference with the senator while Nicole packed. Pilar clung to her as she gathered what few belongings she'd amassed since getting back to the States, including some clothes and toys for Pilar. Oreo, clearly recovered from the ruckus earlier in the day, hopped up on the bed and tried to curl up in the suitcase. Pilar's face brightened when she saw Oreo, and she left Nicole's side in order to pat the cat.

Daniel, who'd accompanied Nicole to her bedroom, sat on the opposite side of the bed with his bad knee stretched in front of him. He knitted his brow as he watched Pilar with the feline. "That's not the cat I rescued for you, is it? The one I got from the storm drain was orange."

Nicole paused in folding a nightshirt and shook her head. "No, that's Oreo. He's a more recent addition to the family. Boudreaux is around here somewhere. Boo is an old man now." She cast a glance to Pilar and Oreo, remembering the events of that afternoon. "You know, Oreo and Boudreaux may have saved us today. They ran when the trouble started, but managed to trip up one of the gunmen, buying me a few seconds to grab Pilar and get to the safe room." She grinned at Daniel. "They're heroes."

He tugged a corner of his mouth up and scratched Oreo behind the ear. "Sure, they get all the credit."

Nicole placed her hand on his arm and held his gaze. "Not all. I'm fully aware that you risked everything to help me. Again." She bit her bottom lip. "I'm not sure I can ever repay you for—"

He gave a disgusted grunt. "I don't want repayment."

"I only mean—"

"Is this everything you need?" He made an impatient gesture toward the suitcase. "We have to get moving."

Fine. So he didn't want her gratitude. Nicole raked her fingers through her hair and turned on her toes to check her room for anything else she wanted to pack. Boudreaux sat in the door to the hall blinking at her sleepily. Shooting a glance back to Pilar, Nicole said, "We're taking the cats."

Daniel jerked his chin up. "What?"

"Look at her with Oreo." Nicole waved a hand toward the little girl, who stroked the black-and-white cat and snuggled close to Oreo's furry warmth. "The cats calm her. Comfort her. And…I've missed them. Why can't they go?"

Daniel rolled his eyes in resignation. "Whatever. But they stay inside. There are alligators where we're going."

"Alligators?" Nicole whipped a look of concern toward Daniel.

He raised a hand, forestalling her arguments. "It's perfectly safe."

"Why won't you tell me where this safe house is?"

"Because if you don't know, you can't tell your father." When she scowled, he added, "Or anyone else."

Nicole let her shoulders droop in surrender as she moved to the back of her walk-in closet to retrieve the cats' travel cages. Boudreaux saw the carrier and headed under the bed.

Nicole pointed to the absconding feline. "Grab him."

Leaning from the bed, Daniel scooped the old orange tomcat up and eyed him. "So we meet again."

"It's okay, Boo. We're not going to the vet this time." Nicole held out the cage, and Daniel guided the wiggling cat inside. Pilar gave them a curious look when they caged Oreo, as well, and zipped up Nicole's large suitcase.

"We're taking the kitties with us, okay?" she told Pilar, and fumbled for a few words of Spanish. *"Llevémonos los gatos con nosotros."*

Pilar gave her a weak smile and nodded as she scooted close to Nicole's side again.

"I'll get your bag." Daniel pushed off the bed and positioned his crutches under his arms. "You and Pilar go on down to the truck. Jake can get the cats."

Nicole hoisted her suitcase from the bed and extended the handle for rolling. "Don't be silly. You're on crutches."

He tried to nudge her aside. "I responded to your 911 on crutches, didn't I?"

She nudged back with her hip, noticing how hard and lean his body felt as she brushed against him. "True. And I'm sure you could wrangle my suitcase down the stairs and out to the truck, if you had the chance, but…" She started toward the door, wheeling the luggage with one hand and holding Pilar's hand with her other. "So can I."

Nicole bumped her suitcase down the steps from the second floor, feeling the weight of Daniel's disgruntled scowl following her.

At the bottom of the stairs, she met her father's frown and sighed. Somehow her father's disapproval bothered her less than Daniel's, a switch from years past that didn't escape her notice.

"I still think this is a mistake." The senator stormed toward her, blocking her path. "Let me hire protection for you. Your safety is my concern, not these guys'."

"I trust Daniel and Jake, Daddy. They're who I want."

"At least take my Kevlar vest with you, in case there's more shooting," her father pleaded.

"I'll be fine, Dad. Really." When Jake took the suitcase from her, she motioned toward the second floor. "The cats are upstairs in travel cages if you'd get them, too, please."

Jake arched an eyebrow and glanced to Daniel. "We're taking pets?"

Daniel swung to the door on his crutches, then paused and rubbed his temple. "Apparently."

Jake lifted a hand in concession, then tugged on the brim of his cowboy hat. "This is your gig."

Daniel faced her father and narrowed a steely stare on him. "If you want your daughter to be safe, don't breathe a word of any of this to anyone. The fewer people outside this room who know, the better."

Her father puffed out his chest and squared off with Daniel. Quickly, Nicole wedged herself between the men and patted her father on the shoulder. Pilar scuttled with her, holding tightly to the hem of her sweater. "I'll call when I can, Daddy."

"No, you won't," Daniel grated.

Senator White aimed a finger at Daniel. "Listen here, pal. Don't you try to—"

"Dad, stop!" Nicole knocked his hand down and divided a frown between the men. "We're all on the same side here.

Can't you two stop warring with each other for even a little while?" She smacked a kiss on her father's cheek and flashed him a taut grin. "Love you. Try not to worry. And you be careful, too."

Jake finished loading the truck, squeezing the cats' cages on the backseat next to Nicole and Pilar, and they got on the road just as the night blanketed the city. Pilar curled against her and fell asleep not long after they reached the dark highway bridge that crossed the marshes surrounding the city. After the first few miles, Oreo and Boudreaux ceased their plaintive mewls, and the truck grew quiet.

In the tight space of the backseat, surrounded by darkness, Pilar huddled against her, Nicole experienced a déjà vu that sent a shudder to her bones. Gritting her teeth, she battled down the panic that tried to climb her throat. *You're not in that cage anymore. You're safe. Keep it together.*

Sucking in a deep breath, she sought out Daniel's profile, reassuring herself with his presence. The lights from the dashboard cast harsh shadows over the rugged lines of his face, and she couldn't help but flash back to the night her hands had traced his chiseled cheeks and square jaw while her body had been tangled with his. That night he'd been smiling, his dark eyes alight with warmth and humor. Her heart pattered with longing. She missed his smile. She had yet to see it since he'd swooped in to save her from her Colombian prison.

"Now that we're on the road, can you tell me where you're taking me?" she called over the road noise. Roused by her voice, Oreo meowed, as if to say, "Yeah, where are you taking us?"

Daniel turned in the front seat and met her gaze. "My turf."

"Excuse me?"

"With my bum knee, I need every advantage I can get against these cretins. We're going someplace I know inside out." He cast a narrowed gaze out the side window and muttered something to Jake she couldn't hear.

A tickle of suspicion crawled up her back. "Meaning?"

"We're going to the bayou."

Daniel peered through the darkness to the weathered house on the bank of a southern Louisiana bayou. He'd spent many nights in the old wooden home. Set on a pier foundation with a wide front porch and a tin roof, his *grandmère's* one-hundred-year-old house looked exactly as it had the day he'd come to live there as a newly orphaned boy.

From the bayou waters, the eyes of creatures large and small reflected the headlights with a preternatural glow. Daniel had learned to respect the wildlife as he grew up, but Nicole and Pilar would have to be taught basic precautions. As beautiful as the moss-draped bayou was, the murky swampland teemed with hidden dangers.

"The circuit box is just inside the back door," he told Jake as he handed him a key. "Turn the power on while we unload, will ya?"

Jake nodded, jammed his cowboy hat on his head and climbed out of his truck, leaving his headlights burning, the only illumination on the house, other than the gibbous moon.

Daniel slid out of the truck and pulled his crutches from the backseat, along with one of the cat carriers. Nicole whispered to Pilar, who sat up, rubbing her eyes and glancing around warily.

"Whose house is this?" Nicole asked, rolling the kinks from her shoulders and craning her neck to gaze through the windshield.

"Mine now." Daniel massaged his sore knee, stiff after sitting so long. "It was my grandmother's and her parents' before that. *Mémère* left it to me when she died three years ago."

Behind him the security light blinked on with a hum that

said the power had been restored. One by one lights came on in the windows, indicating Jake was making his way through the rooms, checking things out.

Nicole popped open the truck door and climbed out, then helped Pilar jump to the ground. After circling the front bumper, she took a cat carrier in each hand and looked up at him. "Lead the way."

Slinging his duffel over one shoulder, Daniel planted his crutches on the soft earth and headed inside. The warped front steps creaked as he climbed them, and he batted a large cobweb out of his way as he hobbled to the front door. He gave the grimy window a quick knock, and Jake opened the door and stood back.

The musty smell of mildew and age assailed him, and as he limped into the familiar living room, he imagined he could still smell *Mémère's* crawfish gumbo and spicy boudin cooking on the gas stove. When his grandmother didn't round the corner from the kitchen and spread her arms for a hug, a pang settled over him. The house seemed lonely, lifeless without *Mémère*.

"I'll grab the suitcases," Jake said, moving to the door. "Which room do you want them in?"

Roused from his memories, Daniel waved a hand toward the back of the house. "Put Nicole in the master bedroom and the girl next door. I'll sleep on the couch."

Nicole stiffened. "No. Pilar stays with me." She stroked the child's head and shrugged. "I doubt she'd stay in a room by herself, anyway. You can have the master bedroom."

Daniel lifted a shoulder and pulled a dusty, protective cover from a stuffed chair. "Whatever."

In their travel carriers, the cats meowed and pawed at the cages' doors. Nicole squatted to peer in one carrier, cooing to the feline inside. "Can I let them out?"

"Go ahead." Daniel moved to the next piece of furniture

and yanked on the sheet cover. A plume of dust rose in the air, and Pilar sneezed.

Yeah, with the accumulated dust and mildew, the house would be full of allergens, but it was secluded, safe. He'd take a stuffy nose over Colombian mercs any day.

Nicole opened the first cage, and the old orange cat crept out, giving the air a cautious sniff. "What do you think, Boudreaux?"

When Nicole pointed to the other cage and nodded to Pilar, the little girl crouched to open the second carrier. The black-and-white cat trotted out and gave an unhappy meow before taking off to explore his new digs.

"How long has this place been shut up?" Nicole asked, joining him in uncovering the furniture and using a corner of one of the sheets to wipe dust from a lamp table.

Daniel wadded up the dirty sheet in his hands and tossed it in a corner on the floor. "Last time I was here was two, two and a half years ago, I think, right before I left for Colombia on an undercover mission with Alec."

"Is there any food here or other supplies?"

Daniel dragged a hand over his mouth and grunted. "May be a thing or two. I'll ask Jake to bring in some supplies for us first thing in the morning."

"What did I do?" Jake asked with a grin as he backed through the front door hauling in Nicole's rolling suitcase and his duffel bag.

"He's volunteered you to go shopping—" A loud crash and the predatory howl of a cat cut Nicole off. More rustling and thumping drew everyone's attention to the back of the house.

Jake and Daniel exchanged a telling look, and both drew weapons from under their shirts. Adrenaline kicking and his muscles taut, Daniel moved down the hall on his crutches as silently as he could while keeping a grip on his handgun.

Pressing his back to the wall, he slid a hand into the first bedroom and turned on the light.

Empty.

Drawing a deep, quiet breath, Daniel sidled farther down the hall and repeated the process at the next door. When the lights flashed on, he swept his gaze over the twin beds, scarred dresser and rag-rug-covered floor.

In the center of the room where he'd slept as a teenager, Nicole's black-and-white cat stood with an arched back and ears plastered to his head, hissing at a fat, disoriented-looking raccoon. While his chest loosened a degree with relief not to find anything more threatening skulking in the shadows, he kept a wary eye on the raccoon. A frightened animal of any size could prove dangerous, and raccoons could carry rabies.

"Casse-toi!" he shouted, waving a hand at the critter. As if animals at his *grandmére's* spoke Cajun French by default. "Scat!" he added, in case this raccoon preferred Southernisms.

Jake eyed him and chuckled. "Scat?"

He shrugged. "Always worked for my grandmother."

The raccoon turned and waddled to a bookshelf, where he climbed up until he reached a hole in the drywall and scampered through.

"Looks like someone's been living here, after all." Jake shoved his gun back in the waistband of his jeans.

Daniel groaned. "And chewed a hole from the attic." He stashed his own gun away and looked around the room for some way to block the varmint's hole for the night. "I'll have to evict the rascal tomorrow and make some repairs."

"Sounds like fun," Jake said, his tone dripping sarcasm. He knocked his cowboy hat back enough to scratch his forehead. "I can stay a day or two and help out if you want."

Daniel shook his head. "Naw. I have another assignment for you, if you're willing."

"I've got some personal time coming. I'm game."

Daniel nodded his appreciation, then frowned as a thought occurred to him. He pulled out his cell phone and checked his reception. "Hmm. Signal's weak, but it might do in a pinch. You have a satellite phone in the truck by chance?"

"No, but I can get you one."

Daniel nodded. "Thanks, cowboy." The satellite phone might be overkill, but with Nicole's life at stake, he'd rather not risk being incommunicado should trouble arise.

And lately, trouble seemed to be following Nicole.

The next morning, Nicole dug her phone from her purse and walked over to a window, searching for the best possible reception, which proved to be rather dismal. When her call was answered, she smiled at the voice at the other end of the line. Stiffly formal, yet familiar and oddly comforting. Some things never changed. "Hi, Daddy. It's me."

"Nicole!" Instantly, warmth tinged with worry suffused the businesslike tone. "Where…you? Where…take you? Are you…right?"

She leaned her head against the window and closed her eyes. "I'm safe, and… Daniel's asked me not to tell you where we are."

"Damn it, Nic—! I'm…father. I…right to know. Does LeCroix really think…going to let anyone or an…hurt you? That's ludicrous."

"Not you, necessarily, but…it's just a precaution."

Through the crackle of static, she heard her father sigh. "If he thinks…shut me out of this situation, I—"

"No one is shutting you out. I promise I'll check in with you from time to time so you know I'm safe. Okay?" Static answered her. "Daddy?"

"You had a call…from Ramon Diaz at the…embassy."

Nicole perked up and crossed the room to a different window, still searching for a clearer connection. "What did he say?"

"The judge has disappeared. Mario…heard about the attempted kidnapping…went into hiding."

"Wait, are you saying *Pilar's father* is missing now?"

"In hiding. He doesn't trust…because of the attack here involving you and Pilar. Diaz isn't happy about you disappearing…Pilar, either. She's a Colombian citizen and you're—"

A loud burst of static cut him off.

"Dad?" Nicole checked her phone. Her screen read, *dropped call*. She tried to call her father back, but couldn't get a strong enough signal now to place the call. "Fudge."

So…Pilar's father was in hiding, as well? Great. How was she supposed to reunite him with Pilar now? Stewing over this turn of events, she carried her phone into the kitchen with her, in case her father called back.

Pilar was sitting at the kitchen table with Jake and Daniel, watching with wide, wary eyes as the men conferred.

"Good morning." She sent Pilar a smile, and the men acknowledged her with mumbled greetings. Her stomach rumbled, and she turned to the cabinets to search for food.

"We're making a list of supplies Jake will get when he goes out in a few minutes. If you have any preferences, speak now."

"Coffee," she said emphatically, then checked the counter for a coffeepot. She sighed her relief when she spotted one. "Fresh fruit and vegetables. Milk. All the stuff a little girl needs for a healthy diet. Cat food and litter for Oreo and Boudreaux." She chose to ignore Jake's eyeroll as he scribbled these items on the list.

Nicole fixed the only breakfast she could find in the empty cupboards. Instant oatmeal that Daniel warned her was likely several years old. When the kettle water boiled, she stirred up two bowls of instant oatmeal and grimaced. "Add eggs and whole grain bread to the list for breakfasts."

Jake winked at her and scribbled on his list.

She put the two bowls on the table and watched as Pilar bowed her head over her breakfast, then crossed herself before eating. Though not Catholic herself, Nicole had attended a Catholic high school and had numerous Catholic friends growing up, and it touched her to see the young girl practicing her faith even after all she'd been through.

"I need ammunition for both my Sig .45 and my .22 hunting rifle," she heard Daniel say, even though he spoke in a hush. She shivered, hating the idea of loaded weapons around Pilar, even if she understood the need.

Daniel must have sensed her gaze, because he glanced up at her and narrowed an all-business look on her. "Can you shoot?"

Alec hadn't bothered to ask when he'd shoved the automatic weapon in her hands as they fled the jungle. "I can pull a trigger, but I make no promises about what I'll hit."

Jake and Daniel exchanged a look before Daniel returned his attention to her. "I'll teach you to handle a gun. I want you ready next time those cretins show up."

"Next time?" Her grip tightened around her spoon. "I thought the point of hiding out here was so there was no next time."

Daniel shrugged and ducked his head to study his notes. "We have to be prepared for anything. No hideout is foolproof."

Learning to shoot. Hiding from assassins. Dodging bullets. When had her life become so…*hazardous?*

Daniel hitched his head toward her phone, which she'd left on the end of the table. "And another thing…no cell phone. A signal can be traced. If you have to use a phone, my cell is encrypted."

"Oh." Guilt nibbled at her. "So…I guess I should tell you that I called my father this morning."

Daniel sent her a tell-me-you-didn't look, then scrubbed a hand over his face. "Okay. We'll deal with it."

"There's more."

Jake and Daniel both raised worried gazes to her.

Nicole glance quickly to Pilar, who stared bleakly at her oatmeal. "Her father heard about the kidnapping attempt somehow. He's gone into hiding. Ramon Diaz, my contact at the Colombian embassy, called my father's house to tell me that, and my father let Diaz know we'd moved Pilar to a safe house. Diaz is upset, presumably because he wasn't informed."

"No one can know we're here," Daniel interjected, anticipating her next argument.

She studied Daniel's unshaven jaw and dark, serious eyes, and a ripple of uneasiness shimmied through her. Her guardian could well be the most dangerous element in this equation. Dangerous to her sanity, her heart, if she didn't figure out how to rein in her wild obsession with him.

Knowing he was sleeping in the next room, Nicole had spent hours staring at the ceiling last night, wishing she could curl up next to his muscular body. Imagining a young Daniel growing up within these walls and becoming the mysterious man he was today had teased her brain in the late hours. The idea of living under the same roof with Daniel for who knows how many days made her skin feel too tight and her blood hot.

She shifted her gaze to Jake, a rugged, incredible-looking man in his own right, yet the powerfully built, sandy-haired pilot didn't stir Nicole's deepest passion the way Daniel did—and always had.

Pilar poked at her oatmeal and sent Nicole a sad look.

"You don't have to eat it if you don't like it, *mija*." The gray-beige goop reminded her, too, of the gruel they'd eaten in the jungle. Nicole shoved her bowl away and pushed her chair from the table.

The sights and sounds of the attack at her father's house flickered in her memory, and Nicole shuddered. If she hadn't gone to check on Pilar when she had yesterday, would the men have succeeded in kidnapping her? And why had she left the girl alone in the first place?

She'd assumed her father's house was safe. Why wouldn't it be? How could she have known such terrible men were already on their trail?

The questions pounded at her temples. What she and Pilar needed was an activity to keep them busy, something to distract them from thoughts of the men who'd attacked them. Cleaning the safe house topped that list.

Nicole raked her hair back from her face and remembered the picture of Mario Castillo she'd received just before the attack yesterday. The photo was still folded in the pocket of her pants. "Wait here," she told Pilar. *"Espérate aquí."*

She hurried to the bedroom to retrieve the crumpled picture, then smoothing the paper against her chest as she returned, she sat next to Pilar and laid the photo on the table. "Do you know this man?" she asked. *"Conoces a este hombre?"*

Pilar leaned forward to examine the photo, and her eyes widened, lighting with happiness. *"Papi!"*

Daniel and Jake glanced over from their huddle.

A thrill raced through Nicole, not only hearing Pilar speak at last, but seeing the pure joy and longing on the girl's face. She smiled and nodded, pulling Pilar into a hug. "Good. That's so wonderful."

"May I see that?" Daniel asked, holding a hand out.

Nicole passed him the crumpled sheet. "That's the judge who's in hiding. Mario Castillo. That picture had just been faxed to my father's home office yesterday when the men attacked. So we have our confirmation of who she is. *Whose* she is."

Daniel studied the photo a moment, then passed it to Jake. "Will you see if—"

"I'm on it." Jake shot Daniel a smug grin as he interrupted. "Do you want me to bring him here when I find him or meet you somewhere?"

Nicole cleared her throat. "Um, gentlemen. May I remind you that I already have the Colombian and U.S. embassies working on this? They're the ones who faxed me the photo and got in touch with Castillo yesterday."

Daniel leaned back in his chair and angled his stubbled chin as he regarded her. He lifted one eyebrow. "And may I remind you that your contacts are likely the ones responsible for leaking Pilar's location to the men who tried to kill you? Until we know what and who we are dealing with, Jake will be doing our legwork in Colombia, looking for Castillo."

His gaze hardened to a scowl as he glanced at his injured knee, and Nicole didn't need to ask how he felt about relying on his teammate to do his fieldwork while he babysat them and nursed his bum leg. Sympathy she was sure he wanted no part of tugged at her. He'd already sacrificed so much for her and Pilar, but losing his mobility—and therefore his position on his black ops team—had to be the hardest for him to accept.

The men finished their discussion, and Jake headed out to buy supplies. Daniel patched the raccoon hole in Pilar's bedroom, leaving the attic repair for when Jake could help him, then moved to the living room where he began cleaning his guns.

Nicole cleared away their untouched breakfast and turned to the girl who now clutched the faxed photo of her father close to her chest. "Well, we might as well start our cleaning in the kitchen." She found a rag and turned on the faucet at the sink. The water that sputtered out was a rusty shade of brown and smelled like eggs. Nicole wrinkled her nose and glanced at Pilar. "Yuck."

Pilar scrunched her nose, too.

After running the water for a few minutes, the accumulated dirt and smell in the pipes cleared enough that Nicole felt comfortable using the water with some liquid soap she found in a cabinet to wash the dishes and wipe the counters, table and chairs. As they worked, Nicole continued the quasi game she'd played with Pilar in their cage in Colombia. Moving through the kitchen, she pointed to objects and told Pilar the English name for each item. Though Pilar never repeated the words, her bright eyes reflected intelligence, and Nicole felt sure the child was soaking the information in.

They'd nearly finished wiping down the kitchen and all the pans when Oreo sauntered in, tail twitching and something furry in his mouth. Nicole jumped back with a screech.

Startled, Oreo dropped his prize. The white fuzzy thing didn't move.

Daniel scrambled from the living room into the kitchen, his gun at the ready. "What happened?"

"Oreo had something in his mouth…." Nicole nudged the wooly thing with her toe, realizing it was a toy. "At first, I thought it was alive. Sorry. I didn't mean to alarm you."

Pilar picked up the toy, a small stuffed lamb that looked like it came from a child's fast food meal, and held it out for Oreo to sniff.

"Hey, where'd he get that?" Daniel asked. "Lamby was mine when I was a kid."

"Lamby?" Nicole's cheek twitched with a grin.

"Cut me some slack. I was five." Daniel stepped closer to reach for the lamb, but Oreo swatted at the small stuffed animal and snagged it with his claw. "Hey, *minou,* gimme—"

Pilar giggled as Oreo batted Lamby across the floor, and she chased down the hall after the cat.

Nicole covered a laugh. "If Lamby is an heirloom you want protected, I'll get it back from Oreo...."

"Pfft." Daniel waved a hand and sighed. "It's a cat toy now."

Nicole cocked her head and tried to read Daniel's expression. "But if it's important to you..."

Daniel hitched his head toward the hall where Pilar played with Oreo, giggling. "Listen to her. That's more important than some old dusty toy."

Nicole's heart swelled, and smiling warmly, she caught Daniel's gaze with her own, held it. "That's the Daniel I remember."

Something in his hard gaze shifted, softened, but before Daniel could reply, Jake burst through the back door, his arms loaded with bags. "Ho, ho, ho. Santa came early this year." Jake set the bags on the kitchen table, then aimed a thumb at the door. "There's more in the truck. A little help?"

"Pilar?" Nicole headed out the back door, crooking a hand to tell the girl to follow. When Nicole saw the pile of groceries and supplies mounded in the bed of Jake's truck, she stopped to stare. "Geez Louise, Jake!"

Jake shrugged as he marched past her. "Tell me about it."

Daniel swung next to her on his crutches and paused. "There a problem?"

She motioned to the huge pile of supplies. "Just how long do you think we're staying?"

His returned gaze was hard and flat. "As long as it takes to make sure you're safe."

Chapter 8

Jake left for Colombia to search for Judge Castillo as soon as they'd unloaded the supplies from his truck. Jake was one of the best agents the black ops team had, and Daniel felt confident the native Texan could track down Pilar's father within a week or two.

Over the next two days, Daniel watched Nicole buzz around his grandmother's house, cleaning up a storm. Guilt nibbled at him every time she picked up a rag or broom, as if her housekeeping was an indictment against him and the safe house he'd provided. Or an unspoken commentary on the home of his youth.

At first, he tried to ignore her, but that exercise was futile. If Nicole was around, she had his full attention. When he tried to help, she shooed him away.

"Cleaning keeps me busy, and if I'm busy I'm less likely to dwell on things that are out of my control." She rinsed her rag in the kitchen sink and headed back outside to wash the porch windows. "Besides, I had enough idle time while I was held captive to last me a lifetime." She aimed a finger at the sofa. "You should sit. Rest your knee. You've earned it."

Daniel raised his hands in surrender and settled on the couch, frustrated with his own idleness.

Pilar found a children's book in a storage box of his childhood things and brought it out to the living room. She sat next to him and opened the cover. A fuzzy warmth filled Daniel's chest. He wasn't sure what to do with the tenderness he felt toward the little girl. He hadn't spent a lot of time around kids, except when he was supposed to be in soldier mode and not focusing on things like how sweet a little girl's smile could be or how a child's laugh could lighten even the tensest mood. Living with Pilar over the past two days, watching her interact with Nicole, cast his protective duties in a whole new light. Pilar had an innocence and vulnerability that stuck under his ribs and crowded his heart.

The first day, as she'd clung to Nicole, Pilar had looked at him with a heartbreaking mix of wariness and hero worship. He was the brute with the guns and the loud voice and the gruff appearance who'd rescued her from even scarier men. He hated the idea that he frightened the girl, so by the second day, he shaved the black stubble that made him look like a thug. When she glanced his way, he made an effort to smile, and with no immediate threat warranting barked commands, he consciously lowered his volume and softened his tone.

Not only did his efforts seem to calm the little girl, but Nicole noticed the changes and sent him appreciative smiles that shot straight to his soul. Though he wanted more from Nicole than her gratitude, Daniel welcomed the points he scored with her because he'd built a good rapport with Pilar.

He didn't know where things with Nicole might go. They had a lot of crap in their way—like her father. But his body ached for her, and his heart bled a little more every time he thought of the happiness he'd known with her for one magical night. If they could get past their differences, could they recapture that bliss, that passion? Or would he always be *that guy from the bayou* to her…a convenient chump from the wrong side of the tracks to use and discard when he'd served his purpose?

A niggle of irritation poked him for the umpteenth time. Nicole's pride had been hurt when he'd walked out on her five years ago. She was determined to rehash the events of that morning, root out his reasons for leaving and exact her pound of flesh for his slight. But how could he relive the pain and humiliation of that morning? His pride and dignity had already suffered one nearly crippling blow thanks to her. He was no glutton for punishment.

The crinkle of yellowed pages drew his attention to Pilar and the book in her lap. The text was in Cajun-English dialect, and the girl stared at the pages, frowning.

He'd heard Nicole chanting English words to Pilar many times in the kitchen or bedroom when they were alone, and he wondered if the English lessons were helping the girl's comprehension at all. Scooting closer to Pilar and readjusting his injured leg, he pointed to the book in her hands, *Cajun Night Before Christmas*. "May I?"

When Pilar handed him the book, looking chastened, he reassured her with a wink and a warm smile. The shadows in the girl's eyes dissipated, and she flashed him a shy grin. Flipping to the first page, Daniel studied the pictures, nostalgia stirring an ache in his chest.

"My *grandmére* used to read this to me when I was little," he told her quietly, knowing she wouldn't understand. "Even when it wasn't Christmas." He pointed to the bearded man in his sleigh. "There's Santa Claus…'cept around here, we call him *Père Noël*, Father Christmas." He glanced down, looking for any signs of recognition in her face. "Oh, yeah. Y'all celebrate with *El Niño Jesús,* right?"

Now Pilar's face lit with a smile.

Daniel had an idea and pushed off the sofa to hobble to a cabinet across the room. He dug in a pile of dusty books until he found the photo album his grandmother had kept of him and his parents. Planting himself next to Pilar again, he turned the pages of aged photos until he found one of himself at about age three. "See, that's me." He pointed to the picture, then to himself. "Daniel."

Pilar examined the picture with a small furrow in her brow, then glanced up at him, a wide smile brightening her face. He turned the page and found another picture of himself with *Mémère.* "That's my *grandmère.*" He motioned around them. "This was her house."

As Pilar looked around then back at the photo, Daniel sent a glance to the front window where Nicole was scrubbing madly. As if feeling his gaze, she paused in her work and met his stare. When she spotted Pilar beside him, the book spread between them, she smiled. Warmth expanded in his chest until he could barely breathe. Damn, Nicole was beautiful.

Pilar tugged on his sleeve and pointed to another picture of him as a young boy, wearing wet cut-off jeans and a sappy grin while he showed off the catfish he'd caught. "*Oui,* that's me, too."

On the next page, he tapped a picture of himself at about five years old, pouting. "Look-a dat *bahbin!*" he said with a thick Cajun accent, remembering what *Mémère* used to say about that photo. *"Quoi faire tu braille?"*

Pilar laughed and imitated his exaggerated pout.

"Oh, just what we need in this house," Nicole said as she walked back into the living room from the porch, her tone wry, "a *third* language." She sent him a teasing grin and headed back into the kitchen to rinse her rag again.

"De rien," he called after her.

As she returned from the kitchen with the rinsed rag, Nicole spotted the picture album he held, and her teasing grin faltered. "What's that?"

"Nothing." He gave her a dismissive shrug. "Just some old pictures of my grandmother's."

"Can I see?" Nicole joined him on the sofa, her thigh brushing his as she settled close enough to see the photos, the lemon scent of dish soap clinging to her.

"Go ahead," he said, trying to sound casual, even though his heart thrashed as hard as that catfish in the picture had flailed when he'd pulled it from the water. He loosened his grip on the album so Nicole could angle it toward her.

Daniel's gut tightened, suddenly all too conscious of how Nicole might react to the Cajun lifestyle depicted in the photos—isolated, poor, living off the bayou. His grandmother had never received a formal education, never embraced modern conveniences and technology. Daniel had been the one to update the house with modern amenities in recent years.

But as out of date as this house had been, the Gatreau family's tiny shack on stilts, deep in the bayou, where his grandmother had been raised, was even more primitive. He'd pointed Alec and Erin to that bayou shack when they'd needed a hideout last winter.

Pilar carried *Cajun Night Before Christmas* to a chair across the room and settled in to study the pictures, while Nicole perused the photos.

A sunny smile lit Nicole's face, and she pointed to the proud boy with his catch. "Is this you?"

"Yeah." His voice sounded tight. Willing his muscles to relax, he forced the air from his lungs. "Yours truly."

Nicole's blue eyes brightened, and she laughed—a happy sound of discovery, not derision.

Daniel slid a covert side glance to her, studying her reaction as her gaze moved from one picture to another.

"Oh, my gosh," she chuckled, "I bet you hate that picture. Look at your pout!" She met his eyes, her lips twitching with humor. "Were you a grumpy little boy, Mr. LeCroix?"

The urge to kiss her teasing grin slammed him so hard he had to catch his breath before he could reply. "No more than most. I'm smiling in all the other pictures."

Her attention returned to the photo album for a moment. When she raised her head again, warmth filled her face.

"So you are." She smoothed a finger over one of the photos, and his skin reacted as if she'd stroked him instead. "That's the smile that stole my heart the night we met."

Stole her heart? The phrase sent a shock wave through him, though with effort, he masked his surprise, suppressed it. His smile hadn't been enough to build a relationship on after she'd used him in her rebellion against her father years ago.

His fingers tightened on the photo album as a familiar knot of bitter disappointment swelled in his chest. He couldn't allow himself to forget the pain and sense of betrayal he'd known that morning and in the months that followed. He'd buried himself in special operations training, praying he could forget Nicole and the hope she'd crushed in that overheard phone call to her father. But he'd never completely erased her from his heart or his mind. And now, here he was sharing the house he'd grown up in with her, protecting her from an unknown threat…and in danger of falling for her all over again, if he didn't find a way to fight the old feelings stirring to life again and keep her at arm's length.

"Oh, there's the requisite I-lost-a-tooth shot." Nicole angled another grin at him, and he ignored the acceleration in his pulse. "Do you remember what the tooth fairy brought you?"

"I didn't have a tooth fairy."

"What?" Nicole sounded truly offended on his behalf. "Why not?"

"Doesn't matter. I had a good childhood," he said, hearing the note of defensiveness in his tone. "I had plenty of reason to be happy, to smile, even though I lost my parents when I was twelve. We didn't have much materially, but I never knew it. What we lacked in things, my parents and *Mémère* made up for in the love they gave me."

"Oh, Daniel…" Nicole stared at him with a certain sadness in her eyes. A bittersweet smile that felt too much like pity to Daniel tugged her lips.

He closed the photo album with a grunt and shoved to his feet, wincing when a sharp ache shot through his knee. The pain only fueled his frustration with the elusive dissatisfaction that nagged him. "I'm not looking for sympathy! I have no regrets from my childhood. I'm proud of my family, my heritage."

Pilar raised a startled looked, and Nicole blinked her surprise at his outburst. "As you should be. I never said otherwise."

Daniel sucked in a deep breath, his nose flaring and his hands fisting at his sides. *Get a grip, man.* She *hadn't* said anything derogatory about his Cajun roots. Not today, anyway, and not since he'd brought her home from Colombia. But being with her in this house had him on edge.

"Forget it," he grumbled, picking up his crutches and heading outside. "I'll be on the porch."

The weight of Nicole's stare followed him as he left, and his gut tightened. Like a storm rolling in from the Gulf, a showdown between them was coming, and he dreaded the fallout.

Nicole carried her glass of iced tea toward the front porch but stopped behind the screened door when she spotted Pilar sitting with Daniel. He sat in one of the rocking chairs with his injured leg propped on a large bucket he'd turned upside down, and Pilar stared at the ugly red surgical scar visible through Daniel's knee brace.

"Pilar," he said softly, and the little girl glanced up. He crooked his finger, motioning her closer. She walked to his side, and Daniel put an arm around her shoulders, turning her and pointing toward the bayou. "Look."

Nicole looked the direction he indicated and spotted a beautiful blue heron strutting through the water, searching the shallows for fish.

Pilar angled her head to grin at Daniel, and Nicole's heart tripped. The little girl had a beautiful smile, and Nicole's spirits lifted seeing the child happy at last. Was it the new hope Pilar had of being reunited with her father that made her feel safer, more cheerful, willing to smile?

No sooner had that thought filtered through her mind than Daniel flashed a warm grin back at the little girl. Now Nicole's heart thundered. When he smiled, Daniel could melt the hardest heart. This was the man she'd fallen so hard for five years ago at the Mardi Gras ball, the man with whom she'd spent a sensual night and with whom she'd envisioned her future. Perhaps part of Pilar's happiness had to do with Daniel. She couldn't blame Pilar for developing a crush on the handsome man who'd rescued her twice.

With a flap of its massive wings, the heron took flight, and Pilar tracked the bird with her gaze, until it disappeared behind the cypress trees that lined the bayou. Pulling her chair closer to Daniel's, Pilar settled in, staring again at the injured knee.

"Te duele?" Pilar asked in a tiny voice, her finger lightly touching Daniel's scar.

Nicole was so startled to hear Pilar speak, she gasped.

Pilar and Daniel both swiveled their heads toward the door

where Nicole stood. Caught spying on the duo, Nicole pushed through the screen door and took the rocking chair next to Daniel's. "She asked if your knee hurts."

He shot Nicole a strange look, then arched one black eyebrow and said dryly, "Thanks."

"Wh—"

Before she could finish, he turned back to Pilar and, with a devastating smile, replied, *"No mucho. Espero que la cicatriz tan horrible que tengo no ahuyente a las chicas bonitas."*

Pilar giggled and shook her head. *"No creo."*

Nicole kicked herself mentally. Hello? The guy had worked undercover in Colombia for who-knows-how-long. Of course he spoke Spanish.

He met her stunned, somewhat embarrassed look with a smug grin. "I told her I hoped my ugly scar didn't scare away all the pretty girls. She said it wouldn't."

"I'm sorry. I forgot you would know Spanish because of your work in South America."

"Instead, you assumed I couldn't understand her. Why?"

She blinked, taken aback by the bitterness behind his question. "Well…most people wouldn't have."

"Most *Cajuns* wouldn't? Is that what you mean?"

She bristled. "What is that supposed to mean? I'm not a bigot!"

He waved her off. "Forget it."

Nicole tensed and leaned toward him. "No, explain. Why do you think I would make any judgments about you based on your heritage?"

"You have before."

She sputtered a laugh. "What? When?"

He rolled his eyes and shook his head, frowning. "Are you kidding me?"

Nicole spread her hands. "No. Please enlighten me."

A muscle jumped in his jaw. "The night we spent together, five years ago."

Her pulse sped up, remembering the sensual glide of his body against hers, the heat of his kisses and the breathy moans of satisfaction they'd both made. But she couldn't recall anything he could have misconstrued as bigotry. She shook her head. "Still clueless. What did I do?"

He glanced at Pilar, and Nicole noticed the girl's worried frown for the first time. Even if she couldn't understand the words, Pilar could obviously tell from the tone of their voices and their expressions that the conversation had turned angry and personal.

"Dang it," Nicole fussed under her breath then flashed the girl a forced smile. "*Todo está bien.* Everything's all right, *mija.*"

Pilar looked skeptical and shifted her gaze to Daniel.

With a lopsided grin, he turned up a palm and shrugged. *"Alguien debe haber puesto un insecto en su desayuno."*

Again Pilar giggled.

"What did you tell her? Something about breakfast."

Daniel gave Nicole a nonchalant glance. "That someone must have put an insect in yours."

Rolling her eyes heavenward, she leaned closer to Daniel. "We're not through with this conversation." She kept her volume low and shot Daniel a pointed look. "We have to talk about it eventually… Soon, preferably."

"Let it go," he returned flatly.

Gritting her teeth, Nicole huffed her exasperation, then met Pilar's gaze and pointed at Daniel. *"Él está loco."*

"Sí, loco." Daniel wiggled his fingers on either side of his head and crossed his eyes.

Pilar laughed and snuggled closer to Daniel's side. *"Sí."*

Nicole grinned, touched by Daniel's attempts to bring Pilar out of her shell. "Well, it seems we're all in agreement."

Daniel grunted and returned his gaze to the still waters of the bayou. "Pilar, my dear, have you ever been fishing?" He met the girl's eyes and repeated the question in Spanish.

When she shook her head, Daniel seized his crutches and hoisted himself out of his chair. "Then I'm going to teach you."

He limped to the other end of the porch and grabbed two cane poles that leaned against the house. Leaving one of the crutches behind, Daniel started down the porch steps and hitched his head, signaling Pilar to follow. "Come on, tadpole. Let's catch dinner."

Pilar's glance asked approval from Nicole.

"Go on." She waved her away with her fingers. *"Te puedes ir."*

Her expression curious, Pilar rose from her seat and joined Daniel on the lawn, taking the fishing pole he handed her.

"Be careful," Nicole called, not sure if she was more worried about Pilar, experiencing the wildlife of the bayou for the first time, or Daniel, dealing with his injured leg on uneven, sometimes murky terrain.

Daniel tapped the walkie-talkie clipped to his hip. Jake had purchased the short-distance radios for just this type of circumstance. At the moment, Nicole's was still sitting in the charging cradle plugged in the kitchen outlet.

He leveled a penetrating gaze on Nicole. "Keep your radio close. If anything seems off, if you so much as think a mosquito has gotten in the house, call me."

Nicole straightened. "I thought we were here because it is so remote, so safe. Do you really think—?"

"No. I think you'll be fine. And I'm only going a few yards down the bank to my old pirogue dock." His eyebrows lowered, deepening his scowl. "But I'd rather not take any chances. There's a gun in the first kitchen drawer. If you need it, don't hesitate to use it."

* * *

After Daniel and Pilar left, Nicole carried Daniel's encrypted cell phone out to the porch, hoping to get more than one bar of reception so she could check in again with her father. The connection was marginally better outside, so she settled in the rocking chair Daniel had vacated and held the phone to her ear.

After assuring her father that she was fine and refusing once more to tell him where they were, Nicole asked if Ramon Diaz had been in touch.

"He's called every day, Nic. He's getting pressure from his government to bring Pilar home before this turns into a political issue. You are holding the child of an important Colombian official, you know."

"I know, Dad, but Daniel thinks we—"

"LeCroix? He shouldn't even be involved in this! He's trouble, Nic. He's up to something. I know he is."

"He protecting us the best way he knows how."

"He has an ulterior motive. Just a few months ago, he swore to my face that he'd destroy me. How can you trust him?"

"Daddy, stop. Please?" Nicole rubbed her eyes and groaned. "Can't you two put your differences behind you and realize that we're all on the same side? This bickering and hostility between you two..." She opened her eyes in time to see a turtle scuttle from a log into the brown bayou. "Well, it hurts me. I care about you both. Deeply. And—" She stopped abruptly when she realized what she'd said.

She had deep feelings for Daniel. But what feelings? Gratitude, certainly. He had saved her life several times. Admiration, yes. Daniel had risen far in a short time and made a difference in the fight against terrorism. Lust? Definitely. In spades.

"Nicole." Her father's wary tone intruded on her reflection. "Are you telling me you're in love with this man?"

A tremor shot to her core. "I…don't know. He's changed since I knew him before."

He scoffed. "Did you ever *really* know him?"

Nicole scowled. "What do you mean?"

"Well, you had a reckless one-night fling with him a few years ago, but then he left town and… I thought that had been the end of it."

Out of habit, Nicole bristled a bit at the word *reckless*. When she did something impromptu—like leaving her nursing job to help at a medical mission camp in a poverty stricken area of Colombia—she was reckless. When her father made snap decisions, he was bold and daring.

Then the rest of his comment resonated inside her. "What do you know about his leaving town?"

Her father hesitated. "Only what you've told me."

"I never said he left town. Even when I left for Colombia, I still had no clue what happened to him. The Navy wouldn't tell me anything, and he never called. I…" A chill of suspicion slithered through her. "Daddy…what…" She took a slow breath for courage. "What did you do?"

"Do? I don't know what you mean, what did *I* do?" Her father might be good at bluffing with reporters and his colleagues, but she heard the slight wobble in his tone.

Acid pooled in her stomach. What part had her father played in keeping her and Daniel apart? Was her father behind the bitterness that Daniel felt toward her? "How did you know he left town?"

"Like I said, I thought you told me that. But it's been years, honey." He laughed stiffly. "I've slept since then."

"Fine. I'll ask Daniel." Nicole rolled her eyes. Liked he'd tell her! Keeping mum about the past was one thing Daniel had in common with her father.

"Nicole, I just don't want to see you get hurt again. I remember how you felt when he walked out on you last time. Who's to say he won't abandon you like that again?"

His question cut her to the quick, because he'd hit on the very fear she'd been skirting around for days. *Don't fall for him again. Don't let yourself form those old attachments to him,* she'd warned herself. Not only had he made no promises for the future, he sometimes acted like he couldn't wait to be rid of her. So why was he here with her at all? She'd give anything to be able to read that enigmatic mind of Daniel's, see past his shuttered expression. Years ago, he'd worn his heart on his sleeve. He'd been open about his passion for her, his hope for the future, his zest for life.

His black ops work, she realized with a sinking heart. They'd trained him to hide his thoughts, show no emotion.

"Nicole?"

When her father spoke, she yanked herself from the silence into which she'd lapsed. "I don't know what will come of my relationship with Daniel, Daddy. But for my sake, if you two could put your differences to rest and at least be civil..." She sighed, wondering if such a truce was even possible.

"So...you are looking for a future with him? You have feelings for him? Real feelings? Because any adoration you have for his heroics in rescuing you is not enough to build a relationship on."

Nicole pinched the bridge of her nose. "I'm aware of that."

She heard her father blow out a breath. "All right. I'll do my best to accept him. For your sake."

She opened her mouth to tell him his concession might be premature, that there was nothing between her and Daniel to accept. But the murmur of voices called her attention to the bank of the bayou where Daniel and Pilar were making their way back up to the house.

Just the sight of Daniel, his skin a deeper bronze after only an hour in the sun, made her pulse stutter and her breath snag in her lungs. The bright daylight accentuated his ebony eyes and the masculine cut of his cheeks and square jaw. He flashed Pilar a white smile as they crossed the yard, and a bayou breeze ruffled his black hair. Her fingers twitched around the cell phone, remembering the silky feeling of his hair threading through her fingers as they'd made love. His dark Cajun features easily topped her list of reasons to love his heritage.

"I just want what's best for you," her father said, interrupting her ogling and sensual memories of Daniel.

Nicole cleared her throat. "Thank you, Dad. I've got to go now." She started to disconnect then added, "I love you."

"Same here, sweetheart. Be careful. And call again soon so I know you're okay."

"I'll try." She tapped the disconnect button and set Daniel's phone aside just as he and Pilar reached the foot of the porch steps.

He sent her a dubious look. "Who was that?"

She shook her head, dismissing the call as trivial, and focused her attention on the fish dangling from the line Pilar held. "You caught some!"

The girl's face lit with excitement, and she held up their catch—two good-size catfish and one very small fish Nicole couldn't identify. Keeping her tone cheerful and bright, she asked Daniel, "Isn't that third one too small to keep?"

He smiled back, keeping up the pretense. "Yeah. But there was no way I was going to make her throw back the first fish she'd ever reeled in. That'd just be mean."

"Cena!" Pilar said, beaming. *Dinner.*

Nicole braced a hand on her hip. "I hope you don't think I'm cleaning those!"

"Squeamish, are we?" Daniel asked, using the porch railing and one crutch to help him hop up the steps on his good leg.

"Just sayin'."

When he reached the porch, he stepped toward her, so that she had to angle her chin up to meet his eyes. So that he was near enough for her to feel his body heat, near enough to smell traces of the soap he'd used in the shower that morning. His proximity caused a quiver deep in her core. The intensity of his gaze as he hovered over her shot longing through her like liquid fire.

For the first time in days, she saw a vibrance and...*life* in his expression that had been missing since he'd woken up in the hospital. Here at his grandmother's home by the bayou, he was in his element. More than that, teaching Pilar to fish, seeing the girl's joy, clearly fed his soul. Though he'd never admit it to her, she could imagine how his injury and the loss of his job with the black ops team had bruised his ego and his sense of purpose. For an alpha male control freak like Daniel, those blows had to have been crushing.

Still holding her gaze, his wide chest so close that he brushed against her when she took a deep breath for composure, he asked, "You know how to make hush puppies and slaw?"

Sarah Beth made the best hush puppies Nicole had ever put in her mouth. Maybe she could call her father's housekeeper for help. "I can try."

Daniel arched a skeptical eyebrow, then shrugged. "Then I'll take care of the fish. Cleaning. Seasoning. Frying. Deal?"

She twitched a grin. "You're on."

With a satisfied nod, he moved away, and Nicole felt the loss to her marrow. Like losing her bedcovers on a winter night, she felt a cool emptiness course through her.

"You okay with her helping me clean the fish?" he asked, taking the string of fish from Pilar.

Nicole frowned. "I'll leave it up to her if she wants to watch, but I don't like the idea of her using a knife."

Daniel glanced toward the bayou before facing Nicole

again. "I was her age when *mon père* learned me how to cut up *la barbue.*"

Nicole folded her arms over her chest and gave Daniel a measuring scrutiny. Had his thick Cajun accent, mixed Louisiana French and English, and blatant use of a common, though grammatically incorrect, Southernism been for her benefit? With a prickle of uneasiness, she recalled his earlier accusation that she held a negative bias against Cajuns. On the contrary, she admired the resilience, traditions and sense of community in the Cajun population. She envied Daniel the unconditional love and support he'd had from his family, while she'd struggled to win her father's approval or five undistracted minutes of his time.

She raised her chin and kept her tone neutral. "I'm sure your father taught you well, but you asked if I was okay with Pilar cleaning fish. And I'm not. You do the cutting, okay?"

Pilar watched them with wide, inquisitive eyes, and Daniel gave her an oh-well glance and a shrug, before starting toward the side yard. "How do you say 'worrywart' in Spanish?"

Dividing a look between Daniel and Nicole, Pilar bit her lip, clearly undecided about who to stay with, then scurried after Daniel like a puppy. Nicole couldn't blame her. Given the chance, she'd spend every minute she could with Daniel, too. Especially the kind, smiling version of himself that he showed Pilar.

Nicole turned to go inside, wondering how long they'd be in hiding here with Daniel. And more important, what would happen once Daniel felt they were safe? Would he disappear from her life again without a word? Would he give their relationship a second chance?

Back in the kitchen, she began searching the groceries Jake had brought in, pulling out the ingredients to make hush puppies, but her mind dwelled on the one question that seemed at the root of everything with Daniel. What had happened five years ago that changed his feelings for her and made him leave without a goodbye?

For her sanity's sake, she had to find out, had to get the truth. Tonight.

Chapter 9

Nicole quietly closed the door to the room she shared with Pilar and tiptoed back to the living room. "Well, I don't think we'll be hearing anything from her until morning. She was asleep before her head hit the pillow."

Daniel paced across the room, using only one crutch for support, then turned and walked back the direction he came. "Wore herself out running around the yard today."

Nicole watched him retrace his steps with a knit in her brow. "I'll say. After being cooped up in that cage in Colombia, I can't blame her for wanting to run herself ragged." She stopped behind the couch and propped her hip on the back of the sofa. "Speaking of which, what are you doing? Shouldn't you be resting your knee?"

"Not if I want to walk without a crutch again. Physical therapist in the hospital told me to use my knee, not let it get stiff. Put more weight on it every day."

Nicole sent him a worried frown. "Does it hurt?"

"Not as much as it used to."

She watched him stalk back and forth, clearly making progress in his recovery, but a far cry from the agile special ops agent who'd stolen through the jungle to rescue her. Did he hold his injury against her? Was that why he seemed so angry with her most of the time?

She wiped a sweaty palm on the seat of her blue jeans and looked for an opening to hash out his grievances. Knowing he wouldn't appreciate her dancing around the issue, she squared her shoulders and dove in head first. "Tell me what happened that morning at the hotel. Why did you leave? What did I do?"

Daniel stopped midstride and whipped his head toward her.

"And don't say I already know," she said, aiming a finger at him. "Because I don't. I've never understood why you left, why you never called or answered my messages."

He sighed heavily and scowled. Cursed under his breath. "Do we have to talk about this?"

She tamped down her rising frustration. "Yes, we do. Because I deserve answers." She tapped her chest with her finger, fighting the hurt that swelled in her chest, still as sharp and ruthless as that morning years ago. "I deserve to know why you broke my heart, why you abandoned me. Why you stayed away for so long."

Daniel closed his eyes and gritted his teeth, making the muscle in his square jaw jump. With a harsh exhale, he met her gaze evenly. "I heard everything you told your father."

The mention of her father hiked her frustration level up a notch. She didn't want to beat that drum again.

"Daniel, I—" But she hesitated, catching her protest before it escaped her lips.

His expression didn't have that shuttered quality it had had in the past when she broached this topic. The wall that said he was shutting her out. She thought back to that morning, replaying the details.

She'd awakened in Daniel's arms, exchanged sleepy good-morning smiles and a languorous kiss…and rolled out of bed to answer her cell phone. Her father had been looking for her, wondering why she was late for a political brunch.

Nicole's gut clenched as she struggled to recall exactly what had been said in that conversation. She'd still been angry with her father for his blind disregard for her feelings, his manipulation and dictatorial attitude toward her life. Because of the deeply personal issues between her and her father and so that Daniel could sleep if he wanted, she'd taken the phone in the bathroom and prepared to shower. And not seen Daniel again until he appeared from the dark of night in the Colombian prison camp.

She spread her hands and shook her head, at a loss. "I remember taking his call, but…I can't remember what I said that—"

He scoffed. "Of course you don't. Because it meant nothing to you. It was no big deal."

She bristled at his bitter tone. "I argued with my father. I remember that. And that argument was not nothing to me. It changed everything. You changed everything for me."

He snorted his disbelief.

She drew a steadying breath, not wanting to let the discussion evolve into another fruitless shouting match. "I'm sorry, but I just don't recall any specific thing I said that you would interpret as offensive."

His obsidian eyes drilled into hers. "You flaunted the fact that you'd slept with 'that guy from the bayou.' You told him you knew his feelings about me and that was the point." Anger and hurt washed over his face, disproportionate to the comments he quoted.

"But what—?"

"There was more. But that's the gist." His entire body was tense, vibrating with pent-up emotions.

"And that upset you?" She shook her head, confused. "I don't get it."

He bit out another sour curse. "It was the way you said it, Nicole. I heard the meaning behind what you said." A husky rasp thickened his tone, and he jerked his gaze away, visibly steeling himself, grappling for control over his pain and fury.

Nicole held her breath, waiting as he shifted his weight uneasily.

When he raised his gaze to hers again, shadows flickered over his face and a storm brewed in his eyes. "You *used* me, Nicole. You used me, because I represented the worst-case scenario to your father. It wasn't bad enough that you had a night of indiscretion, but I was bayou scum."

Nicole gasped, stunned silent by his accusation. The depth of his pain and anger toward her stole her breath, gnawed her soul. How could he have believed such things about her after the intimacy they'd shared the night before?

Color rose in Daniel's cheeks as he growled, "You couldn't wait to rub your walk on the wild side in Daddy's face. You practically chortled with glee as you told him how we'd done the nasty, repeating for him that I was a *Cajun,* so that he wouldn't miss just how low you'd sunk in your scandalous rebellion. You didn't give him a name, because who I was didn't matter. Only *what* I was."

"That's not true," she whispered, her voice choked with dismay.

He curled his lip in a snarl. "I was the butt of the joke you pulled on Senator Daddy."

She shook her head, reeling, stung by his accusations. "No. You're wrong."

"Am I? You didn't sleep with me to prove a point to your father?"

Her stomach lurched. She had been making a statement to

her father. Just not the one Daniel believed. "You misunderstood. I didn't think of you that way. I'm not a bigot."

His glare was skeptical.

She sighed. "Yes, I was mad at my father, and I flaunted our night together to make a statement, but I cared about you. I wanted to see you again, if—"

"The facts say otherwise." His tone was cold. The bitter anger that rolled off him left her trembling and sick inside.

"What facts? You didn't give me a chance to explain! You left the hotel without telling me where you were going, where I could reach you, how I could—"

"You knew where I was. And you made sure I didn't stay there long enough to cause trouble. You and Daddy certainly arranged for me to be transferred out of state fast enough."

Nicole blinked her confusion. "I don't know what you're talking about."

He scoffed and sent her an impatient frown. "You sure about that? Why else would I get singled out for an exclusive black ops program less than twenty-four hours after sleeping with you? Your father's fingerprints were all over that transfer."

Nicole recalled her father's earlier comment about Daniel leaving town after the night they'd spent together. A prickle raced down her back. "Maybe my father's, but not mine. I was heartbroken that you'd left." Her voice cracked, and she paused to clear her throat, swallow the knot of frustration and disappointment choking her. "I called the Naval base looking for you and kept running into dead ends. I left messages…."

Daniel's gaze narrowed. "You didn't know about the transfer?"

She battled the tears that burned her sinuses. "I swear I didn't. Not until now."

He turned, shaking his head in denial and lifting a disgusted look to the ceiling.

"I never knew where you went," she persisted, "or what happened to you until you rescued me from Colombia." As soon as the words left her mouth, a whole new flood of questions washed through her alreadyspinning thoughts. Her knees buckled, and she braced an arm on the back of the couch to keep from crumpling to the floor. "All this time... you've hated me."

Daniel jerked his chin down and swung a stunned gaze toward her.

Her mouth dried. "You've believed such terrible things...." Her thoughts shifted again, scrambling to keep up as she saw the past five years from a fresh, startling perspective. "But...if you hate me so much, why..." A tremble started in her core, spreading until her entire body shook. "Why did you risk your life to save me? Wh—why are you here now? What's your game?"

An unfathomable expression of shock darkened his face. The tension coiled in him was a palpable vibration that charged the air. "You think I *hate* you? Are you insane?"

"You said—"

Daniel threw his crutch aside with a clatter and closed the distance between them in two stiff strides. Trapping her between the back of the couch and his large body, he captured her head between his hands, his fingers digging into her scalp. Nicole's heart lurched at the flash of heat that blazed in his eyes as his mouth crashed down on hers so hard and fast their teeth clicked and she bit her tongue.

She, in turn, curled her fingers in his hair and returned his frantic kiss with her own desperate need. A thrum of desire surged through her veins, hot and fast. A rumble of satisfaction rose from her throat, and Daniel slid a hand to the base of her back to pull her closer. She tasted blood from her cut tongue but didn't care. She'd waited too long for this, dreamed of having Daniel back in her arms. The kiss was rough, untamed, but his mouth felt right against hers. Preordained.

When Daniel finally tore his mouth from hers, his breathing was ragged, as if he'd just run a long distance. He still held her nape with a firm grip, and his eyes blazed with a dark, dangerous fire.

"I got you out of Colombia," he said in a low growl, "because the thought of you being in the hands of those rebel bastards made me crazy. Knowing they could be starving you, hurting you, *touching* you haunted me. Made me sick."

Nicole raised her hands to stroke his taut jaw. "Oh, Daniel…"

"I have tried every day for the last sixty-three months to get you out of my head. Wanting you is a physical ache I live with every minute of every hour."

Nicole's heart tripped, and her eyes filled with tears. As romantic as Daniel's words were, his expression and his tone reflected misery and frustration rather than rapturous love. The incongruity twisted in her chest.

"I can't erase the memory of how you felt beneath me, how sweet your hair smelled, how warm your kiss tasted, how erotic your moans were when I pushed inside you."

She caught her breath, recalling that earth-shaking moment. Feeling the proof of his current arousal pressed against her belly, her body pulsed with the same anticipation and heat as the night they'd made love.

He sucked in a shallow breath, his eyes fierce. "I wish to God I could hate you, Nicole. Maybe then I could break this hold you have on me. Maybe then I could stop wanting you and missing you so much I hurt." His voice dipped to a whisper. "Maybe then I could move past the betrayal I felt that morning, hearing you tell your father I'd only been the lowly means to your rebellious end."

When he tried to step back, she grabbed his shirt in her

fists and met his gaze with a determined stare of her own. "I never said that. Whatever you thought you heard, you were wrong. I've never thought of you as anything but heroic and thoughtful and maddeningly sexy."

He frowned and turned his head, but she grabbed his chin and dragged his face, his gaze back to hers.

"Listen to me, Daniel. You stole my heart that night in New Orleans." Her voice cracked, but she forged on. "And you broke it the next morning when you left me."

His mouth tightened, and his brow furrowed, as if hearing this truth pained him. She plowed her hands into his hair, pulling him closer. "I felt betrayed that morning, too. But it didn't change my feelings for you. You're not the only one who couldn't forget. Except I'm *glad* you were in my head all those months."

He squeezed his eyes closed, clearly trying to shut her out. Giving him a firm shake, she waited until his gaze met hers again before she continued. Tears dripped onto her cheeks and strangled her voice, but she needed him to hear her out. "My memories of you kept me sane while I was caged like an animal in that godforsaken prison camp. I clung to the hope that I'd survive and see you again. Hold you again. Make love to you again."

He stiffened, his expression tormented. He seized hold of her, framing her face with his hands. "Damn it, Nicole…."

Her gaze drilled his. She was determined to make him understand how she truly felt. "I wasn't entirely surprised to see you when you rescued me, because deep inside, I knew you'd come. I'd prayed you'd come for me. And I—"

"Stop!" he rasped, his eyes suspiciously bright. Beneath her hand, his heart thundered, hard and fast.

Drawing a ragged breath, she licked her tears from the corner of her mouth. Daniel's eyes tracked the path of her tongue, and with a groan, he captured her lips again. His kiss was gentler this time, but no less needy, no less toe-curlingly seductive.

Nicole wrapped her arms around his neck, and he angled his head to deepen the kiss. When he drew harder on her mouth, she responded with equal fervor. When he backed off and soothed her lips with tender kisses, she sighed at the sweetness of his caress. When he searched with his tongue, she met him, stroke for stroke. Tangling, teasing, savoring…

Nicole tugged his T-shirt out of her way, eager to feel the heat of his skin, feel taut muscle and sinew. Soon he'd slipped a hand under her shirt, and his fingers closed over her breast. His palm abraded her beaded nipple through the thin satin of her bra, and the rush of sensation that washed through her stirred a moan from her throat. Without thinking, she hooked one leg around his hip, straining to feel him closer, hating the clothing barrier between them.

"Mon Dieu!" he rasped, and remembering his hurt knee, she panicked briefly that she'd hurt him somehow. But those thoughts fled as he cupped her bottom, lifted her and tumbled with her over the back of the sofa and onto the cushions.

He stretched across her, his weight pressing her into the soft couch, their bodies aligned so that there was no mistaking his desire for her. She wrapped her legs around his, canting her hips forward to rub against his steely length. His breath hissed through his teeth, and with shaking hands, he shoved her shirt and bra up and off of her. With hot, obsidian eyes, he drank in the sight of her, then laved the peak of each breast with his tongue, molded them with his fingers.

Nicole gasped and writhed beneath him, burning and trembling as her need built. She helped him push her jeans down her legs, kicking them to the floor. When he insinuated a hand between her legs, the intimate stroke of his hand shot liquid fire to her core.

"Daniel!" She teetered on the brink of climax, felt herself

careening toward that sweet oblivion, free falling. "Not…yet. I want you…inside me."

He pressed a warm kiss to her lips, then nuzzled her ear. "It's all right. There'll be more. Let go, *cher.*"

The whispered endearment was her undoing. The rich rumble of his voice rolled through her, and the tenderness in his tone melted her bones and pierced her heart. He sank two fingers inside her, and she shattered with a soft cry. She clung to him as she floated back to earth, wanting to weep with joy and love. After so long, she was finally back in Daniel's arms.

His day's growth of beard scraped lightly as he trailed nibbling kisses along the curve of her throat. "We should move," he murmured against her skin. "We're too exposed here."

She tipped her head to meet his gaze. "You think Pilar—?"

"Anyone." He jerked his head toward the front window and door to the porch. "I want to see my target before he sees me."

The reminder that dangerous men were looking for them sent a shiver down Nicole's spine.

"Don't worry, *cher.*" He dragged a crooked finger along her jaw. "I always get my man."

A cocky smile tugged the corner of his mouth, and Nicole grinned. "I can imagine."

Daniel sat up, pulling Nicole with him, and his gaze grew smoky once more. "I've waited a long time for this."

She brushed a kiss on his cheek. "Too long."

With amazing agility and strength, he swept her into his arms and rose from the couch, despite his injury. Nicole struggled, wanting down. "Daniel, no! Your knee!"

"Is fine." His level gaze echoed his assertion. "Let me do this."

She opened her mouth to argue, but having seen the pain and frustration in his eyes when he dealt with his injury over the past several days, she knew she couldn't deny him this chance to reclaim his sense of his manhood. She laid her head on his shoulder and looped her arms around his neck, and as he carried her back to the master bedroom, her heart swelled with affection for her stubborn hero. She caught his occasional grimace but knew he'd rather die than let the ache in his knee interfere with his gallant gesture. Once they were in the room where he'd slept the past nights, he kicked the door closed and followed her down on the mattress.

She fumbled with the button at his fly, murmuring, "You, sir, are overdressed."

"Roger that." He caught her mouth for a quick kiss before rolling on his back to toe off his shoes. Once he'd worked his jeans past his knee brace, she skimmed her hands down his chest to his briefs, pushing them down his legs to join the jeans on the floor.

"That's better." She flashed him a sultry smile, then swung her leg over him to straddle him. He moaned his satisfaction when she settled on top of him, and the teasing light fled his face. His dark eyes held hers, the intensity and hunger in his expression sending ripples of anticipation through her blood.

Once he'd stripped off his shirt, Daniel picked up where they'd left off on the couch. His hands covered her breasts, tweaking and arousing. His kisses ravaged her mouth and explored her bare skin. He moved unerringly from one erogenous zone to another, as if…

"You remember what I like," she said on a breathy sigh as he kneaded and nibbled a sensitive spot at her nape.

He pulled back to meet her gaze, his hands still stroking her. "I memorized everything about you. I remember it all. Every." He kissed her. "Last." Kiss. "Inch."

Her hand smoothed over his chest, and she sighed. "I thought I'd memorized you, but—" She traced a jagged scar on his shoulder. "You've changed." Her fingers drifted to another scar, pale against his tanned skin, and a dull ache jabbed her heart. "I don't think I want to know how you got all these." She let her finger trail to another pucker in his skin. Clearly a healed bullet wound. She shuddered. "You lead such a dangerous life. I hate the idea of you facing death as a regular part of your—"

"Led." His fingers closed around hers, and he pressed his lips to her palm. "Past tense. I've been benched from field-work, remember?"

She laced her fingers with his and resumed her position on top of him. "I know you're disappointed, but…I can't say that I'm sorry. I want you safe."

He tucked her hair behind her ear, his expression serious. "As I want you."

Nicole bent down to kiss him, lingering over his lips, sa-voring the heat and passion. Then, wrapping her fingers around his arousal, she covered him, first with the condom he had waiting and then with her body, taking him deep in-side her. Lacing her fingers with his, she moved with him, the pumping sway of their bodies causing a sweet tension to coil at her core. Closing her eyes, she recalled their first night together and the promise their future held. The magic in their lovemaking. *Say my name.*

Daniel moaned as she rode him, and in her mind, she was back on the rumbling helicopter in Colombia, holding his hand as his eyes, wild with pain, searched hers. *Say my name.*

Her chest contracted remembering the heartache in his eyes when she woke in his hospital room. *Say my name.*

She opened her eyes and met the ebony gaze that had been full of fear when he'd burst into her father's bullet-riddled of-fice to save her from the hired gunmen. *Say my name.*

"Daniel," she whispered in his ear, "I'm here, Daniel. I'm yours."

His grip on her hand tightened. "Nicole…*cher,* I…"

Whatever he'd planned to say was lost as he inhaled a sharp breath and shuddered with his climax. She followed him into the fray, her body inundated with blissful sensation. "Oh, Daniel…"

When she was spent, she collapsed against him, her heart hammering, her lungs panting for air. Silently he held her, his fingers strumming her spine, threading through her hair.

After a moment to catch her breath, Nicole tipped her head back to see his face, and she scraped a fingernail along his stubbled chin. "That was…pretty great, huh?"

He tonelessly hummed his agreement, flashed her a lop-sided smile. "No argument here." Silently, he stared at the ceiling for a while before adding, "Damn shame, though."

Nicole propped on an elbow to get a better view of his expression. "What is?"

"The blistering heat between us."

She drew her eyebrows together. His now-serious expression nipped her neck with apprehension. "How is good sexual chemistry a bad thing?"

He spared her a glance before studying the ceiling again. "It muddies the water. Complicates the real issues."

Nicole's felt her stomach swoop in dread. "Meaning?"

"My job, my reason for being here, is to keep you and Pilar alive. Anything else is a distraction."

"Including how we feel about each other," she concluded with a sinking heart.

"Yeah."

And there it was, the protective wall slamming into place around his heart, keeping her distant. She shoved down her hurt, determined not to let her disillusionment show. "So this was just sex. Nothing more?"

"Has to be. I can't afford anything else. Not until this mess is over, anyway."

She released a breath slowly, careful not to let him hear the tremor that seized her. "And after this is over?"

He was silent for so long she wasn't sure he planned to

answer. But, finally, his low voice rumbled through the dark room like distant thunder. "I don't know."

Squeezing her eyes closed, she battled down the sting of disappointment as she curled against his body and rested her head on his chest. Her body was sated, but her heart craved more. She wanted what she feared she might never have from Daniel…his love.

Chapter 10

The next morning, Daniel's side of the bed was empty when Nicole woke. A chill filled her, burrowing to the bone, when she thought of the empty hotel room she'd found after her shower the last time they'd made love. Within minutes of making love last night, Daniel had been withdrawing again, erecting the barriers that kept his heart off-limits to her.

She curled her fingers into the sheets on his side of the bed. The covers were cool. He'd been gone for a while. A knot twisted in her chest, and her pulse kicked. Had he left the house, abandoned her and Pilar?

She drew a slow, calming breath. He wouldn't leave them here. Not with kidnappers after Pilar, men willing to kill anyone who got in their way. Daniel was first and always a protector, a defender. No wonder he was so good at guarding his heart.

Sliding out of bed, she padded over to Daniel's duffel bag and found a T-shirt to wear until she could get her own clothes from the room where Pilar was sleeping. His shirt hung almost to her knees and held a trace of his scent, a sexy combination of man and fresh air and soap. Just that hint of Daniel turned her insides to mush and stirred a flutter in her veins. Surviving his disappearance from her life had been hard enough last time. She wasn't sure she had the strength to handle losing him again. But how did she get past his defenses? Why did he still feel he had to hold her at arm's length?

Maybe she'd be better off guarding her own heart, giving up her delusions of a future with Daniel. She wanted roots, children, cats, a house with a garden and a husband who was there for her every night, physically and emotionally. But Daniel craved danger, adventure. Except for his partner and friend, Alec, he'd been a loner most of his professional life. Could she really expect Daniel to settle down and be content with home and hearth?

The tinkle of a child's laugh drifted to her from down the hall, and she headed to the kitchen to check on Pilar. As soon as she opened the bedroom door, the smell of bacon and fresh coffee greeted her, and Nicole's stomach rumbled. In the kitchen, Pilar sat at the table, a plate of toast and eggs in front of her and a grin on her face. Daniel stood over a pan of sizzling bacon, a pair of tongs in his hand and a chef's apron that read *Laissez les Bon Temps Rouller!* draped over his bare chest—presumably to protect him from popping grease.

Nicole was busy ogling Daniel's wide shoulders and gauging his mood in the wake of their night together, when a chipper voice said, "Good morning, Señorita Nicole!"

Jerking a stunned glance to Pilar, Nicole blinked...grinned. "Good morning, Pilar." Turning back to Daniel, she widened her eyes in query.

He lifted a muscled shoulder, his mouth twitching with amusement. "Don't look at me. I didn't teach it to her. I was as surprised as you when she greeted me that way."

"I taught it to her while we were in Colombia. That and a few other words and phrases. I just never knew if she was retaining any of it since she wouldn't speak."

Daniel turned back to the bacon, flipping the slices in the pan. "Apparently she did."

"Apparently. I'm just…relieved that she feels safe enough now that she's talking again."

He shot a glance over his shoulder at the little girl, then raked an encompassing look at Nicole. She felt his slow, heated perusal like a physical caress.

He arched a black eyebrow, but his expression remained neutral. "That shirt's never looked better."

She flashed him a crooked smile, hoping to elicit one from him. "Hope you don't mind my borrowing it. My clothes got left in the living room last night."

"Pas du tout."

She deflated a bit. Though he seemed in a pleasant mood, an improvement from his grim scowling earlier in the week, he also seemed reserved, except where Pilar was concerned. She watched with a prick of envy as he offered the little girl one of his smiles. "Is it good? *Está bueno?*"

Pilar bobbed her head. *"Sí."* The little girl paused and grinned. "Yes! Good."

Daniel winked at the little girl then shifted his gaze to Nicole. He hitched his head to the coffeepot. "There's coffee."

"Thanks. Smells wonderful." She padded over to pour herself a cup, watching Daniel from the corner of her eye. As she sipped from the ceramic mug, Boudreaux rubbed against her legs, greeting her with a meow. "Hey, Boo. How are you, old man?"

She squatted to pat him and scratch his cheek, which earned her a purr of appreciation. Oreo sat in the chair next to Pilar, eyeing the eggs on her plate and sniffing the air. Casting a quick, guilty look to Daniel, whose back was turned, Pilar plucked a bite of egg from her plate and fed it to Oreo. When she discovered Nicole watching her, the little girl's eyes widened.

Nicole sent her a wink and a grin, then gave Boudreaux a final pat before rising to her feet again.

"Thought I'd take Pilar out in the pirogue today. My family still has a shack in the bayou where my grandmother grew up." Daniel shot her a hooded glance that seemed to be daring her to judge him for his family's simple, live-off-the-land history. "The fishing there is the best in the swamp."

Nicole smiled pleasantly. "I'm sure she'd love it."

He stepped closer to her, holding her gaze. "Want to come with us? I promise not to let the alligators get you."

Daniel stood near enough that she could smell the soap from his shower. Mingled with the mellow aroma of fresh coffee and frying bacon, the scents were a feast for her senses. She laid a hand on his chest, and his heart thumped strong and steady beneath her palm. "I'd love that."

"After breakfast, then." He slid a hand into her hair and nudged her forward for a quick kiss.

Relief flowed through her at this indication that he didn't regret their lovemaking, even if he viewed their liaison as merely an outlet for their sexual chemistry.

A giggle reached them from the table, and they turned as one to find Pilar grinning at them. Daniel cocked an eyebrow. "Should I not have done that in front of her?"

"Didn't your parents kiss in front of you?"

"All the time. But we're not her parents."

Nicole squeezed his shoulder and brushed another kiss across his lips. "Is that bacon ready yet? I'm starved."

"Help yourself." The heat in his eyes as he massaged the nape of her neck with his fingers said he was also hungry… for her. A tingle raced through her from his touch, and just the intensity of his dark gaze made her bones feel as if they were melting.

As he pulled away, he whispered, "Beautiful," so quietly she almost missed it.

While Daniel tended to the bacon, Nicole collapsed in a chair at the table, her legs trembling with the rush of adrenaline and passion Daniel had stirred in her.

Pilar practiced her English throughout breakfast, correctly naming each food they were eating and repeating the list of birds and animals she'd seen the day before while fishing. The scene felt so natural, so blissfully domestic, that Nicole couldn't help but imagine what it might be like to sit around a table with Daniel and two or three children who had their father's dark Cajun good looks.

I can't afford anything else. When Daniel's words replayed in her head, Nicole forced the fantasy of family dinners with him, along with the stab of heartache, to a back corner of her mind. She and Daniel still had a lot of work to do before that dream stood even a remote chance.

With the long, sturdy pole that he dug out of his grandmother's storage garage, Daniel guided his old pirogue through the muddy bayou water, the way to his family's old shack as familiar to him as his own reflection. Nicole and Pilar sat together at the opposite end of the long flat-bottomed boat, pointing out wildlife to each other. A family of turtles on a log, an egret wading in the shallows among the ancient cypress trees, a nutria lumbering along the shore. Smiling to himself, he kept quiet whenever they passed a snake coiled on a branch above them or when he spotted a pair of alligator eyes watching them from the murky depths. He monitored those potential threats, ready to take action if needed but not willing to frighten the females unnecessarily.

As the skiff glided through the water, Daniel's attention drifted to Nicole over and again. Images and sounds from last night flashed in his memory, making his entire body hum and his nerves jangle. Sleeping with Nicole hadn't tamped the fire inside him. The first touch of his lips to hers had been gasoline on the smoldering embers. He hadn't imagined he could burn any hotter for her, but he was discovering new things about himself every day since returning from Colombia with her.

For instance, he found himself enjoying quiet time with Pilar and caught himself wondering what it might be like to take his own daughter fishing or teach his son to bait a crawfish trap. Before this week, he'd never considered himself a father figure. After all, what father spends ninety-nine percent of his time infiltrating dangerous cartels and street gangs in the world's seamiest neighborhoods, then goes mucking through muddy jungles or lurking in remote caves for days waiting for his human prey to make a wrong move?

Except those days were over for him, thanks to his bum knee. So where did that leave him? How did a guy who'd spent so much time in the field make the transition to a life of bedtime stories and lazy afternoons with a fishing pole?

And where did Nicole fit in the picture? He gritted his teeth as a sharp pang of longing gouged his heart. Since that fateful morning five years ago, he hadn't allowed himself to envision a future with her. The parts of that dream his pride hadn't squelched, his life on the black ops team had made impossible.

But last night, having her in his arms, burying himself deep in her welcoming warmth, had revived a glimmer of his youthful optimism. That seed of hope burrowed deep inside him, taunting him and raking his heart with painful illusions of what could never be. His life and Nicole's were still as different and incompatible as ever. They both had a mountain of issues to deal with, careers that took them all over the planet, and ambitions for the future that had no room for family. And she had loyalties to her father that Daniel would never ask her to deny. Because family mattered. *Mémère* had taught him that, and he believed it, even when it meant accepting that Senator White was a permanent fixture in Nicole's life.

Last night had been soul-shaking, and he refused to regret any part of it. But he couldn't let Nicole believe it was more than what it was—hot, even-better-than-he-remembered, burned-into-his-DNA sex.

He watched Nicole tuck her hair behind her ear and laugh at something Pilar said in broken English, and a fist squeezed his lungs. He'd survived without her before, and somehow he'd find a way to move on this time, as well. Once Pilar was back with her father, he'd launch a new career and put Nicole behind him, just like he had five years ago.

When the old shack came into view, a bittersweet nostalgia settled over him. As a boy he'd loved coming out here with his father to fish, and when he'd grown older, he'd taken on the job of caring for the tiny house on stilts for his grandmother, who'd loved to tell him happy stories about her childhood in the swamp.

As they approached, he tried to see the weather-beaten shack through Nicole's eyes. The warped and rotting wood, the rusty tin roof, the moss-covered walls and dingy windows. Yet the shack wasn't a total disaster, since he'd made some repairs and cleaned the inside a few months back, before directing Alec here to use the house as a hideout from the men tailing him.

The pirogue bumped the rickety dock, and Daniel lashed a rope from the boat to a post.

"Can we go inside? I'd love to see where your grandmother grew up," Nicole said as she climbed out onto the floating wooden platform at the base of the stilts.

"Sure. Let's unload the boat, then I'll give you the fifty-cent tour." Daniel handed her the cooler with the lunch they'd packed and gave Pilar the set of cane poles and tackle box.

"Want help?" Nicole asked, offering her hand to help him negotiate the awkward gap between the dock and the pirogue.

He waved her away with a scowl. "I can do it." When he stood, the boat rocked, and unable to put his full weight on his bad leg, he fumbled for balance.

"Daniel." Nicole shoved her hand at him, her blue gaze steady and determined. "Don't be so stubborn. Give me your hand."

He hesitated, hating to appear weak in any way in front of her, but finally grasped her arm at the elbow while she grasped his arm and pulled him onto the dock beside her.

"Thanks," he grunted, then set to work moving their cane poles to the other end of the platform where they'd be fishing.

As promised, he took Nicole and Pilar for a quick tour of the two-room shack, but getting inside required climbing a ladder made of two-by-fours nailed to one of the stilts. Daniel ascended the rungs by pulling himself up until his good leg had a foothold, then performing another pull-up to repeat the process. He didn't give the tactic a second thought until he saw the gleam of appreciation in Nicole's eyes as she squeezed his biceps and wiggled her eyebrows. "Impressive. I like."

In deference to the little girl watching them, he limited his response to grin and a smoldering gaze. But later...

Nicole turned and took in the decor. "Hey, not bad."

Despite its outer appearance, the shack had several new items of furniture, including a new mattress on the bed. He'd paid extra to the delivery man for his help to bring it out on a boat and carry it up the two-by-four ladder. The living space had a small table, a couple of chairs and a kitchen area where he could cook over a camping stove. The tiny back room was a bathroom with a shower, sans hot water, and a toilet hooked up to an underwater septic tank.

"See? All the comforts of home," he said, pulling a wry grin.

Nicole gave him a dubious grin, and Pilar, standing at a window, stared out at the water. "Fishing?"

Daniel chuckled. "Yes, fishing. Let's go."

For the next hour, they tossed their lines off the small dock, swatting mosquitoes and working with Pilar on her English. Despite their chatter, which Daniel knew was scaring away most of the fish, they managed to hook a couple medium-size crappie. When Nicole's line pulled taut, Daniel wrapped his arms around her to help pull in a struggling catfish. The excitement in her eyes when they dragged the catch onto the dock spun a mellow warmth inside him.

"Aye-ee!" Nicole whooped in her best Cajun accent.

"Aye-ee!" Pilar echoed, and Daniel laughed.

"You're pretty pleased with yourself," he teased.

She flipped her hair behind her. "Of course I am. I've never caught a catfish before. This is a red-letter day!"

He raised his eyebrows. "You grew up in Louisiana and never...?" Daniel shook his head. "Well, this *is* an occasion, isn't it?" He pulled her closer and dropped a kiss on her lips. "Congratulations, *cher.*"

They took a picture with his cell phone, then released the fish at Nicole's request.

"My work here is done." She laid her pole aside and headed toward the two-by-four ladder. "I'll be right back. Bathroom break."

"Check the seat for spiders before you sit down," he called to her, earning himself a frown of dismay. He grinned and cast his line into the water. "I'm just sayin'."

"Check the seat for spiders?" Nicole grumbled as she marched back to the tiny bathroom. "Not funny." Though, if she was honest, she should be glad the shack had such facilities at all. She could be holding it until they got back to Daniel's house.

Nicole squeezed into the small bathroom and forced the rusty slide bolt into place. Turning, she eyed the toilet warily before lifting the lid and leaning forward to search for creepy crawlies. No spiders but...

The reek of sewage wafted up in a redolent wave that caught her off guard. Gagging, she staggered back a step and gasped for a fresh breath.

But the stench filled the tiny room, filled her nose, filled her memory. In an instant, she was back in her pen in Colombia where the stink of the outhouse and prisoners' waste, of fetid mud and decay hung in the air, an inescapable reminder of the squalor she'd lived in.

The thread of panic and terror she'd held forcibly at bay

since coming home jerked tight around her throat like a garrote. Her vision blurred, and she panted for air as a clawing, frantic horror engulfed her.

Sweat popped out on her face. Her heart thundered. The walls shrank around her.

Spinning toward the door, desperate to get out of the tiny room, she scrabbled with the slide bolt. Her legs shook, and her hands trembled. But the lock wouldn't budge.

Chapter 11

Trapped! She was trapped!

Mewls of fright punctuated her choppy gasps. She had to get out! Had to—

Giving up on the bolt, she slammed her hands on the door. Out! She had to get out!

She heard the guards' cruel laughs. Saw the chain-link fencing. Felt the desperate despondency. The fear. No!

Tears dripped onto her cheeks. "No! No, no, no! Let me out! Please God!"

She barely recognized her own voice, strangled by anxiety and panic, unable to pull herself back from the edge. Screaming, terrified, she battered the door with her fists. "Noooo!"

Over her own moans of fear, the thump of uneven footsteps reached her ears. "Nicole? Nicole! What's wrong?"

"Help me!" she sobbed. "Please!"

The door rattled. "Unlock the bolt."

"I—I can't. I—help me!" Her head spun as she panted shallowly for air. "T-trapped…"

"Okay. Stand back."

Numbly, Nicole stumbled a step away from the door, until her back hit the opposite wall. She squeezed her eyes shut, quivering to her marrow. A cage. Leering guards. Mud. Bugs. Heat. Despair. No, no, no! Not again!

A loud thump sounded at the door, then another. The door buckled, shook. Finally, the slide bolt tore away from the wall, and the door crashed open.

She jerked a startled gaze up, gulping the fresh air.

Through the opening, Daniel frowned at her, rubbing his shoulder. "Nicole? *Cher,* what—?"

"I…I smelled…the camp," she muttered between gasps. He knees gave out, and she slid to the floor. "Prison camp… I couldn't…get out. Trapped… Oh, God—" She buried her face in her hands and sobbed, "So…sc-scared."

Warm arms wrapped around her, and a smooth, deep voice crooned, "It's okay, *cher.* You're safe now. You're free."

Nausea rolled through her, and she shoved Daniel aside to retch in the toilet. Only to catch another waft of putrid stench in the process. "Oh, God," she moaned as the horror crashed down on her again.

"Hey, take deep breaths, Nic. You're hyperventilating." Daniel put a hand under each of her arms and pulled her to her feet. "C'mere, *cher.* You're safe. Breathe for me, Nic."

She stepped to the tiny sink to rinse her mouth out, then cast a sodden gaze toward him, too battered by her roiling emotions and dark memories to do anything but crumple against him. "Hold me. Please."

"Ah, *cher.* Always." He scooped her into his arms and carried her into the main room, where he sat on the bed with her in his lap. "Let it out, Nicole. You've held it in too long. You've earned the right to fall apart a little."

Fall apart.

More like disintegrate. She clung to Daniel's broad shoulders and let his presence, his strength wash through her. If she had to come unraveled, she could think of nowhere she'd rather be than in Daniel's arms. Hiding her face in the curve of his throat, she curled her fingers into his shirt and held on tight, shuddered.

"Let it out," he murmured, and caressed her back.

She'd tried so hard to be strong. To keep it together for...

"Pilar," she whispered.

"Is fine." He stroked her hair, kissed her forehead. "I told her to wait outside. I'll check on her in a minute."

Nodding, she closed her eyes, fought to get her ragged breathing under control. "I'm sorry. I just—"

"Don't," he growled, his arms tightening around her. "Don't you dare apologize. You're human. And you've been through hell." He wiped the moisture from her cheeks. "To be honest, I've been waiting for this. I knew it was coming."

She raised a forlorn look to him. "Because I'm weak."

He huffed an exasperated sigh. "No. Because I've seen enough hardened soldiers suffer breakdowns after a trauma to know PTSD can affect anyone. And you have a tender heart. You care. You let things in, including the horrible, evil things men are capable of." He threaded his fingers through her hair and massaged her scalp in a slow, relaxing caress. "It will get to anyone after a while."

"I was fine until...I smelled the septic gasses..." She shivered and nestled closer, savoring the heat of his body. "And then...it was like I was back there...in Colombia...in that pen."

"Smell is one of the most closely linked senses to memory." He slipped a pack of breath mints from his pocket. "This might help get the stink out of your nose."

Nicole accepted a mint gratefully and sucked hard on the

candy. After drawing and exhaling a lungful of musty, though septic-stink free, air, Nicole hummed her agreement. "I've heard that about smell and memory. I know the sm-smell of cut grass…reminds me of my mother."

"Cut grass?"

"Not because she mowed our lawn." She forced a staccato laugh. "But because I used to work in our flower garden with her, pruning roses, weeding daylilies, planting tulip bulbs. You'd think the smell of flowers or soil would make me think of her, but it's grass. Our yard man was almost always out at the same time, mowing, so…" She sucked in another tremulous breath, feeling a fresh rush of tears. "I miss her so much."

Daniel pressed a kiss to her head, squeezing her again in his embrace. "Shrimp boil reminds me of my *grandmére*. For the obvious reasons."

They were quiet for several minutes, except for her soft sniffles as she cried, releasing months of tension and fear and heartache. The silence was comfortable, soothing, and Daniel's gentle ministrations lulled her frantic pulse back to a normal rhythm.

"Nicole?"

She tipped her chin up to meet his gaze and was startled by the pain that flashed in his dark eyes.

"Did they…" He paused, clenching his teeth, as if his question was to vile to speak. "Were you…raped?"

Placing a hand on his cheek, she shook her head. "They knew I was an American, that my father was a senator. I think they left me alone because they feared an American retaliation if any harm came to me. They were in a better position to negotiate with my dad for my release if I was unhurt."

Relief flooded his face, and he sighed. "Thank God."

"I like to think that, in that way, my dad was protecting me, even from thousands of miles away."

Daniel twitched a quick lopsided grin. "Yeah."

Her returned smile faltered as another memory crowded her brain. "But…" A shudder rolled through her.

He cupped her chin and stroked her cheek with his thumb, his expression morphing to reflect her own gravity. "What?"

"There was another woman there for a few weeks. I don't know who she was or where she came from, why they were holding her, but…" Her stomach churned with bitterness. "The guards raped her…almost every day. They made sure I saw." She bit her bottom lip as fresh tears welled in her eyes. "I wanted to help, but I…couldn't. I felt so helpless. Hearing her scream was…a whole new kind of hell."

"Merde," he muttered under his breath, his jaw rigid and anger clouding his eyes.

"When Pilar arrived, I made it my mission to protect her." The maternal determination that had motivated her to guard the little girl surged through her now. "Taking care of her… saved my sanity. Comforting her, shielding her, teaching her, keeping her spirits up gave me something to take my mind off my own plight."

Daniel traced her jawline with the back of his fingers, his attention fully focused on what she was telling him.

"I felt like, in some small way, I had control again. I could protect Pilar, if I did nothing else."

"And soon she'll be going home, thanks to you."

Nicole sighed. "Seeing her leave will be hard. She means a lot to me."

"I can tell." His eyes held a soft glow of compassion and concern that burrowed deep inside her, chasing away the chill her memories of the prison camp evoked.

But here she was safe. Here she was protected. Here she was…loved?

Nicole searched Daniel's expression, and although he'd never professed any feelings for her other than lust, she could've sworn she saw affection and commitment in the way he looked at her. Or was that wishful thinking?

Her heart kicked, and suddenly she needed his kiss more than she needed her next breath. Plowing her fingers into his hair, she dragged his head down and caught his lips with hers. A quiet rumble of satisfaction hummed from Daniel's chest, and he cradled her nape as he angled his mouth for a deeper kiss. Unlike the frantic urgency that had ignited their passion last night, the tenderness of Daniel's lips echoed the comforting gentleness he'd shown her since breaking down the bathroom door to reach her. The warmth of his lips flowed through her like a balm, soothing the last jagged edges of her frayed nerves and filling her with a sense of security and belonging she hadn't experienced since…the night they'd shared in New Orleans five years ago.

After breaking free of her father, she'd buried herself in her nursing career, traveled with the medical mission to Colombia, dedicated herself to guarding Pilar, but only Daniel had given her the deep-seated joy and fulfillment that satisfied her searching heart.

Nicole tangled her fingers in his thick hair, savoring the sweet sensation of holding him, tasting him, feeling the answering tremors that shook him, just as her own body trembled with desire and an overwhelming joy. When he traced her lips with the tip of his tongue, she welcomed him with a soft sigh of pleasure. After a moment, Daniel gentled the kiss again and pulled away to look into her eyes.

"Are you okay? No more flashbacks?" His concern was etched in tiny lines beside his eyes and the softening in his penetrating gaze.

She stroked his cheek and nodded. "Thanks to you." She closed her eyes as he placed a small kiss on her nose, her eyelids, her forehead.

"You're strong, *cher*. Don't forget that. And you are safe now."

When she felt his lips on hers again, she wrapped her arms around his shoulders, wanting to hold him close forever. Wanting that moment to last. Wanting—

A frightened squeal rang through the shack. Tensing with alarm, Nicole and Daniel broke apart, and she scrambled, two steps ahead of him, toward the ladder.

"Daniel!" Pilar screamed. "Daniel!"

"Pilar?" Heart thumping, Nicole scurried down the first few rungs of the two-by-four ladder, only to run into the little girl clambering her way up. "*Mija,* what's wrong? *Qué te pasa?*"

Pilar tugged at Nicole's leg, then pointed toward the water. "*Una serpiente! Una serpiente!*"

Inching down next to the little girl, she looked out at the bayou and saw a snake swimming away, his body wiggling as he glided through the murky water. Nicole shivered.

"He's gone. It's okay, *mija.*" Nicole guided Pilar down the last steps to the dock, allowing Daniel room to descend.

"What did it look like?" he asked. "What shape was its head?"

Nicole shot him a withering glance. "Snake-shaped. All snakes look the same to me." She shuddered and hugged Pilar to her. "Creepy."

With one eyebrow cocked, he divided a considering look between Nicole and Pilar. "I'm assuming our visitor has spoiled your enthusiasm for fishing?"

Nicole nodded. "Kinda."

Heaving a patient sigh, Daniel shuffled toward Pilar's abandoned fishing pole and began to pack up.

Daniel sat at the kitchen table under the pretense of eating a plate of the cookies Nicole and Pilar had baked that afternoon for dessert, but his focus never left the woman snuggled on the couch. She read a book to the drowsy girl in her lap while Boudreaux napped at her feet.

If keeping his mind, his attention off Nicole had been difficult before, now it was impossible. Daniel dragged a hand over his face and exhaled a harsh breath. Over the past few days, she'd systematically chipped away at his defenses until he could no longer deny how important she was to him. How much he wanted her back in his life. How much the thought of losing her again frightened him.

And because nothing had been settled between them, despite their recent cease-fire, losing her was still a real possibility. *Merde!*

The terror that had filled her eyes when he'd busted through the bathroom door at the shack had sucker punched him. Knowing the horrors she'd seen and survived wrenched inside him and fueled the burning anger toward her captors. Realizing how much worse it could have been for her chilled him to the marrow.

Her heartbreaking sobs and tremors had been hard to witness. Wanting to take away her suffering, but being helpless to do more than mutter useless platitudes and provide a shoulder for her tears, left him raw and restless.

Daniel shoved another peanut butter cookie in his mouth and chewed, tasting nothing, his mind preoccupied. Having spent so much of the past five years trying to forget Nicole, Daniel didn't know what to do with the feelings she was awakening in him. His knee-jerk response to her was still to keep his guard up, waiting for the left hook he hadn't seen coming.

But maybe the real knockout punch was her claim that he'd gotten it all wrong five years ago. That she hadn't been using him in her rebellion against her father, that her feelings had been real, that she held no prejudice toward his family history and Cajun heritage. If that were true, if that night had meant as much to her as it had to him, then he'd thrown away a precious gift. He'd walked out on the best thing to ever happen to him. He'd been a damn fool.

"Couillon," he scolded himself under his breath and shoved the plate of cookies away. Folding his arms over his chest, Daniel rocked back in the kitchen chair and listened to Nicole pronouncing words for Pilar to repeat.

"Shirt."

"Shirt," Pilar echoed.

"Shoes."

"Shoes."

"Socks."

The soft brush of fur and a quiet meow roused him from his observation. Glancing down, he found Oreo rubbing on his leg. Lamby lay on the floor near where Oreo paced. Daniel picked up the toy and tossed it across the floor. Oreo scampered after it.

Hearing the skitter of cat feet, Pilar sat forward and grinned at Oreo. "Silly cat!"

When the little girl tried to scurry after Oreo, Nicole caught the back of Pilar's pajamas, bringing her up short. "Nope, it's bedtime."

Bedtime was a word Pilar knew, and she poked out her bottom lip in disappointment.

Nicole cast a disgruntled look at Daniel. "And thanks for getting her riled up again after I spent thirty minutes calming her down for bed."

He spread his hands and gave her a what-did-I-do? look.

She quirked a lopsided grin, taking the edge out of her chastisement.

To redeem himself, Daniel shoved to his feet and clapped his hands together the way his father used to before he'd lay down the law. "C'mon, tadpole. Time to *fais do-do.*"

Pilar continued pouting, and Daniel, using the antique

cane he'd found in his *grandmére's* closet, crossed the room to her. With a fake growl, he wiggled his eyebrows playfully and scooped her under his arm like a football. After a high-pitched squeal that shattered his eardrum, peals of girlish laughter tumbled from Pilar as he toted her back to her bed.

Nicole groaned as she followed them. "She'll never fall asleep now."

Daniel dumped Pilar in the pile of pillows and blankets, and her giggles turned his insides to mush. Nicole wasn't the only one who'd miss Pilar when she went home.

"Now." He arched one eyebrow in a mock scowl and pointed to the bed. *"Fais do-do.* Go to sleep." Then, for good measure, he added the Spanish, *"Duérmete."*

He turned to limp out of the room, and hearing scrambling and rustling sheets behind him, he stopped at the door next to Nicole and faced the bed again. Pilar had crawled out of the bed and knelt beside it, hands folded and head bowed.

He sent a side glance to Nicole, and whispered, "What do you think little girls pray for?"

She smiled at him. "Same thing big girls do. Safety, their family, their dreams. Oh, and to marry Justin Bieber."

He snorted. "Who?"

Nicole rolled her eyes.

After making the sign of the cross, Pilar crawled back into the covers and pulled the sheet up to her chin. Nicole moved to the side of the bed and kissed the girl's head. "Good night, *mija.* Sleep well."

Daniel switched off the light and closed the door behind Nicole. Remembering how they'd passed the evening after Pilar's bedtime last night, he gave Nicole a hungry glance and murmured, "How fast do you think she'll fall asleep?"

She stepped close to him, her hand sliding up his chest and a coy smile tugging her lips. "Not fast enough."

* * *

Thirty minutes later, Nicole had finished straightening the kitchen, and she dropped wearily onto the sofa next to Daniel.

When he opened his arms and patted his chest, she happily accepted the invitation to snuggle against him and rest her head on his shoulder.

"So…I've noticed you've been using a lot of Cajun French and colloquial phrases this week." She tipped her head back to gauge his reaction.

He tensed a bit. "That bother you?"

"Not at all. Except that it might confuse Pilar while she's trying to learn English." She paused. "And…I don't recall you using so much French in the past. "

"I didn't. When I was around anyone except my grandmother, I made a point of not using French and keeping the Cajun accent out of my voice."

"Why?"

He snorted. "You have to ask?"

"Apparently so."

He drew a large breath, as if explaining himself were a burden. "You know the stereotypes about Cajuns in Louisiana. We're uneducated…which in some ways is true. A lot of folks around here, especially the older generations, didn't bother finishing high school, since they made their living off the land, harvesting oysters, crawfish and shrimp. Hunting alligators for their meat and hides. Raising catfish for market." He drilled a hard look on her. "But that doesn't mean we're stupid."

"I know that."

"And yet we're the butt of Boudreaux jokes around the state."

She sighed. "As long as there is ignorance and cruelty in the general population, there will be bigoted jokes. And not just about Cajuns."

"Yeah, well…we're also seen as backward, since some of the older generation have been slow to embrace modern technology."

"Or it could be said that they're trying to preserve traditions passed down for generations. I love the idea that someone values their culture's history enough to do that."

"I—" he started, then snapped his mouth shut, apparently unable to find a counter-argument. "Regardless, most people have preconceived, stereotyped ideas about Cajuns. For instance…when I met my cousin's and your friends on your prom night, your date started calling me Boudreaux as soon as he heard my accent and learned where I was from."

"Grant Holbrook was a jerk. A fact I learned well enough when he abandoned me and went to prom with your cousin when I wouldn't leave the kitten to die in the sewage drain."

Daniel grunted. "Doesn't say much about my cousin, either. Although, in her defense, she saw the error of her ways and has straightened up in recent years."

Nicole smoothed a hand over Daniel's chest. "Last I heard, Grant's still a jerk."

"Yeah, well…he did me a favor. He showed me that I needed to be proactive in the way people perceived me. I had to erase the swamp from my voice and be better than the next guy in everything I undertook. I had to try harder, run faster, be smarter, reach higher and never make excuses. I was determined to prove critics wrong and never let an undeserved stigma keep me from achieving my goals."

Nicole sat up, swinging her feet to the floor, and gave Daniel a narrow-eyed scrutiny. "You know what I think?"

He raised his eyebrows and cocked his head slightly, inviting her to continue.

"I think you're the one who has a problem with your heritage."

Daniel scoffed loudly. "Bull."

"You're certainly sensitive about it. You assumed the worst five years ago when you heard half of a conversation I had with my father. Your prove-the-critics-wrong philosophy reeks of a personal prejudice at the least and an insecurity about your roots at worst."

Daniel's dark eyebrows snapped together. "Wanting to do my best, be the best, doesn't mean I'm prejudiced," he growled. "I love my *grandmére* and everything she taught me about life on the bayou."

"I'm not saying you don't love your family. But—"

"*But* even my parents recognized that they had to move to another part of the state if they wanted to achieve the goals they had for themselves and for me. Cajun people have always isolated themselves. On purpose—with their language, their location, their traditions, their lifestyle…"

"So do dozens of other cultural groups around the country. The Gullah in South Carolina. The Amish in Pennsylvania and Ohio. Hasidic Jews in New York—"

"All right!" He held up a hand to hush her. "Point taken. But that doesn't change the fact that being a member of one of those cultures means living with the stereotypes associated with that culture. I chose to stay a step ahead of the stereotypes. I prefer to eliminate any obstacle before it becomes a problem."

Nicole shook her head and studied him with a heavy heart. "And I find it sad that you saw your heritage as an obstacle rather than a strength."

"I don't—" Daniel's phone chirped, interrupting him, and he checked the screen before answering. "It's Jake."

Nicole's sat forward, anxious to hear what Jake had learned.

"LeCroix."

She watched Daniel's expression closely for clues to what Jake had to say.

"Tell me you found the judge." He jammed his finger in his other ear as if he was having trouble hearing, then glanced up and met her expectant gaze. Answering her unspoken question, he gave a quick nod. "Excellent." When his forehead creased with consternation, Nicole's pulse kicked up. Was something wrong?

"No, no. I can't say that I blame him. Hang on." Daniel met her gaze. "Get Pilar. The judge wants to talk to her. He needs proof that she is with us and isn't in danger."

Of course, the judge would be dubious, need proof of life and his daughter's well-being before he'd cooperate. Nicole nodded and started down the hall. "I'll wake her up."

She walked quietly to the bed where Pilar snoozed peacefully and brushed the hair back from her face. "Pilar, *mija.* Wake up." Nicole had to jostle the girl and say her name a few more times to rouse her from her slumber. When she had the girl's attention, she motioned for her to follow. Taking Pilar's hand, she led the groggy girl into the living room.

Pilar squinted against the light and blinked curiously at Daniel, her expression reflecting apprehension.

Daniel held out the cell phone and smiled his reassurance to Pilar. "Your father wants to talk to you," he said in flawless Spanish.

"Papi?" Pilar's eyes widened, and she snatched the phone from Daniel. *"Papi? Papi!"*

Nicole watched the hopefulness in the child's eyes morph to joy, then Nicole's eyes filled with tears as Pilar's puddled with moisture and the child's small shoulders shook.

She pieced together parts of the conversation as Pilar half laughed, half sobbed to her father. Yes, she was fine, she was safe, she told him. Miss Nicole has taken care of her. She was trying to be brave, she said, her chin trembling, and a tender ache stole Nicole's breath. Pilar missed him, missed her mother and sister. She sobbed harder now, and Nicole recalled what they'd learned about her mother and sister being murdered in front of her.

Her heart breaking, she wrapped Pilar in a hug that she knew could never take away the horrible memories or replace the family she'd lost.

Pilar sniffed loudly and told her father, *"Te quiero."* I love you.

She handed the phone back to Daniel, who stroked her head and flashed her another encouraging grin as he raised the phone to his ear. "Jake?"

Pilar buried her face on Nicole's shoulder. She held Pilar and rubbed the girl's back while she followed Daniel's end of the conversation.

"Good enough? Will he trust you?"

The hard lines in his face relaxed a degree, which Nicole took as a good sign.

"Where are you? Do you have a tail?" Daniel shifted his gaze away, clearly concentrating on what Jake was telling him. "How long will it take you to get him out of the country?" He paced a few steps, then turned and limped back toward her. "I just think we need someplace out of the way, neutral ground to make the transfer. Somewhere we know we aren't being watched."

Nicole tried to get Daniel's attention, using hand signals and mouthing, *Why not here?*

He dismissed her idea with a shake of his head, then told Jake, "Good idea. I'll look into getting a boat."

A boat? Nicole furrowed her brow.

"When will you be there? It'll take us a couple hours to reach international waters."

She blinked. They were boating out into the Gulf of Mexico?

"Right. I'll handle that from my end. Text me the GPS coordinates of the rendezvous point. Yeah. Okay. See you then." He thumbed the disconnect and looked up at Nicole with a sigh.

"We're taking Pilar to meet her father out on the Gulf?"

He jerked a nod. "That's the plan." He paused and twisted his mouth in thought. "I have to rent a boat by tomorrow night. We're meeting Jake and Castillo in roughly thirty-six hours."

"We can use my father's cabin cruiser. He keeps it docked at a private marina on Grand Isle." Still hugging Pilar close, she held her hand out for the cell phone. "I'll call him now and make the arrangements."

Daniel shook his head and tucked the phone in his shirt pocket. "I've told you I don't want him involved in this. We have to keep a low profile."

"He's not—" Nicole stopped herself, feeling her blood pressure rise. Before she hashed this out with Daniel, she needed to put Pilar back to bed.

She nudged the girl back by the shoulders and smiled warmly. "You'll see your father—*Papi*—soon. I promise. *Pronto.*"

Pilar nodded, a bright hope in her eyes, though Nicole couldn't be sure how much Pilar understood. Had her father explained anything in their brief conversation?

She led Pilar back to the bedroom and tucked her into bed. As she waited for the girl's eyes to droop and her breathing to deepen with sleep, Nicole mentally rehearsed her argument in favor of including her father in the loop, allowing him to help. With one call, she could arrange for her father's forty-foot cabin cruiser to be fueled, stocked and ready for them within hours.

After pressing a light kiss to Pilar's forehead, Nicole walked back out to the living room and, crossing her arms over her chest, she faced Daniel. "I trust my father."

"Good for you," he said without looking up from the map he was studying. "I don't."

"Because he's just like you."

Now Daniel glanced up, his eyebrow arched skeptically. "Excuse me?"

"The reasons you hate my father—his interference in our relationship five years ago and his giving up your cover to General Ramirez's men—he did both because he wanted to protect me. As extreme and ill-advised as they seem to us in hindsight, he just wanted to save my life. You've done some pretty extreme things for the same reason. Because you both care about me."

Daniel tensed his jaw, making the muscle jump. "I care about you, yes. I'm nothing like your father."

She ignored his denial, taking a seat beside him and spreading her hands in entreaty. "What's more, I care about both of you. I *love* both of you."

Though he clearly tried to mask his reaction, she saw the telltale twitch in his muscles, as if he'd received an electric jolt. She caught the flicker of heartbreaking emotion and surprise that passed over his face in an instant, before he slammed the protective walls back in place.

He dropped his gaze back to the map, but his hands weren't quite as steady now. "The fewer people involved, the better our chances of getting Pilar back to her father safely." He tossed her a side glance. "That is what you want, isn't it?"

"Of course, but my father already knows about Pilar. Seems to me, keeping the boat arrangements within the circle of people already privy to our situation is the wisest move." She thrust her hand out for the phone. "Let me call him. We don't have time to find another boat and still make our meeting with Jake and Castillo on time. I'll ask him to arrange for us to get the key from the marina manager."

Daniel stared at her, his dark eyes bright with penetrating

intensity. Finally he growled under his breath and slapped his cell phone in her hand. "Warn him not to breathe a word of this to anyone. He's not to tell the marina manager anything except to have the cruiser ready to sail by sunrise."

Nicole nodded and gave him a grateful smile, careful not to appear gloating. His capitulation was a small victory for her, but she didn't presume to believe he was ready to cede the war with her father. Still, it was a step in the right direction. Maybe there was hope for them yet.

Chapter 12

The plan was simple. Drive to Grand Isle, take Senator White's cabin cruiser out into the Gulf of Mexico, rendezvous with Jake and Judge Castillo at the set GPS coordinates. After he handed Pilar over to Jake and her father, Jake would deliver the judge and his daughter back to the judge's safe house in Colombia via the same means he'd gotten Castillo out of the country. With Pilar no longer in her custody, the threat to Nicole should be eliminated, and his protection would no longer be needed. They'd be free to go their separate ways. Easy peasy. Clean and simple.

He should feel relieved. This mess was almost over. Mission accomplished.

So why was his chest contracting so tightly he could barely breathe? Why were his nerves jumping and his pulse racing like he'd just run a marathon?

Nicole rode silently in the passenger's seat of the rental car they'd picked up in Baton Rouge. He'd chosen a rental company that would send a driver to his grandmother's house to get them and take them back home tonight. He cast a side glance at Nicole.

I love both of you.

He'd waited half his life to hear her tell him she loved him. And, *damn it,* when she had, her father's presence had overshadowed what should have been his. He'd even had to friggin' share Nicole's declaration of love with the infernal man. Daniel gritted his teeth. He couldn't ask Nicole to exclude her father from her life for his sake, so any future he tried to build with her would always include the man who'd offered him to the enemy like a Thanksgiving turkey. Her loyalties would always be divided.

Irritation plucked at him, and he shifted in the driver's seat, restless and ready to get out to sea.

"We're almost there," Nicole said, reading his mood correctly. "The road to the marina is just past this turn a few miles."

He nodded and used the rearview mirror to check on Pilar. The little girl met his gaze in the mirror, and her doelike brown eyes turned his heart inside out. Nicole wasn't the only one who'd miss Pilar. And wasn't that a kick in the pants? A hardened undercover counter-terrorist agent letting a little girl's giggle and innocent eyes burrow under his tough hide. "*Pronto,* tadpole. *Pronto.*"

Pilar nodded, and her grin reflected her eager anticipation of seeing her father.

When they reached the turnoff to the marina, Nicole directed him to the crushed-shell parking lot and aimed her finger to a large boat moored at the end of the wooden pier. "That's it. The *Serendipity.*"

Daniel cut the engine and studied the cabin cruiser. "The marina manager has the key?"

"He's supposed to. I'll get it and meet you two down there."

Daniel climbed out of the car and retrieved the cane he'd been using the past two days. The loose shells made walking more difficult, and he had his head down, watching his step, when Nicole gasped.

He looked up to see what had startled her, then followed the path of her stunned gaze to the manager's office.

Senator White stalked down the sidewalk toward them. On his heels were two well-dressed Hispanic men.

Daniel stiffened, alarms clanging in his head and white-hot fury roiling inside him.

He'd given her a clear mandate, specific directions. No one else could know about their meeting with Jake. Her father was not to be involved or informed of their plans beyond their need to use the boat for the day.

Had she defied his directives and betrayed his trust? *Again?*

Acid bit his gut hard as he saw his future in clear focus—Nicole deferring to her father, Nicole not trusting him, Nicole second-guessing him and undermining their relationship because of her shaky faith in him. Which, in truth, meant he had no future with Nicole.

Swallowing hard, Daniel choked down the bitter taste of his hurt and anger, and cut a narrow-eyed gaze to Nicole. "I told you your father couldn't be trusted. Apparently, neither can you."

A wounded look crossed her face, and she opened her mouth to defend herself. But Daniel knew all he needed.

"Take Pilar and go wait at the boat. I'll handle this." He hobbled forward, hating the disadvantage he was at because of his damn knee. With his free hand, he unzipped his jacket for faster access to the sidearm in his shoulder holster. The patter of footsteps behind him told him Nicole and Pilar were following him rather than doing as he'd ordered.

When he sent Nicole a glare, she raised her chin and scowled back. "He's my father. *I'll* talk to him."

"Nicole, honey, how are you?" The senator's booming voice reverberated across the marina. He drew Nicole close for a hug, and she gave her father a tight smile and a peck on the check.

"Dad, what are you doing here? I told you we didn't need help with the *Serendipity*."

The senator cocked his head. "Just the same, it is my boat, and I prefer to be the one who pilots it. Besides, I thought it would be nice to have the opportunity to get to know your Mr. LeCroix better."

Her Mr. LeCroix? What did he mean by that? Daniel wondered but shoved the thought aside in the interest of more pressing matters. Like the two men standing with Nicole's father.

"Who are you?" Daniel asked the men, his tone less than polite.

"Ramon Diaz," the taller of the two men said, stepping forward to shake Daniel's hand. "I'm the attaché to the Colombian embassy who has been working with the senator and Miss White in returning Pilar Castillo to our country. And this—" he indicated the shorter yet well-muscled man with him "—is Jorge Menendez, my associate."

Daniel sized Menendez up. The bulge at the waist of his coat was, no doubt, a gun, and the eagle eye with which he regarded the group told Daniel the term *bodyguard* might be more accurate than *associate*.

Diaz turned to the little girl, who scuttled closer to Nicole's legs, giving the stranger a wary scrutiny. "And this, I presume, is Pilar."

Nicole shook Diaz's hand, as well, her expression guarded. "What brings you here today, Mr. Diaz?"

The attaché chuckled. "I'd think that was obvious. Pilar

Castillo is a Colombian citizen, and I'm here to take custody of her."

Daniel tensed and, from the corner of his eye, saw Nicole square her shoulders.

"We've been in New Orleans for days," Diaz continued, "trying to make just such arrangements. But you disappeared with her."

If he was simply here to take custody of Pilar, why did Diaz feel he needed a bodyguard for the meeting? Was the muscle for his protection or for Pilar's? Did he expect trouble from the goons who'd tried once to kidnap the girl?

"How did you know we would be here?" Nicole asked, echoing Daniel's next thought.

"The senator told me," Diaz returned blandly.

Nicole sent her father a stunned look, which the senator met with a guilty frown and shake of his head.

"I called him to see if he'd had any news from you, Miss White," Diaz explained, "and he filled me in on your little jaunt today."

"Only after you threatened to go to the media with accusations that I was an accomplice to kidnapping and harboring an illegal immigrant," Senator White growled, then shot Nicole an apologetic look. "I'm sorry, honey. I was in a bad position, and God knows the last thing I need is any more scandal or bad press."

Nicole scowled her disappointment in her father and faced Diaz. She gave the attaché a tight, businesslike grin. "Well, as much as I appreciate your help in finding Pilar's father and keeping this whole situation amicable, the truth is your assistance is not needed. We've found Judge Castillo and are meeting him today to return Pilar to his custody."

Daniel's gut dropped, and he gritted his teeth. *Merde!* Why had she told Diaz their plans? Too much was still at risk. Too much could still go wrong. Embassy official or not, Diaz was a wild card, an unknown, and Daniel didn't trust him.

Diaz and Menendez exchanged a startled look.

"Castillo is coming here?" Menendez asked.

"No," Nicole said. "Were going to him. Meeting him at a neutral location."

"Where?" Diaz asked.

"Doesn't matter," Daniel cut in before Nicole could show all their cards. "We have the matter under control. Your embassy doesn't need to get involved."

"LeCroix, is it?" Diaz asked shifting his attention to Daniel. "We are already involved… As is proper protocol." His eyes narrowed as he shoved his hands in the pockets of his dress pants and twisted his mouth in a thoughtful moue. "But I'm not an unreasonable man. If you have a custody transfer set up, there is no point in changing those plans."

Daniel's neck prickled with suspicion, but Nicole released a relieved sigh and flashed a bright smile. "Thank you."

"On one condition," Diaz added.

Nicole's smile dimmed, her eyebrows pulling together in a dubious frown. "What condition?"

"We accompany you to the rendezvous point to verify the exchange for the Colombian government."

Daniel squeezed the grip of his cane. "No way in hell."

Blinking her surprise, Nicole shot him a dark look. "Daniel, why—?"

"No. We go alone, as planned." His returned look asked her to trust him. Their plans had been leaked, but he could still salvage the mission. All that mattered was seeing Pilar safely delivered to her father. He only asked for Nicole to have faith in him, give her cooperation.

Diaz heaved an impatient sigh. "It seems to me you have but two choices. One, you allow us to go with you and verify that the girl is, in fact, given back to her father, or two, I call the local sheriff and Coast Guard and have you arrested for kidnapping, child endangerment, child trafficking and anything else I can make stick. This will become an international incident, because I will see to it your government is called to task."

"Now see here," Senator White started, aiming a finger at Diaz.

"Dad." Nicole gripped her father's arm and sent him a pleading look for calm. Turning back to Diaz, she employed another ingratiating smile. "Mr. Diaz, what if we verified the transfer for you. We could send you proof, say pictures of Pilar with her father, or—"

"Pictures can be altered," Menendez countered.

Daniel cursed under his breath. "We're wasting time here."

Pilar's wide brown eyes darted from one man to the next, clearly alert to the tension in their voices. Daniel gave her a brief considering glance. His goal was to get Pilar back to her father. Diaz had thrown a monkey wrench in that plan, but not an insurmountable obstacle.

As much as he hated changing their plans, getting locked in a diplomatic stalemate benefitted no one. He nailed a grim stare on Diaz. "Fine. You can go with us and verify." He hitched his head to Menendez. "But your *associate* stays here. Take it or leave it."

Menendez glowered at Daniel before exchanging a silent but pregnant look with Diaz. The attaché sniffed and scratched his nose, then nodded. "*Sí,* he will stay here."

Menendez's expression clearly displayed his hatred of this plan. "Diaz—"

The attaché raised his hand to quiet his associate. "Shall we go, then?"

Senator White rallied, as if afraid the situation could backfire if he didn't hurry. He put a hand on Nicole's and Pilar's shoulders and directed them down the pier.

Daniel opened his mouth to stop the senator but reconsidered. If things went sideways, the senator was safer on the *Serendipity* with them than alone here with Menendez. Sighing his resignation and taut with apprehension, Daniel followed the rest of the group to the senator's cabin cruiser.

While the others boarded, Daniel slipped out his cell phone, hoping to send Jake a quick text, warning him that the attaché and senator were accompanying them.

No signal. *Enfer!*

The two-way radios they'd brought for communication with Jake would only work when they were within five miles of him.

Before Diaz could enter the living space, Daniel pulled him aside and searched him for weapons. He found the man's 9 mm Beretta in an ankle holster and confiscated it, much to the attaché's displeasure.

"This is a simple custody transfer. Why would you need a weapon?" Daniel asked coolly.

"Because the same people who took Pilar in Bogotá, who tried to kidnap her in New Orleans, are still out there. Anything could happen."

"I've thought of that, and contingencies are covered." With a nod of dismissal, Daniel strode inside the main cabin.

While Nicole's father headed to the cockpit and piloted them out of the marina, Nicole opened an overhead bin and removed a child-size life jacket for Pilar. After helping the girl into hers, he showed the men where the other life preservers were stored in case of emergency, then followed the girl out to the bow to watch the waves. Diaz followed the women outside and planted himself in a deck chair.

Joining the senator upstairs in the cockpit, Daniel stepped close to Nicole's father, so his low tone could be heard over the rumble of the engine and whipping slipstream. "Do you keep any weapons onboard?"

The senator cut a startled look to him, then nodded to a compartment beside them. "I have a loaded gun—a Colt .45 single-action revolver that was my grandfather's—locked in there. I thought it was prudent to have some means to defend myself and my passengers in light of recent news about pirates and the violence crossing the border out of Mexico."

Daniel arched an eyebrow. "If you're looking to defend yourself against pirates and drug runners, you better consider an automatic rather than a single action." He sighed. "But keep the Colt handy. Just in case."

The senator gave Daniel a long, hard look. "Listen… LeCroix, I know we have a lot of history. You have every right to hate me and what I did."

Daniel gave him only a brief glance of acknowledgment before setting his jaw and turning his attention to the Gulf.

"I'm not proud of some of the things I've done. But I'd do them all again, if it meant saving my daughter's life. She is everything to me."

Daniel kept silent, searching the horizon for signs of trouble.

"Nicole has deep feelings for you, LeCroix."

Though he tried not to show any reaction to that statement, Daniel felt his muscles give a telltale twitch.

"And because of that, I'd like to bury the hatchet."

When the senator paused, Daniel glanced at him. "Bury it where? In my back?"

Nicole's father shook his head. "I'm trying to offer a truce. A cease-fire for my daughter's sake."

Flexing and balling his hand in agitation, Daniel faced the senator. "I have deep feelings for Nicole, too. I'd like to think we have a future together, but recent events have proven that's nothing but a pipe dream."

The senator drew his gray eyebrows together. "Recent events?"

"Like our extra passenger, Diaz. You put your political well-being ahead of your daughter's safety."

The man's eyes widened. "I didn't—"

"I don't trust you, and I'm learning I can't trust Nicole when it comes to you, either."

Senator White raised his chin, and his expression hardened. "Do not ever question my motives regarding my daughter. Her safety and happiness are my top priority. Always."

"Then act like it." Before heading back down to the lower level, Daniel slapped a scrap of paper with the GPS coordinates of the rendezvous spot on the dash and aimed a finger at the locked compartment. "Have your weapon ready in case it's needed."

On the ladder to the main deck, Daniel cast a glance to the senator to be sure he'd complied. Nicole's father slid the Colt revolver in the waist of his pants at the small of his back and met Daniel's gaze with a nod.

Nicole stood with Pilar at the bow of the *Serendipity,* trying to soothe the knots in her stomach and cool the burn in her heart. If the tension over the Colombian attaché's surprise appearance and her impending goodbye to Pilar weren't enough, Daniel's earlier caustic comment ate at her, leaving her stinging and raw.

I told you your father couldn't be trusted. Apparently, neither can you.

Daniel had avoided her for the past hour and a half as they cruised out into the Gulf of Mexico, and she had tried to stay busy, keep her mind off the newest rift between them, by entertaining Pilar.

The little girl had shaken off the tension from the confrontation on pier, clearly focused on seeing her father, the seagulls clamoring near the boat, and the spray of water splashing her face as she hung over the railing at the bow.

Suddenly Pilar's face brightened, and she pointed toward the horizon. *"Papi!"*

Shielding her eyes from the glare of sun, Nicole squinted at the spot Pilar indicated.

"Mira, Nicole! *Papi!"* Pilar squealed and waved an arm excitedly.

Sure enough, a small boat with two men aboard rocked in the waters ahead of them. One of the men, his hair as black as Pilar's, stood and waved an arm back at Pilar. The second man wore a telltale cowboy hat.

The girl's shouts and excitement brought Diaz and Daniel to the railing, as well. Daniel lifted a pair of binoculars and confirmed that the other boat was Jake and Pilar's father. "Anchor here!" he shouted to the cockpit. "Let them come to us."

Her father gave a nod of understanding, and the drone of the *Serendipity*'s engine quieted.

Daniel raised a hand radio to his mouth. *"Serendipity* to Connelly. You there, cowboy? Over."

"Roger that. Over," Jake's voice crackled over the radio.

"We have extra company. Over."

"So I see. What's the plan? Over."

Daniel cast a glance at Diaz and scowled. "Same plan. We're anchoring here. Copy?"

"Roger that."

Daniel's jaw tightened, and he stared across the Gulf at the small fishing boat that was even now turning toward them. Raising the radio to his lips again, he added, "Greek protocol."

Nicole furrowed her brow, shooting him a question in her glance. He returned a hard stare but said nothing.

Having dropped anchor, her father came down from the cockpit and joined her at the bow railing. He put his arm around her shoulders. "You've done well, Nicole, caring for Pilar the way you have. You can be proud."

A bittersweet pang sliced through Nicole's chest and squeezed her lungs. She stroked Pilar's head and winked at the girl when Pilar angled her a grin. "It's hard to let her go. I'll miss her so much."

Her father patted her arm. "I know you will. But you can stay in touch."

When she moved to hug her father, her hand brushed something hard at his back. A gun. She gave him a puzzled look.

"LeCroix's idea," he said quietly.

Pilar bounced on her toes, clapping her hands, as Jake steered the fishing boat within a few yards of the *Serendipity*. "*Papi!*"

From the fishing boat, Mario Castillo beamed at his daughter and blew kisses. "Pilar! *Mija!*"

Diaz crowded in next to Nicole and her father at the railing, and Castillo's attention shifted to the new face. And his smile faltered.

Nicole barely had time to register the judge's reaction before chaos erupted.

Castillo pointed an accusing finger at Diaz.

Diaz snatched the gun from her father's back. Aimed at the fishing boat. Cocked the hammer and fired. Jake jerked and stumbled backward, and Castillo shrank to a crouch.

Pilar screamed, and adrenaline surged through Nicole. Fear and stunned confusion sent her pulse skyrocketing.

Producing a gun from under his jacket, Daniel swung his weapon toward Diaz. "Drop it!"

Jake lunged at Judge Castillo and tumbled with Pilar's father into the water on the far side of the fishing boat.

His primary target hidden behind the fishing boat, Diaz turned his weapon toward Daniel. Cocked the hammer.

As Nicole turned to grab Pilar, ready to take evasive and protective measures, her father tightened his grip on her shoulders and shoved her behind him.

"No! Pilar!" Panic swelling in her chest, Nicole fought to get past her father, but he held her arm tightly and shielded her with his body.

"Nicole, stay back!" her father growled.

Daniel and Diaz glared each other down in a deadly game of chicken. Nicole stared in horror at the weapon aimed at Daniel, and a numbing terror swept through her, strangling her breath.

"Drop the weapon," Daniel snarled, his dark eyes flinty and unyielding.

"Not until Castillo is dead." Diaz reached Pilar in one giant step and, snaking an arm around her, he hauled her back against him in a death grip. "He is responsible for my brother's murder!"

The girl's eyes rounded, wild with fear, and she cried, "Nicole!"

Only someone who knew Daniel the way Nicole did would have noticed the small tic in his jaw muscle, the slight catch in his breath. Diaz's move had rattled Daniel. Because Daniel loved Pilar.

Diaz cut a quick glance to the water, holding Pilar between him and Daniel. A human shield. "Come out, Castillo, or your daughter will die!"

"No! Don't hurt her! Please!" Nicole cried. Fear pooled like ice water in her veins, and Pilar's pleas shredded her heart.

"Let the girl go," Daniel grated through clenched teeth.

Diaz shook his head. "No, *señor*. She is my bait to draw out *her traitorous father!*" He shouted the words toward the water.

"You are the traitor, you BACRIM coward!" Splashing sounds preceded Castillo's appearance in front of the boat as he swam toward the *Serendipity*. "All of you who murder innocents in our streets and poison our children should be hanged!"

Diaz saw his opportunity and fired at the judge.

"Castillo!" Jake shouted, swimming with one arm from the protection of the fishing boat. Blood trailed Jake in the water, and his other arm hung loosely at his side. Nicole's gut tightened with concern. Jake needed a doctor, but they were miles from shore.

Despite his injury, Jake seized the back of Mario Castillo's shirt and dragged him back toward safety, even as Diaz cocked the gun again and squeezed off another shot. Re-cocked.

From her peripheral vision, Nicole saw Daniel shift, edging toward Diaz. But the movement, slow as it was, drew Diaz's attention back to Daniel, as well. Without hesitating, the attaché fired.

"Daniel!" she screamed, terror sluicing through her.

The bullet flew wide to the right. With a two-handed grip, Daniel aimed at Diaz but clearly had no shot, not with Pilar in the way.

Wearing a gloating grin, Diaz thumbed the hammer back with a click and tightened his finger around the trigger.

Nicole felt her father's muscles tense. His hands released her, and instantly, without a second thought, she lunged for Pilar, jerking her free from a distracted Diaz.

But even as she pulled Pilar close, she watched, as if in slow motion, as her father sprang toward Daniel, as a bullet hit his back, as he knocked Daniel from his feet and lay motionless on the deck. "Daddy!"

Then Diaz spun toward Nicole, his lip curled in disdain, and he pointed the gun at her.

Chapter 13

Daniel shoved the senator off him in time to see Diaz whirl toward Nicole and Pilar and take aim. An icy fear unlike anything he'd ever experienced stole his breath. Nicole!

Acting purely on training, muscle memory, instinct, Daniel jerked his gun up and fired. Fired again. Didn't stop until Diaz crumpled on the deck, his eyes fixed and lifeless.

As the concussion dissipated over the Gulf, Daniel lay still, the aftershock of adrenaline sending a shiver through him. He cut his gaze toward the woman he'd thought, just seconds earlier, he could lose forever. Another shudder rolled through him. "Nicole!"

She jerked her head up from her protective huddle over Pilar. Terror filled her eyes as she looked first to Diaz's body, then at him.

"W-we're all right." Tears spilled from her eyelashes, and she lowered her gaze to her father. "Daddy?"

Daniel holstered his weapon and rolled to a seated position beside the man who'd taken a bullet meant for him. Nicole's father had saved his life. That truth sat in Daniel's gut like a rock, and he shoved the thought aside to deal with later.

The senator lay on his back, and though his eyes were open, he didn't move. No blood showed on the front of his shirt, which was a bad sign. No exit wound meant the bullet had likely ricocheted around inside the man, wreaking havoc with his internal organs.

When Daniel pressed his fingers to the man's neck, searching for a pulse, a thready wheeze issued from the senator's mouth. "Nic—"

Nicole scurried across the deck to her father's side. "Daddy? Oh, thank God!"

The senator's eyes turned toward his daughter. He gasped for a breath. Raised an arm.

"No, lie still, Daddy. Let us help you." She stroked his head with a trembling hand and sniffed as she cried. "How badly are you hurt? Can you breathe?"

Daniel fumbled with the shirt buttons at the senator's throat, loosening the collar to help him draw air.

"Back," he wheezed.

"Pilar!" Castillo's voice rang from the water.

Daniel glanced over his shoulder as, sobbing, Pilar jumped to her feet and reached over the railing toward her father. *"Papi!"*

"Daniel?" Jake this time. "A little help here?"

"Give me a minute! We've got a man down!" he shouted back.

Nicole met his gaze. "Jake's injured, too. The shoulder, I think."

The senator made a strangled noise and tried to sit up. Grimaced and groaned. Wheezed.

Daniel finally freed the buttons at the senator's neck, and as he worked the lower buttons, he discovered a stiff, unyielding garment beneath the senator's undershirt. Startled, Daniel flattened his hand against the garment, feeling the material and weight, confirming his suspicion. His gaze connected with the senator's, and the man read his expression, gave a small nod.

"Kevlar," Daniel mumbled, then gave a chuckle of relief. He caught Nicole's hand to capture her attention, and when her panicked eyes darted up to his, he flashed her a crooked smile. "He's wearing Kevlar. A bulletproof vest."

Nicole's mouth opened, recognition brightening her eyes. She turned to her father and laughed through her tears. "The vest Mama bought you when…"

"Thought…it was…prudent." This time when her father tried to sit up, Nicole helped him, and Daniel worked the senator's dress shirt up to reveal the point of the bullet's impact.

Senator White moaned, then rasped, "Knocked the…wind outta me. Hurts to…draw breath."

"I bet." Daniel sat back, rubbing his own aching knee, which had taken a blow when the senator knocked him down. "You don't have a bullet in you, but you could easily have a broken rib or bruised lung." Guilt kicked Daniel, along with an uneasy gratitude.

He'd sworn he'd hate White forever for his part in keeping him away from Nicole. For betraying his and Alec's cover and putting their lives in peril while they were on a mission in enemy territory. For dividing Nicole's loyalties.

Daniel swallowed the bitterness those memories still stirred in him and met the senator's gaze. "Thank you."

Still panting for air, White nodded. "Because…my daughter…loves you."

Nicole gasped, and fresh tears puddled in her eyes. She divided a look between her father and Daniel, and bit her lip. "Oh, Daddy…" Carefully, she leaned in to hug her father's neck. "I love you, too."

"No, *mija!*" Castillo's shout drew Daniel's attention back to the scene that had been playing out as background noise behind him.

Pilar had climbed under the railing, and before he or Nicole could scramble to stop her, the little girl jumped into the Gulf.

"Pilar!" Nicole cried, dashing to the bow. Daniel groped for his cane and met Nicole at the rail. Below them, Pilar swam into her father's arms and was greeted with tears and kisses and admonishments for her impetuous leap into the water.

Spying them at the rail, Jake called, "Hey, I'm feeling a bit like shark bait down here, bleeding like this. Could you drop a ladder so we can come aboard?"

"Roger that, cowboy," Daniel returned, then faced Nicole. "Help them out of the water. I'm going to raise anchor and find a first aid kit. Then we need to radio the Coast Guard and have them alert the police on Grand Isle to pick up Menendez before we reach shore."

Jake grunted as Nicole shoved a wad of sterile gauze into the hole in his shoulder, and Daniel cringed in sympathy. Even though the bullet had passed through and done minimal damage, Jake had to be hurting like the devil. "At least it's not your gun arm."

Jake nodded. "There is that— Ow!" He sent Daniel a gloomy look. "My own fault. You warned me, and I didn't take enough precautions."

"You warned him? Is that what that Greek protocol business was about?" Nicole asked.

Jake nodded. "As in, the Greeks should have been more wary of their Trojan gift. Proceed with caution." Shifting his attention to the father and daughter reunion across the room, Jake hitched his head toward Castillo. "You oughta debrief the judge so we can vamoose before the Coast Guard arrives."

Daniel glanced at Nicole. "You got this?"

She nodded. "Of course, it would help if the patient would *sit still.*"

Twitching a grin at Jake, Daniel stepped over to the cluster of overstuffed chairs where Castillo and Pilar were huddled together, wrapped in blankets and alternately chuckling and crying.

"You speak English," Daniel stated, confirming what he'd gleaned from the day's earlier events.

Castillo nodded. "Enough to get by."

"You recognized Diaz," Daniel said, getting right to the business at hand. "How did you know him?"

Castillo clutched Pilar to his chest and met Daniel's gaze levelly. "I grew up in the same neighborhood with Ramon and his brothers."

"What did he mean when he said you were responsible for his brother's murder?"

The judge snorted. "Carlo was not murdered. He was executed for his crimes." His eyes darkened. "Carlo and their youngest brother, Hector, joined a BACRIM— how do you say—? A street gang…."

"Go on," Daniel answered with a nod, well-familiar with the criminal gangs that were the scourge of daily life in Colombia, dangerous hordes of competing drug runners, rebel factions and lowlifes exploiting the civil unrest in the country as an excuse for lawlessness and personal gain.

"When he came before my court, I gave him what he deserved. Death sentence. His brothers said I was traitor to him. That he was fighting other gangs to keep the neighborhood safe." He scowled darkly and shook his head. "But no one is safe while he runs his drug traffic through our streets and poisons our children with his *cocaína*." He paused and stroked a hand down Pilar's head, his expression sad now. "It was after this that they attacked my family. They murdered my wife and daughter and took Pilar. Only if I, ah…" He fumbled as if looking for the right word. "Obey their demands, turn my eyes away from their crimes, will I get Pilar back."

"Did you do as they asked?"

The judge sneered at Daniel's question. "Never! I will not surrender my country to these criminals!" He looked down at his daughter, his face crumpling in anguish, and he made the sign of the cross. "God forgive me, I couldn't give in to them, even if it cost my daughter's life." He drilled a hard gaze on Daniel. "We are at war with these BACRIM. The drug cartels and traffickers. They have—what's word? Infil—"

"Infiltrated?"

Castillo nodded. "Infiltrated too many *policía* and government posts already."

Daniel sighed heavily. "Like Diaz did in the embassy here in the U.S."

Pilar whispered something in Spanish to her father, and he kissed her head. *"Sí."*

"Is she all right?" Daniel asked.

Judge Castillo smiled. "Eager to get home."

Daniel frowned. "In light of everything, her kidnapping, the threats against you and the turmoil in your country, you still want to go back to Bogotá?"

"I must. It is our home, and we cannot let the evil win. We will go home to fight for what is right." Castillo must have read Daniel's concern for Pilar in his expression, because he grunted and added, "I will be hiring a bodyguard for Pilar. More protection at our house." He arched an eyebrow. "Would you or Jake be interested in the job?"

Daniel tugged a wry grin. "A few months ago, I might have jumped at the offer but…" He rubbed his injured knee. "I'm not the man for the job anymore."

Castillo cut a telling look toward Nicole. "For many reasons. Pilar tells me you and Señorita White are in love."

Daniel's gut rolled, and he battled down the bitter taste of betrayal he'd shoved aside earlier when they'd encountered the senator, Diaz and Menendez at the pier. "I'm not sure what we are. But...I don't see a future for us. It's...too complicated."

Judge Castillo leaned back in his chair, a disappointed glare fixed on Daniel. "Too complicated? For the man who rescued my daughter and her lady-guardian from a rebel camp?" He shook his head and narrowed his eyes. "No. Nothing is too hard if it is also what is right. If you love her, you will not say it is too complicated and walk away."

Daniel opened his mouth, unsure what to say, but Jake saved him the trouble of a response when he strolled up behind them.

"All done here." Jake gingerly tested his freshly wrapped shoulder with his fingers. "I think it's time we hit the road... or the water, in this case. Judge Castillo, are you ready to go?"

Castillo nodded and nudged Pilar, whispering to her. The girl's eyes widened, and she searched the room until her gaze landed on Nicole, who was still packing up the first aid kit. Scooting off her father's lap, Pilar ran across the room to her surrogate parent. "Nicole..."

Daniel couldn't hear what Pilar told Nicole, but reading Nicole's expression was simple enough. Melancholy, the bittersweet ache of goodbye.

Nicole dropped to her knees and wrapped Pilar in a firm embrace. With her eyes squeezed shut, she clung to the little girl. "I'll miss you, *mija*. You are so brave and strong. I know you'll do great things with your life," she told her in stilted Spanish.

Pilar said something softly that made Nicole's face crumple with grief, and she squeaked, "I love you, too, *mija*."

Seeing Nicole's pain, knowing how much he, too, would miss Pilar, Daniel was blindsided by a wrenching ache in his chest. His airway tightened, and he had to clear his throat to loosen the knot of emotion. When Nicole and Pilar joined the men, Judge Castillo shook hands with Daniel and Jake and gave Nicole a kiss on each cheek. "I can never thank you enough for the love you have shown my daughter, the care you've given her and the risks you've taken to bring her back to me."

"There is one thing you can do," Nicole said, wiping her cheeks. "Stay in touch?"

Castillo nodded. "Of course." Taking Pilar's hand, he looked to Jake. "We are ready."

But when her father turned to leave, Pilar tugged her hand free and threw herself against Daniel's legs. "Goodbye, Daniel."

Shifting his weight to his good leg, he bent and lifted Pilar in his arms for a bear hug. He kissed her head, and through the fresh onslaught of emotion choking him, he rasped, "*Adios,* tadpole."

When he set her back on the ground, Pilar took her father's hand, and they followed Jake out to the deck. Daniel paused at the door and looked back at Nicole, who sat on a sofa with her face buried in her hands. "You coming to see them off?"

"No." Lifting her head, she swiped at her red eyes and shoved to her feet. "I'd better go check on Dad."

Without another word, she headed back to the small bedroom where her father was resting. Daniel watched her go, and wondered to himself— if saying goodbye to Pilar hurt this much, how much more would it hurt when he and Nicole went their separate ways?

Because he still had a bad feeling in his gut about where they were headed.

The Coast Guard met the *Serendipity* a couple miles from shore. In addition to examining her father's injury and reaching the same conclusion as Nicole had—significant bruising but no broken ribs, a diagnosis that they would still confirm with X-rays at the closest emergency room once they reached shore—the Coast Guard officers took an initial incident report on the shootings. As they had all agreed to ahead of time, Nicole, her father and Daniel gave truthful accounts of how the senator and Diaz acquired their wounds.

Diaz had joined them for a day trip to discuss business. The senator kept the gun on the boat in case of trouble from pirates or drug runners. He had the gun tucked in the waist of his pants, and Diaz snatched it and threatened them all with it. When Daniel produced his own weapon to defend them, Diaz fired, the senator knocked Daniel out of the way and took a bullet in his Kevlar-protected back. Diaz turned toward his weapon on Nicole and Daniel fired to save her. Initial forensic analysis supported everything they reported, as would later tests. Nicole was confident the case would be closed as justifiable homicide. No mention was made of Pilar, her father or Jake.

When the Grand Isle police were alerted to Menendez's possible connection to the attack the week before at the senator's home, they located him in a small diner near the pier and held him as a material witness. Before they left the Grand Isle police station, Nicole and her father were told that Menendez had clammed up, sitting like a rock, stoically staring straight ahead when questioned. Nicole could only surmise the man's silence was largely due to his links to Diaz and the criminal gang in Bogotá responsible for killing Pilar's family. They also learned that the Colombian embassy denied any association with the thug, but produced an extradition request for his for crimes in Colombia. By nightfall, Menendez was on a plane back to South America, and she and her father were released from police custody to return home. As she walked out to the police department parking lot, Nicole breathed a giant sigh of relief to have that chapter of her life behind her at last.

She couldn't regret her time with Pilar, though, or that the tumultuous past weeks had brought Daniel back into her life. Pain pinched her heart when she remembered Daniel's biting assertion that morning that he couldn't trust her and the cool distance he'd kept from her throughout the day. She'd been as surprised as anyone to see her father and Diaz on the pier but hadn't had an opportunity to defend herself.

By the end of the physically exhausting and emotionally wrenching day, when she found Daniel waiting for her in the police department parking lot, her hurt had grown a callus, and she bristled at the idea of having to defend herself. She was tired of proving herself and reiterating her loyalty to him. After all they'd been through, all the past hurts and misunderstandings, she needed Daniel to love and trust her unconditionally.

She helped her father get settled with a pillow in the passenger seat of his Caddy, then met Daniel, who leaned on the hood of the rental car they'd picked up just that morning. Had it only been that morning? Geez, it had been a long day!

"You okay to drive him back to New Orleans?" Daniel asked as she approached.

She nodded. "I'll stop for coffee somewhere, but I'm fine. What about you? Are you headed back to your grandmother's tonight?"

He gazed into the darkness avoiding her eyes. "Probably. For a day or so. I need to see about my leg. Talk to a surgeon about a knee replacement. After that…" He lifted a shoulder in a dismissive shrug.

She studied his rugged profile in the harsh bluish parking lot lights, and her stomach swooped. His jaw was rigid, and the jumping muscle in his cheek spoke of his lingering anger with her. She sighed, too weary to verbally spar with him tonight.

Why, oh why, out of all the men in the world, had she fallen so hard, so completely in love with this hardheaded, temperamental, obstinate man?

Dreading his answer, but needing to know where he saw their relationship, she asked, "Will you call?"

He didn't respond for a moment, and with each second that passed, Nicole felt her heart slowly cracking, as if a thin wedge were being driven in one tap at a time. Finally, he lowered his eyebrows in a scowl and shot her a dark look. "I don't see the point." *Tap.* "You and I...have never really fit." *Tap.* "I think it's time we both let go of the fantasy we created that night in New Orleans and admit that we could never work."

Tap.

Tears of frustration burned her eyes. "Daniel, you haven't given us a chance to wor—"

"Good night, Nicole." He pushed away from the hood and popped open the driver's door. "I'll get your cats back to you by the end of the week."

She gaped at him. Stunned. Stinging. Furious. "Daniel?"

He paused only long enough to give her one last look, his eyes full of regret. "Take care of yourself. You deserve it."

Without another word, he lowered himself into the rental car and cranked the engine.

Crash. Nicole struggled for a breath as the shards of her shattered heart sliced her chest and left her bleeding inside. She stood motionless, aching to her marrow as she watched him drive away. Only after his taillights had faded into the night did she muster the strength to stumble back to her father's Cadillac.

He sent her a worried look as she turned the ignition key and backed out of their parking space. "Everything all right, honey?"

And because she'd never lied to her father before, she cut a quick glance to him and answered simply, "No."

* * *

Two days later, while sitting out on the porch of his grand-mére's house, Daniel received a text message from Jake saying Pilar and her father had been successfully returned to the safe house in Colombia, and Jake was on his was back to his home in Texas for some recuperative time for his shoulder injury. After reading the message, Daniel set his phone aside and gazed at the bayou, bored out of his skull and missing Pilar and Nicole like crazy. He knew he might never see Pilar again, yet the girl had shown him the joys of fatherhood and given him hope that someday he'd have children of his own.

Children with Nicole's stunning blue eyes and breathtaking smile…

He smacked a fist on the arm of the chair and bit out a curse.

Stop it! You made the only decision you could. Look at the contrail of pain and hurt you two have already left behind you. How could he put his heart at risk again? Just two days ago, she'd broken her promise not to tell her father about their plans. How could he trust her allegiance in the face of that betrayal? No, he'd already suffered enough anguish over Nicole, her self-serving father and her lack of faith in him.

Because…my daughter…loves you.

Daniel shifted restlessly in the rocking chair as the senator's words replayed in his mind. Nicole's father had saved his life…for Nicole. That sacrificial gesture didn't jibe with the ugly picture of the senator he'd locked in his brain for the past five years. Readjusting his perception wasn't comfortable. Neither was admitting he could have been wrong about what had really happened that morning in the hotel room in New Orleans.…

I think you're the one who has a problem with your heritage.

I love you both. Love you.…

With a growl of consternation, Daniel ground the heels of his hands in his eyes and leaned his head back on the rocking chair. Why did things between him Nicole have to be so confusing, so complicated?

If you love her, you will not say it is too complicated and walk away.

If he loved her? *Enfer!*

He'd loved her since the day he met her. That was what had made her betrayal hurt so much. Except…if he were to believe Nicole, she hadn't betrayed him. She'd been rebelling against her father's ideals, but she'd been invested, she'd wanted to be with him, given him her heart.

The buzz of his phone cut into his frustrating rationalizations.

Snatching up the phone, Daniel checked the caller ID, secretly hoping it was Nicole, but saw his partner's number instead. "So Alec," he said by way of greeting, "Erin kick you to the street yet?"

"Hello to you, too," Alec returned, sounding happier than ever. "And, no, for some reason, Erin loves me and seems quite happy to put up with me."

Daniel twitched a small grin, relieved to have the distraction. "She's a keeper."

"That she is. Especially after seeing her endure twelve hours of labor. The woman is my hero."

Daniel sat up straight. "Labor? She had the baby?"

"This morning. A boy. He's a little small, since he's a couple weeks early, but he's got strong lungs and a head full of his mother's blond hair." Pride filled Alec's voice, and Daniel couldn't help but smile.

"That's wonderful. Congratulations to you both."

"Thanks." Alec heaved a contented sigh. "I tell you, Lafitte. I never thought life could be this good. Marriage, family…you should try it."

"Yeah, maybe someday." He let his gaze drift out to the dock where he and Pilar had fished, and his heart twisted.

"Someday? Dadgum, Lafitte, haven't you kept Nicole waiting long enough? When are you going to wise up and tell her how you feel?"

Daniel pinched the bridge of his nose and sighed. "That ain't happening. Just a couple days ago, I told her we were through."

"Through? Wha—" Alec huffed. "What's that word you called me? *Coullion?*"

Daniel cocked his head, surprised to hear Alec tossing the Cajun term back at him, the term he'd used to shake Alec out of his stupor when he was prepared to let Erin slip away. "Yeah, *coullion.*"

"Because I'd say it applies to you, too. You're a stubborn fool if you give up on Nicole. I was only with her a few hours, but I could see how much she loved you. Do *not* let her get away, Daniel. I will come down there and kick your ass if I have to."

Daniel grinned. "I wouldn't presume to pull you away from your wife and baby like that."

"So you'll call her? Apologize? Beg her for a second chance if you have to?"

Daniel groaned and shook his head. "I— It's not that simple."

"Yeah, well, *hard* isn't in your vocabulary," Alec countered. "I've seen you take on three armed guys with your bare hands and come out alive. I've seen you get past security at a drug lord's fortress and get back out without even waking the guard dogs. 'Not that simple' merely means you have to dirty your hands a bit." Alec paused, and Daniel heard the cry of a baby in the background. "Look, the nurse just brought Ethan in. I need to go."

"Okay. Well, give Erin my best."

"Daniel, do you love her? Because that is what it boils down to, man. If you look at it that way, it is real simple."

Daniel squeezed the cell phone, and his chest tightened. "Yeah. I do."

"Then do right by her, okay?"

Nothing is too hard if it is also what is right. The judge's stilted English bounced through his memory.

"Thanks, Alec. Congrats again." Daniel disconnected and set the phone aside. *Do right by her.*

An energizing warmth flooded his body when he whittled away all the debris that had been cluttering his view of his relationship with Nicole. Alec was right. If he loved Nicole, wasn't that all that really mattered? Couldn't they sort out all the rest if they clung to their love for each other? After all, their feelings for each other had already survived the tempest of the past five years.

He glanced down at his knee brace and began calculating his next moves. Before he could ask Nicole to build a future with him, he had to settle a few matters. He wanted to schedule his knee replacement surgery and get on the road to recovering full use of his leg.

And he had unfinished business with her father.

Three days later, Daniel knocked on the door to Senator White's garden district mansion in New Orleans. The woman who'd been with Nicole on the day of Pilar's attempted kidnapping answered his summons and smiled when she saw him. "Daniel LeCroix, my hero! How nice to see you again."

He offered a polite smile to the housekeeper. "And you, Sarah Beth. Are the Whites home?"

The clack of shoes on hardwood preceded Nicole's appearance behind her father's housekeeper. "Daniel!" Her expression was both heartbreakingly hopeful and cautious. "Come in. What...what brings you here?"

Sara Beth took her leave, and Daniel focused on the woman who'd filled his dreams for the past ten years. Though surprise and concern filled Nicole's face, he couldn't help but notice how the past several days of rest and nourishment had put more color in her cheeks and flesh on her bones. She looked beautiful, and his heart responded with a pure, sweet pang of affection.

"I can't stay long. I'm on my way to the surgery center for my knee replacement now, but...I have some business to discuss with your father first. Is he home?"

Her brows furrowed with suspicion. "Yeah, but...what business?"

"Where can I find him?" he asked, purposely avoiding her question.

She stood back, worry etched in tiny lines around her eyes. "He's in the den. I'll take you."

Heart drumming, he followed her to the spacious room at the back of the house, already repaired after the gun battle with the kidnappers from a few weeks earlier.

"Dad, you have company," she said rousing her father from the television.

Senator White stood slowly and faced Daniel, his curious, somewhat wary expression matching Nicole's. "LeCroix." He offered his hand and Daniel shook it, meeting the man's eyes squarely.

"Senator. Are you feeling better?"

He tipped his head a bit. "Still a little sore and moving slowly, but I'm doing all right. What can I do for you?"

"I have something important to ask you."

Nicole moved next to her father, biting her lip. "Daniel, what's going on?"

He met her eyes briefly before giving her father his full attention. "Senator, I've been in love with your daughter since her prom night ten years ago. I believe I've demonstrated my willingness to do whatever it takes to protect her, even if it costs me my own life."

White glanced at Nicole, then gave Daniel a brief appreciative smile and tight nod. "Indeed you have."

"Sir, I promise you that nothing will change in that regard. I will always love, protect and defend her, no matter your answer."

He quirked a bushy gray eyebrow. "My answer? I haven't heard a question yet."

"Dad!" Nicole scolded.

Daniel wiped his hands on his pants and cleared his throat. "You're right. Senator White, will you grant me the honor of your daughter's hand in marriage?"

Nicole gasped, and her hand flew to her mouth.

White grinned and regarded his daughter with love in his eyes. "Daniel, my boy, I've learned not to make decisions where my daughter's life is concerned. She's a headstrong and capable woman with a mind of her own. If you want to marry her, she's the one you need to ask." He turned back to Daniel, adding, "For my part, however, I give my blessing and wish you many years of happiness."

Daniel twitched a grin, relief pricking the bubble of tension filling his lungs. Shifting his cane, he faced Nicole, his heart thundering. "Nicole, I—"

"Yes!" she cried and flung herself at him so hard and fast he dropped his cane in order to catch her. As a result, his balance faltered, and they nearly toppled.

Senator White laughed. "Honey, once again, I didn't hear a question."

Tears of joy leaked onto her cheeks, and she pulled back from his embrace just far enough to send him a grin. "Sorry. You were saying?"

He flashed a lopsided grin. "I was wondering if you'd drive

me to the hospital, so I don't have to put my car in long-term parking."

She mock-scowled and poked him. "Of course, I'll drive you. Anything else?"

He captured her face between his hands and sobered. "Only this…I love you. I've loved you for years, and I promise to love you the rest of my days on this earth. I can't imagine my future without you in it." He pulled a small pouch from his pocket and took out his grandmother's ring. "*Mémère* wanted me to give this to my bride." He slid the antique ruby and diamond ring on her finger. "Will you be my wife?"

Fat tears dripped from her spiky eyelashes, but a smile of sheer bliss and love lit her face.

"I love you, too, Daniel LeCroix." She wrapped her arms around his neck and kissed the breath from him. "I've waited a long time for this moment. And through the years, my answer has never changed. Yes, I'll be your wife. Absolutely yes."

* * * * *

"I don't date, Sheriff Harrison."

"Look, about the kiss—I didn't plan that. That's not why I was waiting in the garage for you. I mean, you do eat, don't you?"

"Of course, I do. But you don't owe me anything. I was just doing my job today. I don't need any thanks from you. And I certainly don't want to be any more trouble to you. So, good night."

Mules weren't the only stubborn thing his folks had raised on their ranch. Boone pulled back the front of his jacket and splayed his hands at his hips. He didn't get why he was so attracted to this prickly city woman who had to be as wrong for him as his ex-wife had been. But he clearly understood his duty as an officer of the law, and as a man.

"You may not need any thanks, but I don't leave a lady in trouble…"

First published in Great Britain 2012
by Mills & Boon, an imprint of Harlequin (UK) Limited,
Eton House, 18-24 Paradise Road, Richmond, Surrey TW9 1SR

© Julie Miller 2012

ISBN: 978 0 263 89574 2
ebook ISBN: 978 1 408 97257 1

46-1112

Harlequin (UK) policy is to use papers that are natural, renewable and recyclable products and made from wood grown in sustainable forests. The logging and manufacturing processes conform to the legal environmental regulations of the country of origin.

Printed and bound in Spain
by Blackprint CPI, Barcelona

KANSAS CITY COWBOY

BY
JULIE MILLER

MILLS & BOON

Julie Miller attributes her passion for writing romance to all those fairy tales she read growing up, and to shyness. Encouragement from her family to write down all those feelings she couldn't express became a love for the written word. She gets continued support from her fellow members of the Prairieland Romance Writers, where she serves as the resident "grammar goddess." This award-winning author and teacher has published several paranormal romances. Inspired by the likes of Agatha Christie and Encyclopedia Brown, Ms Miller believes the only thing better than a good mystery is a good romance.

Born and raised in Missouri, she now lives in Nebraska with her husband, son and smiling guard dog, Maxie. Write to Julie at PO Box 5162, Grand Island, NE 68802-5162, USA.

For Steve & Carolyn Spencer
Your dedication to the arts is such a blessing to our community. You're smart, talented, generous people who've raised a wonderful family and are fun to hang out with. Carolyn, thanks for reading my books. And Steve, we'll get you on a cover one day.

Prologue

Boone Harrison never tired of standing atop the rugged Missouri River bluffs and watching the wide, slate-gray water thundering past. The dense carpet of orange, red and gold deciduous trees and evergreens lining every hill that hadn't been cleared for farming or cut out to put a road through blocked his view of the interstate and made him feel like he was the only soul around for miles.

Even though he was partial to the sheriff's badge he'd worn for almost fifteen years now, knew most of the folks in the tiny burg of Grangeport and on the farms and ranches in the surrounding county—and liked most of them—there was something peaceful, something that centered him, about getting away for a ride across his land on his buckskin quarter horse, Big Jim. Feeling Jim's warmth and strength beneath the saddle reminded Boone of where he came from. Smack-dab in the middle of the Missouri Ozarks, his family's home might not be used as a working cattle ranch any-more, but he rented out enough parcels of grazing land to a friend to keep it well maintained and looking like the thriving operation his father and grandfather before him had run.

   Pulling his gaze from the early morning fog off the river some fifty yards below his feet, Boone nudged his heels into Jim's sides and cantered up over the rise toward the gravel road leading back to the house. A small herd of Herefords scattered as he approached the gate, and for a few mutinous seconds he considered chasing after them the way he had when his parents had been running the place. Give him fifteen minutes—twenty, tops—and he'd have them rounded up and on their way to the next pasture.

   But they weren't his cattle. That wasn't his job. Boone was forty-five years old. His folks and his grandparents were gone now, and his brothers and sister had moved on. Buried in the county cemetery, married and raising kids in town, gone to the big city to make a career or simply thumbing their noses at ranch life. Boone might be the only one still living on the land where they'd all been raised, but he had other responsibilities now.

   Leaving the cattle to settle back down to their sleepy breakfasts, he reined in Jim. "Ho, boy."

   The big buckskin snorted clouds of steam in the chilly autumn air as Boone leaned over the saddle horn to unhook the gate. With the skilled precision of the ten years they'd been taking this morning ride together, Jim walked through the gate. Boone refastened it and, with nothing more than a touch on the reins, Jim trotted up to the road.

   Boone had already noticed the tire tracks in the dusty gravel before he topped the next rise.

   Company wasn't part of the morning routine.

   Instantly on guard without making a fuss about it, Boone checked the gun on his belt, then pulled back the front of his jacket to reveal the badge on his tan uniform shirt. He adjusted his Stetson low over his forehead and rode the horse in to see who'd come out to the house so early in the day.

He recognized the green departmental SUV parked behind his black farm truck and knew the news wasn't good. Occasionally over the years, an inmate had escaped from the prison on the opposite side of the river, and his team had been put on alert. More often there was an accident on one of the highways that crisscrossed through town. Sometimes there was a drunk or a domestic disturbance, but his men could handle calls like that without his guidance.

This was something different. Flint Larson, the young man in the tan shirt and brown uniform slacks that matched Boone's own, stopped his pacing and came to face him at the edge of the porch.

Boone reined in Big Jim, and stayed in the saddle to look Flint in the eye. "What is it?" he asked, skipping any greeting.

They weren't so backward that cell phones and landlines didn't work out here. A visit to the house meant something personal. The pale cast beneath the deputy's tanned skin confirmed it.

"It's Janie." Boone's sister, the youngest of the Harrison clan. A failed engagement to the blond man standing on his porch, and the desire for something more than small-town living, had taken her two and a half hours away to Kansas City more than a year ago. "She's dead." Flint's voice broke with emotion before he steeled his jaw and continued. "The office just got the call from KCPD."

Boone crushed his fist around the saddle horn, feeling Flint's words like a kick in the gut. Janie? Hell. She wasn't even thirty years old yet. She was loud and funny. She had an artist's eye and the ability to put her four older brothers in their place. He needed to call those brothers. As the oldest, they'd expect him to take charge of making arrangements. Who were her friends in the city he'd need to contact? What the hell had happened to her, anyway? Driving too fast? An illness she hadn't shared?

He squeezed his eyes shut as the questions gave way to images of growing up in the house and town flashed through his mind. A lone daughter, spoiled by her parents and big brothers, overprotected, well loved. She could be just as rowdy as the rest of them, yet turn on the ladylike charm whenever…

The images froze and he snapped his eyes back open. Hold on. "The police?"

"Yes, sir." Flint shifted on his feet. He had to be feeling the shock and loss, too. "That's not the worst of it."

What could be worse than Janie's bright light being taken from the world?

"Tell me."

"She was raped and murdered."

Chapter One

Police psychologist Dr. Kate Kilpatrick shivered against the chill that lingered in the damp air and tightened the belt of her chocolate-brown trench coat as she hurried along the sidewalk to the crime scene. She hated being cold. And if this early October morning was any indication, then she was in for a long winter.

Impossibly long if she had to face any more visits to this revitalized area of Kansas City and deal with the job she'd been summoned to.

High heels, the KCPD auxiliary identification hanging around her neck, and the confident authority that she'd honed into a suit of armor over the years got the gathering crowd to part and let her pass with little more than a nod or a touch. She spotted the lanky, red-haired detective, Spencer Montgomery, who headed up the serial rapist task force she'd been assigned to, standing near the yellow crime scene tape that blocked the entrance to an alley between a local flower shop and a gutted warehouse building that was being remade into shops, offices and loft apartments. Summoning her courage on a deep breath, Kate turned off her emotions and braced herself for the death and violence reportedly on the other side of that yellow tape.

"Officer Taylor." She approached the tall, brawny K-9 officer who was guarding the scene with the proportionately big and muscular German shepherd panting beside him.

He touched the brim of his KCPD ball cap. "Ma'am."

She grinned up at him. The two had recently become acquainted with his assignment to the task force, as well. "I told you to call me Kate."

"If you call me Pike."

"Done." The nickname was unusual, but the charm was genuine.

The K-9 officer pointed to the trio of police officers conferring next to the wall at the edge of the alley. "They're over there…Kate."

"Thanks, Pike." She stepped around him and the dog to join the rest of the team. "Detective Montgomery."

"Doc." Spencer turned from the conversation he'd been having with his shorter, dark-haired partner and a copper-haired female officer she recognized as Nick Fensom and Maggie Wheeler, an investigator and a victim interview specialist also assigned to the KCPD task force. "The CSIs are nearly done processing the scene where the body was found, and we're conducting an initial canvas of the neighborhood." His report was as measured and concise as the tone of his voice. "Our Rose Red Rapist has stayed true to his pattern. The abduction occurred late at night after the victim closed up the shop for her boss—she was dead by two or three in the morning. This is the dump site, not where the assault occurred—and thus far we haven't turned up any witnesses." He handed over his notebook and let her study the observations he'd recorded. "You ready for this?"

"Not especially." She nodded a good morning to Nick and Maggie. She tipped her head toward the closed-off street behind her. "Is there any way we can thin this crowd out a little bit? And turn off the flashing lights? There's been enough speculation about the Rose Red Rapist escalating the violence of his attacks. All this commotion is only adding fuel to the fire of public panic."

"I'll take care of it," Maggie volunteered. She turned her mouth to the radio clipped to her jacket and started issuing orders.

"Thanks." Kate caught Maggie's hand and squeezed it before she could walk away, silently asking her former patient how she was handling the pressure of the unsolved investigation and the horrible memories the scene in the alleyway must have triggered.

"I'm good," Maggie reassured her, returning the squeeze with a real smile and reminding Kate of the engagement ring the uniformed officer now wore on her left hand. "It's the first time one of the assault victims has been found dead."

"Did you see the body?" Kate asked.

Maggie nodded, her smile fading. "That woman fought hard for her life. But I'm a fighter, too. Doing something to help put that bastard away helps me handle it all. So I'm good. We'll catch up later, okay?"

More friend than counselor now, Kate agreed. "I owe you a cup of tea. Give me a call."

"Will do."

Kate stuffed her hand back into the warmth of her coat pocket as the other woman walked away, and skimmed Detective Montgomery's notes before handing the book back to him. After discovering Maggie's affinity for understanding the victims of sexual assault, Kate's role on the commissioner's task force had shifted slightly. She wasn't a trained investigator, and she hadn't suffered a terrifying attack the way Maggie had, but she understood people. As a trained psychologist who counseled members of the police force and assisted with suspect interviews and criminal profiling, Kate knew how to read a face, a room, an entire crowd. She had a way with words—she knew when to talk, when to listen—and she knew what to say. In a city being terrorized by a serial rapist who'd reappeared in May after a ten-year hiatus, and had claimed his latest victim sometime last night, nerves were on edge.

It was her job to put those nerves to rest.

"I'm assuming you've moved the press to a neutral location?" She turned her attention to the two detectives.

Nick Fensom groused at the camera flash that went off on the other side of the street barricade. "Except for a couple of photographers trying to get a shot of the corpse—" he raised his voice to chide the photographer "—which we've already moved—"

"Nick," Spencer cautioned, quieting his partner.

The shorter man held his hands out in a begrudging apology. "The reporters are in front of the Robin's Nest Florist Shop, where the vic worked."

Just catty-corner across the street from where the previous victim had been abducted outside a local bridal shop. Kate nodded to the shop owner standing at the window of Fairy Tale Bridal, suspecting she and the other women who lived and worked in this neighborhood were beginning to rethink their choice of the trendy, upscale location. Two assaults in just six months—attacks that were brutal, traceless and now deadly—must be making every woman afraid of her own shadow, and every man look like a potential suspect.

Not to mention what news of another rape had to be doing for local business. With a determined intake of breath, Kate looked to her left, spotting the group of television cameras, broadcast vans, microphones and reporters waiting for her to make a statement on behalf of the task force. "I doubt the flower shop owner will be thrilled with this kind of publicity. I'll set up on the sidewalk facing north so the storefront won't be behind me in the picture."

"Good point." The detective reached out to stop a young officer who was assisting with crowd control. A sly glance at his navy blue uniform identified him. "Estes?"

"Yes, sir?"

"I need you to help Dr. Kilpatrick move this crowd of reporters down half a block or so."

"Right away, sir." The young man was barely in his twenties. He was new to the job and eager to please the senior officer. "Dr. Kilpatrick."

"Hi, Pete." She knew the rookie cop from a couple of counseling sessions on anger management issues he'd had that had carried over from his off-duty life into his work. "How are you doing today?"

"Haven't gotten myself into trouble yet."

"Good to hear." Kate summoned the necessary smile to send him on his way. She wore a more serious expression when she handed the notebook back to Detective Montgomery. "It's my understanding that the

Rose Red Rapist *hasn't* stayed true to his pattern. The woman he attacked is dead?"

Spencer nodded. "Blow to the head. M.E.'s office has her now. They'll have to tell us if it was intentional or the result of the struggle—maybe the vic saw his face or managed to get away, and he did it to stop her."

Two things that hadn't happened with any of the Rose Red Rapist's previous—surviving—victims. Changes in a perp's behavioral patterns could mean something as simple and tragic as silencing a witness to his crimes. But it could also indicate a psychotic break—a dangerous development that meant his attacks would become both more frequent and more violent.

Kate had counseled plenty of assault victims before, but she'd never been assigned to work on a case where the victim hadn't survived. "And we're sure it's our guy? And not a sick coincidence?"

The crime lab liaison assigned to the task force, Annie Hermann, approached the opposite side of the crime scene tape, holding up a bagged red rose in her gloved hand. "I don't know anyone else who leaves one of these with his victim. I'll run an analysis, but I'm betting it came from the flower shop where she worked."

"That's gutsy." Detective Fensom lifted the tape for the petite brunette in the navy blue CSI jacket to join them. "Buying a flower from the woman you plan to attack later? She probably looked him right in the face."

"Could be why he killed her," Annie theorized. After a moment's hesitation, she tucked her curly dark hair behind her ear and crossed beneath Detective Fensom's arm to join their circle. "Maybe he was a regular customer and she recognized him by the sound of his voice, even if he did wear a mask to hide his face the way his other victims describe. If she called him by name, that could have been her death sentence."

Kate offered another, more disturbing explanation. "Or maybe rape is no longer satisfying enough for our unsub to display his power over the women he attacks."

Spencer Montgomery tucked his notebook inside the front of his suit jacket. "Yeah, well, let's keep that tidbit of information to ourselves. The city's already on edge. If they believe it's a onetime thing, and not an escalation in the violence of his attacks, we might ease somebody's fears."

Kate nodded her agreement and inhaled another fortifying breath.

"Go work your magic, Kate," Spencer encouraged her. "You calm this chaos down and we'll finish up here."

"Right. We'll debrief later at the precinct?"

Detective Montgomery nodded. "This afternoon, if possible."

"Keep me posted."

As the detectives and CSI went back to work, Kate pulled up the sleeve of her coat to make sure her watch was visible. Short and sweet was the key to a successful press conference. She was already formulating a brief statement and would set a time limit for entertaining questions. When she was done, she'd send the press away to make their preliminary reports and tell the residents of Kansas City to remain cautious but not to panic—that KCPD was on the job. Then she could get back to her office at the Fourth Precinct to get some real work done on unmasking a serial rapist turned murderer and get him off the streets.

Kate raised her hands to silence the onslaught of

questions that greeted her and took her position on the sidewalk. She pushed aside a microphone that had gotten too close to her face and squinted as the bright lights of numerous cameras suddenly spotlighted her.

"Ladies and gentlemen, if I could have your attention, please." As her eyes adjusted to the unnatural brightness, some of the faces in the crowd began to take shape. She recognized Gabriel Knight, a reporter for the *Kansas City Journal* and one of KCPD's harshest critics. She knew Rebecca Cartwright, another reporter who happened to be the daughter-in-law of KCPD's commissioner, and who would no doubt put a more positive spin on things than Knight would.

She hesitated for one awkward, painful, debilitating moment when she spotted Vanessa Owen, a woman who reported local news for one of the city's television stations. Vanessa's caramel skin, dark brown hair and smoothly articulate voice had become a fixture on Kansas City televisions. She'd once been a fixture in Kate's life, as well. Vanessa had been a good friend, a sorority sister from college who continued to move in the same social circles as they established careers and marriages after graduation. The story between them that mattered the most had thankfully never been aired, though at times like this, the events that marked the end of their friendship still burned like a raw wound in Kate's chest.

But Kate was here to do her job, just as Vanessa was here to do hers. This wasn't personal. *Suck it up, counselor. You're in control here. KCPD made you spokesperson for the task force because they know you can handle it.* And with that mental pep talk sending her emotions back into the protective vault inside her, Kate blinked and moved on with the job at hand.

Beyond that first row of reporters, the lights and flashes and eager crowd made identifying others in the sea of faces nearly impossible. "I'm Dr. Kate Kilpatrick. I'm a police psychologist and public liaison officer with KCPD."

Gabriel Knight didn't wait for any further introduction. "Is it true that the Rose Red Rapist's latest assault victim is dead?"

Biting her tongue to maintain a patient facade, Kate looked straight into the reporter's probing blue eyes. "I will be making a brief statement on behalf of the department and the task force investigating the attack, and then I will have time for a handful of questions."

"Make your statement," Knight challenged.

Kate eased the tension she felt into a serene smile and included the entire gathering, including Vanessa Owen, in her speech. "A twenty-eight-year-old woman was sexually assaulted in this neighborhood last night, sometime between ten p.m. and three o'clock this morning. There was a rose left at the scene, indicating the attack was committed by the man—" she paused and held out her hands, placing the blame for their perp's notoriety squarely where it belonged "—*you* have dubbed as the Rose Red Rapist."

"Kate, is the woman dead?" Vanessa stole Gabriel Knight's question before he could ask it.

Although she bristled beneath her coat at the liberty her old friend had taken in addressing her by name, Kate merely nodded. "Yes. We are in the preliminary stages of a murder investigation—"

"Who was she?" Vanessa followed up.

"—and pending more exact information and notification of the family, I can't give more details at this time."

"Kate," Vanessa prodded. "You have to give us something."

She looked straight into the camera beside Vanessa. "This is what I can tell you. We *will* find this man. The task force members investigating these crimes are top-notch specialists—the best in KCPD. I guarantee that we will not rest until this attacker is caught and arrested."

A commotion at the rear of the crowd diverted Vanessa's and Gabriel Knight's attention for a moment, but the cameras were still rolling, so Kate continued with the briefing. "Rest assured that KCPD and the commissioner's task force are doing everything in our power to identify the attacker and ascertain whether or not this crime is related to the attack that occurred in May, or to others that have occurred in previous years."

The shuffling of movement and *Hey's* and *What the's?* in the crowd behind them finally garnered Gabriel's and Vanessa's attention, too.

The spotlight faded as cameras turned to see what the fuss was about. Normally, Kate was relieved when the cameras turned away to give her the privacy she preferred, but she had to say what she was required to say. "KCPD urges the women of Kansas City to practice common safety procedures. Don't walk alone after dark. Lock your cars and doors. Carry your keys or even pepper spray in your hand, and be sure to check under and around your vehicle before approaching it. Remember that KCPD is offering free self-protection workshops, or you can look into classes offered elsewhere. And finally we ask that everyone remain vigilant...."

Kate's voice tapered off as the lights followed the parting of the crowd, splitting like a crack in an icy lake, and heading straight toward her.

"Sir, you're gonna have to..." She thought she heard Pete Estes's voice, but it faded into the growing buzz of the crowd.

She spotted a cowboy hat and broad shoulders a moment before Gabriel Knight was pushed aside and a man dressed in a tan-and-brown uniform and insulated jacket stood before her. His eyes, dark like rich earth and shadowed by the brim of his hat, captured hers.

"Who are you?" Vanessa asked beside him. "Are you connected to this investigation? Has KCPD called in outside help?"

But the questions went unheeded as the dark focus of the man's eyes never left Kate.

"Are you in charge here?" His dark voice was just as coolly efficient, just as menacing, as the gun and badge next to the hand splayed at his hip.

Rarely at a loss for words, Kate cursed the splutter of hesitation she heard in her voice. But she shook off the foolish reaction and came up with a diplomatic answer. "I'm part of the task force that's in charge— Hey!"

Apparently, something she'd said was good enough for him. Immune to the flash of lights and uncaring of the public recording of the scene he was making, the cowboy closed his grip around Kate's arm and pulled her aside. If he hadn't been wearing a badge that identified him as law enforcement, Kate might have protested further.

"Lady, I've been driving ever since the report came over the wire early this morning."

"What report?"

With the interview effectively ended, she quickened her pace to keep up with his long strides. And though she tugged against his hand, his hold on her never wavered.

"What can you tell me about the woman you found in that alley?" he demanded.

"Excuse me, but we have rules about how a press conference is conducted here in Kansas City. We also have rules about interdepartmental investigations. If you need to speak to someone about a case, then you—"

"I'm only interested in this case." She nearly pitched off her pumps when he abruptly stopped to test the door on a nearby storefront. That same strong hand kept her upright and pulled her inside the boutique beside him, beyond the flashes of cameras and noise of the reporters and curious onlookers. Once he released her and shooed away the store clerk who offered to help them, Kate could face him. Only then did she see the jet-black hair with shots of silver at the temples. Only then did she clearly make out the chiseled jaw and six feet or so of height. Only then did she detect the scents of leather and man and some unnamed emotion that made her back up half a step.

"Who are you?" she asked.

This time, he answered. "I'm sheriff of Alton County."

Alton County? Central Missouri? "What are you doing here…?" Temper turned to confusion. She sputtered again while her brain shifted gears. "How do you know about the murder? We haven't even released her name to the public, pending notification of her family."

"You've notified them," Sheriff Cowboy stated. "My name's Boone Harrison. Jane Harrison is…was…my baby sister. I want to know who the hell killed her, and what you're doing to find him."

Chapter Two

Boone paused at the doors leading from the medical
examiner's lab into the morgue and autopsy room. He
pulled off his hat, working the brim between his fingers
as he looked through the glass windows to the stainless
steel tables inside.

He watched a dark-haired woman in blue scrubs and
a white lab coat working beneath the bright lights at
the middle table. She wore gloves and a surgical mask.
And as she circled around the table, the front of her lab
coat gaped open, revealing a baby bump on her belly.

But it wasn't the pregnant medical examiner who
had his attention. He wasn't even shocked by the tray
of wicked-looking tools or the cart filled with saws and
hoses, glass containers and evidence bags.

Boone touched his fingers to the cool glass partition,
wishing he could reach through the glass and erase the
images before him. It wasn't his first dead body or even
his first murder. But it was his first and only baby sister lying there—her life cut short, her beautiful laugh
silenced forever.

His jaw ached with the tight clench of muscles holding back the tears and curses. And his gut was an open

pit of anger, grief and failure, eating him up from the inside out.

"You don't have to do this, Sheriff Harrison." The firm, slightly husky tones of the blonde woman standing beside him filtered into his brain, tossing him a lifeline back to the reality at hand. Dr. Kate Kilpatrick stood shoulder to shoulder with him, viewing the same scene he was, maintaining a calm strength he couldn't seem to find within himself. "Certainly not right now. Give us some time to work first, and then I'll call you. I promise."

He flattened his palm against the glass and pushed the swinging door open. "I need to see her."

Startled, the medical examiner looked up from her work. She zeroed in on Boone and straightened to attention. "You shouldn't be in here. Hi, Kate."

"Sorry, Holly." Dr. Kate's hand on his arm slowed him a step, giving her the chance to reach the steel table before he could. "Dr. Holly Masterson-Kincaid, medical examiner. This is Sheriff Boone Harrison from Alton County." But she wasn't much of a wedge when it came to stopping him. Boone moved in beside her, looking down at the raven-haired woman on the table. "He believes the victim is his sister."

"Well, then, he really shouldn't be in here right now." The M.E. reached for the sheet draped at the foot of the table. "I'm just about to start... Hey!" She swatted Boone's hand from across the table. "Don't touch her. Please." She covered the body up to the shoulders as gently as if she was tucking a child into bed. "There may be evidence on her."

"I won't compromise anything."

"Sheriff?" He felt Kate's hand on his forearm again,

but there was more comfort than warning in this particular touch, and his gaze locked on to the elegant, pale, practically manicured fingers resting on his sleeve. "Perhaps we should wait outside and let the doctor work."

But he'd already seen the bruises on Janie's knuckles and the torn fingernails. He'd already noted the sticky-looking mat of hair beneath her head, indicating the blow that had ended her life. The worst of the bloody wound was hidden from view. There was nothing the M.E. or the police psychologist needed to hide from him. The loss had already imprinted itself in his brain, and deeper—in his heart. Boone's sister had been a firecracker in life. He couldn't remember ever seeing her this still, not even in sleep.

But the shell of the girl he'd grown up with was still there.

"It's her. It's Janie." He lifted his gaze to the moss-colored eyes looking up at him. But the emotion there quickly shuttered, neutralizing their color to a grayish-green before Dr. Kate pulled her hand away. With that unconscious bit of caring denied him, Boone cleared his throat and looked over at the dark-haired doctor. "Jane Beatrice Harrison. Named for both our grandmothers. She's twenty-eight. Born and raised on a ranch outside Grangeport, Missouri. Moved to K.C. about a year ago. She's single, but dating, I think. Worked at a florist's shop. Taught evening art classes at one of the community colleges here."

The M.E. picked up a computerized clipboard and started logging in some of the details he was sharing.

Boone's breath got stuck in his chest and he exhaled a big sigh before he could continue. "I talked to her on the phone just last week. But I haven't seen her since the Fourth of July. The family gets together for a big celebration—fireworks, food. One of my brothers has a cabin on the lake. She got a sunburn out tubing on the water with our nieces and nephew." Something numbing and merciless was eating its way through every nerve of his body, robbing him of rational thought. "Janie loved those kids."

"Is there anything else you can tell us about her life here in Kansas City?" Dr. Kilpatrick asked. "Any specifics about her daily routine?"

The answers drifted out of his brain. For a few moments, it seemed it was all he could do to stay on his feet and take in the world around him. Boone was aware of the two women processing everything he'd said. Holly Masterson-Kincaid was dark, dressed in white. Her hair was long and wavy and anchored in a ponytail at her nape. Kate Kilpatrick was fair, dressed in deep chocolate brown. Her hair was short and chic, with every strand falling into place. Both women were in their thirties, although he guessed the blonde to be slightly older than the brunette. Both women had their eyes on him, watching him with a mix of trepidation and concern. *Get it together, Harrison.*

Man, that Dr. Kate was a cool customer. He'd practically abducted her to get the answers he needed. He'd been bossy and on edge, yet she'd stayed calm and composed when she'd had every right to slap his face or call for backup to haul him away. She could have blown him off as the crazy out-of-towner stomping into their official territory, yet she'd answered every question with clear, if guarded, precision, and offered to bring him to the morgue herself.

Some part of his foggy brain knew she was probably running interference, keeping him away from the CSIs and detectives investigating the crime scene and talking to potential witnesses. But she could have called a uniform to drive him through town. She could have arranged for a receptionist to guide him down to the building's basement morgue. Instead, she'd volunteered to handle the ol' bull-in-the-big-city country boy herself. That took a lot of compassion, and probably more guts than the woman realized.

If Kate Kilpatrick could keep it together on a morning like this, then maybe he'd better do the same. With a nod that was directed to the highly trained law enforcement professional pushing its way through the emotions inside him, Boone summoned the detachment that had gotten him through a lot of disturbing crime scenes and graphic traffic accidents. "Has the body been cleaned up yet?" he asked.

The M.E.'s lips parted, in surprise, he supposed. But she set aside the computer pad and answered in a tone much less clinical than the one he'd used. "I was in the middle of processing when you showed up. If you'd given me some advance notice—"

"There was some jewelry she always wore." Boone brushed his fingertips against the collar of his shirt. "A necklace of my mother's. Three or four silver and turquoise rings she'd made. Janie was an arts-and-craftsy kind of gal. She took a jewelry-making class once."

The M.E. pointed to the paper envelopes and plastic sheaves on the table behind her. "The rings are in evidence bags, waiting to go to the lab upstairs. I didn't see a necklace. But there are clear signs of a struggle."

She looked back across the table to Kate, with a look

that could only be described as a plea for help. When Boone refused to budge, Dr. Kilpatrick nodded, giving her some sort of permission to continue sharing information with him. He needed to know everything—no matter how gruesome, no matter how tragic. His only solace right now was information—and the justice it would lead him to.

Resuming a mantle of detached practicality, Dr. Masterson-Kincaid pointed one of her gloved fingers at the thin, purplish-gray bruise bisecting Janie's delicate collar bone. "That would explain this mark. Looks like a chain around her neck was ripped off. Perimortem, judging by the bruising."

Another treasure stolen from his family. "Did the bastard take it as a souvenir?"

The blonde beside him shook her head. "That doesn't fit the profile. The Rose Red Rapist hasn't collected tokens in the past, but it is important to note. Maybe he overlooked it when he was cleaning up the scene."

"Back in that alley?" Boone would make time for a detour to search the place himself.

Kate shook her head and stepped aside to pull her cell phone from her pocket. "The body was found at a secondary location, like the others. But if we can locate the necklace, we might just find our primary crime scene." Her gaze slipped up to Boone, no doubt assessing how much information from their interchange he was taking in, as well as what he intended to do with that information. "Can you give me a description of the necklace?"

"A sterling silver locket. Heart-shaped, with a picture of our folks inside."

"I found a trace of some sort of metallic substance

in her hair—could be a piece of a broken necklace. I'll call Annie and Detective Montgomery to alert them to keep an eye out for it."

Dr. Masterson-Kincaid circled around the table, urging both her guests to clear the space around the examination table. "I'll give you some privacy while you're making your call. I need to take a break and phone my husband, anyway." She rested her hand on her belly and crossed to the double swinging doors. "Ever since we got the news about the baby, he's become a little more overprotective. If that's possible. Um." Boone glanced over his shoulder as she waited at the door to get his attention. "Take a few moments to grieve with your sister, Sheriff Harrison. But when I get back, I *do* need to get work. Alone."

"Thank you, ma'am."

"And remember, don't touch anything."

Boone nodded.

After the dark-haired woman left, Kate apparently decided to give him some space, too. "I'll go out there to make my calls, allow you some quiet time—"

"Don't." Not understanding the impulse, but not questioning it, either, he reached out and grabbed Kate's arm. He tugged her back to his side and turned, ignoring her startled gasp as he pulled her into his chest and hugged his arms around her. "Not yet."

"Sheriff, I…"

For a few moments, she stood there, rigid as a barn board, her arms down at her sides, her nose pressed into his chest. He knew he'd surprised her, knew he was taking liberties with a woman he barely knew. But he needed human contact right now. He needed the reassurance of a beating heart. He needed something strong to hold on to, something soft to absorb the pain and the rage and the grief roiling inside him that threatened to drag him down to his knees and bring him to tears.

As unexpected as the contact might be, there was a sensitive side to the police psychologist he must have tapped into. He felt her slender frame swell against him with a deep breath. And then she nudged her chin up onto his shoulder, wound her arms around his neck and stretched up on tiptoe to hug him back.

"Hush." She whispered soft words against his ear. Meaningless syllables that soothed him. "I'm so sorry, Boone. Shh."

Her body was flush against his, her arms around his neck and shoulders clinging almost as tightly as he held her. Boone buried his nose in the delicious scent of her honey-blond hair and let the grief overtake him in deep, stuttering breaths.

He held on as he purged the onslaught of emotion. Sensation by sensation, the blinding need eased and his body and spirit revived. Kate Kilpatrick was of average height, but the high heels she wore lengthened her legs and made her just the right size to fit against him like a hand to a glove. There was nothing remarkable about the shape of her body other than that the subtle curves were all there, in just the right places. She was a sophisticated blend of jasmine shampoo and woman and class.

She was businesslike yet compassionate, strong in body and resolve, yet she was the softest thing he'd held in his arms in a long time. At this moment, she was everything he needed.

But his timing couldn't be worse.

With something else waking inside him—something

that was more about family and the job, more about protecting one's own than it was about himself—his wants, his needs and the beautiful woman who'd assuaged them both for a few stolen moments—Boone pulled his hands up to Kate's shoulders and abruptly pushed her away.

He needed the chilly rush of air-conditioning filling the gap between them. He needed to see the self-conscious splotches of color on Kate Kilpatrick's cheeks. He needed to watch her straighten the front of her coat and tug the sleeves back into place.

He needed to see her fixing her personal armor around her so he could do the same himself.

"Sorry about that, ma'am," he apologized.

"Not a problem, Sheriff." She smoothed her short hair back behind her ears. "Sometimes grief can be too much to bear. And I was here."

"You've already done more for me than you should." And yet he had to ask her to do something else. As of this moment he knew Kate Kilpatrick better than anyone in Kansas City, now that Janie was gone. They were virtual strangers, yet she was the closest thing he had to a friend right now. She was also the best source of information he'd found thus far. Dr. Kate was a pipeline straight to the detectives who were working Janie's case. He glanced over to give his sister one last loving look, before facing the police psychologist's guarded expression. "I want to see the crime scene and any evidence your team has on Janie's murder and the previous rapes that bastard committed."

The green eyes blinked. Dr. Kate was shaking her head. "Sheriff Harrison...Boone...you need to take your sister home. You need to take care of your family right now."

He set his hat on his head, adjusting the crown to its familiar, comfortable fit. He closed his fingers around the crisp sleeve of Kate Kilpatrick's trench coat and the warmer, softer woman underneath, and walked her to the door with him.

Her psych degree and whatever heat was simmering beneath that cool exterior might have her programmed to be all touchy-feely with his emotions. But he didn't have the time to feel right now. "I need to work."

THE MAN PEELED OFF his shirt and tossed it into the hamper beside the socks and pants he'd worn last night.

His eyes were glued to the television across from his bed, and on the haughty blonde being interviewed on the morning news show. He paused, stripping down to his skivvies. The bitch was looking right at him, taunting him.

"We will find this man. The task force members investigating these crimes are top-notch specialists—the best in KCPD. I guarantee that we will not rest until this attacker is caught and arrested."

His gaze dropped to the bottom of the screen as the press conference was interrupted. He didn't really notice the cowboy or the commotion of wonky camera angles and muffled sounds as the reporters scrambled to pursue them. He was reading the words scrolling across the bottom of the screen—*Dr. Kate Kilpatrick, KCPD police psychologist and task force liaison officer.*

A shrink. He could just bet that woman wanted to get inside his head. Change him. Fix him.

A familiar resentment boiled inside him. *"We will*

find this man?" he mocked. "You wish. You've got nothing on me, woman." She thought she could threaten him, intimidate him into making a mistake. This one looked right at him and challenged him. Yet she looked all sympathetic, like she thought she could help him. Like he needed help. "I didn't do those things. There's nothing wrong with me."

Dr. Kate Kilpatrick was all blond hair and sharp tongue and classic beauty. She looked so much like *her.* She sounded like *her.* That entitled, smarter-than-him attitude was just like *her.*

Despite everything he'd done, despite the promises he'd made, *she'd* talked to him as though he wasn't good enough, as if he was some kind of broken thing that needed to be fixed.

The rage spilled over into his veins. She was trying to humiliate him. Publicly. Again.

A nagging voice of reason piped up in his head. *It isn't her. You know she's a different woman.*

No. Women like that were all the same.

He could feel the irritation crawling beneath his skin. They took. They demanded. They emasculated. If they ever deigned to notice him, that is. A woman like that—so confident, so beautiful—she'd look right through him. *You don't know that,* the voice argued. *Don't let her get to you. She'll make trouble for you if you let her get to you.*

"She won't get to me." He read the name scrolling across the bottom of the screen again. Kate Kilpatrick. She'd mocked him. Right there on television, for all the world to see.

He rolled his neck, scratching at the itch beneath his skin until he realized there was blood beneath his fingernails. Feeling the sticky stain on his fingertips more than the pain in his forearm, he dashed into the bathroom to check the mark in the mirror—to assure himself that *he* had put the mark there. There was no DNA that the brunette from the flower shop had taken from him.

He'd never make a mistake like that.

Breathing away the momentary panic, assuring himself that no woman had dared to get the better of him, he turned on the water in the sink and let it run hot before he picked up the soap and plunged his hands beneath the spray. After he'd washed his hands, using a brush to get rid of any trace of blood or skin beneath his nails, he opened the medicine cabinet. He pulled out rubbing alcohol, medicated ointment and plastic bandages to doctor the scratch he'd made, reveling in the sharp bite of pain that cleared his thoughts.

You were too smart. Too careful. The voice praised him, stroking his ego and fueling his pride. *You didn't make any mistakes.*

"Damn right I didn't." His heart rate slowed and his breathing evened out as the utter self-assurance of his actions returned.

Once he had finished doctoring his wound, he returned to the bedroom to remove the last of his clothes. Using his undershirt as a barrier to keep from touching any buttons, he picked up the remote and turned off the blonde liar and the morning news.

Then he stepped into the shower to clean up and get dressed for work.

Chapter Three

"You let Janie close up the store all by herself that late at night?" Boone braced one hand on the cash register and leaned over the counter at the Robin's Nest Florist Shop.

"I trust her with my keys. She's my assistant manager... Trusted. She *was* my—"

"After eleven o'clock? In the dark? Knowing that bastard was running around out there?"

"We close at nine p.m. Why was she here that late?"

"You tell me."

Boone couldn't keep the raw tinge of frustration out of his voice, and knew that the clipped tone and deep pitch and bulk of his shoulders were probably more intimidation than the brown-haired woman hugging the design book to her chest could handle. But damn it all, that redheaded detective in the suit had run him out of the alley where Janie had been found, and then set up a brick wall of a K-9 cop and his German shepherd sidekick to keep him away from the crime scene.

Normally, he was a patient man, a methodical investigator. But this crime burned far too close to the heart. His family was his responsibility, and he'd already failed if his sister had suffered so and ended up dead. He needed answers to why this unthinkable act of violence had happened—and he needed them sooner rather than later if he was going to have any chance of assuaging the guilt and rage and grief thundering along with every blood cell in his veins. If KCPD wouldn't let him comb through the crime scene with fresh eyes, then his next best avenue was to retrace Janie's steps yesterday and start talking to the people she'd had contact with.

The jingle of a bell over the shop's front door should have served as a warning to rethink this interview.

"We're closed today." The woman glanced at the intruder, maybe hoping for a polite escape, but the approaching customer only made him lower his voice and lean in closer.

"How long had Janie been working for you?"

The shopkeeper's blue eyes darted back to his. "Almost a year."

"And those were her regular hours? Did she close every night?"

"We traded off." She tried to look away again.

"Was it a regular routine? The same nights each week? Something that anyone watching this place for any length of time could pick up on?"

The blue eyes widened in shock and focused on him again. "I didn't realize I was putting her in danger like that. Yes, I suppose she'd had the same schedule for a couple of months—"

"Are you Robin?" Boone sniffed jasmine in the air a split-second before the softly articulate voice beside him spoke. The blonde in the brown trench coat rested a warning hand on his forearm, and the skin beneath his jacket danced at the unexpected touch.

Suspicion colored the shopkeeper's voice. "Yes?"

The lady cop psychologist who smelled better than any fragrance in the floral shop extended her hand. "I'm Dr. Kate Kilpatrick, KCPD. I'm a psychologist with the department and a public liaison officer."

The other woman set her design book on the counter and reached over to shake Kate's hand. "I'm Robin Carter. I own this shop."

Dr. Kate's steady voice and calm presence were quickly defusing both the florist's fears and Boone's own unthinking rudeness. "My colleague, Sheriff Harrison, here brings up a good point. For women, especially, it's smart to vary your schedule from time to time when it comes to personal safety. I know it can be hard to close the shop at different times, but don't work late every night, park in different locations, have someone meet you here from time to time, and so on." Perhaps sensing that he had a dubious control over his emotions again, she pulled her hand away and tucked it into the pocket of her coat. "People with predictable routines make themselves easier targets for a mugger or rapist to ambush."

The shopkeeper's skin paled beneath the blush on her cheeks. "I never thought of that. I'll make sure my entire staff knows. Thank you."

Boone's emotions might be in check, but that didn't mean he was finished here. "Ms. Carter and I were just having a little chat."

"Say, do you mind if I ask you a few questions?" Did Kate Kilpatrick just nudge her shoulder between him and the counter? Pushing him out of this conversation? Her move was subtle, putting a few more inches of protective distance between him and the woman he wanted to talk to. "Where were you last night? When was the last time you actually saw or talked to Miss Harrison? And was she alone?"

Fine. Questions he would have asked. As long as they got answered, he wouldn't nudge back.

"I had to leave early in the afternoon for a doctor's appointment." Kate waited expectantly—a patient ploy that often made a witness nervous enough to keep on sharing information to fill the silence. The woman had interrogation skills, for sure. Robin Carter tucked a lock of coffee-colored hair behind her ear and continued. "I was at the Lyddon-Wells Clinic. I've been going through in vitro procedures, trying to get pregnant via a sperm donor. You know, single career woman—biological clock ticking and all that. Yesterday the doctor called me in for a pregnancy report. Janie knew it was important to me, so she volunteered to switch nights with me. I left at three-thirty, and except for any customers she might have had, she was alone."

"Did you get the results you wanted?"

Robin hugged her arms in front of her and shook her head. "It didn't take this time, either. He suggested I look at adopting."

Boone didn't pretend to know about how a woman might feel if her hopes for a pregnancy fell through. His ex had put off starting a family year after year until he finally realized that she'd put their marriage on hold, too.

But apparently, Kate understood. "I'm sorry about the baby. Do you know who Janie was seeing?"

Boone tipped his hat back on his head at the abrupt change of topic. Catching the witness off guard was another smart tactic. He'd learned all the same interrogation strategies, but Dr. Kate's skills put his to shame today.

"No," Robin answered. "But I think it was pretty serious."

That was the first Boone had heard of a new man in his sister's life. Screw keeping his distance. He leaned forward again, his chest butting into Kate's shoulder. "Janie was in a serious relationship?"

The shopkeeper's gaze shot back to his, and Boone let Dr. Kate shrug him into a less-threatening position again. "She stopped talking about her love life, er, who she was dating, these last few weeks. Wouldn't go out for a drink with me after work anymore. Now that I think about it, she was secretive a lot lately. I'd interrupt a personal call and she'd quickly hang up. I invited her to bring a date to a staff party and she came alone. Left early, too."

"You don't have a name for this mysterious boyfriend?" Boone asked.

"I don't remember her ever mentioning it. And if he came to the shop, I never knew about it. She didn't treat anyone more special than her usual friendly self." Robin pulled a tissue from the apron she wore and dabbed at the sheen of tears in her eyes. "I'm going to miss that smile. Sorry I can't be more help."

Kate reached across the counter to squeeze the other woman's hand. "You've been a big help already, Robin."

Kate might be signing off on this interview, but Boone needed more. "Do you have any idea where she would have met this guy?"

For the first time during the entire conversation, Kate tipped her face up to his and looked him straight in the eye. Reprimand noted. And ignored. He opened his mouth to follow up, but Kate beat him to the punch. "I understand what you mean about devoting all that time to your career." He'd bet there was a kinder, gentler expression on her face when she turned back to the shopkeeper. "Other things get…overlooked." And then she was stepping back, nodding toward the front door. "Shall we?"

Boone ignored the unspoken command to exit stage right and pulled out his wallet to hand Robin Carter a business card. "If you think of anything, don't hesitate to call me…or KCPD," he added before Kate could correct him. He paused for a moment to tip the brim of his hat to Robin. "I'm sorry about earlier, ma'am. I'm a little upset today. But I appreciate your cooperation."

The woman sniffed back her tears and summoned a smile, appeased by the apology he'd owed her. "I can't imagine what you're going through, Sheriff. Janie was a sunny, vivacious spirit—and so talented. I'm sorry for your loss."

"You two were good friends?" Robin nodded. "Then I'm sorry for your loss, too. I'll send word about the arrangements for her services when I know them."

"I'd like that. Thank you."

Finally content to leave—for now—Boone turned to the door and gestured for Kate to precede him.

He'd barely closed the door behind them when Kate stopped in the middle of the sidewalk. She crossed her arms and tilted her face to challenge him. "You're going to scare away all our potential witnesses if you dive down their throats like that."

"I'm sorry if I scared the lady, but she had answers we needed."

"No, she had answers *I* needed. That the *task force* needed."

The lady's dander was up, all the way from the top of that honey-gold hair down to the soles of those ridiculously high, undeniably sexy heels. "Did Montgomery send you after me? I don't think your lead detective likes me," he asked.

Those mossy-green eyes held his for a moment before she turned and strolled up the street. "Where's your truck?"

Boone grinned behind her. Nice dodge. He'd take that as a yes, that Spencer Montgomery had called in cool, calm and eye-catching Dr. Kate here to corral him away from the investigation. He moved into step beside her. "How do you know I drive a truck?"

"You're a cowboy, aren't you?"

The muscles around his mouth relaxed with an actual laugh after too many hours of being clenched tight to stop up the emotions roiling inside him. He pointed a few parking spaces farther ahead to the black, diesel-powered Ford he'd driven in from Grangeport. "Yes, ma'am."

"I could tell that those boots weren't just for show."

Boone glanced down at the brown leather that was scuffed and broken in, and, okay, maybe tinged with a bit of the aroma that had driven his ex-wife off the ranch and out of his life. Although Boone hated to think of anyone as a stereotype, he supposed the Stetson and boots and badge stated exactly who he was, inside and out.

He wondered if the sophisticated facade and cool-as-a-cucumber demeanor said who Kate Kilpatrick was on the inside, as well.

Any curiosity about the pretty blonde vanished at her next comment. "The M.E. said she'll release your sister's body early tomorrow morning. Maybe you should be making those arrangements you mentioned instead of scaring away my witnesses."

He stopped beside the truck, his shoulders lifting with a weary sigh. "I can help. I've been at this job a long time and I know Janie better than any of you."

"I'm no rookie, either, Sheriff. I know Kansas City. And I know the Rose Red Rapist and how he works." She pulled a hand from her pocket and turned to face him once more. What was it about this woman's gentle touch on his arm that made each skin cell wake and warm beneath her fingers? "I'm also a psychologist. I've worked with several officers who've had to deal with the loss of a partner or a loved one, or even the death of a suspect. You need time. You need to grieve. You need to help the others in your family who are dealing with this loss, too." The warmth and subtle connection between them left when she pulled her hand back into the pocket of her coat. "Let us do this difficult work."

"Dr. Kate...." That's how he'd heard her introduce herself more than once, and that's the name that landed on his tongue. "I'm the oldest brother in my family, and our parents are gone. Janie was my responsibility. Finding who did this feels like my responsibility, too."

She nodded, perhaps understanding his guilt, or perhaps just eager to move him along out of the police department's way. "Please. Go find a hotel for the night. Did you come here by yourself? Is there someone you should call?"

Dr. Kate could maneuver a conversation six ways to Sunday, and a man had to stay on his toes to keep up—

or probe beneath that chilly control she maintained over her thoughts and feelings. He was interested in taking on the challenge, but right now he was too tuckered out emotionally to be a worthy adversary. So he relented and let her chase him off KCPD territory. For now.

"I'm a big boy, ma'am. Been taking care of myself a long time now." Boone circled around the hood of the truck and opened the door, but paused before climbing inside. "I'm glad Montgomery sent you to handle me. I'd have punched him by now."

Her chin tipped up as though his bluntness had taken her aback. And then her pink lips curved into a soft smile. "You're quite the charmer, aren't you, Sheriff?"

That glimpse of warmth through a chink in her armor made Boone feel like smiling, too. Yep, there was at least one thing he liked about Kansas City. He climbed in behind the wheel and started the engine. Then he pulled a contact card from his wallet and rolled down the passenger-side window to share one last word with Dr. Kate Kilpatrick of KCPD before driving away. "You need me for anything—you find out anything about this murder—I expect a call."

She stepped forward to take his card and it disappeared into the pocket of her trench coat along with her hand. "I will."

"See you later, Doc."

"JUST ONE QUOTE, Kate." Vanessa Owen had shown up at the precinct offices late in the afternoon, thankfully without her cameraman, and ambushed Kate the moment she stepped off the elevator onto the third floor. "I know we have history—and I know a lot of it was pretty bad—but this isn't personal."

"Nice speech." Kate took note of the visitor and press badges the dark-haired reporter wore around her neck, and quickly chucked the idea of having the doe-eyed beauty tossed out on her generous backside. Kate was in charge of public relations for the task force, after all. But that didn't mean she had to stand here and give Vanessa an exclusive interview when she'd already made a formal statement to the press earlier in the day. Skirting around the reporter, Kate headed for the temporary refuge of her private office. "If you'll excuse me, I have work to do."

When she turned the corner into the hallway leading to her office, a uniformed policeman with a buzz cut of brown hair jumped out of the chair where he'd been waiting and startled her. "Dr. Kilpatrick?"

"Pete." Kate pressed a hand over her racing heart and retreated half a step from the frantic young man who'd assisted her with controlling the crowd of reporters just that morning. "Do we have an appointment?"

"No. But my girlfriend called me at work and she said—"

"Pete." Kate stopped him before whatever the latest demand his girlfriend had requested of him turned into a full-blown rant. "I can't hold your hand through every crisis. Now we've talked about ways to improve your communication skills. Try one of those strategies to tell her what you're feeling. You have to practice them."

"But she said she'd leave me."

Vanessa invited herself into the conversation. "Officer, you interrupted us. I suggest you make that appointment."

"Vanessa."

"Five minutes of your time, Kate." Now Vanessa

was ignoring the young man altogether. "That's all I'm asking."

Keeping the irritation out of her tone, Kate patted the officer's shoulder, giving him a little encouragement. "Go on home, Pete. Talk to her the way we practiced. If it doesn't work out, I'll try to fit you into my schedule tomorrow."

"Thanks." He glanced up at Vanessa, then back to Kate. "Thank you, ma'am."

"You don't deserve five minutes." As soon as Officer Estes had disappeared around the corner, Kate resumed the walk to her office. "You can't talk to my clients that way."

"You were dismissing him already." Vanessa quickly caught up with her, refusing to be ignored. "Look, we are both professional women doing our jobs. Let me help you. Let me help the department's reputation—"

At that, Kate stopped and faced her. "There's nothing wrong with KCPD's reputation."

Vanessa arched a skeptical eyebrow. "You've been investigating the Rose Red Rapist for months—even longer, if the department's claim is true that he's the same man who committed a series of unsolved attacks and then disappeared for a few years." Vanessa pulled a phone from her purse and prepared to text whatever Kate might say. "Give me something to help calm the fears of the women in this city. I'm happy to give them your spiel about smarter ways to protect themselves. But my viewers want information about the crimes that have already happened, not just a public service announcement. They want to know KCPD is making progress. That there's hope the crimes will stop and that this deviant will be put away for the rest of his life."

Kate checked her watch. Unless someone else was running late, Spencer Montgomery had already started the task force debriefing on the day's events. But leaving Vanessa with an unanswered question would only encourage the woman to come back.

She knew better than to publicize the unsub's penchant for sterilizing both the victims and the crime scene after the rape had occurred—that was a fact they were keeping to themselves to help eliminate bogus hotline tips and rule out evidence from assaults committed by someone else. But she'd probably already shared more of the profile than she should. She needed to be the stronger woman here and not let her emotions dictate her interactions with this particular member of the press.

"This is off the record because we don't have the proof yet…." She waited for Vanessa's nod of agreement before continuing. "But after careful study of the behaviors in each of the attacks, we believe our unsub has been hurt, humiliated, possibly even abused, by an important woman in his life. The assaults are a punishment, a means to…reclaim his power, to prove that he's stronger, smarter, than the woman who damaged him. Unfortunately, the attacks probably have nothing to do with the actual victims. In his mind, they all represent this one woman to him. He's proving to himself that she lacks the power to ever hurt him again."

At least Vanessa had the grace to look appalled and slightly terrified of Kate's description of the monster who was preying on the women of Kansas City. "And do you have a list of suspects who fit that description?"

But Kate had said enough. "I have a meeting to get to. If you'll excuse me."

With a noisy huff of exasperation, Vanessa fell into step beside her again. "That's it? Psychological mumbo-jumbo about a man you're no closer to identifying than you were five months ago?"

"We're making progress, Vanessa, but that's all I can share right now."

"Can I at least tell my viewers that professional women are more likely to be targeted than others? You're talking about assertive women—confident, successful women, right?"

Kate stopped and looked Vanessa straight in the eye. The implication was obvious. "Yes. Women like you and me."

After a momentary pause, Vanessa nodded. "Thank you for the insight, Kate. I'll share the warning, along with the safety tips you gave at the press conference this morning. I'm glad we can move past what happened between us and do what's right for the greater good of the city."

Well, at least one of them had evidently moved on from the tragic events that had ended Kate's marriage. Even though the humiliation and pain of just how she'd discovered Brad and Vanessa's affair had dulled over the past five years, a big scar remained on Kate's ability to trust in personal relationships. She certainly no longer believed in the friendship she and Vanessa had shared.

Without further comment, she turned her back on the reporter. Once Kate was alone in the empty hallway, her shoulders sagged with the need to catch a quiet moment to herself before she joined the task force meeting. She untied the belt of her coat and unhooked another button. The high heels would go next if she had another five minutes to decompress. But, "Oh, hell."

The door to her office was already open. Had she forgotten an appointment? She hurried the last few steps, then halted in the doorway.

"Oh, double…" She swallowed the rest of her unladylike curse as the sheriff with the coal-black hair unfolded himself from one of the visitor's chairs and stood.

"Dr. Kate." Holding his hat in his big hands, Boone Harrison nodded a greeting to her. With his insulated jacket draped over the back of the chair, she got a better idea of how broad shoulders and solid muscles filled out the dimensions of the tan-and-brown uniform he wore. The silver in his hair indicated he might be five to ten years older than she, but there was nothing over the hill about the fitness of his body, and he seemed as comfortable in his own skin, and as laid-back about the authority he exuded, as any man she'd met.

There was something basic and unpretentious about the masculinity imprinted in every rugged line, deeppitched word and chivalrous gesture of Boone Harrison. And as much as his relentless and poorly timed refusal to leave her and KCPD alone to do their work annoyed her, she couldn't deny a rusty feminine awareness sparking to life inside her at every encounter with the man.

Taking a deep breath and forcing her weary muscles to smile, Kate unhooked the last button and shrugged out of her coat as she circled around her desk. She draped the coat over the back of her chair and smoothed the sleeves of her cashmere cardigan, diverting her focus to distract her traitorous hormones for a moment.

"Who's taking care of Alton County while you're here in Kansas City?"

"I've got deputies." A tall, broad shadow loomed over her as Boone approached the desk. "Since I'm staying the night to escort Janie home in the morning, I thought I'd check in to see if any progress has been made on your investigation."

She'd thought she'd gotten rid of him after their meeting at the florist's shop that morning. So much for a five-minute respite to recoup the emotional energy she'd expended throughout the day. After the long day she'd had—counseling a retired cop who was dealing with the recent death of his wife, as well as a young officer who'd been particularly surly about being assigned to temporary desk duty, observing witness interviews and trading carefully chosen words with reporters who were just as intent as Vanessa Owen to get the inside scoop on the Rose Red Rapist's latest attack—the last thing Kate needed was to deal with Sheriff Tall, Dark and Determined here.

Five minutes free from drama was apparently too much to ask for right now. Maybe if she quickly sent Boone Harrison on his way, though, she could at least close the door and enjoy two minutes of silence before joining the next meeting. "You've got a hotel room already? They fill up pretty fast this late in the day, especially south of town where the new crime lab and M.E.'s office are. Maybe you'd better—"

"I've got a room. But I'd sleep in my truck if I had to." A soft gray Stetson landed in the middle of her desk, followed by two broad hands braced on either side of it and the earthy, warm scent of the man leaning over them. Kate tilted her gaze up to a pair of whiskey-brown eyes that were entirely too close to hers. "Thought if I made an effort to be a little more civilized than I was this morning, you might be more inclined to share some information."

Didn't the man understand personal space? And had that breathy little catch of sound really come from her?

"You were understandably upset this morning. But that doesn't change the facts. You're out of your jurisdiction, you're too emotionally connected to the victim, and I don't have any details I can share with you right now." She slid a stack of files from beneath his hat and hugged them to her chest, straightening away from the desk and putting some distance between them. At least work was marginally less stressful than dealing with Marshall Hot-Shot here. She knew the expectations of her at KCPD. She knew what her clients needed from her. However, she wasn't as comfortable with persistent men and these flutterings of awareness. "I'm running late to a task force meeting right now."

"Perfect." He snatched up his hat. "I can sit in and listen."

"No." That had come out more aggravated than authoritative. She fixed a friendly smile on her face and tried again. "I've got your card. I'll call you when we're finished."

"Who was that woman pestering you out there?"

So was he truly observant? Or just plain nosy? Her arms tightened around the shield of papers she clutched to her chest. "A reporter."

"Did you tell her anything you haven't told me? I'm a cop and I'm family." Observant, she decided, reading the stern set of the lines beside his eyes. "I don't want to be surprised by anything I read in the papers or see on the evening news."

His reasoning made her stop and think. And relent. Her run-in with Vanessa had reminded her of just how frustrated and helpless not knowing the truth had made *her* feel five years ago. Boone Harrison wasn't leaving town until morning, anyway, so at least she could keep track of him and know he wasn't interfering with their investigation if he was in the room with them. That was how she'd present it to Spencer Montgomery, too.

"Fine. Detective Montgomery won't be happy about it, but I'll clear it so you can sit in and listen." Kate came around the desk, pointing a warning finger at Boone. "But not a word, remember? And anything you see or hear in that room has to remain confidential."

"I know how to keep my mouth shut."

Somehow she doubted that. But she only had so many fights in her on any given day, and this one was sorely testing her limits. "Let me go in and talk to Spencer first. This way."

"After you."

A half hour into the meeting and Kate wondered if she'd made the wrong decision. Although Spencer Montgomery wasn't pleased to have an unplanned visitor sitting in with the task force, he'd agreed that keeping the sheriff in sight was less worrisome than having him running through the city like a pinball let loose in a machine, conducting his own investigation into his sister's murder, impacting witnesses and giving off the impression that the task force couldn't get the job done on its own.

Still, it couldn't be easy, even for a veteran officer

of the law like Boone, to listen to the gruesome facts about his sister's rape and murder.

Spencer sat at the head of the boardroom table, his suit and tie looking remarkably fresh for this late in the day. He was speaking to his partner, Nick Fensom, a short, stocky, streetwise contrast to the buttoned-down task force leader. "Dr. Masterson-Kincaid says the traces of vinegar match what we found on his previous victim?"

"Yeah. The bastard cleaned her up after he raped her." Nick ran his fingers through his short, dark hair. "It doesn't make sense, though. If he took the time to get rid of any DNA after the sexual assault, then why leave the bloody mess we found when he dumped the body in the alley?"

Boone's hand fisted on his thigh in the chair beside Kate's.

"Nick," she warned, feeling the raging emotions coming off the sheriff in waves as he struggled to hold them in check.

"Sorry, man." Nick looked across the table and apologized. "I've got sisters, too. I get so angry when I see how he treats these women."

"You're an open book, Nick." Spencer chuffed his partner's shoulder in a masculine show of compassion. Then he steered the meeting back to the facts. "Anything else we can get from the M.E.'s report?"

Annie Hermann, the CSI attached to the task force, opened the folder in front of her and fanned out the papers and photos inside, digging through them until she pulled out a computerized sketch and set it on top of the scattered items. "I took pictures of the fatal head wound, and had Holly make a mold of the unusually deep wound track." Her dark eyes glanced up nervously, apologetically, perhaps, at the big man sitting between her and Kate. "Is it okay if I go into the details?"

The tension in Boone never eased, but he turned his head toward the petite woman beside him. "Do it."

After a murmured apology, Annie continued. "Holly says the blunt-force trauma was definitely the COD. But what he hit her with isn't immediately apparent. It's almost as if she was impaled by something. Nothing I found at the dump site seemed to fit. Of course, that's not the primary crime scene, either. I plan on going through our database and running simulations to figure out what kind of tool or instrument made that wound."

Spencer nodded. "Let us know as soon as you determine the weapon. If it's something unusual, maybe specific to a certain profession, that could help narrow our suspect and crime scene searches."

"Will do."

Boone's eyes remained transfixed on the drawing. Thankfully, it wasn't an actual picture of his murdered sister. Kate was about to warn Annie to pick up her mess, or act on the impulse to give Boone's fist a supportive, sympathetic squeeze beneath the table herself, when he reached for something else from the stack in front of Annie.

He picked up an 8 x 10 photograph and studied the jewelry displayed beside the cataloging number in the picture. Kate leaned forward, watching his eyes narrow in concentration. She quickly sat back when he turned his focus past her to where Spencer Montgomery sat at the head of the table. "May I comment, Detective?" he asked.

"If you can tell us something new." Spencer seemed

wary of inviting Boone into the discussion. But he was too smart a cop to overlook a possible lead, even if it did come from someone outside the task force. "We've all got a description of the necklace you said was missing."

"It's not that. All this other jewelry, this handmade silver and turquoise stuff—I've seen Janie wear it." He pointed to the smallest round object in the photo. "But this ring is something new."

Kate pulled the photo in front of her to study the jewelry in question. "A ruby and diamonds set in white gold? A lot of diamonds. That's expensive."

When Maggie Wheeler, the red-haired police officer sitting opposite her, asked to see it, Kate slid the photo across the table. "It looks like an engagement ring." She twirled her left hand in the air to show off the simple solitaire set in gold that she wore. "I saw designs like that when John and I were shopping."

"Was your sister engaged?" Spencer asked, studying the photo himself as it made its way around the table.

"No."

"In a relationship?"

Boone shook his head. "Nothing serious enough to warrant a gift like that. At least not that I knew of."

Feeling the subtle shift from helpless anger to focused purpose from the man beside her, Kate voiced the information Boone was probably already sorting through inside his head. "Robin Carter, the victim's boss, at her shop this morning said she thought Janie had been unusually secretive lately. And that she'd stopped dating."

Spencer's sharp gray eyes challenged Boone. "Could she have been involved with someone she didn't tell you about, Sheriff?"

Annie tucked a curly dark lock behind her ear. "Not every woman confides in her family when she's in a relationship."

Nick Fensom scoffed at the notion of a woman keeping her mouth shut. "My sisters do. Sometimes, I can't shut 'em up about the latest stud or hottie or whatever name they're calling them."

"Really?" Annie bristled at the amusement in Nick's tone. "Women with good sense confide in you?"

"My family's close, Hermann. We talk." He shrugged off her sarcasm and leaned back in his chair. "Unless the guy's trouble. And then they keep it a secret because they know I'll check him out—and run him off if he's no good."

Unless the guy's trouble. Even Nick went silent at the implication of what he'd just said. The words hung in the air around the table, and a group decision was silently made.

Nick groaned. "She would not have been dating our unsub, would she?"

"You said this guy was faceless in the city," Boone reminded him, "that he blends in so well that no one suspects him of being *no good.*"

"Thank you for the heads-up, Sheriff." Spencer closed the folder in front of him and stood, dismissing them all to do their work. "Let's find out who Jane Harrison was seeing."

Chapter Four

"Dr. Kate—do you have a minute?"

"Sorry, no."

"Coward." Even now, Kate could recall the expectation she'd read in Boone Harrison's warm brown eyes before she'd turned her back on him and scurried down the hallway to her office where she'd closed the door... and locked it. "No," she insisted to herself, not bothering to stifle the yawn that stretched nearly every muscle in her face. "You're a survivor, Kate. You did what was necessary to get through this day."

After saving the notes she'd been typing up on her laptop, Kate slipped off her pumps and curled her cramped toes into the carpet beneath her desk. She'd stayed at the office far longer than she'd intended. But once the duty shift had changed on the main floor and the buzz of voices diminished, she'd finally found the calming quiet and solitude she needed to recharge her batteries and prioritize the demands on her time and emotional energy once again.

As the task force meeting ended, she knew that Boone Harrison had wanted to say something more to her. Maybe he was even going to ask her to dinner so he could continue grilling her for answers to his sister's murder. Or maybe he simply wanted to pass the time with the most friendly face he'd found in Kansas City so that he wouldn't have to be alone with his thoughts and his grief the rest of the night.

But she'd reached the limits of patience and compassion for one day. The man had barged into her well-ordered life, bullied his way past her personal defenses, and tapped into a dangerously unreliable part of her psyche—her heart.

The counselor in her was inclined to listen to his helplessness and anger. The woman in her wanted to ease the guilt and grief that was almost too much for even a strong, mature man to bear. But she had to handle this investigation with her brain, not her heart. She had to manage her life with the same strict logic.

Caring led to vulnerability.

Vulnerability made her an easy mark for heartbreak and betrayal.

Forgetting either of those two truths would lead Kate down the same path that had nearly destroyed her five years earlier.

She'd known Boone Harrison for only a day—he didn't even qualify as a friend. She owed him nothing beyond the professional courtesy extended to him by the department. And as much as part of her wanted to help him get through not just this day but also the ongoing adjustments he'd face after losing someone he'd been so close to, Kate was too smart to let things with the sheriff get personal and make a mistake of the heart again.

So she'd left her coworkers behind. She'd sent Boone on his way with a smile and the very real excuse that she still had work she needed to complete before her day ended.

Now, with only the lamplight over her desk and the words on the laptop screen to keep her company, Kate wondered at the emptiness she'd chosen for herself in the name of emotional survival. She'd certainly never advise one of her clients to handle hurts and disappointments this way. But that was the point, wasn't it? She couldn't take on the issues of all her clients and visiting sheriffs, manage the image of the task force, reassure the frightened citizens of an entire city *and* deal with drama in her own life without losing her patience, draining her compassion, blowing out a few brain cells and winding up being no good to anybody. She had to protect herself like this, right?

Made sense.

Maybe she could dispel this unfortunate case of second-guessing her choices today by conducting a little exercise she sometimes used with clients who bottled up or misdirected their emotions.

Kate raised her arms over her head and extended her legs, stretching out the kinks in her body from head to toe before collapsing back into the chair with a weary sigh. She imagined how her impromptu interview with Vanessa Owen might have gone if she didn't exercise such self-control.

"Get out of my face, you witch. You've already taken enough from me. You won't get another damn thing out of me."

"I'm only doing my job, old friend. Please help."

"You already helped yourself to my husband. Your treachery killed him. You killed my marriage, my abil-

*ity to trust and did serious damage to my self-esteem.
You don't get to ask for favors from me."*

*"You were a fool not to know what was going on,
Kate."*

*"Maybe. But I learned to never be made a fool of
again."*

Feeling a bit of satisfaction, Kate nodded. That was
closer to what she'd really wanted to say to Vanessa
Owen.

And how could she have handled Boone Harrison
differently? Spared herself the full-body hug and dark
eyes that penetrated her emotional armor and awoke
something tingling and feminine and needy inside her?
How should she have reminded herself that it was duty,
not compassion, that had forced her to accept his company so many times today?

"Get your hands off me, you clod."

"But you like it when I put my hands on you."

Kate startled in her chair and sat up straight, glancing around her office as though the words had been real
and spoken out loud for the wrong person to hear. She
was supposed to be purging her resentment and frustration, reclaiming control of her emotions. This wasn't
the time to indulge a subconscious admission. She had
enough conflict battling it out in her head without inviting a latent sexual attraction into the mix.

"Try again," Kate advised herself. She inhaled a
cleansing breath and replayed this morning's press
conference in her mind, envisioning what she should
have said to the buttinsky sheriff who'd demanded answers from her.

*"Handle your own problem, cowboy. I have a job
to do."*

Better. Maybe she should have sicced Boone and Vanessa on each other, and then half the stresses of Kate's day would have become someone else's. After a brief introduction, Kate could have slipped away. Boone would have politely stood, and removed or tipped his hat when Vanessa entered the room. Vanessa would have been charmed by the old-school chivalry. And then she'd have tried to take advantage of it. She'd appreciate an interview with a family member of the rapist's latest victim. She could exploit Boone's unsanctioned investigation to attract viewers and ratings.

But Boone was more cop than country bumpkin. He'd be too smart to be taken in by Vanessa's charm. Vanessa would be intrigued by a challenge like that. Kate could visualize the sheriff and the reporter strolling off together, each primed for a battle of wits and will while Kate sat alone in her office, oblivious to the secret alliance, just as she'd been oblivious to Brad and Vanessa's affair until the police had called about the heart attack in his mistress's bed....

Kate swore at the unsettling turn of her thoughts. "End the damn exercise, already."

She rolled her chair back in front of her laptop, typing in a few more words before an unexpected revelation from the mental exercise gone wrong popped into her head. "They'd keep their relationship hidden from me," Kate murmured out loud.

She flashed back through her day—Robin Carter's speculation that Janie Harrison had been seeing someone, the picture of a very expensive ring, changes in behavior, unexplained gifts—secrets that neither family nor close friends knew.

In hindsight, Kate recognized the similarities from her own past.

"Jane Harrison was seeing a married man. Or possibly a student—someone she'd get in trouble over for having a relationship with." Although a student was less likely to have the money for that ruby and diamond ring—unless he'd come from a wealthy background or had stolen it. And a thief wouldn't take that necklace and leave all those rings behind. All were specific leads the team could look into.

Energized by the possibility of narrowing down their suspect pool, and welcoming the distraction to the wayward turn of her thoughts a moment earlier, Kate turned to her desk computer and typed her suspicions and reasoning into an email and sent it to the other task force members. Then she pulled out a phone book and put in a call to the community college where Jane Harrison had worked.

Although evening classes were in session, she discovered that the business offices had already closed for the day. Ignoring her frustration over the delay in getting some answers, she gathered her thoughts and left a succinct message on the line for the director of the Fine Arts department: "…that list should have class rosters, departmental colleagues—anyone she might have come into contact with on campus. You can reach me here at KCPD, or on my cell if I'm out of the office, to arrange a meeting to go over the information. Thank you."

Feeling reenergized by that bit of deductive reasoning and the small but potentially significant breakthrough she'd just made on the case, Kate decided it was time to call it a night. The clock on her wall and the rumbling in her stomach confirmed it. She slipped her swollen toes back into her high heels, packed her laptop into her shoulder bag, pulled on her trench coat and shut off the lights.

This day was done. Soup and salad, a steaming hot bath and one of the food shows she liked to watch on television were waiting for her at home.

After checking out with the overnight desk sergeant, Kate rode the elevator down to the first floor and stepped outside. The cool autumn air whipped her hair into her face. She paused on the entryway's top step to brush her bangs off her forehead and blink the grit carried by the wind from her eyes.

A glimpse of movement, of someone more shadow than substance, darted beyond the limestone railing and vanished out of sight. Kate's breath jolted through her chest. She captured her hair behind each ear and turned her face away from the swirling air currents that promised rain, peering into the night to double-check what she'd seen. It was probably someone taking a shortcut through the grass or hugging the building to avoid the battering wind blowing from the north.

But a closer look revealed no one, nothing, stirring besides the crispy, thinning leaves on the trees lining the sidewalk, and the swaying steel and flickering illumination of the street lights and traffic signals nearer to the street.

Irritated with how easily she'd been startled, Kate relaxed with a cautious sigh, and she cinched her coat more tightly around her waist. Fatigue had made her senses unreliable, she reasoned silently. She'd seen the shadow of a branch or a bobbing circle of light from the corner of her eye and mistaken it for something more sinister.

She'd been profiling too many suspects lately. With a shake of her head, she crossed down the wide stone steps to the sidewalk. She swept her gaze from side to side as she walked down to the street light at the corner, alert to any other signs of movement. But she doubted she'd see anything unless her imagination conjured it. There weren't many cars heading downtown past precinct headquarters, and even fewer pedestrians on the block.

If she'd left when the shift had changed three hours earlier, the sidewalks on either side of the street would be filled with coworkers heading for home or a night out on the town. With the threat of rain driving everyone indoors as quickly as possible, there were only a few other brave souls out and about, carrying briefcases and backpacks, hunched down against the wind as they hurried from the government buildings, courthouses and legal offices in the area to their cars or the nearest bus stop.

"Smooth move, Doctor," Kate chided herself. Her heels clicked against the concrete, echoing her increasing heart rate as she neared the crosswalk that would take her to the parking garage across the street. She deserved the little rush of nerves that quickened her pace. She hadn't even followed her own safety advice that she'd given to the women of Kansas City that morning. She was alone. After dark. Walking to her car in the same garage where she'd been parking for years. Not smart. With a serial rapist turned killer hiding on the streets, was it any wonder she'd been able to spook herself with nothing more than wind and shadows? "Real smooth."

But surely this wasn't a terrible risk. The parking garage was across from a police station. The street lamps might be undulating in the wind, but they were working. And even though she fit the profile of the women he attacked, this wasn't the neighborhood where the Rose Red Rapist had abducted his last two victims.

Still, she was more than uncomfortably aware of the man in dark brown coveralls approaching the same intersection from one of the side streets. He wasn't any taller than she, but from this angle, most of his face was obscured by the sweatshirt hoodie he wore beneath the insulated jumpsuit. Kate made a point of standing in the circle of lamplight as he joined her to wait for the traffic signal to change. For a split second, she considered crossing against the light, but, like Murphy's Law, the traffic that had seemed so sparse a few moments ago now showed up with three cars and a truck to keep her on the sidewalk.

She was vaguely aware of the man glancing in her direction, but studiously kept her eyes focused on the traffic in front of her. "Looks like a storm's coming," he said politely enough, his voice a gravelly whisper.

Kate nodded, sidled half a step closer to the streetlight, then stepped off the curb as soon as the vehicles had cleared the intersection. Either put off by her lack of a response, or waiting for the light to change, the man held back while she darted across the street. She'd already circled around the crossbar gate at the garage's entrance when she looked back to see the man step onto the sidewalk behind her and turn toward the open-air parking lot just south of the parking garage.

Expelling her paranoia on a relieved sigh, Kate hurried to the elevator and pushed the call button. She was grateful to see the doors open immediately and that the car inside was empty. She stepped inside and pushed the button for the sixth floor.

"Dr. Kilpatrick?"

Not Pete Estes again. Resentment fisted in her chest. The kid needed to grow up.

"Hey! Wait!"

Kate pushed the Door Close button. Not the most professional of responses, but she just couldn't deal with his issues and hold his hand right now. She'd already gotten her nerves worked up with the man at the corner. She wouldn't be a very patient listener right now, anyway.

"Dr. Kate!"

She might have heard someone calling her name again, might have imagined the muted crunch of quick footsteps over the concrete. But when a dark blur of shadow rushed toward the elevator, she gripped the side railing and punched the Door Close button over and over, speeding the process to be alone and safe inside the elevator.

She didn't imagine the deep-pitched curse before the doors squeezed shut.

"Pete," she sighed at the young man's desperation to save his relationship with the girl he'd gotten pregnant. Kate couldn't be sure if those footsteps had changed course to take the stairs, or if that was her own pulse hammering a warning signal in her ears. Either way, her brain had kicked into overdrive, driving out both pity and fatigue.

She was embarrassed to realize she hadn't given better thought to her own safety at this time of night. It worried her to think the man outside the elevator had truly meant her harm. Would Pete Estes really turn his temper on her? Or maybe it hadn't been her client at all.

Her name had been splashed all over the television and papers this morning. She was a fixture in the department. A lot of people knew her name.

Was it possible for the man in the coveralls to keep to the shadows and move quickly enough that he could have been the movement she'd spotted beside the precinct's front steps, the stranger at the street corner *and* the man rushing up inside the parking garage? Surely, he'd have to fly like the wind gusting outside in order to be in all three places. And maybe she was believing the worst of an innocent man—or two innocent men—or even three—when each encounter could be explained away by coincidence, regret at the chance she'd taken by walking out here alone and her overly analytical way of thinking.

Nonetheless, Kate had her keys out and her pepper spray in hand when the elevator reached the sixth level and the doors opened. She heard an engine gunning somewhere in the distance. But that wasn't the noise that alarmed her.

"Oh, no." Did she trust that coincidence could also explain away the footsteps she heard coming up the stairs behind her?

Chances were, someone whose legs were fueled by the aggravation of missing the elevator was climbing his way to one of the garage's upper levels. Or maybe a reporter had been lying in wait, ready to ambush her with questions the way Vanessa Owen had. If the man was half as determined as Vanessa, he wouldn't let six flights of stairs deter him from getting his story. Of course, there was Pete. And the man in the coveralls.

And the sound of an engine speeding up and circling through each level of the parking garage beneath her feet.

Maybe she'd been foolish to reason away those instincts that warned her to be wary of any man approaching her at this time of night.

Kate spotted her Lexus against the far wall and quickened her steps. Normally, she didn't park so far away, but the garage had been nearly full when she'd returned for the task force meeting that afternoon. Now, there were a handful of cars to the left and right, but hers sat at the end of the row, facing away from her. So very far away.

The timbre of each footfall changed as the man behind her left the steel grate stairs and followed her onto the solid concrete of the parking level.

Followed her?

Squeezing the pepper spray in her fist, Kate broke into a run.

She'd covered the length of the garage before she realized that the pattern of footsteps behind her hadn't changed. She was running, but the man behind her wasn't. Kate halted at the trunk of her car and whirled around.

Her words came out in breathless derision. "Stupid woman. You stupid…freaked-out…"

The man hadn't followed her at all. In fact, he was nowhere to be seen. He must have veered off into another parking lane and hadn't been after her at all. Danger wasn't closing in on her. She was just letting her emotions spin her imagination into overdrive.

Cursing the pinch of her shoes and her readiness to believe the worst of the men in the world around her tonight, Kate tapped the remote to unlock her car. She tugged the strap of her purse back over her shoulder, opened the car door and froze.

The man in the coveralls might not be chasing her. There might not be any client or reporter in hot pursuit. But someone definitely had her in his sights.

The squeal of tires over the pavement barely registered as she moved around the open door to read the message scrawled across her windshield in bright red.

Lies, Kate. Lies! was all it said.

And the wilted red rose tucked beneath a wiper blade left no doubt who the message was from.

"Please be paint." She reached out to touch one finger to the sticky exclamation point. Her stomach plummeted as she quickly pulled back, rubbing the vile evidence across her fingers in her efforts to get rid of it. There was no way to know if it was human or not, but she was 99 percent sure it was blood.

"I don't understand." Shock dampened her hearing to the noises around her. She tried to force logic into her brain, tried to make sense of a bloody threat that didn't fit the profile of the opportunistic rapist the task force was after. How had he found her? What connections did he have, how long had he watched, to know this car was hers? What did the message mean?

Why was she still standing here, contemplating this frightening mess?

Kate took a step back, then another.

A hand closed over her shoulder and she screamed.

"Whoa, whoa, whoa." Boone deflected the stinging attack of pepper spray as Kate spun around, twisting her wrist and knocking the vial to the concrete. "Kate." The canister rolled out of sight beneath her car and she came back swinging. He caught that hand, too, and pinned it against his chest, willing her to see through her panic and identify him. "Kate! It's me. Boone."

"Boone?" Her hands balled beneath his, curling into the front of his jacket.

"Yeah. Pain in the butt? Won't go away?" Now that the weapon was gone and the fists were accounted for, he eased his defensive hold on her. "Sorry I startled you, but you didn't hear me. I tried to catch you on your way into the garage, but your mind was someplace else."

Apparently it still was. That soft green gaze bounced from his chin to his chest and up to the brim of his hat before meeting his. "What are you doing here?"

Now, what would make a sensible woman take off running like that? What would put that dazed look in her eyes?

"I was parked outside on the street. I've been waiting for you to get off work." He dropped his voice to little more than a whisper, hushing her the way he'd croon soft words to a skittish colt. "I saw you were walking to your car by yourself and I tried to catch you, but you took off. I thought I'd better grab my truck and find out where you were parked before I missed...oh. Okay."

One second she was staring at him as if he was talking gibberish, the next she was walking into his chest, latching on with a death grip that pinched the skin beneath his uniform.

"You're shaking like a leaf." Boone had no problem wrapping his arms around her and resting his chin against the silky crown of her hair. He did have a problem with the clammy chill of skin he felt at her nape. He had a very big problem with the vandalism he spotted on her windshield when he sought out an explanation for Kate Kilpatrick's uncharacteristic display of confusion and vulnerability. "Come here."

That she willingly followed when he led her to the far side of his truck to block her view of the bloody message alarmed him even more. Although his instincts were to check out her car for any further signs of tampering that could endanger her, Boone temporarily contented himself with scanning the deserted floor of the parking garage over the top of her head.

He reached beneath his jacket to unhook the catch on his holster—just in case—before wrapping his arm back around her shoulders and backing her up to his truck to put another layer of protection between the unseen threat around her. He hadn't seen anybody who'd seemed out of place going in or out of the garage in the three hours he'd been waiting for Kate to get off work. When the shift had changed in the KCPD offices, folks had walked straight in and driven back out. A few might have stopped for a few minutes to chat each other up, but he hadn't seen anybody lingering where they shouldn't be, or sneaking around as if they didn't want to be seen. He'd never even dozed off, but had spent the wait time on his cell, making calls to his brothers and checking in with his deputies back in Grangeport.

Whoever wanted Kate's attention must have done this after the shift change, once her car had been left sitting in the remote corner by itself, facing away from the few vehicles still remaining on this level. Crowded or not, that was pretty brave, walking into a garage used by cops, support staff and legal types, and defacing the car owned by the police psychologist investigating him.

As if he needed any more proof that the man who'd raped and murdered his sister was dangerous.

"Hey." He liked the feel of this woman in his arms, liked the smell of her perfuming every breath, liked the way she held on like she had no intention of letting go—he liked it a lot more than he should for practically being strangers. He hadn't expected the patient, cinched-up, textbook ice princess to be so clingy, so... female. But every cell of his body had been trained to serve and protect. With every beat of his heart he knew that understanding whatever was happening here would lead him one step closer to finding the man who'd murdered Janie. "You keep holding on to me like this, Doc, and I'm going to start to think you like me."

It was a few seconds more before she pulled away without a word. Well, hell, he'd just been teasing, trying to get a smile out of her, trying to get her to talk and clue him in on what seemed to be far more than a tasteless prank. But she was looking at his jacket where she had crushed it in her hand. Maybe the woman was a little shocked. She looked surprised to discover how she'd latched on to him, and equally fascinated by the movements of her fingers, smoothing out the wrinkles in the quilted material, unconsciously petting his chest and triggering a tiny leap of electricity beneath his skin with each gentle stroke of her hand.

"I thought someone was following me. I guess it was you."

"I called out to you when I saw you get on the elevator, but you must not have heard me. I had to circle through every level to find you, but I drove up here as fast as I could."

Boone almost regretted the loss of contact as Kate

stuffed her hands into the pockets of that tightly wrapped coat, and a cool mask slipped over her expression. "You mean you didn't just come up the stairs?"

Her skin was still a little too pale for his liking, but whatever had spooked her—she'd moved past it.

"I was looking for you," he said. "I drove up here, Doc."

"Did you see anyone else? There was a man on the corner—I thought he was going on down the street, but…oh, damn." A fist came out of her pocket and shook the air. "I didn't look at his face. I didn't want to make eye contact and encourage him. How could I be so stupid? What if that was him? What if we just lost our unsub because I was too afraid to look?" She swung her arm out toward the message dripping from her car. "And what does that mean? 'Lies'? What have I lied about?" She wiped at the smear of red on her fingers. Ah, hell. That wasn't paint. "I don't understand. I don't like it when I can't figure out—"

"Take a deep breath, Doc. You're all right."

"No, I'm not. This is all wrong."

Boone gently grasped her by the shoulders and turned her back to face him. He pulled a bandanna from his back pocket and dabbed at the offending mark on her hand. "I didn't see anybody else on this level of the garage. You're safe."

He glanced at the empty space around them one more time, ensuring that was still the case.

But her head trembled back and forth in a subtle *no*. She doubted the sincerity of his words and was getting set to argue some more.

And then, because he'd been in pain all day long, because she'd been rattled by a justifiable scare—because their emotions were too raw and too near the surface to ignore—Boone palmed the back of Kate's neck, dipped his head and pulled her mouth up to his for a kiss.

Her lips parted on a startled gasp. Her warmth rushed to meet him with one breath and hastily retreated with the next. And then a heavy sigh of release relaxed her mouth beneath his and he felt her leaning in ever so slightly. The kiss was hard. It was gentle. It was quick. And even as he savored the hesitant softening and pliant grasp of Kate's lips against his, Boone was pulling away, wondering what the hell had gotten into him.

He stared at Kate for a couple of breathless seconds, taking quick note of the velvety skin at her nape, the artful curve of her pink lips and the thumping of his pulse that charged his body with the desire to kiss her again. Vivid impressions. But none were as clear as the question clouding her verdant eyes.

Why?

Boone pulled his hand from her neck. "You with me now, Doc?" He reasoned away the impulse to kiss her by rationalizing that a peck on the mouth was a far less violent and far more pleasurable way to snap her out of that panic attack than a slap across the face would have been.

Her head moved in the slightest of nods and she pressed the bandanna back into his hands. "If things are safe and no one else is here, there's no need for you to stay—or to—" her fingers wavered in the general vicinity of her mouth "—do that."

"Do *that?*" he echoed. He should apologize for overstepping the boundaries of friendly acquaintances. But Boone wasn't about to start lying to Dr. Kate or to himself. Yeah, he was incensed by everything that had happened today that led up to that impromptu embrace. But he wasn't sorry he'd kissed her. Chances were, however, she was sorry about kissing him back. "Are you okay, Doc?"

She tilted her chin and pasted on a smile. But the white-knuckled grip she still had on her keys didn't fool him. "Thank you for coming to my rescue, but I'm fine."

She was forgetting the badge he wore—and that inexplicable connection forming a bond between them that couldn't be dismissed with a polite thank-you. "We're not going anywhere until you call for backup, have the lab take pictures and analyze that…graffiti, and you file a report."

Kate nodded, dismissing him again. "I'll do that."

Boone stuffed the bandanna back into his pocket, but he wasn't budging.

"Why are you still here, anyway, Sheriff?"

"I realized I never thanked you for everything you've done for me today. I know I didn't give you much of a choice, but you were still mighty gracious about it." The wind whistling through the garage had nothing on the chill Dr. Kate was trying to throw his way. "I figured we both had to eat. Figured maybe you'd let me take you to dinner. To show my appreciation."

"I don't date, Sheriff Harrison."

"Look, about the kiss—I didn't plan that. That's not why I was waiting in the garage for you. I mean, you do eat, don't you?"

"Of course I do. But you don't owe me anything. I was just doing my job today. I don't need any thanks from you. And I certainly don't want to be any more trouble to you. So, good night."

Mules weren't the only stubborn thing his folks had raised on their ranch. Boone pulled back the front of his jacket and splayed his hands at his hips. He didn't get why he was so attracted to this prickly city woman who had to be as wrong for him as his ex-wife had been. But he clearly understood his duty as an officer of the law, and as a man.

"You may not need any thanks, but I don't leave a lady in trouble. I didn't see anyone following you, but that doesn't mean it didn't happen." He inclined his head toward her car. "And clearly someone was here." Easily overriding Kate's protest, Boone slid her purse off her shoulder and handed it to her. "Trust me, kissing you was no trouble. But I promise to keep my hands to myself. Make the call."

"ARE YOU SURE YOU'RE OKAY?" Maggie Wheeler asked, handing Kate a cup of hot tea and sitting beside her on the rear bumper of the ambulance that had been called to the sixth floor of the KCPD parking garage.

"I'm fine," Kate insisted, wrapping her trembling fingers around the warmth of the insulated cup. She appreciated the supportive gesture and true concern from her friend, but hated to see such a big fuss being made over one vandalized car. What she hated more was that the entire task force and several more uniformed officers and a trio of paramedics had shown up in the past hour or so to make a fuss over *her*. "I'm grateful for the tea, Maggie, but don't you think all of this is a little bit of overkill?"

The garage had been deserted an hour ago, but now

it was a beehive of activity. Annie Hermann hovered over the windshield of Kate's car with a flashlight and a cotton swab, verifying that the disturbing message had indeed been written in blood. Pike Taylor's dog Hans had his nose to the concrete, pulling his handler with him along an unseen trail around car tires and concrete pillars toward the elevator. Detectives Montgomery and Fensom had their heads together discussing possible implications of the attack, while two officers unrolled yellow crime scene tape across the top of the stairwell where Pike's dog had stopped to sit and tell his handler that he'd identified a particular scent.

Yet for all the bustle of movement and buzz of conversations, there was one lone figure off by himself, pacing beside the black pickup truck he'd been forced to move to the far side of the garage. Kate's gaze reluctantly drifted over to Boone Harrison's slow, purposeful strides. He was like a hungry mountain lion, waiting for the right moment to pounce on his prey—or perhaps more like a new kid in school who hadn't been invited to join the other students on the playground.

She knew he was anxious to dive into the middle of the investigation, to find answers that would purge his guilt and give him the healing satisfaction of justice for his sister. She understood why he was still here, and was glad that he'd been there to hold on to when she'd been too rattled to think straight. But the man should go home to his family. At the very least, he should go to his comfortable hotel bed and get some much-needed rest instead of wearing a path in the concrete.

And then the pacing stopped and the dark eyes found hers across the distance between them. Kate's fingers tightened around her tea and she huddled inside the blanket the paramedics had draped around her shoulders. What was it about the small-town sheriff that sparked that low hum of electricity inside her and short-circuited her ability to focus on the job at hand?

Her lips burned at the memory of Boone's mouth pressed against hers. Her pulse quickened with the desire to lean against his sturdy chest and feel his solid arms around her again.

She wasn't quite sure why he had kissed her, or why she had stretched up on her tiptoes to kiss him back. There were sound reasons why people in stressful situations turned to each other for comfort and acted out on latent attractions. But she had never given in to such mental weakness before. And she couldn't quite fathom what sort of weakness Boone Harrison possessed that would lead him to such a physical solution to dealing with her panic.

Then Boone turned and his hat shaded his eyes, masking the intensity that she just now realized had left her staring at him like some sort of dumbstruck teenager.

Seriously, Kate? she chided herself, turning her own attention to the tea in her hands and swallowing a mouthful of hot liquid that burned her tongue and knocked some common sense back into her head. *You're too old and too smart to be distracted by a man.* She could ill afford to be blinded by emotions or hormones or whatever it was that made her forget that she'd known Sheriff Harrison for less than twenty-four hours, and that the bulk of that time had been spent arguing with the man or reminding him that he was getting in the way of the work the task force was doing. She'd paid a heavy price for trusting her feelings and believing that the people she cared about had her best interests at heart. She wouldn't make that same mistake again.

While Kate organized her thoughts and evaluated her actions, Maggie continued the conversation. The tall redhead gave a wry laugh beside her. "You should have seen how Detective Montgomery rolled out the cavalry when my ex came after me earlier this year."

Kate inhaled a deep breath that flared her nostrils and gave her time to respond appropriately. "Yes, but your ex-husband had a violent history," Kate argued rationally, suppressing the gut-tightening possibility that someone as abusive as Maggie's late husband had set his sights on her. "There's a big difference between a man trying to kill you and one who just wants to scare you." She nodded toward the detectives at her car. "And that's all our unsub is trying to do—we've rattled his confidence by making some headway in our investigation. He's just reminding us that we haven't identified him yet, and challenging us to step up our efforts to catch him."

Maggie's freckled face creased into a frown. "That's how the violence starts, Kate. With a threat, with intimidation. It doesn't take much more for the fear a stalker instills into every breath you take to become something dangerous or deadly."

A chill that even the hot tea couldn't penetrate shivered through Kate. But she still summoned a brave smile. "I thought you were here to cheer me up."

Maggie dropped an arm around Kate's shoulders and gave her a friendly squeeze. "You're such a strong woman, Kate. I'm sure you'll be fine. But I don't want you to make light of a threat like this. Don't take unnecessary chances. If you feel like someone is after you, and wants to hurt you, let one of us on the task force know. We're going to fight this guy together."

Kate nodded her understanding. "He doesn't get to win."

Maggie smiled again. "Exactly."

"Back it up, pal."

Kate and Maggie both turned at the deep-pitched warning from the parking-garage ramp. Sheriff Harrison had left his truck to stand nose-to-nose with Gabriel Knight, the reporter who covered KCPD's activities for the *Kansas City Journal* newspaper. Only the plastic crime-scene tape and a few inches of attitude separated the two men.

"Oh, no." Kate set her cup down on the ambulance's bumper and let the blanket fall to the concrete at her feet as she hurried over to run interference.

Gabriel Knight was grinning, sarcasm evident in his expression. "Are you the new guard dog on the task force, Sheriff? It *is* sheriff, right?"

Boone didn't bother answering the questions. "That press card hanging around your neck doesn't give you the right to trespass on a crime scene. You might have gotten past the cops downstairs, but you're not getting past me."

"You got in my way this morning, cowboy," the reporter challenged, "but you won't get in my way again. There's a story here."

"Boone." Kate touched his elbow, silently urging him to retreat a step. "I'll handle this." When he straightened his arm to keep her from moving past him, Kate bristled to attention. He was protecting her again. And she didn't need that kind of chivalry right now. "This is *my* job."

He glanced down over the jut of his shoulder at her. "Do you know who messed with your car? Does anyone know? What if it's this guy?"

"Are you accusing me—?"

Boone ignored the reporter's interruption. "I think you'd be a little more cautious about who you let approach you until we get some answers."

"And I think you'd be a little more respectful about departmental protocol." And a little more respectful of the job she'd been trained for. "Creating a scene and alienating the press is not the kind of PR we're looking for."

Gabriel Knight was still looking for his story and the tension between Kate and Boone was feeding right into it. "The grapevine says a task force member received a threat from the Rose Red Rapist. Were you threatened, Dr. Kilpatrick? Is that why Sheriff Cowboy here is so adamant about protecting you?"

Kate turned her frustration on the dark-haired reporter. "Mr. Knight, we're not ready to give a statement yet."

"Is there a problem?" A voice that could be counted on to remain cooler than anyone here entered the conversation. Spencer Montgomery pulled back the front of his suit jacket and splayed his hands at his hips, calmly asserting his authority and making his disapproval of a confrontation on his crime scene clear. "How did you get wind of this threat, Mr. Knight?"

A cocky grin curved the reporter's mouth. "I have my sources."

"If your sources are withholding information key to my investigation—if *you're* withholding information—"

"Can't solve these crimes without my help, Detective?"

Spencer didn't take the bait. "Two things. One—" he took a step toward Knight "—KCPD doesn't talk to you until we're good and ready. So you've got nothing but rumors and hearsay that you can't print. And two?" Kate retreated a step as the red-haired detective turned toward Boone. "Go home, Harrison. I'm glad you were here for Kate. But we've got the investigation covered without your help."

Every muscle in Boone's arm clenched beneath her touch and Kate, not realizing she still held on to him, wisely pulled away.

"You get it right, Montgomery," Boone warned. "All of it." His dark gaze skimmed over Kate, perhaps saying a reluctant goodbye, or maybe just warning her to watch her back, before he met Spencer's icy stare again. "Or I won't care whose jurisdiction it is. I'm finding my sister's killer."

"This isn't right."

He skimmed through Gabriel Knight's article in the *Kansas City Journal* and looked at the black-and-white photo again.

"You're wrong, Dr. Kilpatrick." His breath felt heavy in his chest, making it hard to breathe as he looked at the image of the striking blonde with a dozen microphones and bright lights framing her pale features. "I didn't do the things you said."

He read through the article a third time, and then a fourth. The pungency of the paper's black ink burned his sinuses and stained his hands. The report was extremely well-written. It seemed so plausible, so real.

But it was filled with lies. Kate Kilpatrick and the task force were spreading lies.

Leave it to a woman to ruin his good name again.

He spread the offending article over his desk and smeared away the newsprint beneath his hand. Over and over. And over again until the pressure and friction ripped a hole in the middle of Kate Kilpatrick's earnest expression.

It's not her, a gentle voice inside his head tried to reason. *She doesn't know you. She doesn't know the truth. She can't hurt you.*

Any woman could hurt him if he let her.

No.

"You're damn right, no." He fisted the torn paper in his hand and tossed it into the trash.

And then he saw the black ink on his hands—as vulgar and damning as the red blood he'd washed off his gloves before carefully disposing of them. *She* hated it when he was dirty like this. He hated it.

His chair spun like a tornado behind him as he shot out of it and dashed into the connecting bathroom. He washed his hands and scrubbed beneath his nails three times before he felt the stain of his deeds leave him.

For now.

A knock on the door to the outer room kept him from turning on the water for a fourth time. He dried his hands, then used the towel to open the bathroom door and hurried out to greet his visitor.

"Where have you been? You're late." He verbally pounced on his guest, even before she could shake the water off the umbrella drenched by the thunderstorm raging outside. He watched in horror as dozens of water droplets spotted the carpet.

"It's just water," she said. "Relax."

But he couldn't help the compulsion. He dropped down to his knees and pressed the towel into the rug, soaking up each remnant of rain before the marks became permanent.

He was surprised when she didn't make a joke or grouse about him taking the towel to her wet shoes as well, before she could track any mess farther into the room. *Don't be a fool,* the voice inside his head warned. *She isn't your friend. You can't trust her. You can't trust any woman.*

But the woman knelt beside him, stroked his hair. She laid her hand over his to still his frantic movements. "It's all right," she whispered against his ear. Her loyalty to him was absolute. It had to be. "I know your secrets. I will always keep them for you."

"You'd better," he warned her.

She took the towel from his hands and urged him to his feet. "Go back to work. I'll finish cleaning up."

Chapter Five

"They aren't making any progress, are they, boss?" Flint Larson knocked on the open door behind Boone, announcing his presence before entering Boone's office at the Alton County sheriff's station.

"Not enough to suit me." Boone scrubbed his fingers over the square lines of his smoothly shaved jaw. The midday news broadcast out of Kansas City featured an update on the Rose Red Rapist assaults and murder. Vanessa Owen, the reporter who'd been hassling Dr. Kate outside her KCPD office, filled up most of the screen as she talked about "unsubstantiated leads" and the police being "closemouthed" about the potential witnesses and suspects they were interviewing.

There were uniformed police officers in the background, along with men and women and cameras and heated side discussions. But there was not one mention of the threat that had been made against Kate.

Boone's eyes were fixed on the cool blonde facing the crowd, answering questions from other reporters at a KCPD press conference. Dr. Kate Kilpatrick looked as beautifully sophisticated and composed as he remembered. Her serene facade and articulate words were no doubt a reassuring panacea for a city living in fear. But he was drawn to the darting focus of her moss-colored eyes. The movement was subtle, but he'd seen her furtive glances more than once in the past few minutes. It was as though she was on guard against an off-camera threat.

Did she have reason to be afraid? Had she received another sick message painted in blood? Had there been another type of communication from the Rose Red Rapist? Was there some other man she clung to like a lifeline when her emotions broke through those barriers of self-control and overwhelmed her?

That classy composure had gone right out the window that night in the parking garage. He hadn't had a woman hold on to him that tightly since...hell, he'd never known a woman so desperate to hold on to someone. It was like Dr. Kate had two settings—the I've-got-it-all-under-control ice queen and the passionate, compassionate firebrand that he suspected came out only under such dire circumstances.

Flint leaned a hip against Boone's desk and sat back to watch the end of the broadcast. "Is that the lady you were talking about? The police psychologist who cleared the red tape for you with KCPD?"

"Yep."

"She's been on the news before, talking about the attacks. I can see why they'd put her on camera. She's a looker."

Boone rolled his gaze up to his deputy. "She's the task force's press liaison. And a trained criminal profiler. She knows what she's talking about."

"Maybe she's good. But she's not doing us any favors." Flint arched a golden brow with skepticism. "Has she called you with any updates? Like finding the man who gave Janie that ring you mentioned?"

"Nope. Out of sight, out of mind, I guess."

Although the sweet-smelling psychologist with the cool reserve and passionate grip had never been far from his mind these past few days. Had the woman just been playing him the same way she was working those reporters? Promising phone calls? Keeping him in the loop? Or had that been her assignment the day he'd gone to K.C. to bring his sister home? Do or say whatever it took to get that bullheaded country boy out of KCPD's hair.

If Kate Kilpatrick thought some heavy conversations and a few touches would get rid of him, then she and the entire task force were mistaken. He'd cleared his schedule for a week—and was prepared to take a sabbatical from his duties as sheriff if necessary—in order to get back to the city and track down the answers he needed. If they decided to cooperate with *his* investigation, Boone would allow it. But if they got in the way of finding Janie's killer—or tried to distract him with the good doctor again—then cooperation was off the table.

"Shall we head out?" Flint stood as soon as the news story ended and Boone turned off the TV. "Colt, Shane and Lucas are waiting for you outside."

Hearing his brothers' names reminded Boone of his immediate responsibilities. The four Harrison men had weathered a lot of ups and downs together throughout their lives. Their bond of blood and friendship made them each stronger. They'd need that strength today.

"Is everything ready?" Boone asked.

Flint nodded. "The traffic's been cleared off the courthouse square, and I lined up a couple of the off-duty guys to lead the procession out to the cemetery following the service. I put the word out, too, that everyone was welcome out at the ranch for potluck and reminiscing."

Good. Just how Boone had ordered it for today. After three days of rain had swept through nearly all of Missouri, he'd even gotten the sunny skies he'd wanted for Janie's sake.

There was really only one thing wrong with the way things were running in Grangeport today.

"Come on, boss." Flint put on his hat and headed for the door. "We've got a funeral to go to."

Boone nodded. He checked the gun at his waist, straightened his tie and grabbed his hat off the coatrack beside the door. Then he headed outside to greet the dark-haired man wearing a bolo tie and business suit.

"Colt." He shook his next oldest brother's hand and pulled him in for a hug. As they separated, Boone looked beyond him to the frail woman waiting in a truck beside the curb. "Will Sally be able to make it today?"

Colt's wife had been battling cancer for several months. He turned and winked at the blonde, who blew Boone a kiss. "She's tired, but she's having a pretty good day. She probably won't be able to make the reception, but she insisted on attending the service."

Boone tipped his hat to his sister-in-law. "Good. That would have meant a lot to Janie. It means a lot to me, too."

"I don't think I could get through today without her." Colt's chest heaved with a deep sigh. "I'm not sure how I'm going to get through any day without her."

Boone squeezed his brother's arm. "She's got good doctors, Colt. We'll just keep praying."

"I finally got the rug rats settled down." Shane Harrison, the third-born son of the family, joined them on the sidewalk in front of the sheriff's office. More lawyer than cowboy, the single dad nonetheless wore a Stetson that he pulled off to warn his ten-year-old son back into his truck to keep an eye on his younger sisters. "If they're not being ornery, they're crying. I don't think they've quite grasped that 'Aunt Jane's gone' means they won't see her again."

Boone offered Shane a wry grin. "If you figure out how to explain it to them, then you can explain it to me."

Shane opened his arms to exchange a hug. "That's one answer I don't have. All I want to do is wrap them up in a hug and protect them from days like this."

Lucas, the Harrison clan's youngest brother, strode up to the gathering. "Any word on who's responsible for today yet, Boone?" The tallest and biggest of them, Lucas wrapped each of them in a bear hug. A cop in the nearby college town of Columbia, Missouri, he, too, wore a gun and badge like his oldest brother. "I can't tell you how bad I want to shoot something today."

Assuming the mantle of family leadership as he had since their parents' deaths, Boone tried to calm his youngest brother's temper as well as offer the strength and reassurance they all needed. "I'm working on it, Lucas. KCPD is going to give us answers. We'll see justice done. I guarantee it." He swept his gaze around the strong circle of family. "But today we need to focus on Janie. And on all the friends and loved ones who are going to miss her, too."

"Not a problem," Colt assured him.

"Whatever you say, big brother," Shane agreed.

Lucas made them all smile again. "But tomorrow we kick somebody's butt, right?"

"*I* kick somebody's butt," Boone clarified, giving his youngest brother a teasing swat to the shoulder. "Let's do this. Let's honor Janie."

They each headed to their respective trucks to get the procession to the church started. The service and reception afterward were just formalities to appease their guests.

As far as Boone was concerned, Janie couldn't really be laid to rest until he had the man who'd murdered her behind bars. Or lying in a grave of his own.

SPENCER MONTGOMERY PULLED IN behind the long row of vehicles lining the drive up to Boone Harrison's ranch. "I need you to work your magic on Sheriff Harrison again, Kate."

"My magic?" She'd spent fewer than twenty-four hours with the small-town sheriff, yet in that short time she'd argued with him, reasoned with him, consoled him…and kissed him. Sounded more like out-of-control craziness rather than any kind of magic.

But bless Spencer Montgomery's sensible soul. He hadn't been talking about any male-female vibe she'd felt with Boone. "You've got a way of reading people, even on their worst of days. I need you to put those profiling skills to work and get these people to open up and tell us about the victim."

"Worst of days," she echoed, thinking back to the day she'd buried her husband, and how the day had been as much about painful gossip and feeling like a fool as it had been about grief. She'd been asked a lot of questions that day, too.

"Did you know Brad had a heart condition? That he had a mistress?"

"Do you think she made him take that performance pill?"

"You must be devastated, finding out this way that your husband had been lying to you for months. How do you feel?"

"And she was a good friend?"

"Poor thing. What are you going to do?"

She'd picked up the tattered remains of her heart and pride, grown a lot wiser, and poured herself into her career.

"Has to be done." Spencer turned off the engine and pocketed his keys.

Kate wished she could turn off her concerns as easily. The setting might be different, the tragedy these friends and family would be talking about was different, but a lot of the scene here in the countryside west of Grangeport felt familiar. She glanced around at the groups of people gathered near different cars, the children climbing over a fence and running to a swing set and fort to play. There were elderly women carrying casserole dishes up to the broad front porch that wrapped around the log and stone house where Boone lived.

She spotted him immediately at the top of the porch steps, along with three other similarly dark-haired men she guessed to be younger brothers, shaking hands and trading hugs with the guests attending this reception. The necessary armor that had gotten her through Brad's funeral and the career she'd devoted herself to softened as her heart went out to Boone and his family. "As a counseling psychologist, and not a profiler, I'm rethinking the wisdom of this idea. It looks like the entire population of Grangeport is here. They need time to mourn."

"We don't have the luxury of time with this guy. So far, all our leads have taken us to crackpots and dead ends." Spencer reminded her why they'd driven two and a half hours from Kansas City. "There has to be someone Jane Harrison was close enough to that she shared her secrets—a brother, a friend. The longer it takes us to find out who she was having that affair with, the more time we're giving our rapist to blend back in with society and fall completely off our radar until he strikes again."

Kate nodded, sharing another grim truth. "And now that his violence has escalated to murder, we need to catch him while his nerves are still a little unsettled by what he's done—before he decides he can get an even bigger rush of power from killing his victims."

Spencer adjusted the dark lenses of his sunglasses over his pale eyes and opened the car door. "I don't want our investigation to turn into a search for a serial killer. Been there, done that."

Kate knew the toll that working the Rich Girl Killer case over the last couple of years had taken on the typically unflappable Detective Montgomery. He'd solved the crimes, and a SWAT team had taken out the killer when he'd gone after Spencer's star witness. And while the notoriety of the detective's success on painstakingly difficult investigations like the RGK murders had gotten him the appointment to lead the task force, Kate knew from confidential meetings as counselor and client that there was a lot of damage eating away at the soul beneath his unemotional exterior.

"Me, either." Understanding that victims and their families weren't the only ones who benefitted from a speedy resolution to a crime, Kate unfastened her seat belt. "Let's do this and then leave these people alone to grieve."

Kate tensed at the familiar *ding-dong* of her phone alerting her to an incoming text message. There were a lot of people—clients, coworkers, friends—who might send her a text. But she had three days' worth of reasons she wanted to ignore the summons. But with Detective Montgomery waiting patiently for her to check it, and an unpleasant task waiting to be completed as quickly as possible, Kate inhaled a soft breath and opened her phone.

I'm coming for you, Kate. To silence your lies. You'll never catch me.

Kate's blood chilled in her veins.

"Is that another one from him?" Spencer asked.

He'd seen the vandalism of her car, and the message that had been left for her in some poor cat's blood. The task force was also monitoring the strange reports and vague threats coming in through KCPD's anonymous tip line. The task force knew she'd been contacted via text message by someone they suspected could be the killer. But no one knew how many texts and calls she'd been receiving on her personal phone every time her image appeared on TV or in the newspaper. Annie Hermann's lab had determined the personal calls had come from an untraceable, prepaid cell. Since Kate's name was listed as the public contact person on the task force's investigation, there was no way of knowing if the threats were coming from one person, or if she was being vilified as the scapegoat for frightened citizens who only wanted to feel safe again.

She could relate.

"No." Kate snapped her phone shut and tucked it into her coat pocket.

"Kate." Spencer wasn't buying the lie.

She confirmed his suspicion. "Let's get this over with and find Jane Harrison's killer. Then the threats will stop."

"Sounds like a plan."

Her doubts set aside by the needs of the case, and her fear put on hold behind a smile, Kate opened her door and stepped outside into the crisp, sunny air. As if drawn by a magnet, her gaze sought out Boone again. But the pull of a magnet worked both ways, and an unexpected shiver of awareness danced across her skin when she saw that Boone's eyes were already focused on her. Despite the bustle of activity between them, he'd noticed her arrival.

Had he noticed the fear that made her tremble the way she had that night in the parking garage, too?

Kate hesitated for a moment, snared by the probing depth of his focus on her. She couldn't remember her own husband ever being so attuned to her presence, able to make her feel like she was the most important woman in the room, or—a couple carrying a sleeping toddler walked past, diverting her attention—like she was the only face in a crowd that mattered.

It was a heady, warming—uncomfortable—feeling, considering the day and the details about his sister she needed to share. Secrets had nearly ruined Kate's life.

She couldn't imagine they'd be any easier for Boone and his family to learn about, either.

"Shall we?" Spencer asked, tapping the roof of the car and snagging her attention away from Boone. "I'll keep my distance, since Harrison likes to butt heads. Maybe I can find some local residents who are willing to talk to me. But I need you to talk to the family."

"Of course."

With Kate's first step, the heel of her navy blue pump sank into the mud and sucked the shoe right off her foot. Not a good omen for the success of this visit. But she was nothing if not professional. A little cool mud between her toes and an anonymous threat on her cell phone wouldn't keep her from doing her job—even if she did feel as if she had Fish Out of Water stamped on her forehead. Boone had been the odd man out that day in Kansas City, but it hadn't stopped him from relentlessly pursuing the truth, coming to her rescue and giving her a memorable kiss. With nary a high-rise in sight or a smooth sidewalk to traverse, Kate was far from familiar territory. But she wouldn't let the awkwardness she felt inside keep her from doing right by the woman whose life these people were celebrating here today.

Spencer had joined a gathering of sheriff's deputies, and Kate's shoes were ruined by the time she reached the steps below Boone on the porch. A young deputy with sun-bleached hair nudged Boone and inclined his head toward her. "Boss."

Boone spared a moment to make eye contact and tip the brim of his hat, but he wanted to finish a conversation with the couple in front of him first. "Irene." He leaned in to trade a light hug with the slender brunette. "I'm glad you drove in from St. Louis."

The woman caught Boone's fingers and squeezed them between hers. "I'm so sorry, Boone. I know you and I parted ways some time ago, but Janie was my friend. She was such an outgoing, talented girl. I'll miss her."

Kate watched him extricate his fingers from the woman's grip. "We all will." He reached around her to shake the shorter man's hand. "Fletcher. Thanks for coming."

"I feel like I knew your sister, since Irene talks about your family." He glanced around at Boone's brothers. "There's the muscle, and the brain, and the quiet one. You're the leader. I guess that made your sister the good-lookin' one." The man named Fletcher laughed, but when Boone didn't join in, he sobered up. "I meant that as a compliment. Losing her is a real tragedy."

"Yep." Boone stretched his arm down the steps toward Kate, inviting her to join them. "Dr. Kate? There's someone I want you to meet. This is my ex-wife, Irene, and her husband, Fletcher Mayne."

Awkward was the word of the day as Boone's fingers folded around hers and he pulled her up to his side and dropped his arm behind her, aligning them together as friends, or, perhaps, even a couple. But the introductions had stopped, and the fingers pinching the nip of her waist reminded her of all the well-wishers she'd endured at Brad's funeral. Kate covered the silence by holding out her hand. "I'm Kate Kilpatrick. I'm a... friend of Boone's."

Irene seemed slightly taken aback, but by what, Kate wasn't sure. "Really. You're a doctor?"

Was the woman checking out her clothes?

"She lives in K.C.," Boone added.

The woman's blue eyes widened even further. "Really?" She lifted her blue eyes to her ex. "Boone, you don't like the city." And then it was back to Kate. "You got this big lug off the ranch? How did you two meet?"

Irene's husband reached for Kate with a smooth, buffed and manicured hand. "Forgive my wife's curiosity. I'm Dr. Mayne. But call me Fletcher. I'm a surgeon. And you?"

"Counseling psychologist."

"Nice to meet you." He linked his arm through his wife's and guided her toward the front door. "Come on, Irene. Boone has other guests to talk to."

Once the storm door swung shut behind the exiting couple, Kate scooted away from the faintly possessive stamp of Boone's touch. "What just happened?"

His chest expanded with a deep breath beneath the Western tailored suit coat he wore. "I'll tell you that if you tell me why you're here."

"I need to ask some follow-up questions. Get some personal insight into your sister's life."

Someone jostled against Kate's back and Boone pulled her over to the porch's wood railing, where he sat, putting his warm brown gaze level with hers. "You could have used a phone for that."

Kate's fingertips danced against her palms as she fought the urge to touch the lines of strain that had settled a little more deeply beside his eyes from when she'd last seen him. "If you don't have the answers, I'm guessing someone around here will. It's a little awkward, but the people who can give us the best information about the hometown girl are probably here today."

"Don't you upset anybody."

"I'll do my best not to." She pointed to the front

door where Irene and Fletcher Mayne had gone inside. "And the introduction to the ex? She thinks you and I are an item."

"Let her think it."

"Boone, we hardly know—"

"Fine." He put up his hands, warding off the rest of her friendly reprimand. He tipped his hat back on his head, revealing more of the jet-black sheen of his hair and the extent of the emotional drain these last few days had taken on him. "Let's just say I've about had my fill of making nice and socializing today. I can't fault Irene for maintaining a friendship with my sister." His voice dropped to a husky whisper, and Kate leaned in closer to listen. "But she left me for that man. She didn't want my children, didn't want this place—and finally decided she didn't even want me. And now she shows up with him?" A wry grin creased his rugged features. "Kind of tough on a man's pride, I suppose."

On a woman's, too. Understanding Boone's pain far better than he knew, Kate followed the instincts of her hand and heart. Her thigh brushed against Boone's knee when she reached out to cup his cheek and smooth her fingertips over the grooves beside his eyes. "All of the emotions—hurt, grief, anger, pride—come to the surface at a time like this. No one would think any less of you if you took a few minutes for yourself."

"*I'd* think less of me." Her hand vanished against his face as he covered it with his. He rubbed his warm, sandpapery skin against her ticklish palm, sensitizing every nerve ending where they touched. Just when she thought she needed to say something, do something, move closer or pull away entirely, Boone turned to press a comforting kiss into her palm before pulling her hand down to his lap and lacing his fingers together with hers. He glanced down at her muddy shoes. "Irene was sizing up the mess on your designer clothes. It was a big reason why she left."

It took Kate a split second to move past the unfamiliar liquid warmth seeping from her hand into the rest of her body. When had comfort and understanding turned into something else? "The mud?"

"All the country living that goes with it. You're a lot like her, you know. Sophisticated. Urban." Boone's thumb continued to stroke over her skin, making it difficult to concentrate.

"Is that good or bad?"

"It just is. Sorry about the shoes. We'll talk later, okay? If you'll excuse me, I need to check on my brothers. Make sure they're holding up okay. Food and refreshments are inside." Kate stuffed her hands inside the pockets of her coat to combat the chill as Boone abruptly released her and stood. He adjusted his Stetson squarely on his head and then moved past her to greet an elderly couple coming up the stairs. "Jack. Shirley. Thank you for coming."

And just like that, the unsophisticated country boy without the M.D. behind his name had maneuvered his way out of answering any of Kate's questions regarding the case.

For the moment.

Kate chuckled softly to herself, admiring how slyly Boone had accomplished his goal of getting out of difficult conversations—and he'd done it with a teasing grin, a hushed voice and quick thinking. She had a feeling Irene and the new hubby, who clearly made a lot of money and liked to talk more than he should, had no clue that they'd just been played by a good ol' country boy.

Of course, the frissons of awareness still fluttering beneath her skin were clear evidence that she'd been played, too. But Kate didn't seem to mind as much as she'd expected. Boone had promised her *later*. And for today, for now, at least, she'd believe that promise.

A pair of shoes and a smidgen of trust were tiny sacrifices to make for coming here.

As she grasped the porch railing and surveyed the beehive of activity around her, she knew there were plenty of people here who might have the answers she sought. Kate crossed to the front door and went inside the log cabin house.

She'd start with the two people she'd just met.

"THANKS, ROBIN." Kate stepped back as Jane Harrison's friend and former employer, Robin Carter, opened her car door. "Have a safe trip back to K.C."

"I will." The floral designer tossed her purse onto the passenger seat, but paused before getting in. "And you'll keep me in the loop if you find out anything about the man who attacked Jane? I told the women who work for me about the safety tips you suggested, but it's still a little scary to be working in that neighborhood. And here I thought it was an exciting, ideal place to open a business."

"It still is. Just keep practicing those safety precautions." Kate had been glad to find someone at the reception she already knew, even if it was just a witness she'd interviewed. "And if you think of any other details about Janie's life these past few months—even something you may have overlooked as insignificant—give me a call."

"I've got your card. Take care."

"You, too." Kate retreated back to the fence as the other woman turned her car around in the gravel drive and headed back to the highway.

She'd learned all kinds of things about Jane Harrison this afternoon. Janie had been a real tomboy growing up. She'd excelled at 4-H and in showing horses, in particular. She'd worked at a diner in town on the square and been elected homecoming queen in high school. She'd studied art at Stephens College in Columbia, Missouri, opened a studio that had failed as soon as the Ozarks tourist season had ended, and had planned a big wedding to the high school quarterback, which she'd called off just a few months before moving to Kansas City.

All interesting stuff—a testament to how well-loved a young woman she'd been. But none of it was helping to narrow down the search for a confidante who could say who Janie had been seeing in K.C. No one here seemed to have any idea about the mystery man in Janie's life.

Turning toward the dramatic beauty of the orange, pink and gold sunset falling behind the dark brown outlines of Boone's family home, Kate sought out the man who'd been avoiding her all afternoon. The crowd in attendance had thinned considerably, lessening Boone's responsibilities as host. And his ex-wife and her second husband had driven away more than an hour ago, making an excuse to depart almost as soon as Kate had brought up the subject of Jane Harrison and her dating life. So there was no reason for Boone to be hiding from anyone.

Unless, of course, it was her.

Maybe the hushed words and sensuous hand holding had been a diversion to keep the conversation from turning to painful subjects. For a few minutes on his front porch, they'd shared an intimate link that, logically, she had no reason to believe. And yet she'd fallen for them—she'd believed that the sheriff had truly needed her for a few moments to recoup his strength, and would seek her out before she had to leave.

Whether she'd been a fool or not, Spencer Montgomery was counting on her to make that connection to Boone again. And with those disturbing threats promising to follow her until this case was closed and Jane Harrison's killer was behind bars, Kate intended to get the job done.

The air was cooling as the sun sank closer to the horizon. Kate pulled the collar of her trench coat up around her neck as she followed the road back to the house where she'd last seen Boone. But a sad sound, a drawn-out breath, a moan of despair, drew her attention to a shiny green pickup truck as she walked past.

As soon as Kate realized she'd stumbled onto Boone's young blond deputy sitting on the rear bumper, looking at a photograph in his wallet and fighting to stem the tears rolling down his cheeks, she raised her hand in an unspoken apology and backed away. But the moment he saw her, he shot to his feet. He snapped the billfold shut and swiped at his eyes with the back of his hand.

"I'm sorry." Kate apologized out loud this time, hating that she'd intruded on the private moment. "I didn't mean to interrupt. I wasn't sure what I'd heard. I was concerned."

"It's all right, ma'am." He gave his face another swipe. "Did you need something?"

The pink tip of his nose gave an indication of how long he'd been crying. She wasn't sure if it was the counselor or the investigator or something else buried deeper inside her that made her take a step closer and ask, "It's Deputy Larson, isn't it?"

"Yes, ma'am. You can call me Flint."

"Are you all right, Flint?"

"I will be. I guess."

She dropped her gaze to the wallet still clutched in his hand. "What were you looking at?"

"Silly for a grown man to cry, huh?" But he rested his forearms on the tailgate of the truck and opened his billfold to a fading photograph.

"It's sillier for him not to care at a time like this." Kate went to stand beside him to look at the picture of a couple at a high-school prom, judging by the matching gown and tux, and corsage the young girl wore on her wrist. The raven-black hair was long and straight, but there was no mistaking Janie Harrison. And the boy was a younger version of Deputy Larson. The high-school quarterback. "You and Janie used to date?"

He nodded. He caressed the photo, then quickly folded his wallet and tucked it into his back pocket as a sniffle hinted at the tears he was suppressing. "We dated in high school."

"I'm sorry for your loss. Today must be hard for you."

Could Flint be the potential link to Janie's past that she'd been looking for?

"I reckon."

A frustratingly brief answer. But Kate had a lot of experience getting people to open up and talk. A direct question relating to a murder was rarely the best way to begin a conversation.

It didn't take long to get an inspiration. She stepped around the scratched-up steel ball of the truck's trailer hitch and ran her fingers along the polished metal die-cut of a rearing stallion that had been mounted over the rear taillight. The reverse image of pawing forelegs and a flying mane covered the opposite taillight.

"Wow. This is some truck." She nodded to the thick, deeply treaded tires that jacked it up higher than a regular pickup. "Looks like you need a stepladder to climb into it."

"No, ma'am." Flint grinned and relaxed a bit. "But the long legs help."

"These decorations are unusual. They look custom-made. Is that the right term?" She looked up at Flint, expecting to see pride in his four-wheel baby. Instead, his nostrils were flaring with emotion again. "Did I say something wrong?"

Flint shook his head. But he smiled before the tears could come. "Janie designed those. She was one of a kind. She was in shop class when the other girls were learning how to cook and sew." He tapped his fist against the customized light cover. "One time I told her that driving this truck made me feel like riding a herd of wild horses, and when my next birthday rolled around, she'd made these."

This pickup was only a few years old. "So you were more than high school sweethearts?"

"I loved that woman. We were together a long time

after graduation. I asked her to marry me. She said yes and made me the happiest man on the planet. But she had her sights set on something out there in the big world. She wanted to be an artist. Somebody famous, I guess." He nodded up toward the house. "Sort of like Irene leaving Boone. She couldn't make her dreams come true here in Grangeport, either."

So it wasn't just the mud Boone's ex had had an aversion to. "What is it that Irene wanted to do?"

"I don't know. From what I hear, she throws parties and raises money for charity. Sounds boring to me. Her doctor came breezing through town one summer on his way to the lake." Flint tilted his head in a conspiratorial nod. "The next thing you knew, they were running away together. Maybe she just wanted to be swept off her feet."

The excitement of a new, illicit relationship had certainly been temptation enough for her husband. No wonder Boone had reached for her and claimed her. At least she would never have to feel the sting of running into a happy ex with the person chosen over her. "Irene cheated on Boone while they were still married?"

Flint nodded. "At least Janie had the heart to end it with me before she left." His gaze drifted off to a distant place and tears glistened in his eyes again. "I thought that was the saddest day of my life. But this…puttin' her in the ground breaks my heart. I always thought that somehow we'd end up together."

She laid her hand over his fist where it rested on the tailgate and gave him a sympathetic pat. The bruises on his knuckles indicated he might have been doing more than crying and looking at photographs as a means of dealing with his grief. "How did you hurt yourself?"

"Punched a wall at the office when I heard the news."

"I'm so sorry." Although a knife of guilt twisted in her gut at taking advantage of the young man's grief, Kate needed more information. "Did the two of you ever talk? After she moved to Kansas City?"

"If she needed a flat tire changed, or wanted to know how to fix a leaky toilet, she'd call." He pulled his hand from beneath hers. "I don't think she wanted her brothers to know she wasn't as independent as she claimed she was."

"She still called you for favors like that?"

"Not lately."

"Because she had another man in Kansas City who'd take care of those things for her?" After a long moment, Flint nodded. "Did she ever say who it was?"

"I never caught a name. It was some guy at school where she taught evening classes. I think she started to feel like the city was home, instead of Grangeport. The phone calls got fewer and farther between." He hooked his thumbs in the belt of his uniform and stepped away with a deep breath. "She didn't need me anymore. I guess she was calling him."

"Doing okay, Flint?" The deep voice from behind Kate explained why the deputy had suddenly straightened to attention.

The young man winked at Kate. "The doc here was listening to my troubles."

"She's good at that." Boone's hand skimmed Kate's back as he moved up beside her. "I know you're scheduled for duty tonight, but if you need some more time, I'll find someone to cover for you."

"That's okay, boss. I'd rather stay busy." He pulled

his keys from his pocket before nodding to them both. "Ma'am. Boss. Hopefully, it won't be a slow night."

"And I always hope that it is." Boone pulled Kate aside until Flint Larson had started his truck and sped off down the road, throwing up plenty of mud onto the clean chassis. "So I'm guessing you're not here to console me. And I know Detective Montgomery isn't." He pointed up to the porch where Spencer stood in a semicircle with Boone's brothers and carried on a conversation. When Kate turned up the driveway to join them, Boone caught her hand and tugged her in a different direction—across the yard toward the barn and other outbuildings. "I've been following the news broadcasts with your reports. Doesn't sound like you've got any leads."

"We're keeping some of our suspicions and information out of the press." She let her hand rest inside his without really holding on. "We still have some follow-up questions we need to ask about your sister, and I think Flint just pointed us in the right direction. Did she ever mention the name of a man at the college where she taught? I think that's the missing boyfriend we're looking for."

He shortened his stride to accommodate the careful steps her high-heels forced her to take across the grass. "You don't think Janie was dating the Rose Red Rapist, do you?"

"No. I don't think so. He's an opportunistic rapist, not a planner. It wouldn't fit his profile." She tightened her grip, telling him without words that she knew these details were difficult for him to hear. "But I do think finding this boyfriend will give us key information about Janie's activities right before she was attacked.

This mystery man may have been the last person to have contact with her. Maybe she said something, or he saw someone…"

His fingers squeezed almost painfully around hers. "What was wrong with this guy that she kept him a secret from me and the rest of us—even from her friends in Kansas City?"

"I think he was married," Kate stated quietly.

Boone shook his head and pulled away. "No. She wouldn't do that. She knows what I went through with Irene. She wouldn't wreck someone else's life."

"She was young and pretty and vibrant, according to everyone I've spoken to here today. What man wouldn't fall in love with her?"

"Falling for her, I get. But Janie having an affair with a married man?"

"Sometimes you can't help who you fall in love with. And he probably lied to her—told her he was leaving his wife, or that they'd grown apart and the marriage wasn't any good." Her own bitterness filtered in. "He's a selfish man, trying to have the best of both worlds— the stability and reputation of a marriage plus the thrill of a conquest."

Kate heard the words tumble out of her mouth and wished she could pull them back when she saw how Boone's gaze narrowed and his lips flattened into a grim line. It was so rare for her to misspeak like that, to utter words without thinking of the consequences, that it shocked her into silence. Had that been Brad's excuse for his affair with Vanessa? He couldn't help who he fell in love with? What lies had he told Vanessa about his marriage to Kate? Had Boone's ex made the same hurtful excuses to him? "I…I'm sorry. I'm sure Janie meant a lot to this man. And I'm sure she didn't mention him to you because she wanted to spare your feelings."

"Unlike you."

She reached for him. "Boone—"

"I'm sorry, too." He backed away, avoiding her outstretched hand. And then he tipped his face to the evening sky and cursed before nailing her with a raw look. "I can't do this right now. Every nerve in my body is fried. Give me an hour to decompress if you want me to think straight." He took a couple of steps toward the barn before looking back over his shoulder at her. "Unless you want to go riding with me?"

Kate's eyes widened. "On a horse?"

For a moment, his expression darkened, intensified. Kate's mind leapt to the idea of riding…other things. Her cheeks felt feverish in the cooling air at the thought of helping Boone assuage his grief with something much more intimate than a conversation.

But if he'd been thinking of a roll in the hay, he never let on. He blinked and the invitation she'd imagined seeing there was gone. "That's generally the way it's done."

She couldn't keep playing these games with him. Barging into her life unannounced. Unexpected kisses. Holding hands, blunt words. He made her say things without thinking and messed up the necessary order of her life. He'd gotten too far into her head already. Way too far.

"If we could just do this now," she begged, "then I could get back to the city, you could get back to your life and we could both get back to work."

He strode away, clicking his tongue against his teeth and calling to a big, tan-colored horse in the corral beside the barn. "I need one hour to myself, Doc. Grange-port isn't that big. I'll find you when I'm done."

"Boone—"

"One hour."

Why was she chasing after him? She forced herself to stop. "Promise?"

He stopped and looked at her then. "Why would I say something if I didn't mean it?"

"Not everyone who makes a promise keeps it."

Kate tilted her chin against the brown-eyed scrutiny.

"I do." He opened the corral gate and grabbed the horse's halter to lead it into the barn. "I'll find you in an hour."

Chapter Six

He didn't have to look hard to find her.

By the time Boone had rubbed down Big Jim and stowed the tack, night had fallen, and the family and guests from Janie's reception had all left. In fact, the only vehicle left in the drive was his own black pickup.

So where was Kate?

Boone ran to the house's mudroom entrance off the kitchen. She'd made such a fuss about him getting back in an hour—okay, so it had been seventy-five minutes—that she'd probably taken off with Spencer Montgomery and gone back to Kansas City. His tardiness was probably all the proof she needed to believe he wasn't a man of his word.

"Kate?" he shouted. Before he'd taken that ride out to the bluffs and back to clear his head and purge the worst of the sadness and rage that had been simmering beneath the surface all day long, she'd seemed desperate that he keep his promise to return to discuss the task force's investigation. And she'd seemed equally certain that he wouldn't. "Kate!"

He tracked his mucky boots straight into the kitchen before he saw her standing at the coffeemaker, pouring a couple of mugs of what smelled like fresh, hot java. The aroma of home-ground beans and the subtler scent of Kate herself filled his nose and drained the fight right out of him.

"You're here." He offered the lame greeting, wondering at the relief coursing through his system.

She picked up one mug and carried it across the kitchen to him. "You said you'd come back to talk."

"I wasn't sure you believed me."

"I wasn't sure I did, either."

Humbled by her honesty, and determined to convince her that she could count on him to do what he promised, Boone took the mug she offered and took a sip of the fragrant, reviving brew. "Thanks."

Relieved to know she hadn't gone and as ready as he was ever going to be to talk about his sister's secret life, he handed the coffee mug back to Kate and took a few minutes to hang up his hat and jacket, and take off his boots back in the mudroom. After securing his gun and badge in a drawer near the back door, he grabbed the broom and swept his trail out of the kitchen. "If my mother was still alive, she'd have a cow over me tracking this mess into her house."

He was curiously pleased to notice that Kate hadn't just made coffee, but had truly made herself at home. She'd kicked off the shoes and hose she'd totaled and was padding around the kitchen in a pair of Boone-sized white socks. When she saw him watching her feet, she thinned her mouth into an apology. "I hope it's okay if I borrow these. I found them folded up in the basket in the laundry room. My toes were cold."

"Not at all." The cotton socks were an odd contrast to the tailored skirt and blouse she still wore, but he liked the homey, not quite so uptight, twist to her wardrobe.

Even something as unsexy as a pair of socks perked up his awareness of Dr. Kate. Could be it was just a little rush of possessive appreciation at the idea of her wearing his clothes. He crossed to the polished oak table where she'd put his mug of coffee. She'd set a place for her mug and cell phone at the opposite end. Just two place settings. Good. "Where's Montgomery?"

She stood at the microwave, watching a plate with a paper towel draped over it spin around. "He went with your brother Lucas to a place called Nettie's for dinner."

"It's a bar up in town that serves sandwiches and appetizers."

The microwave dinged, and she plucked out the steaming paper towel and tossed it into the trash beneath the sink. "I cleaned up a bit and made up a plate of leftovers for you, in case you were hungry, too." She set the plate of casserole samplings on the table and gestured for him to sit. "I know at events like this, the host doesn't usually eat much."

"I didn't. Thanks." He waited for her to sit before he picked up his fork and joined her. She wound her fingers around her mug to warm them while he tasted the cheesy mac and beef and something crunchy with an Oriental tang. He hoped she'd eaten while he was out. He hoped she was ready for the question that had been nagging at him since he'd saddled Big Jim. "So why don't you trust me, Doc?"

"Oh, it's…" green eyes met his across the length of the table, then discovered something fascinating in the depths of her coffee "…it's not you."

Boone took another bite. "So who *do* you trust?"

Her gaze searched the cabinets now. "I don't suppose you have any tea instead of coffee around here, do you?"

"Nobody, huh?"

The mossy-green eyes found him again, conceding trust issues. He had to give the woman credit. Whatever thoughts were running through her head looked like they were pretty tough to sort through. But she wasn't shying away from them.

"Flint told me about your wife—your ex-wife," she amended. "I wanted to apologize for those things I said before at the barn. I know how it feels, when the person you love and have pledged your life to cheats on your marriage. I was letting some of my own feelings get into the mix, and my words wound up being hurtful, and I'm sorry." Irene's infidelity was old news. He appreciated the apology, but hearing some selfish lowlife had treated Kate the same way? Boone stabbed his fork in a meatball and waited to hear the rest. "I, um—the reason Vanessa Owen and I were arguing outside my office, why we don't get along well is—"

"Was she the other woman?"

"Yes. And I felt particularly stupid about the affair because I didn't find out about it—I had no clue—until my husband had a heart attack and died while he was… in bed with her."

"That's rough." Boone forgot the food and reached across table to pry her hand off the coffee she held. He rubbed his thumb over her knuckles, concerned by the chill he felt there despite the warm mug. "I wondered about your husband. You're too smart and too pretty to have never been attached to anyone. He's the stupid one, if you ask me."

"Thanks." She turned her hand in his. "I think the

same way about Irene." Her mouth softened with half a smile. "I spent half an hour talking to her and Fletcher, and somehow the conversation always came around and ended up being about him."

Kate's smile triggered one of his own. "Self-centered jerk."

Tiny lines crinkled beside her eyes when she laughed. "I think Flint was right. She's probably bored out of her mind with that guy."

"I don't know. She said she was bored here, too."

"With that gorgeous sunset I saw tonight? And all the friendly people?"

She'd noticed the sunset? Boone laced his fingers together with hers and studied her expression until her cheeks dotted with color and he was certain her appreciation for the scenery around here was genuine. "Maybe you have less in common with my ex-wife than I gave you credit for."

"Is that a compliment?"

"Definitely."

Despite the blush, an unsmiling gravity returned to her expression. "So, are we okay?"

The glimpse of vulnerability in this normally confident woman touched the places that were raw and hurting inside him. Without releasing her hand, he stood to walk around the table and tug her to her feet. He heard a formal gasp of protest when he palmed either side of her waist and pulled her to him until his thighs could feel the warmth of hers against them. "I want to be more than okay with you, Doc."

She braced her hands in the middle of his chest and leaned back. "Boone—"

"I know you're cautious and guarded and like to

think things through. But right now I just want to feel."
He smoothed the silky, honey-gold bangs off her forehead and pressed a kiss to one golden brow. "I want to
forget all I've lost and grab hold of something good."
He watched the caution light go on in those pretty green
eyes as he kissed first one cheek and then the other.
The pale skin warmed with heat beneath each caress,
and the tips of her fingers curled into the muscles of
his chest. "I want you to admit that you're feeling what
I'm feeling, and find out what good places those feelings can take us to."

He dipped his head and pressed a gentle kiss against
her lips. They trembled. Parted. He kissed them again.

"I don't think—"

"Shh." Boone pushed a finger over her lips. "I don't
want you to think, Doc. Not about how you've been
hurt in the past, not about how you're worried you'll
be hurt again. I just want you to feel this moment—be
in this moment with me. Trust me. For this moment."

For an endless second, he thought she might not respond to his request. Then she tilted her eyes to his and
nodded beneath his hand.

"Not a word," he reminded her. He didn't want logic
or fears talking her out of the connection he believed
she needed—the same connection he knew he was craving like a thirsty man.

Kate's lips stretched into a smile beneath his fingertip.

With an approving nod and a grateful smile of his
own, Boone removed his finger and leaned down to
capture her lips. But Kate slid her arms around his neck
and rose up on tiptoe to meet him halfway.

Boone's mouth opened greedily over Kate's. She

tilted her face to give him access to every warm corner and soft swell of her lips. He felt the tips of her breasts knotting against his chest as she pulled herself closer. His hands found the sleek arch of her back and the womanly flare of her bottom. He lifted, pulled until he could feel her hips flush against his. He dipped his tongue inside her mouth to taste coffee and heat and the shy welcome of her tongue sliding against his.

The emotions of the day, of the entire week, tumbled together inside him and found an outlet in the white-hot fusion of her lips matching every foray of his, and in the needy grabs of her fingers in his hair, beneath his collar, against his feverish skin.

He had no memory of the ice princess who measured every word and controlled every action. This Kate was open and giving and grasping. She was everything he wanted in a woman, everything he needed. Right now. At this moment.

There were no words, no sounds beyond a gasp for breath or hum of pleasure. There was no thought or reason or doubt. There was only feeling.

The spark of attraction that had been there from their first meeting blazed like a lightning storm between them. And the understanding of two wounded souls coming together in healing passion lit up something close to his heart.

A voice from deep inside his head tried to warn him this was too much, too soon. But the whispering voice was drowned out by pain being assuaged, loneliness being cast aside, trust being nourished and mutual desire being given full rein.

Boone's thighs crowded against Kate's, backing her up against the table as he plundered her mouth. There was zero chill to her fingers now as she unhooked one button, and then another on his shirt to slip her hands inside and brand his skin.

In one fluid movement, Boone lifted her onto the table. If china rattled or silverware danced, he didn't hear it. Blind with need, his fingers found the hem of her skirt and tugged it up her legs. Her thighs were smooth and firm, and opened as willingly as her mouth, welcoming him. Boone pushed impossibly closer between them, nestling his swelling heat against hers.

It was hot. It was passionate. It was perfect.

He hadn't been with a woman for so long. And he couldn't remember ever wanting to be with one as much as he wanted Kate right now. Right here.

A bell rang in head. A mechanical *ding-dong,* like the doorbell, only much, much closer.

"What the…?" Boone dragged his mouth away from Kate's. Who would dare intrude on this moment?

Her breath rushed out in a moist caress against his neck. "Is that…? Where is…?"

He moved his hands to the more neutral location of her back and scanned the kitchen walls and mudroom exit, trying to orient himself to the sound.

"Boone, stop. I need to…" Kate's breathing was as ragged as his own as she pulled her hands from inside his shirt and scooted off the table, forcing him back half a step.

And then he saw light on Kate's cell phone. *1 msg Unknown*

He picked the phone up off the table before she could get turned around. He stepped back to give them each some room to cool off and reclaim some of the sanity he'd encouraged her to abandon. "Got a secret admirer?" he teased.

She snatched the phone from his hand and turned her back on him, putting the width of the kitchen between them. She was straightening her skirt and blouse, fluffing her hair with her fingers, getting that invisible armor into place before she flipped open the phone.

"Isn't it a wrong number?" Everything about her reaction to a misdirected text put him on guard. "Doc?"

"Just a sec."

There was no *just a sec*. The woman was shaking like an autumn leaf on the wind, despite the determined tilt of her chin. And he didn't think it all had to do with the aftershocks of that passionate tête-à-tête that he was still recovering from. Boone crept up behind her on silent feet and peered over her shoulder.

You're not as smart as you think you are, Kate. I will silence you if you don't stop telling lies.

"Son of a bitch."

"Boone!"

He plucked the phone from her hand and read the text a second time. There was no mistaking the threat he read there. Message 10 out of 10. He deflected Kate's hands as she tried to reclaim her phone. Boone scrolled through her Inbox and found seven previous texts from the same unknown caller. Each message was just as cryptic and venomous and vile as the threat she'd just received.

He caught her wrist when she reached for the phone again and held the evidence up to her face. "These are from him, aren't they. The Rose Red Rapist? First he vandalizes your car and now he's stalking you?" He let her pull free and grab the phone from him. "How long has this been going on?"

Her kiss-stained lips and wrinkled skirt warred with the defiance in her eyes. She snapped the phone shut and dropped it into her coat pocket on the back of her chair before facing him. "Every time I appear on television, or I'm quoted in the news—I'll get two or three texts or calls afterward."

"And Montgomery knows about these threats, right? He's putting a stop to them, isn't he?" Boone raked his fingers through his hair as she set that stoic expression into place. "Doc?"

"I'm developing a relationship with him—"

"With a serial rapist?" Anger and fear and misguided bravery were terrific antidotes for the electricity sparking through his system.

He listened in disbelief to the justification for not actively pursuing the threats or throwing away her phone or at least changing her number. "It's key to his profile, I believe. It's a way to smoke him out. He needs to feel superior to strong women—in this case, me. If he fixates on me, then he—"

"He'll rape and murder you, too."

"—won't go after anyone else." Kate's tone grew calmer, more articulate with each ludicrous sentence. She reached up to refasten the buttons of his white shirt and smooth the collar back into place. "He'll expose himself. He'll make a mistake. We can catch him."

That gentle touch, which had tamed his impulsive nature before, barely took the edge off his temper. He closed his fingers around her wrists and pulled them away. "I don't know how Montgomery runs an operation, but here, we do not put innocent people in harm's way for the sake of the investigation."

"Do you want to find Janie's killer?"

"Yes. But I don't want to lose anyone else in the process. I don't even like that you were here at the house by yourself."

Now the ice princess was back. She twisted her wrists from his grip and straightened the cuffs of her blouse. "Fortunately, it's not your call to make, since you're not part of the task force."

She wanted to go there again? He was the one losing the good people in his life. Boone Harrison wasn't about to go down without a fight—be it against a violent killer or the ice-cold logic of a woman whose passion and vulnerability were turning him inside out. "Get your shoes and coat on." He pulled his gun and badge out of the drawer where he'd stashed them and turned toward the mudroom to get his boots. "I'm taking you to Montgomery and we're going to discuss exactly what kind of dangerous mind game you're playing."

KATE DIDN'T KNOW if it was the pinch of her shrunken shoes, the noise from the jukebox and chatter of the bar or the black-haired cowboy arguing every statement she made that was giving her such a splitting headache.

"Let's take this outside," Spencer Montgomery ordered. She doubted that line dancing and country music were the lead detective's taste in evening entertainment, but he seemed to have no problem siding with Boone and reprimanding her about the text messages.

As the small town's sheriff, Boone apparently enjoyed the privilege of parking his truck wherever he wanted, so he'd pulled up onto the sidewalk just outside the front entrance.

As soon as the door to Nettie's closed behind them, there was a blessed reprieve to the decibel level of the noise pounding in Kate's ears. But there was no reprieve in the two-against-one standoff between her and the unlikely alliance of Boone and Spencer.

"How many of these messages have you received?" Spencer asked.

"Eight and counting," Boone answered before she could get a word in.

"Do you mind?" she countered, sensing she'd have a far better chance of reasoning her plan out with Spencer than with Boone.

Especially in the chaotically emotional state he seemed stuck in ever since that make-out session on his kitchen table that she'd foolishly let get out of hand, Kate wasn't so naive to think she'd had no part in how far things had gone. Between his seductive kisses and the hushed confessions they'd shared that had somehow brought them closer, and the bruised ego that truly wanted to believe that a mature, virile man like Boone was into her, she'd let all common sense go out the window. She'd done exactly as he'd asked, turning off the cautious intellect that had saved her from any hurt or humiliation since Brad's death, and simply *felt* the moment.

But she was tired, the headache was throbbing against her skull, and the chance to catch five minutes of quiet time to herself wasn't going to happen here. Maybe Boone could think and function in the midst of emotional turmoil, but she needed to step back and discuss things rationally.

She concentrated on Spencer's cool gray eyes and on the sensible man she knew him to be. "He's contacted me after each of the daily press conferences, and after Gabriel Knight's and Rebecca Cartwright's articles in the *Kansas City Journal*. And there have been two today since this morning's press conference."

Spencer asked to see her cell phone again. "You told me there'd only been a couple of calls. Has there been any physical escalation to these threats beyond the vandalism of your car? Have you had the sense that anyone is following you?"

Did the bullish sheriff pacing behind her count? "No. Only the texts."

The detective scrolled through the eight messages again. "All variations on the same theme. You're sure this is related to the investigation, and isn't something personal?"

"It's damn personal," Boone insisted, stopping at her shoulder.

"But is it a warning to the task force or to Kate specifically?"

She caught her breath at the heat radiating off Boone as he leaned in. "Have *you* gotten any messages that threaten to silence you?"

Spencer handed back her phone and Kate tucked it into the pocket of her coat. "And we're sure the number is untraceable?"

"Annie already checked it out. They're from different disposable cell phones."

"So they could be from more than one person."

"Or from someone who's smarter than you. You need to take her off this investigation, Montgomery," Boone advised. "Or at least put someone else in the public relations spotlight."

"That's exactly what you shouldn't do." Kate flattened her hand in the middle of Boone's unyielding chest and nudged him back a step. "Think about this guy's profile, Spencer. I'm the perfect bait to smoke him out. I'm the enemy he preys on personified. He's made a connection to me before we've been able to nail down a connection to him. If he wants to come after me, then let him."

"Doc!"

She turned to include both men in her argument, feeling a twinge of guilt at the grim lines of strain that had returned to deepen the grooves beside Boone's eyes. "How many women has he already hurt? How many innocent women like your sister have to pay the price for his sickness? It needs to stop." She turned back to her colleague. "People are afraid, Spencer. And I have the means to do something about it. If he fixates on me, he'll break the pattern. He'll make a mistake. Then we can catch the Rose Red Rapist and put him away for good."

"She's crazy," Boone muttered.

"It's a good idea, though." Spencer, at least, could see the merit in taking advantage of the rapist's newfound obsession with her. "From a police procedural perspective."

"Damn good one," Boone agreed.

"Really?" Kate was stunned to hear Boone's support. Or not. "Logically. On paper it may be a good idea." His eyes were unreadable pools of darkness in the shadows cast by the brim of his hat. "Doesn't mean I like it. This guy may never act on these threats. He doesn't confront women—he abducts them in the middle of the night when no one's looking. You can't put her in danger like that."

Kate wanted to reach out to Boone to ease the tension she heard in his tone. But she suspected a reassuring touch wouldn't be welcome right now, so she stuffed her hands into the deep pockets of her coat, instead. "It's not your decision, Boone."

"I know. I'm not a member of the task force. You're not my jurisdiction." His sardonic tone chafed against her ears and made her wish she didn't care quite so much about disappointing him. Or worrying him. Or... just how much did she care about Boone Harrison and what he felt about her?

"She's handled you okay," Spencer pointed out.

"Yeah, but I'm one of the good guys." A tipsy couple came out of the bar and stumbled past them. Boone made eye contact with them long enough to warn them away from the car they were headed to. Only after the man doffed him a salute and the couple walked on down the street instead of driving, did Boone resume the argument. "I have the same goal as your task force—to solve Janie's murder and get this guy off the streets. He's not interested in helping you solve the crimes."

Spencer, at least, was beginning to see the possibilities of the offer she'd made to serve as bait for the Rose Red Rapist. "You'd need twenty-four-hour protection, Kate. And you don't even carry a gun."

"Because I'm not a cop. I only work with them. But I do know how to use a gun."

He nodded. "You'd better start carrying."

She'd need to spend some time on the practice range, too, to refresh her skills. But she'd probably feel safer with her department-issued Glock in her purse, too. "All right."

"Hold on," Boone protested. "You mean you're actually considering this?"

Kate wasn't feeling particularly victorious at the moment. Boone was right. Logically, developing this relationship with the Rose Red Rapist in an effort to draw him out of hiding made good sense. But one woman had already died. Others had suffered terribly at his hands. This was not just a patient she was trying to help to open up and reveal himself. If the threats did become physical, she doubted she'd be able to talk him out of hurting her. Not for long, at any rate.

And could she trust that backup would be there to save her if talking didn't work?

Spencer understood the seriousness of what she was proposing. He wouldn't take advantage of the danger she'd be in just for the sake of solving the case. "We'll have to make at least one protection detail undercover. Too many uniforms around you will drive the unsub off the radar, and you'd be risking your life for nothing."

"She'll have her protection."

Kate tilted her head at the matter-of-fact tone in Boone's voice. He was serious. "I didn't ask you to help with this."

But Spencer seemed to like the idea. "Are you volunteering, cowboy?"

"Wait a minute." Kate wasn't sure who she was arguing with now. "I can't have him around 24/7."

"I thought you two liked each other."

"We do," Boone insisted.

"Makes sense, then. If the two of you are a couple, it wouldn't look out of place to see you together."

Kate's face felt fiery hot. "We're not a couple. He'll get in the way of the investigation. He's…distracting."

"I've never met a more focused woman than you, Kate." Spencer's compliment was meant to encourage her, but her resolve to take on the difficult task of taunting the Rose Red Rapist out of his comfort zone was wilting beneath the conditions being put on her. "Of course, we'll keep pursuing the forensic angle. If we get a lock on this guy's phone or he finds another means of communication we can trace, we'll go after him. But for now I want you to continue following up any leads you have and running the press conferences. Let's put him on the defensive for a change. And someone from the task force, a uniformed officer, or the sheriff here will be watching out for him—"

"And watching over her," Boone added.

"—around the clock." Spencer turned his eyes to Boone. "Can you keep her safe?"

"Yep."

"Then welcome to the team." Spencer shook Boone's hand, then held on to make a point. "Strictly as a consultant. You'll still be out of your jurisdiction, Harrison. So no solo investigation, understood?"

"Understood. I guess I'm heading back to the big city." Boone tipped his hat back on his head, letting the illumination from the streetlamp reveal the promise in his eyes. "Wherever the doc goes, I go."

Chapter Seven

"This is never going to work."

"You can always change your mind," Boone suggested, loosely gripping the steering wheel of his truck as he eased them off the highway into Kansas City's late-night traffic.

"I'm talking about you being here, not the plan."

Kate picked up her purse from the floor of Boone's truck as soon as he turned into the relatively new subdivision where her house was located on the northern edge of the city. She opened the bag and fished for her keys. Getting used to carrying her bag and gun with her everywhere would be an adjustment. Her life seemed to move much more efficiently when she locked up her purse for the day and carried the necessities like keys, lipstick and phone in her pockets.

Once the keys were in hand, she leaned back into the oversize dimensions of the truck's velour seat. "I talk and listen to people all day long. It's emotionally draining. I need some down time at the end of the day— quiet time, alone time. How am I supposed to recover for the next day's work if you're here?"

"You won't even know I'm around."

She rolled her eyes doubtfully and pointed out the next turn.

"I can sleep on the couch or out in my truck if that's the way you want it."

"I do." She thought that offer sounded a little too good to be true.

"But you're not moving from one location to another without me driving you. And if it gets too quiet or I don't have a direct line of sight to you, I'm coming to check it out."

Kate groaned. Since Boone had come into her world just a few short days ago, her life had been more of an emotional roller coaster than anything she'd experienced after Brad's death. She'd carefully reconstructed her daily routine after losing her husband. It was how she coped. "Do you have any idea how much I need my alone time?"

"Who took a ride out into the countryside to get away from it all for an hour or so this evening?" She felt his attention sweep over her before he glanced at the dashboard clock and returned his eyes to the road. "Make that yesterday evening."

The luminous clock said it was nearly two in the morning. And she was feeling every long hour she'd been awake. "But you had the chance to be alone with your horse, or whatever you were doing, and 'decompress,' like you said. How am I supposed to decompress if you're shadowing me all the time?"

"I can teach you how to ride."

Kate snorted at the joke.

"Were you always this much of a control freak, Kate? Or did your husband's cheating do that to you?"

She hugged her purse in front of her, bristling at his questions. "I'm not going to answer that."

"You don't have to." He pulled off his Stetson and dropped it onto the seat between them. Then he scrubbed his fingers along his scalp, indicating that he was feeling the fatigue of the long day, too. "I may not have the Ph.D. after my name, but I can figure people out. You are a passionate, giving, spontaneous woman when you drop the body armor."

"One ill-advised kiss in your kitchen because I let my hormones get away from me—"

"That's what made it so special, so hot. You weren't thinking things through. You were feeling, reacting, trusting your instincts instead of your brain. You wanted me. I wanted you. It was that simple." He pulled up to a stop sign and waited. His eyes were dark and focused and daring her to argue his point when he looked over at her this time. "You may know how to profile people, Doc, but you don't always understand them. Take this crazy idea you've got about 'developing a relationship' with that Rose Red bastard. You're thinking logically. But he isn't. He doesn't care about the plan, and I doubt he'll follow it. He's going to react. Be unpredictable. That's your mistake." He turned his eyes back to the road and pulled out. "Not all of us think things through as carefully as you do, Doc. Don't be fooled into thinking he will."

They rode the rest of the way in silence until Kate pointed out her bungalow. "You can pull into the drive...way."

She grabbed the dash and sat up straight when she saw the garage door standing partway open.

Boone saw it, too. The sudden alertness radiating

off his body and filling up the cab of the truck only increased the uneasy suspicion she felt. "Is it broken?" he asked. "Did you leave it that way?"

"It was closed when Spencer picked me up this morning."

He shifted the truck into Reverse and backed out of the driveway. He drove around the block and pulled up to the house more slowly this time. "Do you recognize the cars around here?"

"It's too dark to see all of them. But of the ones I can make out, yes, they're my neighbors'."

"It may be nothing. The city has had a lot of rain, too, and sometimes all that moisture can mess with the automatic sensors." This time Boone swung around parallel to the curb and parked on the street. Was he anticipating the need to make a quick getaway?

"Wait here a sec." He put his hat back on his head, adjusted the front of his jacket to reveal the official uniform he'd changed into before leaving Grangeport, and pulled his gun from his holster. "I'll check it out."

So he didn't really suspect a faulty sensor in her automatic garage door opener, either. Kate crushed the straps of her purse in her fingers and watched him approach the half-open garage. The only light on the house was over the front porch steps. But there was enough muted light from the nearest streetlamp to see him flatten his back against the siding, tilt his head to listen for sound, and then, with his gun clutched between both hands, duck beneath the hanging door and disappear into the darkness of her garage.

She wasn't aware of holding her breath and counting off the seconds until she reached five. And then her brain finally kicked in over her fear. Boone had gone in there without backup, and the soft leather crushed between her fingers reminded her that her gun was locked up inside the house.

If someone had broken in... If that someone was still there, and he'd found her gun... Boone could be walking into an ambush. An ambush meant for her.

Her purse was on the floor and Kate was out the door. After one step, she stopped to pull off her heels so she wouldn't make any noise on the concrete driveway and walk, and give her approach away. She set one shoe down on the ground and turned the other one around in her fist to use the mud-caked heel as a weapon if necessary.

Kate moved as quickly and silently as she'd seen Boone do, changing course at the last second, thinking that sticking to the light of the front porch would be smarter than following him directly into the unknown darkness of the garage. Ignoring the chill on her bare feet, she crept up the front steps and pulled out the key. She was reaching for the lock when the interior door swung open.

Her startled yelp was punctuated by the storm door smacking into her shoulder. She lost the shoe, lost the keys, lost her balance as a figure dressed in dark colors from head to toe charged out the door and barreled into her.

Kate and the faceless intruder toppled over the edge of the porch and tumbled down together, hitting the edge of every step with a bruising thud.

Dizzy, aching, Kate had the presence of mind to latch on to her attacker, to cushion the crashing fall. When they rolled to a stop, Kate was pinned beneath him. But he wasn't attacking her at all. He was scrambling to his knees, struggling to get away.

"I'm with KCPD. Stop. Boone!" Kate shrieked, grabbing on to a gray hood, a dark brown sleeve, whatever she could reach to hold the perp in place. Adrenaline gave her strength, but freedom motivated her squirming opponent. With his legs straddling her waist, he sat up, jerking the edge of the stocking mask from her fingers to keep his face covered. Kate pushed up on one elbow, desperate to hold on to and identify the intruder, their suspect…the Rose Red… "Boone—!"

A wicked right cross slammed into Kate's face, knocking her to the ground. She'd been struck by something hard and square, a tool rather than a fist. Her cheek split open, burned. Her vision blurred. Her grip weakened and the dark figure slipped away.

Without a threat, without a word—without any attempt to harm her beyond his desire to escape—he left her and ran through her neighbor's yard and disappeared into the murky shadows.

"Kate?" The storm door slammed again. She heard Boone's boots on the stairs.

She rolled over onto her hands and knees and pushed herself up. "There." She pointed to the neighbor's yard. Dark brown coveralls. A hooded face. "That way." She wobbled. "Go!"

The images tried to match up with a memory. Another day. Another attack. She had a brief vision of long legs giving chase. But her balance was a pendulum swinging back and forth inside her head, and she finally gave up on the idea of standing and collapsed onto her burning cheek.

"Kate!" In a matter of seconds, she felt herself being

turned, lifted. And then she was leaning against the solid warmth of Boone's chest. "Doc?"

He was down on the ground with her, cradling her in his lap. Her pillow rippled with muscles and crisp cotton beneath her cheek as Boone holstered his weapon, pulled out his phone to call 911, and wadded up his handkerchief to dab at her wound.

She winced at the sharp pain that stabbed through her entire skull. "It was him. Did he get away?"

"I let him go."

"We had him. The man from the parking garage."

He easily overpowered her protesting hand and pressed the white handkerchief against her cheekbone again. "Honey, you're bleeding. Did you hit your head? Are you hurt anywhere else?" She rode the heavy, frustrated breath that expanded his chest. "What part of 'stay put' don't you understand?"

When he wouldn't ease up on the pressure on her cheek, Kate held on to his wrist to pull herself into a more upright position. The dizziness was subsiding, and the need to prove that she hadn't just done a completely idiotic thing was growing. "My gun is in the house. If I called out to warn you, he would have known you were there. He could have shot you."

"He could have shot *you*." Kate realized that she still had something from her wrestle on the front walk clutched in her fist. Pushing Boone's fingers aside, she took over holding the stained handkerchief against the cut on her cheek and let him adjust his hold to help her sit completely upright. "Uh-oh. I'm learning that look. Doc, what are you thinking?"

"That man was dressed just like the guy I saw outside the parking garage at work last week. The one I thought was following me. But I got a piece of him this time." She held up the black knit glove she'd pulled off her assailant. "This glove would almost fit me. He has small hands."

Boone peered around at the trees and houses and vehicles again, either ensuring the perp hadn't returned or looking for the backup he'd called. "What little glimpse I got of him, he wasn't that tall. Maybe that's why he hits his victims from behind when he abducts them." She used him as a brace to sit up on her knees, and he moved to kneel in front of her. "Did the guy who tackled you seem strong enough to haul a woman in and out of a van?"

"Strong enough, I suppose. He surprised me as much as anything. I'm sure he got a little beat up and disoriented on the trip down the steps, too, so that's probably why I could pull this off him." She held up the glove. "We need to get this into evidence in case there's DNA on it. And we need to call dispatch with a description of his clothes—brown coveralls, gray hoodie, stocking mask—no wonder I couldn't see his face that day."

"I'll call it in, I promise. But we need to get you inside and get that cut cleaned up. If it's bleeding too badly, I'm taking you to the E.R." He pushed to his feet, holding out his hand to her. "Can you get up?"

She folded her hand into his, but paused before standing. She could see the bloodstain on the front of his jacket now. Her blood. His clean white handkerchief was streaked with crimson. No wonder he'd been so concerned and given up his pursuit. She must look even worse than she felt.

Misreading her hesitation, Boone pulled her to her

feet and swung her up into his arms. He caught her behind her shoulders and knees and carried her up the steps.

She pushed against the wall of his chest. "I'm not a damsel in distress. I can walk."

"Well, I'm an old-fashioned kind of guy, so let me do this." She *had* given him a good scare. She could see it in the tight lines in the beard stubble bracketing his mouth. If a little old-fashioned chivalry would ease his concern and keep him amenable to her strategy to catch the rapist, then she'd give herself permission to relax against his strength and heat, and feel a little bit like Snow White being rescued by Prince Charming. Once he'd opened the door and carried her into the foyer, he halted. "Do you have a first-aid kit?"

He didn't set her down. Kate pointed down the hallway. "In the bathroom off the master suite."

But when he carried her through the door to her bedroom, her fingers curled into his chest and the fairy tale ended. Boone set her down, pulled her behind him and put his hand on his gun.

Kate buried her face against his shoulder. "Okay. Now I'm distressed."

"I'm calling Montgomery directly." He turned to gather her in his arms and walk her away from the utter destruction of her most private sanctuary.

But the images had been instantly and indelibly etched on her brain. Slashed pillows and drapes. Broken mirrors and picture glass. Roses scattered all over her bed. And one word, painted in red, on the wall above her headboard.

Silence!

BOONE RUBBED AT THE FATIGUE burning his eyes. The pulsating lights of the ambulance and police cars in Kate's driveway and lining the street in front of her house didn't help the lack of sleep that was pulling at his body. They didn't do much to ease his concern that there was nothing any of these people could do to keep Dr. Kate safe from the bastard who had already killed his sister, either.

A dozen uniformed officers swarmed around the place while he stood on the front walk listening to members of the task force discuss the break-in and the intruder who was probably already home getting some shut-eye.

He understood the intricacies of a long-term investigation, and the patience required to evaluate every possible lead, dismiss worthless intel and decide which pieces of evidence or witness testimony required even more evaluation. But while Spencer Montgomery and the others gave their reports, Boone's attention kept shifting over to the stubborn, barefoot blonde sitting on the ambulance's back bumper. The paramedic tended to the wound on Kate's cheek and checked for other minor injuries while the tall redhead in the KCPD uniform, Sgt. Maggie Wheeler, who was apparently a good friend as well as a coworker, took her statement and kept her company.

For a few brief moments, Kate's eyes locked on to his and the weariness inside him eased a bit. He'd been scared that she'd gotten hurt—sick to think, even for a moment, that he'd failed to protect her the same way he'd failed Janie. A couple of butterfly bandages and an ice pack for the bump on her head, and Kate claimed she was okay. But should a reassuring smile from a woman who'd complicated his life in so many ways in such a short time really have such a profound effect on him?

Normally, Boone wasn't one to question his instincts when it came to people and investigations and doing his job. The one place he'd ever misjudged something important, the one time his instincts had been wrong, had been his marriage to Irene. He'd loved her hard, believing she wanted the same things he wanted—roots, children, a long life together. But once the magic of the honeymoon had worn off and the real work of making a marriage strong had set in, she'd grown more distant. She often had a reason for working late in town, or a business trip to take. She'd secretly stayed on birth control while he'd believed they were working on starting that family. In hindsight, he was glad they hadn't created a child in a marriage that had been falling apart. But he'd thought Irene was the one for him. It had been a tough blow to his pride and his heart to realize that he was only *the one for now* with her.

Now here he was, getting tangled up hard and fast with Kate Kilpatrick. She was a city sophisticate with a Ph.D. who wore sexy, impractical shoes and knew beans about horses—not too unlike Irene. But she had a big, compassionate heart beneath that chilly exterior. She was intellectual in ways he couldn't always fathom but had to admire. And she had to be about the sexiest woman he'd ever put his hands on, especially when he got the idea that those clutching fingers and fiery kisses only worked on him.

Should he be listening to what his instincts were telling him about Dr. Kate? Or should he take a cue from the good doctor herself and spend a little more time thinking things through before he let her into his heart any further?

A whiff of panting wet dog at his feet drew Boone's attention back to the gathering of KCPD task force members.

Pike Taylor, the big cop who'd kept him from crossing the crime scene tape to see where Janie's body had been found that first day he'd come to Kansas City, tossed a knotted toy to his German shepherd companion to reward him for doing the job he'd been trained for. "Hans followed the perp's trail until it went cold. He lost the scent about a quarter mile down on the next street over. I'm guessing the perp got into a vehicle and drove away at that point." He knelt down to play a little tug-of-war with the big dog. "I did a little house-to-house work, too. Nobody we talked to remembered seeing any vehicles they couldn't identify. One guy said he thought he heard an 'expensive' engine gunning out on the street that woke him. But at this time of night, most of them were asleep, so no one saw anything. I gave them Dr. Kilpatrick's description of the intruder and warned them to keep their eyes open and their doors locked. Call us if they see anything. The usual spiel."

Boone shook his head. "This guy was only after Kate. They're all safe."

"Try telling them that." Pike pushed to his feet and glanced around, indicating the lights coming on in nearby homes and shades opening for the curious and the frightened to peek out.

"He's right." Kate brushed her hand against Boone's elbow and he stepped to one side, letting her and Maggie Wheeler join the conversation. "We need to turn off these flashing lights and get some of these vehicles out of here, Spencer, or we're going to cause a panic. And I'm sure the press will get wind of it before the sun comes up, if they aren't already on their way here."

"I'll take care of it, sir," Pike volunteered. "I need to get Hans a drink of water, anyway." He called to another uniformed officer, standing guard beside the yellow crime scene tape marking off Kate's front steps. "Yo, Estes. Come give me a hand."

The young, dark-haired officer hurried over, then jumped back half a step when he startled Pike's dog. The big German shepherd spun around, baring his teeth. Pike shouted one word and the dog dropped to his haunches, then crawled forward to a down position, although his nose stayed in the air sniffing something on the wind.

"He probably smells my girlfriend's dachshund on me." Officer Estes lowered his hands from the surrender position and tucked his thumbs into his belt as soon as Hans gave up his interest in him and Pike Taylor led him away to his departmental SUV. He smiled at Kate like they were old friends. "Dr. Kilpatrick, are you all right?"

"I'll be fine, Pete. Thanks for asking. And thanks for helping out tonight."

"Glad to do it, ma'am." Boone noticed the twenty-something standing up a little straighter under Kate's praise. Then he glanced around the group, clapped his leather gloves together and scooted off after the K-9 cop and his dog. "I'd better get going. What do you need, Taylor?"

Was Boone overreacting to be suspicious of Pete Estes? The dog didn't seem to like him. But that hardly made him a suspect. There were a couple of things, like motive, means and opportunity, to be considered first. After tonight's events, he supposed he'd be paranoid about any man he didn't know addressing Kate.

The others in the circle appeared less concerned. And the kid was doing his job. The ambulance and two of the squad cars pulled away while Detective Montgomery turned to Annie Hermann. "What about the message on the wall?"

The petite CSI cringed as she peeled off her gloves and stuffed them into the pockets of her navy jacket. "Maybe I'm what set Hans off. It looks like more cat blood, but I'll have the lab run it to make sure. I wonder if we should start talking to animal shelters, see if anyone has reported a missing pet. It makes me sick to my stomach to think of how much blood volume it would take to leave these messages."

"Cat lover?" Nick Fensom teased.

She glared at the burly detective. "I've rescued a couple. The messages and vandalism are bad enough. But when I think of the cruelty behind them… Our unsub clearly has no conscience—no qualms about hurting anyone or anything."

Nick patted the petite woman on the shoulder. "I'm sure your tabbies are safe, Hermann."

"They're Siamese." She tucked several unruly dark curls behind her ears and excused herself. "I need to get that glove and these samples back to the lab."

"Can't say anything nice to that woman," Nick groused.

"You need to make an appointment with me sometime," Kate gently chided him. "We can work on those communication skills."

Boone slid his hand behind Kate's back, battling the

urge to wrap his arms around her to shield her from the chaos around them. "Fix him later, Doc. We need to get you out of the open here. Get you someplace safe."

Spencer agreed. "Let's wrap this up. Was there anything taken from the house?"

Boone tried to speed the process along. "I secured her gun. It's in my truck. But this break-in wasn't a burglary. Nothing like a TV or sound system was taken. As for anything personal? Don't make her go back in there and look."

Kate slipped away from Boone's touch and crossed to the yellow tape. "It's okay. Maggie? Do you mind coming with me? We can do a quick sweep. I'd like to get some shoes and a change of clothes before my feet freeze, anyway."

Boone could feel the walls already going back up between him and Kate. Maybe his instincts about her were as off as they'd been about Estes, and that this need burning inside him was all one-sided. Maybe the protective—possessive—turbulence of his emotions was just the result of Dr. Kate being the person who'd been there when he'd needed someone to connect to.

Didn't make it any easier to concentrate on work, though.

Once the two women entered the house, Spencer turned to Boone. "Anything else you can tell us?"

"The perp I chased was a small guy. I'm six foot and he was at least a couple of inches shorter."

Nick Fensom straightened up beside him. "My height?"

"Maybe. But not as muscular." Nick was built like a Mack truck. The man Boone had chased from the house was more of a sports car. "And like Kate said, the guy had small hands."

Spencer jotted the details in his notebook. "Five-ten, wiry build. We'll add that to the description."

"So what about Kate?" Was Montgomery even considering what could have happened tonight if she'd walked in on the guy slashing up her room with a box cutter or small knife? "You're giving up this crazy idea about using her as bait, right? I mean, this guy has found her car, her house—now he's put his hands on her."

The detective tucked his notepad inside his suit jacket. "I offered to move her to a safe house, but she insisted on a hotel room with periodic drive-bys to watch over her for now. I don't think you're going to get her off this case."

Kate herself had something to say about that. "You won't. I'm still your chief profiler and press liaison. I don't want to be locked away where this guy can't reach me at all. I still want to put the Rose Red Rapist away for good."

She came down the stairs with another pair of those sexy high heels she favored on her feet and an overnight bag hooked over her shoulder. If Boone overlooked the two butterfly bandages and puffy bruise forming beneath her left eye, then she was looking the part of the consummate professional again. But he did see the cut and bruising, and with her hands buried in the pockets of that dusty, smudged-up trench coat—hiding the telltale indicators of her true state of mind—he couldn't tell how much of the confident facade was real, and how much of it was a cover for tight fists or trembling fingers.

"But I do need a hot bath, a good night's sleep and some time to myself to think through a theory I have."

The facade was convincing enough for Detective Montgomery. "What theory?" he asked.

"Wait until the next task force briefing. I need to work it out with a clear head first. But it could change the focus of our investigation."

"I look forward to it."

Boone tossed Kate's bag in the back of the truck and cranked up the heat, giving the cab a few minutes to warm up before he drove to the hotel where Maggie Wheeler had made arrangements for Kate to stay. She still had her hands hidden inside her pockets and had leaned back against the headrest and closed her eyes.

He didn't even turn on the radio for company as he waited, thinking she'd nodded off. But a minute later, she surprised him. "I don't think I've been this tired since going through the emotional wringer of Brad's death. I didn't sleep much then, either."

"Avoiding your emotions is how you keep your energy up?"

She opened her eyes and lolled her head to the left to face him. "It's a defense mechanism and you know it, Dr. Harrison."

He grinned at the reference to his earlier claim that he didn't need a Ph.D. to understand people's behavior. "Personally, I think you use up less energy if you just go with the flow of what you're feeling instead of trying to reason out all the potential consequences."

"That can be your dissertation topic when you decide to become a full-fledged behavioral psychologist."

Boone's grin became a chuckle. The woman's clever sense of humor revealed she was a lot tougher than she looked. "So, since we're talking hypotheses…" she giggled at the big word coming out of his mouth "…what's this new theory you have about the Rose Red Rapist?"

Her smile faded and she turned her focus back out to the men and women still working the scene in front of her house. But talking was what she did for a living, and she was willing to share. "I've been thinking this for a while—that this stalking bit doesn't fit the profile of our unsub. Our rapist is a cockroach who doesn't want to be seen. Who is so good at not being seen, in fact, that, after all these years, we have virtually no description of him. I've seen the man in the brown coveralls twice now. A stalker wants someone to know he's there. And after my run-in with that guy tonight… I think we're looking for two unsubs. The rapist and—"

"—a copycat who identifies with him?"

"At least a fan who thinks he's helping him."

As horrible as the thought of having two whack-jobs out there was, Boone could see the logic of her idea. "The guy in your house tonight—the stalker—he may even think he's protecting his…hero…from KCPD, the task force and the face of that task force. You."

Kate nodded. "Me. I'm thinking this unsub is younger. He's following all the publicity of the case, and might see Rose Red as a role model. He has the compulsion to hurt women, to terrorize them—but he hasn't progressed to the stage of attacking them."

Boone's hands tightened on the steering wheel. "What about tonight? He attacked you."

"That was a fight-or-flight reflex. He wasn't expecting to find me there. He just wanted to get away and I was in his path." She faced him again. "He heard or saw the big, scary cowboy coming into the house after him, and ran out the opposite direction."

"And plowed into you."

She reached up to touch the mark on her cheek. "What do you think he hit me with? It wasn't a gun. Or a knife."

"From the pattern of the damage done in your bedroom, CSI Hermann thinks he was armed with a box cutter." Boone stretched his arm across seat to brush her soft golden hair away from the injury. "You're damn lucky you didn't lose one of those beautiful eyes."

He felt her skin warming beneath his touch and leaned across the seat to kiss her. But a firm hand in the middle of his chest stopped him from getting too close. "Not here." She dropped her hand and glanced out the windows. "Not where the others can see us."

"I think they've already got an idea about us, Doc." Boone pulled his hand away, turned on the headlights and shifted the truck into gear. "I'm just not sure you've got the same idea."

His foot was still on the brake when she slipped her hand out of her pocket again. He could see the little tremors in her fingertips as it slid across the seat toward him, out of sight from all the cops and coworkers and curious onlookers outside. Maybe she did have some inkling of that idea.

Boone reached out, swallowed up her hand in his and held on tight.

She offered.

He accepted.

His instincts were telling him to hold on to this woman any way he could. He likened this uncertain relationship to taming a stubborn, ill-used filly. The desire to work with him was there. But it would require patience and practice and building an unshakable trust before she could truly be his.

Now he just had to make sure a raping killer and his blossoming protégé gave them the time he needed to make that happen.

Chapter Eight

The last of the bubbles had popped and gone by the time Kate decided she'd soaked long enough in the hotel room's spacious bathtub. She reluctantly opened her eyes and forced her jelly-soft muscles to wake up so she could unstop the drain and climb out.

She wrapped a warm towel around her middle and crossed to the mirror to run a comb through her hair and fluff the short strands into place. She could wash her hair and relax the tension from her body with a steamy bath, but there was no toning down the evidence of going head-to-head with the intruder who'd broken into her house. Leaning over the sink to get a closer look, Kate gently touched the sickle-shaped cut beneath her eye. Her cheek wasn't as swollen as it felt, but she'd be wearing a natural blue, purple and violet blush for a while.

Every bruise on her body stood out against her pale, freshly washed skin. The chill that shimmied down her spine and raised goose bumps across her arms and legs could be attributed to the variations in temperature between the bath water and the air, but she suspected her sudden inability to feel warm had a lot to do with being up for nearly twenty-four hours, and suddenly, fully, realizing just how close a call she'd had.

Whether she'd confronted the Rose Red Rapist or a wannabe sidekick, her injuries could have been so much worse. She might be lying in the morgue like Janie Harrison had, instead of lying in a hotel bathtub until every cell of her body had finally relaxed. Unable to shake the chill, Kate pulled one of the fluffy white terry robes off the back of the door and wrapped it around her body, towel and all. She tied the sash around her waist and opened the bathroom door.

"It's as rejuvenating as a long ride on a good horse, isn't it." Boone Harrison was stretched out on the sofa in the suite's sitting area, with his feet propped on the coffee table in front of him. His voice sounded drowsy in the room's dimly lit shadows. But Kate had a sense of unblinking eyes focused squarely on hers, as if he'd been watching the closed door the entire time she'd been in there.

Feeling her temperature rising again beneath those warm brown eyes, Kate knotted the robe a second time, wondering if it was possible for him to tell that she'd left her pajamas in her bag in the suite's separate bedroom. "Well, the scenery may not be as striking, but I bet it's a lot easier on the muscles."

Boone rose from the couch and strolled across the room. "Depends on what scenery you're looking at."

He lifted the collar of her robe and pulled it to the base of her throat, covering the top of the towel and stretch of skin she'd inadvertently exposed across her chest.

All the blood seemed to rush to Kate's face as she plucked the collar from his fingers and clasped it together at her neck. His suggestive compliment and teasing smile warmed her in ways a bath and robe could not. Good grief. She was almost forty and blushing like a schoolgirl. Time to check her hormones and remember why they were sharing this hotel suite in the first place.

She moved toward the clock on the coffee table before consciously remembering to breathe again. "It's five in the morning. Do you need help unfolding the sofa bed out here?"

"I got it covered, Doc. I set out the spare pillows and blanket, pulled all the blinds in both rooms—for security's sake, as well as keeping the sun out when it comes up. I verified that one of Montgomery's squad cars has circled the place at least twice. And the Do Not Disturb sign is on the door."

"You've been busy."

He grinned. "You were in there a long time."

She returned his smile, then changed direction toward the bedroom door. "We have permission to sleep in as long as we need before the task force debriefs, but I think we'd better say good night."

If Boone had picked up on the raw nervous energy she felt, he was either too tired or too polite to call her on it. "Everything's locked up tight so you can get some rest, Doc. I still want to jump into the shower if you've left me any hot water."

"A little." She wasn't such a schoolgirl around a mature, virile man that she couldn't throw out a little teasing, too—or appreciate that his presence here *did* make her feel safe. Saf*er,* at any rate. "I'm doing the right thing, aren't I? Drawing this guy out so we can catch him?"

She could tell he still wasn't completely sold on her

theories about the case. "If that bastard or his sick little sidekick shows his face, I will take him out before they can hurt you. I promise you that."

It was a promise she desperately wanted to believe. "Good night, Boone."

"Good night, Kate."

Weary and wrung out both physically and emotionally, Kate changed into her pajamas and crawled under the covers. She'd barely turned off the light and rolled over before falling into a deep, hard sleep.

Exhaustion claimed her body.

But her mind couldn't seem to shut down and let her rest.

From the darkest shadows of dream land she heard laughter. Not teasing. Not funny.

Painful laughter. It was a man's and a woman's voices, mocking her. Wounding her.

Kate thrashed in the bed, fighting to wake herself before the nightmare could claim her. But she wasn't strong enough to spare herself.

"You think you're so smart." Vanessa Owen wandered out of one dark corner of the hotel room as horrid dreams came to life. She walked hand in hand with Kate's husband, Brad. *"You have no clue about men and women and the world, Kate. They don't need you. They'll leave you behind."*

Brad was dressed in the tuxedo he'd worn on their wedding day. The gold ring she'd given him glinted with an unearthly green light. "So smart," he laughed. "So stupid. We all leave."

They walked up to the bed and circled around her. Laughing. Pointing. Kissing. Forcing her to watch their

*happiness while the bed beneath her turned mucky,
spongy like black quicksand.*

"Stop. Don't do this." *Kate argued with the haunting
images to make them disappear. They leaned over her,
pushed her down, surrounded her in the black hole that
sucked her down into the murky abyss. She reached for
her husband.* "I love you."

"Not good enough, Kate." *His laughter deepened,
filled up her ears.*

"You said you loved me." *She caught hold of his
hand, but she was sinking. Drowning.* "You gave me
your word."

"I lied." *He let go of her hand and she plummeted
into the darkness.*

"Stop." *Kate clawed her way to the surface. She
struggled to wake herself, to find her way back to the
real world of light and hope.* "Stop it!"

"So, so smart." *Vanessa leaned over her. Her long,
curling hair dangled in Kate's face, caught in Kate's
mouth and choked her.* "So, so stupid."

"Stop." *Kate tried to brush it away, to speak, to protest—to beg if she must. But her arms were trapped,
her body pinned.*

*The corners of the room swirled with shadows, cir-
cling around, closing in. Other hands were on her now,
dragging her down. Squeezing the air from her lungs.
Stopping up her mouth. Crushing her throat.*

*She tried to scream, but the unseen hands wielded
slashing silver blades. They cut her tongue, sliced her
throat.*

Stop.

Laughter.

Stop.

Darkness.

Stop.

Silence.

"Stop!"

Kate flung herself out of the grasping pit of darkness. The scream tore through her and she startled herself awake.

She clutched at her neck and opened her eyes, unsure what was reality and what was nightmare. She was still in her hotel room. There were still dark corners. Still shadows.

There was one tall, dark, broad shadow, in particular—throwing open the door to stand silhouetted against the light from the other room.

"Doc?"

KATE KICKED OFF THE COVERS that had wound around her body and scrambled onto her knees and across the bed to flip on the lamp.

The small circle of light chased away the darkest of the images that terrorized her. It also gave shape and form to the figure standing in the open doorway.

"Boone?"

"Yeah, Doc, it's me."

His gaze swept around the room. He opened the closet door, checked behind each curtain, then crossed to the bed. Details registered now that the shadows were fading. He carried his gun pointed down at his side. His damp hair glistened like polished onyx, run through with shards of silver. His hastily buttoned jeans rode low on his hips, as if he'd jumped out of bed and run in here, expecting to find an intruder.

The only intruders had been the cruel images conjured by her emotions. Kate's hands fisted at her throat and stomach. She was still breathing hard and deep, and her heart thudded against her ribs.

"I was having a nightmare."

"You think?"

Her gaze dropped briefly to the gun. But the rock-steady gaze and piercing alertness of the man standing above her compelled her to tip her chin up to face him. She pulled the covers into her lap. "I woke you. I'm sorry."

"At least I know you've got a good scream in case you really are in danger."

She knew she was meant to laugh, but couldn't quite summon the sound from her throat. Boone tucked the gun into the back of his jeans and sat on the edge of the bed. He pulled her hands off the covers and rubbed them between his palms. "God, woman, you're like ice. I heard you cry out and came to check. I thought your friend found a way to scale the building and break through a locked window to get to you."

She watched his hands and felt the magic effect they had on her. So rough in texture, so gentle in touch, his big hands were sheltering, soothing—and shared an abundant warmth her nightmare had stolen from her.

"I'm afraid the only danger is inside my head." She squeezed her eyes shut against the gritty sensation of gathering tears. "I think too much, don't I? And then an idea gets stuck in my head and I'm too stubborn to believe any differently." She blinked her eyes open and the evidence of all her frustration, fears and fatigue spilled over. "I can never just leave well enough alone."

"Hey, none of that. You'll get your bandages wet." He caught the first tear with the tip of his finger and wiped it away. He patiently caught another, and another, until she sniffed and regained a dubious control over her emotions. "You want to talk about it?"

She wiped away the next few tears herself and sniffed again. "I'm the counselor. I'm supposed to help other people talk about things."

Boone got up to stack the pillows against the headboard, straighten the covers and tuck them securely around her. The bed shifted when he sat back down on top of the duvet beside her. He leaned back against the pillows and pulled her into his arms, nestling her injured cheek against the firm heat of his chest.

"You talk to *me*," he ordered on a velvety-toned whisper.

The armor surrounding Kate's heart cracked open, without any hope of repairing the protective barrier this time. Without thinking, she wound her arm around his waist, found damp, warm skin to hold on to, and leaned into his strength and comfort.

For several minutes, he simply held her in silence. Kate's head cleared as she drank in the spicy, fresh scent of his skin. She pulled strength from him and felt his abundant heat slowly working its way through her body. The shelter of Boone Harrison's arms chased away the threat from the shadows and her imagination.

Trusting that he meant what he said about listening, she began to open up and share a little about the nightmare, and the realities that triggered it. She talked about her marriage and Brad's affair with Vanessa—how the relationship and people expert had felt like a failure—clueless, betrayed, heartbroken. She talked about rebuilding her life and focusing on her career, how she felt a special affinity for female victims of violent crimes and often did pro bono work helping them find their voice and confidence again. She talked about the things she'd seen the Rose Red Rapist do to a woman, and how driven she felt to get him off the streets so those victims could stand a chance of emotional recovery.

Every fear, every compulsion, had woven its way into her nightmare. The emotions, the personal threats. She'd wanted to fight, to defeat those demons. But she'd been helpless, powerless, a victim herself all over again.

Boone's fingers stroked the hair at her temple. His steady breathing and strong heartbeat evened out the tempo of her own. And he listened. Just as he'd promised. He listened.

"…and I couldn't talk. They humiliated me and hurt me and kept me from speaking. I just wanted somebody to listen."

"I wouldn't worry about that dream." His fingers paused their gentle massage.

"No?"

"Honey, once you get an idea in your head, nobody's ever going to shut you up."

With that, Kate did laugh. She was ready to now. They both laughed. She felt close to another human being. And all was right in her world. For now.

And then another kind of closeness filled the hushed intimacy of the room. Boone tunneled his fingers into her hair, cradling her nape and the side of her jaw as he tipped her head back and kissed her. Kate anchored her hand at his shoulder and held on as he gently, tenderly, explored and reassured. She welcomed him into her mouth, tasting the minty bite of his toothpaste, savoring the catlike rasp of his tongue sliding against hers.

She slid her fingers up into the coal-black silk of his hair and pulled herself more fully into his leisurely, thorough embrace. He kindled an ember of heat deep in her belly, and it spread into every limb, into every cell, until every inch of her, from the tips of her breasts to her once-frozen toes, was on fire.

"Kate." Just as her brain was shutting down and her body's craving to crawl right into his heat was taking over, Boone rolled away.

But he pulled away from the needy clutch of her fingers for only a few moments. He reached behind him and then she heard the heavy thump of his gun being set aside on the nightstand. "Boone?"

"Dr. Kate." He came back to her, scooting down on the bed and quickly reclaiming her mouth as if he'd missed the hungry pressure of their lips joining together as much as she had. He slipped his arm beneath her and palmed her butt. He squeezed and lifted, dragging her to lie more fully on top of him, bunching the covers between them. And as her body softened against the teasing hints of hardness beneath the layers of cotton and batting, Boone shifted the intensity of his kisses into something far more seductive than sharing strength or comfort.

His hands slipped beneath the hem of her long-sleeved tee and the elastic waist of her flannel pants. Every callused stroke against her skin made her want the same freedom to explore the textures of his body. She tugged in frustration at the covers until she could lay her palm over the swell of a flexing pectoral. The muscle quivered beneath her touch. The flat male nipple tightened and poked between her fingers. The crisp dusting of dark hair tickled her sensitive palms.

"Sweet Dr. Kate." His raspy beard stubble grazed along her jaw and the soft underside of her chin as he followed the path of her pulse with his lips and tongue.

Kate arched her neck and then her back, granting him access to every needy nerve ending that longed for his touch. He pulled her up along his body, the shifting covers and friction between them revealing the evidence of his desire.

She snatched at the covers between them, wanting to feel skin on skin. His fingers tugged with a needy lack of finesse, finally pulling her shirt off over her head. Before she could free her arms and toss it onto the floor, his lips reached up and caught her breast in his mouth. She gasped in pleasure at the swirl of his tongue against the pebbled tip and collapsed against his mouth, stabbing her fingers into his hair and clutching his scalp, urging him to deepen the sensual torment of his rough beard and soothing tongue against her most sensitive skin.

And then he was sliding her pants down her thighs, sitting up and spilling her into his lap, reaching between them to unhook the lone button holding his jeans together.

But when she felt the bulge in his jeans pulsing against her, Kate knew a split second of painful inadequacy. She flattened her hand against his chest and pushed. "Wait. Boone, stop."

His chest heaved beneath her hand, and his voice was a ragged gasp. "Did I hurt something?" His eyes were clear, probing, as he captured her face between his hands and brushed his thumb near the bruise on her cheek. "I know you took a pretty hard tumble."

"No, I…" She pulled her hands back to cover her body. "I wanted…"

He bowed his head in a frustrated sigh and rested his forehead against hers. "Ah, Doc. We're going to think this through, aren't we?"

"We've been through a lot in the last few days. We've spent time together, and…" Leaving one arm covering her bare breasts, she latched on to his wrist and tilted her gaze up to his, begging him to understand that this hesitation was all on her. "You may have expectations of me that I can't deliver."

"Honey, I'm not going to force you."

"I know. You would never do that. And God knows you've got the goods…" Kate shrank back from his gaze and felt her entire body heat with embarrassment. "Please tell me I didn't say that out loud."

His worried expression stretched into a Boone-sized grin. "Maybe I shouldn't worry about how much you like to talk. That may just be the best damn compliment I've ever had. And trust me, Doc, the feeling is mutual."

She tilted her eyes to him again. His flattery was wonderful, as much of a stroke to her fragile feminine ego as the proof of his words still evident beneath the covers. But he had to see the logic in what she might be sparing him. "Thank you, but…you have needs, and I—"

Boone swore. He said words she hadn't used in a long time, and he said them twice. "That lowlife bastard scum of an ex didn't deserve you."

The grip he held on her face strengthened, yet somehow gentled at the same time. "When was the last time you were with a man? It was with him, right? And what, he probably stopped sleeping with you and blamed it on too much work or not understanding his needs—and all the time he was screwing someone else?"

Kate read the turbulence in his eyes. She felt it in the shaking control of his fingertips. Had he gone through something similar with his ex-wife? Had Irene ever made this utterly masculine and virile man feel like anything less than he was?

Kate nodded. "Something like that."

He kissed her square on the mouth. "He's not a part of your life anymore, Kate. I am. It feels right. I want this. I want you. I haven't wanted any woman for I don't know how long until I met you. You're in my head day and night. I want to feel those sexy hands all over me."

His vehement argument was making sense. Sort of. "My hands are sexy?"

"What you do with them is." Brad had called her beautiful. A lovely compliment, easy to say. But Boone talked specifics. Striking scenery. Pretty eyes. Sexy hands. "Do you believe me? Please, Kate. I need to know that you believe how much I want you."

She nodded, believing.

"And I need you to believe how much I think you want me, too."

"I do want you. I want this."

His grip on her eased. The smile crept back across his features. "I want you to be completely sure."

Kate dropped her hands to the covers between them. She matched his smile and stretched up to kiss him. "Do you have a condom?"

Leaving time for nothing but feeling, nothing but wanting, nothing but trusting that this was right, Boone fell back against the pillows and pulled Kate with him. In a flurry of bumping hands and laughter, of climbing out of bed and diving back in again, they slipped off clothes and stole kisses and burned away any lingering shadows from the past.

Soon, there were no covers, no clothes, no doubts between them. There was only Boone. Rising over her, sliding inside her, claiming her mouth with the same exquisite thoroughness with which he claimed her body.

Kate clutched his hips between her knees to welcome him more fully. She slipped one hand down between them and touched her fingertips to where they were joined. Boone moaned at the brush of her fingers and his entire body went taut.

"Oh, Doc," he panted against her ear. "Damn sexy."

He thrust one more time, carrying Kate over the edge with him as he poured out inside her.

She hugged him close as his body went slack and he collapsed beside her. They dozed in each other's arms for a few minutes, until the sheet cooled and goose bumps shivered across her skin.

Boone pulled the covers over her and left her for a few minutes. But after she heard the water run in the bathroom, he came back and slipped beneath the covers with her.

He gathered her back into his arms and she studied her ordinary, unadorned hand resting at the center of his chest. "Sexy hands, hmm?"

"Oh, yeah." He splayed his fingers over hers and trapped them against the reliable rhythm of his heart.

She'd opened herself up to Boone this morning, baring far more than her body—sharing more with him than she'd shared with any man, including her late husband. She felt raw inside—curiously content, but emotionally wrung out. She recognized an important breakthrough just as she would recognize one in a client. But she also knew that a mental and emotional catharsis didn't mean she was instantly cured. She had scars on her heart that would still require time and nurturing in order to heal.

But for the first time since she'd learned of her husband's infidelity and death, Kate believed that she *would* heal.

She rested her cheek against the pillow of Boone's shoulder. "Would you stay for a little while? At least until I fall asleep?"

He pressed a kiss to the crown of her hair. "You're not gettin' rid of me."

With that promise to hold on to, she smiled and drifted into a deep, dreamless sleep. She knew she was safe from the demons in her imagination as well as the real ones out there in the world—for now.

She'd take for now with Sheriff Boone Harrison.

She'd trust…for now.

Chapter Nine

"He's not our man," Boone muttered under his breath. He closed the door behind the graduate student who scooted past him into the hallway outside the Fairfax Community College art room and turned to face the older man who'd replaced the student at the makeshift interview table across from Kate.

"Professor Ludvenko?" Kate asked.

Boone took a half step back into the room until a sharp glance from Spencer Montgomery reminded him that he wasn't officially a part of the investigative process here. Biting down on his frustration, Boone anchored himself in his boots and did what he'd silently been told to. *Stay back and watch the door. Make sure this stays a private conversation.*

Door duty? Really? He'd been in the police business at least as long as Kate, and certainly longer than Spencer Montgomery. And now he was stuck watching through glass doors and windows into an empty hallway while Kate and Montgomery interviewed every male on campus who'd had any sort of regular contact with Janie.

This was their fourth interview this afternoon. If this Maksim Ludvenko was the guy she'd been seeing, then Boone really had lost touch with his sister these past few months. The long-haired weasel with the eastern European accent was as far from anyone Janie had ever dated in Grangeport as a chicken was from a horse. He'd much prefer hearing that Janie had been dating that younger graduate student, or the nearsighted academic adviser they'd talked to before that, than this guy. Surely this man was too old for his sister. The fact that the fiftyish art professor would rather pick at paint stains on the table where he sat across from Kate than look her in the eye when she asked a question didn't sit well with him.

Professor Ludvenko was too fidgety, too evasive to not be guilty of something. The more Kate prodded, the more he dodged her questions and protested as though he was the victim. That self-preserving egoism didn't sit well with Boone, either.

"Professor Ludvenko, please." Kate pulled a folder from her purse and opened it on the table between them, displaying far more patience than Boone could have mustered. "We're just asking for information about your colleague. We're not accusing you of anything."

Boone didn't know how Kate could sit there and coolly ask Maksim Ludvenko questions about the classes he taught at the Fairfax Community College, when he wanted to put his hands around the guy's throat and ask him point-blank if he'd had an affair with Janie that had ended so badly, he'd killed her. Or maybe he'd ask if raping strong, independent women was more his style.

"I cannot talk about this here." Ludvenko waved a dismissive hand in the air and glanced up at the red-haired detective circling behind him, ostensibly glancing at the half-finished canvases mounted on easels throughout the room. "Not with this man watching over me or that man there, his eyes accusing me of things I did not do."

Boone nodded at the professor, glad to be included in the conversation, and happy that the man could accurately read his thoughts.

"Then just talk to me," Kate reasoned. "Ignore them. Did you have a personal relationship with Jane Harrison?"

There was no trace of either the mind-blowing passion or the vulnerability she'd shown him early this morning in their hotel room. Dr. Kate Kilpatrick couldn't be ruffled by a lack of proper sleep, a late-night attack by a crazed fan or spending several hours sharing her most personal fears and desires with him. Maybe she could turn her emotions on and off like that, or maybe their time together hadn't affected her as profoundly as it had him. He was falling in love with Dr. Kate. Hook, line and sinker. It would be kind of nice to think she was feeling more than empathy or had the hots for him.

That doubt of hers must be contagious, because this morning he'd been certain the falling-in-love stuff was mutual. And now the ice princess was even harder than usual to read.

But then, maybe the cool, calm and collected act was for Ludvenko's benefit. The professor shot up out of his chair and headed for the bay of windows opening into the hall. "I cannot talk about this now. My wife is teaching accounting upstairs—"

Boone blocked his exit out the door. "Sit down and answer the lady's questions."

"No. I want my attorney."

Montgomery flanked the artist on the opposite side. "You don't think your wife's going to know something's going on then?"

"Sheriff, Detective—it's all right." Kate walked up to the professor and tapped his arm, urging him to face her. "Just have your attorney meet you at the Fourth Precinct offices. We'll take you in and do the questioning there."

"Oh, yes," Ludvenko snapped sarcastically. "That would be so much better." Classes must be changing. All of a sudden the handful of students meandering through the hallway were now thirty or forty people walking past. Ludvenko looked through the windows, catching the eyes of a few curious onlookers. Perhaps he decided getting this over with as quickly as possible was a better choice than climbing into a police car out front and setting all sorts of tongues wagging. "Fine. I will answer your question." He made a sharp reverse turn and returned to his seat at the art table. "I do not date my students."

"Janie wasn't a student. She taught jewelry making and welding sculpture classes. She was a colleague of yours…and your wife's." Kate unhooked the button of the blazer she wore and sat. "Maybe we should ask the other Professor Ludvenko if she knew who Jane Harrison was seeing."

"Fine. Yes. I was sleeping with Jane. But I am not this monster you speak of—this rapist." He waved his hand in the air again. "I did not do the things you are accusing me of."

Detective Montgomery resumed his nonchalant stroll through the forest of easels. "If you think the Rose Red

Rapist is a monster, then help us out. Tell us everything you can about Miss Harrison. The more we know about the night she was attacked, the better we'll be able to narrow down the time frame of the assault. If we know more about her state of mind, about who she talked to that night, about who she saw—then it can put us that much closer to finding her killer."

Boone was developing some grudging respect for the unflappable detective. He was as calm and logical as Kate. On paper, they'd make a perfect match. Sophisticated appearances. Scary smart. Cool under pressure.

While he was…hell. He'd better *watch the door* and keep an eye on the students in the hallway to stop anyone from coming in.

"Janie and I were kindred spirits. She possessed the soul of an artist—like me." So Ludvenko was the creep who'd taken advantage of Janie's big heart and thirst for life. "My wife, she is all about numbers and calculations—a good match for any man. But Janie…she was passion."

Boone was getting irritated. "So your wife holds down a steady job, keeps a good home and enjoys a respectable reputation in the community."

"Yes, my wife is all those things."

"In other words, she's boring."

"Boone," Kate cautioned.

"Harrison," Montgomery warned.

"Yes…no." Ludvenko turned his argument away from Boone and pointed across the table at Kate. "Dorothy is a good wife. Do not trick me into saying things. I will deny them all in court."

Kate seemed pleased to finally have his full attention. "But you and Janie shared common interests—your love for art and learning? A passion for life?"

"Yes. We were drawn together at an artists' retreat we both attended one weekend. We continued to see each other when my wife traveled or worked late, whenever we could."

Man, wasn't this scenario sounding familiar. The roles were reversed, of course, but it wasn't too unlike the excuse Irene had given for straying from their marriage.

"Did you see Jane Harrison last Friday night?" Montgomery asked. "I already checked at the business office—your wife went to Phoenix for a weekend symposium."

"No. She did not." Ludvenko grew defensive at the detective's interruption. "She was scheduled to leave, yes, but Dorothy came down with a cold. Her sinuses were so bad that flying was out of the question." His manic gesticulations had been reduced to picking at paint on the table again. "So I called Janie and canceled our weekend getaway. She was not pleased. And then I read in the paper that she was murdered."

Detective Montgomery had a follow-up question. "And your wife will confirm that you were home with her all night?"

"Yes." He pounded his fist against the table. "I lose the woman I love, and I cannot even grieve for her... because of my wife."

Sarcasm poured through Boone's blood. "I'm crying for you, pal."

"You do not understand what we felt for each other."

"Better than you know. I pity your wife."

When Ludvenko turned back to the relative safety

of addressing Kate, she pointed to the picture of the ruby-and-diamond ring she'd set on the table. "Did you give this to Janie?"

"Yes. For her birthday." His mouth curled with a rueful smile. "She said it would be a better present if I were to leave my wife and we could see each other without hiding from the world."

"You never had any intention of leaving your wife, did you?" Boone accused. "You had your cake and were eating it, too."

"I cannot help what the heart feels." He threaded his fingers through his lion's mane of hair. "I know she deserved better. But I would never hurt Janie. Never."

Kate tapped the photo again. "Did she like this ring? It doesn't exactly seem her style." Where was she going with these questions about the ring?

"It was expensive. It proved my love to her."

Boone snorted.

Both Kate and Montgomery glared him into silence again.

While Kate folded the photo into the file and sat back in her chair, pondering some unknown question, Detective Montgomery walked up beside Ludvenko. "Did she contact you at all that Friday night? Or early Saturday morning? The phone records we downloaded from her cell phone show she called a local motel—the Highway 40 Inn. Maybe she was hoping you'd changed your mind?"

"I told you I stayed home with my wife. Janie did not call me after I canceled. Like I said, she was very angry. Besides, we would not stay at a cheap motel. I treated her better than that. It was always the Muhl-bach downtown. We liked…the historic architecture."

Montgomery pulled his cell phone off his belt and walked away. "The discretion of a doorman and an old-monied hotel didn't hurt, either, I'm guessing."

"One last question, Professor Ludvenko." Kate stood and gestured around at all the projects on display in the room. "Are any of these paintings Janie's?"

"No. As you said, she was a sculptor. She liked working with metals." He pointed to an oxidized copper sunburst hanging behind his desk. "That is her work."

The interview was over, and though Professor Scumbag alibied out for the night of Janie's rape and murder, Boone decided the man was still guilty—of feeding his sister false hopes and breaking her heart. Crimes he hoped Dorothy Ludvenko would make him pay for with a good divorce attorney.

"So who was Janie calling at the Highway 40 Inn?" Boone asked, once they were outside in the crisp sunshine.

Spencer Montgomery was still on the phone as they walked to Boone's truck and his car. "I'll get the motel to fax over a guest list for that night." He paused before climbing in behind the wheel. "Kate, are you up for the daily press briefing?"

"I am." She answered with more confidence than Boone had expected for a woman whose car and home had been vandalized, and who still bore the vicious bruise of her stalker's last attack where there was no hiding it from the cameras. Not to mention the fact that one of those reporters she'd be facing had wrecked her marriage. He wondered if the confidence was real, or a show for the senior officer on her team.

"Get her back to the office in one piece, Sheriff," Montgomery ordered.

"You got it."

Boone opened the truck door for Kate, then got in behind the wheel and started the engine. The ice princess was a little less icy now that Montgomery had driven away. She was studying the photos in the evidence file again, and her mouth was twisted in a perplexed frown. And while he admired her toughness, wisdom and patience as a profiler and interrogator, he was incredibly drawn to this softer, more pensive version of Dr. Kate.

He waited until she tucked the file back into her purse to throw the truck into Reverse and back out of the parking space. If she wasn't going to share whatever was on her mind, then he'd start the conversation. "So we found out Janie's big secret. She *was* having an affair with a married man. And after the way Irene ended our marriage, Janie probably thought she couldn't talk to me about it."

Kate's focus came back from the wheels spinning inside her head. "She may have thought that being the other woman would have hurt you. I get the idea that she didn't want to be a disappointment to her big brother."

Boone shifted the truck into Drive. "She was my baby sister. I loved her. We'd have worked it out."

"Maybe she thought that she was a grown-up now— not a baby anything—and that she should resolve the problem herself."

"That independence got her killed," he muttered with a mix of guilt and frustration. "And we're no closer to finding out who did it."

"You haven't let her down, Boone." The woman sitting across that seat really *could* read people.

He reached over to squeeze her hand. "It sure feels

like it." Grateful for her insight and compassion and how her gentle reassurances soothed him, Boone returned his grip to the wheel and pulled onto the street. "Ludvenko's not our man. Even if his wife hadn't vouched for his whereabouts last weekend, frankly, I don't think he's smart enough to be the Rose Red Rapist. He's too self-absorbed to feel threatened by any woman, and with that temper of his, he'd have made a mistake by now. Left a clue at one of his crime scenes."

"I agree. He's not the Rose Red Rapist. Or Janie's killer."

He glanced across the seat to see those moss-colored eyes waiting for him to ask, "You still think we've got two different unsubs?"

"No." Boone didn't see it coming. "I think we've got three."

"Is it true you were attacked by the Rose Red Rapist, Dr. Kilpatrick?"

Kate blinked through the spotlights and camera flashes to focus on Vanessa Owen, standing in the front row of the KCPD press conference. A dozen or so reporters, their sound and camera crews, concerned citizens from the community and a cadre of plainclothes and uniformed police officers maintaining some degree of order in the Fourth Precinct's first-floor lobby, crushed forward at the sensationalist question.

She wasn't above letting the disdain for her onetime friend show on her face. But she put up her hand to quiet the buzz of speculation and follow-up questions. If nothing else, it was her job here today to calm their fears, and thus the city's, by not allowing rumors and misinformation to be splashed across headlines and television screens.

Only when the noise had quieted down to a few clicks and whirrs of equipment running, did she speak.

"I was *not* assaulted by the Rose Red Rapist." She articulated the announcement as clearly and succinctly as the human voice would allow. "Despite the drama your colleague Ms. Owen would like to capitalize on here today, there have been no reported rapes in the Kansas City area this past week."

Gabriel Knight wasn't about to be outscooped by Vanessa. The newspaper reporter raised his pen for permission to speak. "So what did happen to you?"

Kate pointed to the cut and angry bruise that was too obvious for even makeup to hide under this many lights. "My home was broken into and I sustained an injury trying to prevent the intruder's escape."

"What did the intruder take?" Gabriel asked.

My peace of mind? The idea that I can be safe alone in my own house, among my own things? Out loud, Kate shrugged off the question with a smile. "Nothing."

"There wasn't a threat? There wasn't a warning, about the task force getting too close to making a breakthrough on their investigation? Kate? Kate!"

She ignored Vanessa's questions for now. If the woman wanted to let the past be forgotten and work together as professional women, then by damn, she could speak to her as a professional, and not rely on either the personal connection they'd once shared to earn her any special privileges, or that arrogant sexuality that up until a few days ago had made Kate feel somehow inadequate and inferior to intimidate her.

Vanessa Owen may have once been an emotional

thorn in Kate's side, but now she was just a reporter. Like anyone else in this room, she was no threat to her. No one here, except for the broad-shouldered sheriff with the warm brown eyes that scanned the crowd and occasionally met her gaze to offer silent encouragement, had the ability to get under Kate's skin and mess with her emotional equilibrium.

"Dr. Kilpatrick?" Finally, the dark-haired reporter figured out the snub. There might even have been a note of newfound respect shading her eyes when she asked her next question. "Was there any sort of threat directed toward you from the man who broke into your home?"

"Yes," she answered honestly, earning another buzz of follow-up questions and photographs. "But again, I do not believe the message came from the Rose Red Rapist. KCPD investigates any number of crimes, from simple vandalism to something as heinous as rape and murder."

Gabriel Knight jotted something in his notepad. "So you're telling us that members of the task force have been threatened by someone besides their target?"

Kate swallowed hard, maintaining her composure. "I'm telling you that *my* home was broken into. No one else's. And that KCPD is investigating the break-in. Don't print anything in your paper that isn't true, Mr. Knight."

The dark-haired man winked. "Rest assured, I always check my facts, Doctor."

Kate went on to reiterate the task force's working description of the Rose Red Rapist, compiled after his assault back in May, and on the Janie Harrison attack. They were looking for a young to middle-aged man with access to buildings undergoing remodeling or new construction, someone with long-standing ties to the community who had the ability to move in and out of different neighborhoods and social situations without drawing attention to himself. "Our unsub is in good shape physically, and probably very fastidious about his appearance and his actions."

"That's it?" Vanessa asked. "Another listing of the profile? I suppose you want us to just keep talking about the neighborhood where he abducted his last two victims and murdered a woman last week?"

Did Kate dare mention her theories about the different unsubs? Would she be giving the frightened people of Kansas City a false sense of hope and security if she told them that she didn't believe the serial rapist they were all terrified of hadn't killed anyone?

If anyone besides Vanessa had asked, she might have mentioned it. But Vanessa was goading her into feeling defensive again and revealing more than she should. Kate stuffed her hands into the pockets of the green tweed blazer she wore and waited for the reactive instinct to pass.

A subtle movement from the corner of her eye diverted her attention. Boone was closing in to warn Vanessa to ease up or shut up or get lost or worse. The subtly protective move warmed her, reminded her of his promise to take care of her. But the reminder that she wasn't alone against pushy reporters or anyone else reminded Kate that she could take care of herself. With a shake of her head, she told Boone she was all right and was able to handle the taunt.

A theory was one thing. Proof was another.

It was in the best interests of the department and of

the city itself to withhold information now rather than
to retract it later.

It was in Kate's best interest to deal with Vanessa
herself and not have to rely on anyone else, not even
Boone, to shield her from dealing with difficult people
and awkward situations. "I believe it's helpful to your
viewers and readers to have the description and safety
precautions repeated." She looked straight into the lens
of the camera next to Vanessa. "We will solve this case.
We will find this man. We're learning more about him
every day. But until that time, we must all be vigilant
and protect ourselves. Don't give him the opportunity
to strike again. Thank you."

Having covered all the talking points required of her,
Kate walked away from the podium and wove her way
through the crowd toward the bank of elevators, despite
the barrage of questions that followed her.

"What new things are you learning, Dr. Kilpatrick?"

"If you don't know who broke into your home, how
do you know it's not related to your investigation?"

"Are you in danger, Doctor?"

"Are you afraid?"

An unseen arm jostled against Kate.

"I'd be afraid," a hushed voice warned.

She spun around, expecting to see a face attached
to that threat. But the flash of a camera blinded her. A
very real hand closed around her arm.

Terror fired through her veins and burst out in a
frightened gasp. Instinctively, she plunged her hand
inside her bag and reached for the gun holstered there.

But another hand, one bigger and rougher than hers,
closed over the unseen man's wrist and freed her.

"Go," Boone ordered beside her ear. The wrist he'd

grabbed twisted free and disappeared with its owner into the crowd.

Kate snatched at a handful of Boone's borrowed KCPD jacket and pulled herself up onto her toes, trying to see into the shifting crowd. "That was him."

Him who? Her stalker? A serial rapist? Someone else?

"Boone? Did you see—?"

"Go." He snugged his hands around her waist and pushed her to the edge of the crowd. "You need to get out of here before this gets completely out of control. Are you heading up to your office?"

"Dr. Kilpatrick? One more question."

He squeezed her hand, then nudged her beyond the fringe of the crowd. "I'll hold them back. You go. I'll meet you up there in a few minutes."

"But I heard—"

Another hand closed around her elbow and she flinched. "Come with me, Dr. K. I'll get you out of here."

Boone glared over her head for one quick moment, then dismissed her and her rescuer with a nod before turning away and spreading his arms wide and bellowing to the crowd, "All right, folks, let's see some manners here. Show's over. We're moving toward the front door."

Kate turned and looked into the youthful concern of Pete Estes's blue eyes. Torn by the intellectual need to identify who had spoken that threat to her in the crowd, and the purely instinctive need to get as far away from that threat as possible, she turned toward the chaotic mass one more time—seeking, searching. But she saw nothing but familiar faces she wouldn't suspect and strangers who looked no more threatening than the uniformed officer tugging at her arm.

"This way, ma'am. I've got an elevator waiting."

Sparing one last look at the protective wall of Boone's broad back, standing between her and the danger, she hurried through the elevator doors with Officer Estes. Once inside, he released her. She moved to the side railing to press the third floor button, but he reached past her and pushed the G for the garage level instead.

"Wait, I..." She arched an eyebrow at the young man. What kind of rescuing did he think she needed? "I was going upstairs."

The elevator jerked and began its slow descent.

"Yeah." He unholstered his gun and pointed it at her. "I don't care."

Kate's temperature dropped along with the elevator. But some part of her—the training and intellect—that she relied on when she counseled clients and created criminal profiles kicked in. She slipped her hand into her purse, seeking out the butt of her gun, keeping her nervous energy at bay so that she could think and observe.

It didn't take a profiler or a psychologist to note Pete's wiry build, or how, when she stood in her three-inch heels like this, she could look him straight in the eye.

"Did you get as beat up as I did, Pete, tumbling down the stairs at my house?" The hand holding that gun wasn't that much bigger than her own. "No wonder Pike Taylor's dog went after you. He'd been trailing your scent earlier."

"I thought it was the cat blood. Maybe I hadn't gotten

it all washed off before I answered the neighborhood all-call to secure the scene." He glanced over at Kate, his smile holding no humor. "It was my girlfriend's cat."

"You killed her cat?"

"Thought it'd be less trouble than killing her."

A disturbed young man, indeed. Either he'd lied his way through his psych profile to get into the Academy, or a stress-inducing event was causing him to lose his grasp of right and wrong and reality now. "Pete—"

"Shh." He held a finger to his lips as the elevator stopped. "Not a word. And I'll take that." He slipped her purse—and the gun inside—off her shoulder and tossed it into the corner of the elevator. "When we get off, we're going to walk over to my squad car and we're going to drive out of here."

"There are people working in the garage. Other officers. SWAT Team 1's home base is down here."

He jabbed the gun into her ribs and she winced. "And none of them will get hurt as long as you keep your mouth shut and do what I say."

"Where are we going?" She needed to think—clearly, quickly.

She tucked her hands into her pockets, falling back on the habit of fisting and flexing her fingers there, out of sight, in order to dispel any nervous energy and maintain a calm facade. She fisted a hand in one pocket to keep from crying out loud in relief because, in the other pocket, she discovered another old habit—carrying the important things on her person instead of in her purse. Namely, her cell phone.

She wasn't quite sure what she was going to do with it yet, but she was thinking. As long as she kept her head and didn't panic, she would get out of this. With no more cuts or bruises…or bullet holes. "Pete, I have a meeting to go to upstairs. People are probably already looking for me. This is never going to work."

"I said to stop talking. It just confuses me. It messes everything up. You say all these smart things—they sound good on camera or in some textbook somewhere. But they're not true. They don't work and I'm sick of hearing them." The doors slid open. With his gun hidden beneath his jacket and his free hand wrapped tightly around her arm to keep the gun pressed against her, he pulled her out into the cavernous parking and deployment area for a portion of KCPD's fleet of official vehicles. "Let's walk."

Kate's shoes tapped a familiar staccato on the concrete floor, reminding her of the night she'd heard the man in the brown coveralls following her. There was no longer any stealth to Pete Estes's behavior. His attempts to merely frighten her had escalated into the desire to do her real harm. A sudden shift in the degree of violence he was willing to commit generally meant a psychotic break. She'd been coaching him on his anger issues for a few weeks now, and had seen some progress—in her office. The reality was that something outside her meetings with Pete had triggered the desperate act of kidnapping.

And she had an idea of the cause. "What happened with you and Jeannee? That's your girlfriend's name, isn't it?"

"Ex-girlfriend. No thanks to you." There was the stressor that had triggered his obsessive behavior. He opened the passenger-side door and pushed her into the seat. "Call out to anyone, try to run before I get behind the wheel, and I'll shoot you."

Think, Kate. Think. In the few seconds he took to acknowledge a passing officer and circle around the trunk of the car, Kate pulled out her phone and punched in Boone's number.

She didn't have time for a conversation, couldn't risk an answering ring. Instead, she took a cue from Pete's talent for sending an alarming message in a single word. *Down.*

Kate texted the word, hit Send as the car door opened, dropped the phone back into her pocket and prayed Boone was as smart as he was caring and protective and funny and... The car door closed.

"Where are we going?" she asked again. Although she had a pretty good idea.

"To talk some sense into Jeannee." After shifting the car into Drive, he pulled the gun out and set it on his thigh, reminding Kate the he was armed and she was not. Reminding her, too, that she was the only one in the squad car who was thinking rationally right now. "And if you don't make things right between us, then I'm going to shoot you both."

WITH THE LOBBY AREA CLEARING OUT and the KCPD crew taking control of that crazy mob that had swarmed around Kate, Boone stepped out of the way to let the city cops escort the reporters and drama seekers outside. He wondered what his chances were of convincing Kate to let someone else, who wasn't the target of some crazy guy's threats, take over the public spotlight.

And sure, she'd kept her cool on the outside when the questions had taken a personal turn. But he'd seen the hands disappear. He knew her skin wasn't as thick as she'd like the rest of the world to think it was. He knew what it cost her to face down Vanessa Owen and the memories of an unpleasant past.

Let somebody else take the hits. Let somebody else deal with the grabbing hands and taking the blame for unsolved crimes that had the city on edge.

He wanted Kate Kilpatrick away from all this mess. He wanted her safe.

Boone pressed the elevator button, thinking he'd have at least three floors to come up with some reasonable argument to get Kate to hide away someplace safe for a while—preferably in bed with him. She'd probably acknowledge his argument, come back with some logical counterargument, distract him with the brush of her hand over his arm, and then stubbornly go about doing whatever she thought was right—no matter what it cost her.

Or him.

The elevator opened and Boone stepped inside. He pushed the button for the third floor, glanced down and saw the leather purse crumpled in the corner.

Boone's blood ran cold. He scooped up the familiar bag, caught the sliding door and shoved it back open.

A quick sweep of the lobby and dwindling crowd told him she wasn't here.

"Doc?"

He'd taken a couple of steps toward the front doors to follow the press conference attendees outside when his phone beeped.

He paused to read the incoming text from Kate's phone. "Down." What did that mean?

Boone mentally replayed the last few seconds he'd had Kate in his sights. Final statement. Crowd. Swarm.

Hand on her. Push her toward elevator. She braced her hand against him and...

"She saw something." No. Some*one*.

Boone grabbed the first blue suit that walked by. "What's downstairs?"

He flashed his badge before the officer would answer. "The SWAT garage, equipment storage, squad car parking—"

"Any way to get there besides the elevator?"

The officer pointed to the stairs.

Boone shoved open the door and hit the stairwell. He dialed Spencer Montgomery's number and unholstered his Glock as he waited for the detective to pick up.

"This is Montgomery."

"Code red or blue or whatever you call it here. Get a team down to the basement." Boone shoved open the door at the foot of the stairs. "That Estes kid just took Kate."

Chapter Ten

The cage was coming down over the garage's exit arch.

"What the…?" Pete stomped on the brake of the speeding car. Kate braced her hands and they skidded to the edge of the ramp leading up to the street. "What did you do, Dr. K.?"

They lurched to a stop and Pete's gun toppled to the floorboards. For two milliseconds, Kate considered diving for the weapon herself. But by the time she'd released her death grip on the dashboard and reached for the door handle, Pete had already retrieved the gun and aimed it squarely at Kate's chest.

"Don't you move!"

Kate also saw the silhouette of a cowboy hat in the side view mirror. She turned in her seat as he came up beside the car, with his gun cradled between both hands. "Oh, no, no, no. Boone, wait!"

There were other guns. Too many guns. Detectives Montgomery and Fensom. Maggie Wheeler. She'd texted for help and the cavalry had arrived.

Boone darted up to the front fender and pointed his gun at the driver behind the windshield. "Get out of the car, Estes!"

More movement in the mirror and to her left warned

Kate they were being surrounded. Men she recognized from SWAT Team 1 were slipping into flak vests and aiming rifles.

This wasn't going to end well.

Unless someone with a cool head prevailed.

Kate held her arms up in surrender. Her hands were shaking. She kept her head slightly bowed although she never completely looked away from Pete or the gun.

"Estes!" Boone shouted.

"I need to roll my window down so I can talk to him, Pete, okay? I'll tell him to lower his weapon." She brought her hands back to her lap, softened her voice. "I'm not going anywhere."

Pete's hands were shaking, too.

"Please, Pete." If she was right, this desperate young man didn't really want to harm her. He'd been frustrated, maybe even scared, angry for sure. He'd needed someone to blame for his troubles, someone to pay for his girlfriend leaving, and Kate—the woman who was supposed to fix all that for him and had failed—had become the target of all those unbalanced emotions.

She inhaled a deep, silent breath, trying to stay focused, trying to calm her nerves, trying to remember everything she'd ever learned about talking to someone as troubled as Pete Estes.

He glanced through the glass at Boone's rock-steady hands, then back at her. "Tell him to drop his gun."

Moving slowly so as not to alarm Pete, Kate rolled down the passenger window. The fumes from the garage stung her nose as she leaned her head toward the opening. "Boone, please put your gun away."

"When he tosses his out of the car."

"Please," she begged. She watched the emotions

travel across his face. He was a man of action. He'd promised to protect her. Holstering his gun and letting her take control of the potentially deadly standoff must be like her letting go of her emotions and simply trusting her instincts. She looked up at the tic of a muscle working beneath his steeled jaw. "Pete just needs to talk."

"He should have made an appointment." His eyes never left Pete or the gun trained on her. "Are you hurt?"

"No." She had to make Boone understand that this was one problem that violence couldn't solve. She had to make Pete understand that, too. "I need everyone to put their guns away."

"You have to fix it with Jeannee." Pete's gun continued to shake. "I said all those things you told me to. I told her I was going to be okay about the baby, that we'd make it work. But you lied, Dr. Kilpatrick. She left me anyway." He ground the gun against her shoulder. "She left me."

"Kate?"

"No!" She warned Boone back.

"He left all those damn threats, didn't he? He hurt you that night at the house."

"I'm fine. I need you to trust me on this." She tore her gaze away from Boone and read the desperation in Pete's eyes. "Pete just wants someone to listen. He wanted me to stop talking and listen."

Pete's head jerked with a nod.

"I'm listening now."

It was the first hint of trust, the first sign of being able to reason with him—her first hope that she and Pete both might get out of this squad car alive. Kate leaned her head out the window again. "I need Jean-nee Mercer, Tiger Village Apartments, on the phone right now."

Nick Fensom, standing off to the side in her periph-eral vision, holstered his weapon and pulled out his phone. "I'm on it."

"She may not want to talk." Kate didn't know if Pete had physically abused his girlfriend. But she was guess-ing that with his anger management issues, she'd cer-tainly borne the brunt of his verbal tirades.

Nick nodded his understanding and retreated. "I'll make it happen."

"I need everyone to put their guns away," she said.

The Glock in Boone's outstretched hands must be getting heavy, but he hadn't wavered.

Despite the facts, Kate tried to assure him she had the situation under control. "This isn't a kidnapping, it's a...counseling session."

"Don't make me put my gun away."

"Please, Boone." She saw the sweat beading on his upper lip. "I'll ask Pete to lower his weapon, too."

She looked to the younger man, dropped her gaze to the gun bruising her shoulder. "How about it?"

He pulled the gun from the dent he'd made in her sleeve and the skin beneath. The gun still rested on his thigh, but it was pointed in a less vulnerable position toward her legs. "Thank you." She forced her trembling lips to smile. "See? It's okay."

"All right." At last, he eased his stance and slowly, keeping his hands where Pete could see them, slipped his gun into its holster. He inched closer to her window. "But you're not gettin' rid of me."

It was a promise she wanted to cling to, a promise she was starting to believe.

"Let me ask you a question, Boone." It was a natural excuse for him to move another step closer to her window. "Pete. You and Sheriff Harrison have a lot in common."

"Like what?" he sneered. "If you're gonna talk, you'd better make those words count."

She intended to. "You're both officers of the law. And pretty good ones, too, I think."

She glanced up at Boone, urging him to say something helpful. His handsome mouth was a tight line of doubt. "Yeah, Estes. I've been in this business for almost twenty years. I'm sure you've got a long career ahead of you, too."

Kate slid her hand along the door above the armrest. She wanted to touch Boone, to squeeze his hand, to borrow his strength. But a firmer grip on Pete's gun warned her to pull her hand back to her lap. "Being married to a cop isn't easy. Being in a relationship with one doesn't always work out."

"Kate…" Boone cautioned. It was a risky topic, for both men. Yet she knew there was no one here who could understand Pete Estes's situation better than Boone.

"Sheriff Harrison's wife left him. Like Jeannee left you."

Boone was catching on to her ploy long before Pete. "Yeah, um…the long hours are hard for someone who isn't in the business."

"Sometimes, you're working so hard to establish your career, that you may lose track of what's going on at home."

Pete agreed. "Jeannee said I wasn't spending enough time with her. I didn't help her paint the baby's room."

The other detectives and uniformed officers surrounding the car were slowly lowering their weapons and backing off. But Kate could see it was because the SWAT team was fully armed now and getting into more strategic positions. Kate had to keep Pete talking to distract him from their movements. "I'm sure you feel as badly about that as she does."

"I felt guilty as hell. I want to take care of my boy… or little girl. But I need to spend time on the streets, too." He ducked his head to see Boone through her window. "I have to earn the respect of the people on my beat."

Boone nodded, pretending he and Pete were sharing a moment of camaraderie. "You have to get to know them."

"Right. It takes time. My shift may say I get off in eight hours, but if there's something I have to take care of…"

"You can't leave victims in the middle of a traffic accident." Boone was a natural at getting the rookie officer to talk. "If a crime is in progress, you have to stop it. You can't wait for the next guy to do it for you."

"Exactly. I want to be with Jeannee. But I want to do my job right, too. How else can I get promoted and make more money? I'm going to have a family to support."

Nick Fensom returned to the car, with his hands and cell phone up in the air. Pete raised his gun again and Kate held her breath. "I've got her." Nick had Jeannee Mercer—and the possible end to this standoff—on the line. "I reached her at her mother's place."

Her breath eased out on a careful sigh. "May I take the phone from Detective Fensom?"

"Yeah." Pete was waving the gun again, but this time, it was Boone who held up his hands to warn the SWAT team to hold their fire. "But Cowboy there steps back."

"I explained the situation," Nick said, handing Kate the phone. "She said she'd come down to the precinct. I sent Sgt. Wheeler out to pick her up."

Kate put the cell to her ear and introduced herself. "I'm Dr. Kilpatrick. I'm a…friend of Pete's. He'd like to say how much he loves you. And explain a few things to you."

"Jeannee?" Pete took the phone after an encouraging nod from Kate. "Yeah, baby. I love you, too. I don't want you to be afraid of me. I want to do better by you." The young man was laughing, crying, setting his gun down on his thigh and finally relaxing his guard the more he talked. "I need you to understand where I'm coming from."

They talked for seven minutes and twenty-three seconds, according to the dashboard clock.

At seven minutes and twenty-four seconds, Pete let go of his gun to switch the cell to his right hand.

Enough talking. Kate snatched the gun from his lap. Boone opened her door and pulled her from the car, forcing her down against the protection of the tire and fender and shielding her body with his while the SWAT team swooped in to drag Pete from the car. They put him facedown on the concrete and cuffed his wrists behind his back.

When the SWAT team commander, Michael Cutler, announced the all-clear, Boone pressed his lips against

Kate's ear and whispered, "You probably just saved that kid's life. But next time, Doc? We do things my way."

Kate was shaking so badly when they stood up that Boone was the only thing holding her upright. She curled her fingers into the sleeve of his jacket and held on.

And that was when she realized that Boone was shaking, too.

"THE HEROINE OF THE DAY."

When would the madness end?

Boone closed the conference room door as a round of applause from Spencer Montgomery and the members of the task force greeted Kate's arrival at the late-afternoon meeting. He was bone tired and itching to get someplace where he wasn't running into another cop or reporter who wanted to get close to Kate to either congratulate her for talking her way out of a hostage crisis or get a quote for the evening news and morning paper.

Kate should be in a bed, sleeping.

No, she should be in a safehouse bed, catching up on her sleep.

And if he was in that bed with her, so much the better.

He could tell by the extra-determined tilt of her chin that she was exhausted by the emotional ordeal of the last few days, too. She was working that sophisticated ice-princess facade while he was feeling more raw and less refined than ever after watching that sad, mixed-up kid hold a gun on her. He'd had the shot. He could have taken the young officer out. But Kate had insisted on saving her client's neck as well as her own.

She smiled at their praise and thanked them for their

concern before sitting down at the long table. Boone dropped his hat on top of the table and pulled out a chair to sit beside her, not waiting for an invitation to join the meeting. He'd agreed to be Kate's protector in exchange for access to the task force's investigation.

Until Janie's killer was locked behind bars, and these people could prove that the only danger stalking Kate was now locked away in a psych evaluation cell, he was staying.

"You should hear the press buzzing now," said Spencer Montgomery. Kate audibly groaned at the prospect of going another round with local reporters. "Don't worry. Chief Taylor is taking care of them. I'm relieving you of press liaison duty, Kate."

"'Bout damn time," Boone muttered under his breath.

The detective at the head of the table paused at the interruption. "I hate to say it, but Sheriff Harrison was right. Setting you up as the bait to draw out Estes turned out to be far more dangerous than any risk I'm comfortable with."

"Pete Estes is a troubled young man." Kate still wanted to defend this guy? "If he'd gotten out of the garage with me as a hostage, I'm guessing one or both of us would have died in an inevitable shoot-out. He's confused and hurting and needs a lot of help." She looked to every person sitting around the table, including Boone. Perhaps her gaze lingered a little longer on him. "Thank you for letting me take charge of the situation."

"You've done good work, Kate," Montgomery said. "Your theory about multiple unsubs was right. Estes had a personal beef with you, and tried to cover his tracks with the red roses. But he isn't our rapist or killer."

"I don't think he even knows Janie Harrison's name. His focus was on his girlfriend, and then on me because he blamed me for her leaving him."

"You're eliminating all kinds of suspects for us, Kate. The victim's boyfriend. This copycat stalker." With a nod to the criminologist sitting across from Boone, Montgomery continued. "But I'd pay good money if someone could bring me a viable suspect on this case. We're no closer to identifying the Rose Red Rapist than we were a week ago. Annie?"

Annie Hermann stood to set her big shoulder bag on top of the table with a solid thunk. She pulled out one file after another, sorting through the labels until she found the one she was looking for and handed it off to Maggie Wheeler. "Here. I have the results we've been waiting for from the lab. I know chemical analysis reports can be hard to read, but go ahead and pass them around. I made a copy for everybody."

"And what do these squiggly lines mean to those of us who aren't scientists?" Nick asked, passing the folder around the table.

Boone was willing to back up the five foot two inches of glare Annie shot toward Nick, providing it would either (a) get Kate out of this meeting and into the comparative safety and privacy of their hotel room sooner, or (b) give him the answers he needed to finally let his sister rest in peace.

"I've been working on identifying the silver trace the M.E. found in Jane Harrison's hair."

The folder finally made its way around to him. He remembered a few abbreviations from chemistry class, but he wasn't seeing the familiar symbol for silver on the report. "The heirloom necklace Janie wore was sterling silver."

"Right." Annie pointed to the photo of the tiny, round-cornered square of metal. "That's not sterling. Or even low-grade silver. It's stainless steel. So…" She reached into her bag and pulled out a molded piece of plaster sculpture. "This is the cast I made of the victim's head wound. I'm not sure exactly what it is yet, but this is the weapon that killed your sister. And I believe whatever it is was made out of stainless steel."

Boone picked up the three-dimensional re-creation of the blunt object that had taken Janie's life. It was two-pronged and cylindrical in shape, about the size of his fist. He remembered the M.E. saying it looked like the object had impaled Janie's head when she'd been struck. The two curved prongs protruding at the end were certainly long enough to do that.

"May I see that?" Kate held out her hand and Boone placed the odd-shaped object into her palm. She picked up the photo of the stainless shard and placed it at the end of the shorter prong.

"It fits, doesn't it," Annie reported. "It's a piece that broke off the tip of the weapon."

"Ideas on what it could be?" Montgomery asked.

Kate's shoulders sagged beside him while the others tossed out suggestions of tools and knickknacks. Her skin turned ashen, save for the bruise on her cheek. Boone ignored the decorum of the meeting and slipped his hand behind her back. "Are you all right?"

She turned her eyes up to his, but the soft green irises were focused someplace far away.

"Kate?" Boone's weary muscles rejuvenated with

concern. Meeting or not, he was taking her out of here to get some rest.

But then she sat up straight and turned to Spencer Montgomery. "Did you get that list of motel guests from the night Janie called there?"

"Yes." He thumbed through his leather binder and pulled out the paper. "Here."

She snatched it from Montgomery's hand and skimmed through the list. Everyone was watching her now. Her shoulders dipped again, but then her chin tilted up.

Boone gripped the arm of his chair, waiting for the grim pronouncement stamped across her features. "My theory about a second unsub is still correct. I don't know who our rapist is yet, but I know who killed Jane Harrison." She set down the list in front of him and pointed to a name. "So do you."

Chapter Eleven

"It matches."

Kate had never wanted to be more wrong about a thing in her life. She'd wanted to be wrong about her husband and good friend's affair. She'd wanted to be wrong about Pete Estes and had almost hoped she had the real Rose Red Rapist stalking her instead of a young man so confused and angry about his world that he believed his only outlet was to terrorize her. For Boone's sake, she'd wanted to be wrong about his sister being involved with a married man, repeating the same pattern that had once destroyed his life.

She really wanted to be wrong about this.

But her mind was too sharp. She remembered too many impressions about people. She could never quite shut off that always-thinking-always-evaluating brain of hers.

Kate wrapped the collar of her brown trench coat higher around her neck and hunched down against the stiff wind whipping along Nichols Street, just off the courthouse square in Grangeport, Missouri. She held up the photograph of Annie Hermann's two-pronged murder weapon beside the taillight of Flint Larson's green pickup truck, parked in front of the Alton County Sheriff's Department.

The object in Annie's photo was three-dimensional, but the design was the same.

A rearing stallion. Handmade with love by an artist who enjoyed sculpting in metal. Long mane flying in the wind. Two shapely, slender front legs, curling out from its muscular body. The fragment of stainless steel that had caught in Janie Harrison's hair was the tip of a hoof that had broken off when her head struck Flint's truck.

"I'm sorry, Boone." Kate looked over at the broad-shouldered sheriff, pushing his Stetson more firmly onto his head to withstand the bleak promise of winter blowing through town. Her heart went out to him standing there in stoic silence, his brooding stare fixed on the back of his deputy and good friend's truck.

How did a man stand that kind of betrayal from a friend? From someone he trusted?

Kate knew. And she didn't wish that kind of pain on anyone.

Spencer Montgomery was on his phone, ignorant or uncaring of what the evidence meant to the local sheriff. "I'll get a search warrant for Larson's truck, his home and his office. Looks like there's a decorative ornament missing from the hitch. Let's start snapping some pictures. Sheriff, do you have an address on this guy?"

At last Boone spoke. "You're in my jurisdiction now, Montgomery." His world-weary gaze swept over Kate, too, giving a double meaning to his words. "We do this *my* way."

"Maybe there's another explanation. Someone borrowed Flint's truck or…" Kate took a step toward him, but Boone's hard look kept her from taking another.

"We're not dragging this out. We're not talking it through all day long. The evidence is there. I need to take care of this for Janie."

Spencer put his call on hold and turned around to face him. "You're not talking about some kind of vigilante justice, are you?" He didn't back off the way Kate had. "To flip a phrase you once threw in my face—I don't know how you do things here in Grangeport, but in Kansas City we build a case against a suspect. Then we arrest him and make it stick."

"We do the same thing here in Grangeport, Detective." Boone was moving now, checking the gun and badge and handcuffs on his belt, striding toward the office's front door. "Flint's probably out on a call in a departmental vehicle right now. You make your case. I'll bring him in."

"Boone." Kate caught his arm as he walked past. "You're asking an awful lot of yourself. A good friend murdered your sister."

"And I want to know why. I want him to tell me to my face how he could do this to my Janie."

She shook her head. "You're too close to this. Too angry. Let Spencer do it."

"No."

"Then at least let me come with you."

"Doc…"

He looked her up and down, from the sweep of her bangs down to her jeans and high-heeled boots. And when she thought he was about to make some excuse about how she wasn't dressed for traipsing around the countryside after a murder suspect, he slid his hand beneath the fringe of hair at her nape, angled her head back and kissed her. It was hard and deep and thorough and fast, and Kate latched on to his collar and stretched up to answer with the same raw need inside her.

And then her heels were flat on the ground and Boone's thumb gave a rough stroke over her bottom lip. "I nearly lost you yesterday to one man who was willing to kill the people I love. I'm not going to give anybody else the chance to do it again.

"You stay."

The people I love?

Boone's parting words fueled Kate's steps as she paced circles around the wood-paneled lobby of the Alton County Sheriff's Station. Boone loved her? Or had that been a generic statement about home territory and losing his sister and not being emotionally prepared to deal with another loss?

He loved her?

A good man. An honest man. A loyal, caring man. A man who could kiss her like she was the most precious, fragile thing on earth one minute, and then in the next minute make her feel like the sexiest, most desirable woman he'd ever met. He made her feel safe. He made her feel unsure. He made her feel...period.

A man like that loved her?

"Why would I say something if I didn't mean it?"

"Not everyone who makes a promise keeps it."

"I do."

Kate stopped in her tracks. She stopped thinking. For once, she stood still and simply *felt* the truth.

Boone Harrison loved her.

And she... *Let the past go. Embrace the woman you*

are now, the woman Boone sees. "Don't think it, Kate," she whispered. "Feel it."

She inhaled a deep, cleansing breath, ready to take a leap of faith. "I—"

"Kate!" Spencer Montgomery ran out of Boone's office with another deputy charging behind him. "We have to go."

"Go where?" She grabbed her coat off the bench beside the front door and shrugged her arms into it. "I thought we were meeting Boone here. That he was bringing Flint to us."

The deputy was already out the door, revving the throttle of his departmental SUV and peeling off down the street.

"There's been a change in plans." Spencer opened the door and hurried her outside to his car. "I promised him I wouldn't leave you alone here. Do you have your weapon?"

"In my purse."

"I'd keep it closer than that."

A fist of dread punched her in the stomach. "You talked to Boone? What's wrong?"

"He just called." Kate buckled her seat belt as Spencer mounted a magnetic siren on the roof of his car and took off after the deputy's speeding SUV.

"There's been a situation with Larson."

"What?"

"Do you know what a Mexican standoff is?"

"Yes, when two people hold guns…" Kate's stomach dropped to her feet. "Oh, my God."

"Yeah. Larson's refusing to come in."

"THAT'S CLOSE ENOUGH, Doc."

The Missouri River bluffs in the autumn really were beautiful, Boone thought obliquely, as he adjusted his stance behind a pile of dead pines that had been cut and stacked for burning. But the bluffs paled in comparison to Dr. Kate Kilpatrick picking her way through a stubble of cow pasture to reach the trees near the hunting blind where Flint Larson had holed up. She had burrs stuck to her jeans, dust on her once shiny boots and a Glock on her belt. A KCPD flak vest from Spencer Montgomery's trunk weighed down the naturally erect posture of her body.

"Not another step, Doc." She might be armed, but she herself had said she didn't carry a weapon regularly, and he wasn't sure how well she'd be able to defend herself if her request to talk Flint Larson out of his suicidal threats went south. "Stick to the cover of the trees."

She glanced over her shoulder. "I don't want to be shouting at him."

And he didn't want her close enough where Flint could put his hands on her, either—or where she could take a tumble over the granite and limestone cliffs into the churning muddy water below their position.

"Come on out, Flint," Boone shouted, urging him once again to step out into the open and surrender himself. "KCPD's here now. Please, buddy. Don't make us come in there with our guns. I worry one of us won't make it back out that way."

Flint shouted from inside the stacked lumber and canvas of the blind. "One of us *won't* make it out, Boone. You know that."

"Flint? It's Kate Kilpatrick. Remember that chat we had the day of Janie's funeral?"

"Get out of here, lady!" Flint warned. "I'm not in the mood to talk."

"I remember our conversation. You were quite charming." Kate was some twenty yards ahead and to the west, about halfway between his Glock and Flint's Smith & Wesson, but out of the direct crossfire should this request and refusal to come in and face the charges against him get any more screwed up than they already had.

"That's bull, and you know it." A nearly empty whiskey bottle came hurtling out of the blind toward Kate's position and Boone jerked inside his boots, fighting the instinct to go get her and bring her back out of harm's way. "I'm not coming out, boss."

Perhaps sensing his impulse, Kate looked back to him and held up a placating hand, asking him to stay back. Stubborn woman. She wouldn't be deterred from trying to talk Boone's deputy out of his hidey-hole. She leaned up against the trunk of a crooked pin oak and tried again. "What if I talk for a minute, Flint, and you just listen?"

When Flint didn't answer, she darted up to hide behind the next tree. "Kate," Boone warned.

He knew she was good at this sort of thing—and that he wasn't. But she was just too damn close.

But knowing she was treading on dangerous ground with the Rose Red Rapist case and that crazy kid of a stalker hadn't stopped her yet, the unpredictable danger of a drunken, suicidal man who was armed with at least one gun wouldn't stop her, either. "We know Janie's death was an accident, Flint."

"It wasn't!" he argued, his voice growing more and

more slurred by the alcohol he'd consumed. "I'm sorry, boss. I killed her. I got so damn mad. I pushed and..."

And what? Could he stand here, hiding in the trees, and listen to how his innocent baby sister had fallen victim to someone she trusted? Boone's breath stilled in his chest. But he found Kate's eyes looking back at him, comforting him, calming him, and he found he could breathe again.

"Tell us what happened, Flint." As much as he hated putting her in harm's way on purpose, Boone was praying that she could work another miracle and talk his longtime friend into surrendering his gun. But she was getting nothing but silence.

"Kate, come on back." He couldn't take this. He was beat up inside with love and worry for that woman. He needed her back here where he could put his hands on her and keep her safe. "When night comes, the cold will chase him out."

"Flint?"

Boone swore when he saw Kate inch up to another tree. Screw hanging back. Keeping low to the ground, Boone crept out from behind his cover and ducked into the same copse of oaks where she was positioned. If she wouldn't come to him, then he was going after her. Again. "Doc, you're scaring me. This was a bad idea. At least draw your weapon so you can defend yourself."

Thank God she at least followed that directive. She slowly unsnapped her holster and pulled the Glock into her hands while she kept talking in that calm, even tone of hers.

"We've already matched your truck to the head wound that killed Janie." But she wasn't any more willing to give up on the idea of getting Flint out of here alive than he was. "There are KCPD criminologists and detectives at your house right now, Flint, searching for evidence that you were there that night with Janie."

"They won't find anything." Finally, an answer.

Even Boone froze where he stood.

"Why not?" Kate asked.

"Because I have it here with me." And with that, Flint stumbled out of the blind with his Smith & Wesson in his hand. Boone's gun went up instantly. He closed one eye, getting a bead on the deputy. But Boone's aim wavered slightly when Flint held up the other hand, dangling the silver heirloom necklace from his fingers.

Ah, hell. Flint had killed Janie. There was no longer even a smidgen of hope left inside him that Kate and the task force and their evidence might be wrong. Boone could hear Montgomery and the deputies moving through the dry grass behind him. And every last man was armed, every bullet was aimed at Flint.

"Drop your weapon, Flint," Boone ordered. "As your friend. As your superior officer—"

"I've washed my truck a dozen times since that night." Boone peeked around the tree as Flint's slurred voice came closer. "But I can't get rid of the blood. It's in my head and on my hands and in my heart. I can't clean it all out of me."

"Kate, pull back," Boone warned.

She started to move, but Flint swung his gun around toward her.

"Kate!"

She jumped back and hugged her body close to the tree again.

"You were right, Doctor." She had Flint talking now. "I was Kate's confidant. I'm the good friend she called that night. I drove all the way to Kansas City to fix the problem for her."

"Fix the problem?" Boone swore. "She'd been raped. Why didn't you take her to the police? Or a hospital? Why didn't you call me?"

"She didn't want her brothers to know just how badly she'd screwed up. But she trusted me. She needed me!"

"Being raped is an act of violence, not a mistake a woman makes. I know you loved her," Kate said gently, urging Flint to quiet his temper. "You told me you went to help her whenever she asked. You were a good friend to her. Even after she broke off your engagement. Not many men have the character to do that."

Boone tried to move closer to Kate, to get her back to safety. But Flint swung the gun back toward him and fired three shots down into the ground, pinning him.

"Flint, stop!" Kate shouted. "You'll only make it worse. Put down your gun. I'll talk with you for as long as you want. Just put down your gun."

Flint took a lurching step toward Kate's position. "I loved her. And I thought…"

Boone flattened his back against the tree. Montgomery and the others were too far back. He had to get to Kate before Flint did.

"Keep him talking, Doc."

"You shut up!" Another pair of shots hit the bark beside Boone, throwing a chip of wood across his cheek and drawing blood.

"Flint!"

Boone peered around the tree. "I'm okay, Doc. Get back."

But the woman thought she could talk her way out

of anything. She thought she could help a drunken lost soul like Flint. She thought she needed to protect him.

She had her hands and gun up in the air and was walking into the clearing toward Flint. "Just talk to me, Flint. Okay? Look at me." *No, honey. No, no, no!* She stooped and set her gun on the ground, turning herself into an easy target. "See? I'm not armed. I just want to talk. That's it."

Boone caught Spencer Montgomery's eye and silently gave him the order to circle around behind Flint's blind side. Kate was still in the open. But if she hit the ground when he told her to, Montgomery would have a clear shot to take out Boone's friend.

He hadn't wanted it to come to this. Flint had been halfway to drunk by the time Boone had found him and explained the evidence KCPD had against him. The man had broken down into tears of guilt and regret and penance—or so Boone had believed. He'd let him go to the john to wash his face. The next thing he'd heard instead of running water was the sound of an ATV motor, tearing off across the countryside. Boone had driven his truck as far as the landscape would let him, and then followed on foot. The chase had ended here.

He'd been worried Flint wouldn't surrender.

Now he was beginning to worry about something even worse.

"Kate! You come back to me." Boone smeared the blood off his cheek. He pulled off his hat and tossed it into the grass at his feet, giving himself a slimmer profile, making himself a harder target to hit. He flexed his fingers around the grip of his Glock, mentally preparing himself for where this showdown might be headed.

"If anything happens to her, Flint, you are not leaving here alive."

"It's okay, Boone." How could Kate sound so sweet and calm when his heart was tied up like a branding calf inside his chest? "Flint and I are just talking. Right? Tell me more about that night."

"I went to Kansas City to see her. Janie said she was in trouble and so I went." Flint's throat grew froggy from tears and drink. "I got us a motel room so we could have some privacy. She was all messed up, like she'd been in a fight." Tears burned beneath Boone's own eyelids at all the sad mistakes that had led to such a tragedy that night. "I thought that boyfriend—Max or whatever she called him—had hurt her. I got so mad. I wanted to go after him. But she came out of the room after me. To stop me. She said she loved him. That it would break her heart if I hurt him. She told me she wanted to call him for help, but she couldn't because he had a wife. She was defending him to me!" Boone didn't have to see Flint to understand the rage building inside him. "She called *me* for help. I thought he'd done that to her. Yet she kept going on and on—Max, Max, Max."

"You fought?"

Boone heard a sorrowful gasp, like the last breath of a dying animal. It was Flint. "I didn't mean to. But I pushed—she fell. She hit her head on the hitch of my truck. The one she'd made for me. There was so much blood. She was gone."

"And afterward?"

"I kept the necklace because it always meant so much to her."

Boone risked another peek around the tree. He

swiped the tears from his vision. Kate was right there, close enough for Flint to touch her. *Move, woman,* he begged, silently creeping toward them. *Give me a clear shot.*

"I took her body back to that alley where I'd picked her up. Left the rose with her like that guy had." One step. Another step. "I loved her." Flint shook his head. "I killed her."

"Put the gun down, Flint," Kate asked quietly. "There are cops all around you. Please put the gun down."

"Kate, get down!" Boone shouted, moving out of the trees, raising his gun.

And then the nightmare happened.

Drunk and unsteady, but strong and desperate enough to react to the threat, Flint grabbed Kate, hugged her and the bulletproof vest in front of him and put the gun to her head.

Kate screamed. Boone charged forward until he didn't dare take another step.

If Flint had pointed the gun at him, he wouldn't have hesitated to shoot. But he had Kate.

"Don't make me do this, Flint. It's suicide."

His deputy smiled. "Don't you think I know that, boss?"

"Damn it, Flint. You could have surrendered."

"And live with knowin' what I did to Janie? And to you?"

Kate thought there was still a chance to reach him. "Flint, please."

"No, ma'am. No more." Flint turned the gun to his own head.

"Flint, no," Kate gasped.

"You're right. He won't shoot to save me." He moved the gun back to her temple. "But he'll save you."

"Don't make me," Boone begged. "Let her go."

"Can't do that, boss."

Montgomery shouted from his position. "Cowboy, you got a plan?"

"Yes." Boone's gun never wavered. He looked straight into Kate's beautiful eyes. "I love you."

"I love you," she answered without hesitation, and something warm and perfect and too good to lose blossomed inside him.

"I'll do it, boss." Flint ground the gun into her temple, forcing her head to the side.

"Yeah, Doc. But do you trust me?"

Boone waited. He aimed. He held his breath.

"Yes."

Boone pulled the trigger. He hit Flint in the middle of his forehead and the man who'd killed his sister, who'd threatened the woman he loved, who'd lied, crumpled to the ground. Dead.

BOONE LACED HIS FINGERS TOGETHER with Kate's and walked her to the barn to introduce her to Big Jim and the other horses. She might not know how to ride yet, but she sure had an affinity for petting foreheads and combing manes and holding carrots out in the flat of her hand for long tongues and soft muzzles to gobble up.

A week had passed since Flint Larson's funeral. A lifetime had passed, it seemed, since he'd nearly lost her to a pair of dangerous young men. One, she'd used her skills of talking and listening and thinking on her feet to escape from. The other, he'd used his more instinctive abilities to escape the promise of death. Thank

God she'd finally decided to take him at his word and trusted him to take that shot.

They'd shared their darkest secrets, some incredible passion, and their hearts. She wasn't afraid to get her shoes muddy or tell him to get his filthy boots out of the kitchen.

But Boone's world wasn't perfect. Not yet.

He pulled her to the ladder leading up to the loft and kissed her hand. "Have you ever had a roll in the hay, Dr. Kate?"

"Can't say as I have."

"It beats a hot bubble bath or a long ride on a horse."

She put her foot on the first rung of the ladder, looked over her shoulder and smiled. "Well, it's been a very long, very stressful week. And I think we both need to…decompress."

Boone palmed her butt to hurry her on up the ladder and climbed up behind her. "I like the way you think, Doc."

She liked the quilt he'd spread out over the hay, and the wine and cheese-and-crackers, and condom he'd already set into place, too. "Hmm…this country living has more going for it than I'd ever suspected."

Boone uncorked the wine and picked up the two glasses to pour a little something to set the mood. "We can class it up like you city sophisticates if we have to."

And then he nearly dropped the glasses when he felt her arms sliding around him from behind. "I'm not thirsty, Boone." She flicked his hat off into the hay and brushed her lips against the back of his neck. "I'm not hungry, either."

He set down the wine and goblet, then turned to

gather her in his arms. "I'm starving," he confessed before claiming her mouth with his.

The talking stopped as greedy hands and hungry kisses took over. Boots dropped. Coats and belts and clothes disappeared. Kate's hands skimmed his body, sending shivers through him. She coaxed his nipples to attention, teased their painful tightness with the swirl of her tongue. She drew her nails along his spine and squeezed his butt as he laved her beautiful breasts and sucked the pink tips into pebbled flowers. She wound a firm hand around his swollen manhood and urged him toward her welcoming heat.

He laid her back across the quilt. The crinkle of hay strands breaking beneath them, along with her sweet, moaning gasps, made music in the air. The exotic scent of jasmine in her hair erased the pungent smells of the barn, filling his head with Kate and her giving hands and heart.

When he couldn't stand another moment of being incomplete, Boone entered Kate in a swift, deep thrust. She wound her legs around his hips, hugged her arms around his shoulders, threaded her fingers into his hair. Those sweet green eyes looked up into his for a moment before she tipped her head back and cried out his name. Boone buried his face against her throat and held on as his body tensed at the brink of satisfaction. And then her hands clutched at his back and he toppled over with the roar of his release. He couldn't imagine anything more perfect than being with Kate Kilpatrick.

Now she was in his arms, snuggling close as the autumn air cooled their bare skin. And those sexy hands were trailing leisurely lines up and down his chest and abdomen.

Boone caught her hand and stilled it over his heart before she made him forget why they'd needed to decompress in the first place. "You're not gettin' rid of me, Doc. You know that, right?"

"I'm not trying to." She pushed herself up on one elbow, her kiss-stung mouth marred by a serious frown. "But your job is here. Mine's in Kansas City. I'm not quitting that task force until the Rose Red Rapist is off the streets and the women in Kansas City are safe again."

"I don't want you to quit."

"You live on a ranch and I live in a house that's too big for me—"

"And we both have some emotional healing left to do. I know." He lifted his head and kissed her until that frown eased into a hopeful smile. "We've talked about this before, Doc. We've both been married to people who were with us every day, and yet they didn't stay."

"So how are we going to make us work?" She gently touched the cut healing on his cheek. "Because I really want us to work."

"I want us to work, too." He brushed a fingertip across the fading bruise on *her* cheek. "Whether I go to K.C. and whip those city cops into shape or you come here to Grangeport and give it some uptown class, I want to be with you."

"Well…" He saw the wheels turning inside her head, knew that woman was thinking of something that could change his world. Again.

Boone let his head fall back to the quilt with a resigned sigh. "What?"

"Maybe if you just promise me that we'll keep working on this relationship, I'll believe it. It doesn't have to be perfect right now. But we'll figure it out so that one day soon it will be."

Boone smiled and pulled her down on top of him. "Whatever we do, Doc—we do it together. I promise."

Epilogue

The man turned off the television and laughed.

"What's so funny?"

Everything in him tensed as the woman walked up behind his chair. He hated when she did that. She knew him so well in so many ways that he couldn't do without her. Yet every now and then he got the idea that he didn't know her as well as he should.

He gestured to the chair across from him, inviting her to sit. Picking up some papers from his desk, he sorted through them, making sure they were in order.

"Well?" she prompted.

He didn't like that, either, when she made even small demands like that from him. His nostrils flared as he forced himself to maintain an even rhythm of breathing. Maintaining his anonymity often required a great deal of patience and pretending he didn't care about things as deeply as he did.

He nodded toward the television. "I was watching the latest report from KCPD and their Rose Red Rapist task force."

"And that's funny?"

No, he supposed a woman wouldn't find anything amusing about a rapist who'd attacked with impunity for some time now. "It's funny that they're not making any progress on their investigation. They've solved two crimes in the past week, and neither is the one they were investigating."

She stood and took the papers from him. "You're worried, aren't you?"

"About the task force?" Irritated by the presumption, he stood. He would not let a woman—any woman—think she was superior to him. "Why should I care about what the police are doing?"

She set the papers down—in the wrong pile. His heart thudded in his chest.

As if she could hear the pounding sound against his ribs, she rested her palm against his chest, and made a shushing, soothing sound.

Don't believe her, the voice inside his head warned him. *She's a woman. How can you trust a woman?*

How could he not trust this one?

"I know your secrets," she said. His hands curled into fists at his sides. She took care of him in so many ways, knew him so well. He needed her. And that, perhaps, was why he hated her so much. "And I won't let anyone else hurt you. Ever again."

* * * * *

A sneaky peek at next month...

INTRIGUE...

BREATHTAKING ROMANTIC SUSPENSE

My wish list for next month's titles...

In stores from 16th November 2012:

❏ Colby Roundup – Debra Webb

& Justice at Cardwell Ranch – BJ Daniels

❏ Christmas Conspiracy – Robin Perini

& The Reckoning – Jana DeLeon

❏ Secret Protector – Ann Voss Peterson

& Daddy Bombshell – Lisa Childs

❏ Captain's Call of Duty – Cindy Dees

Available at WHSmith, Tesco, Asda, Eason, Amazon and Apple

Just can't wait?

Visit us Online

You can buy our books online a month before they hit the shops! **www.millsandboon.co.uk**

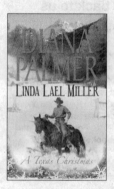

Mills & Boon® Online

Discover more romance at
www.millsandboon.co.uk

- **FREE** online reads
- **Books** up to one month before shops
- **Browse our books** before you buy

...and much more!

For exclusive competitions and instant updates:

 Like us on **facebook.com/romancehq**

 Follow us on **twitter.com/millsandboonuk**

 Join us on **community.millsandboon.co.uk**

 Visit us Online | Sign up for our FREE eNewsletter at **www.millsandboon.co.uk**